Praise for *The Damned of Petersburg*

"If Thucydides and Tolstoy together were commissioned to write a historical novel about the American Civil War, the result would be something like Ralph Peters' *The Damned of Petersburg*. Combining unflinching Thucydidean realism about warfare with Tolstoyan empathy for humanity, Peters re-creates the bloody Petersburg campaign through the eyes and in the words of the men who lived and died during it. Anyone who wants to understand why the Civil War is the defining event in American history should read this deeply researched and beautifully written epic."
—Guy MacLean Rogers, Kenan Professor of History and Classical Studies at Wellesley College and author of *Alexander: The Ambiguity of Greatness*

"The best series of Civil War novels ever written."
—William Martin, *New York Times* bestselling author of *The Lincoln Letter*

"I predict that *The Damned of Petersburg* will be a classic that people will read for the next fifty years."
—Thomas Fleming, author of *The Secret Trial of Robert E. Lee*

"A must-read for Civil War novice and aficionado alike."
—John Horn, author of *The Siege of Petersburg*

"Peters' research is impeccable. His account of life in the trenches is told by the actual participants, from the common soldier to the higher-grade officers. Readers can only feel as if they were participants in that dirty, hot summer of 1864, with death constantly facing them."
—Chris Calkins, author of *The Appomattox Campaign*

"Rich in detail and rendered with a literary flair, this is magnificent fiction that Civil War buffs will want for their libraries."
—*Kirkus Reviews* (starred review)

RALPH PETERS' NOVELS PUBLISHED BY FORGE

Cain at Gettysburg (Boyd Award)
Hell or Richmond (Boyd Award)
Valley of the Shadow
The Damned of Petersburg
Judgment at Appomattox
The Officers' Club
The War After Armageddon

RALPH PETERS' CIVIL WAR MYSTERIES PUBLISHED
UNDER THE PEN NAME "OWEN PARRY"

Faded Coat of Blue (Herodotus Award)
Shadows of Glory
Call Each River Jordan
Honor's Kingdom (Hammett Prize)
Bold Sons of Erin
Rebels of Babylon

and

Our Simple Gifts: Civil War Christmas Tales

Ralph Peters is also the author of numerous books on strategy,
as well as additional novels.

THE DAMNED OF PETERSBURG

RALPH PETERS

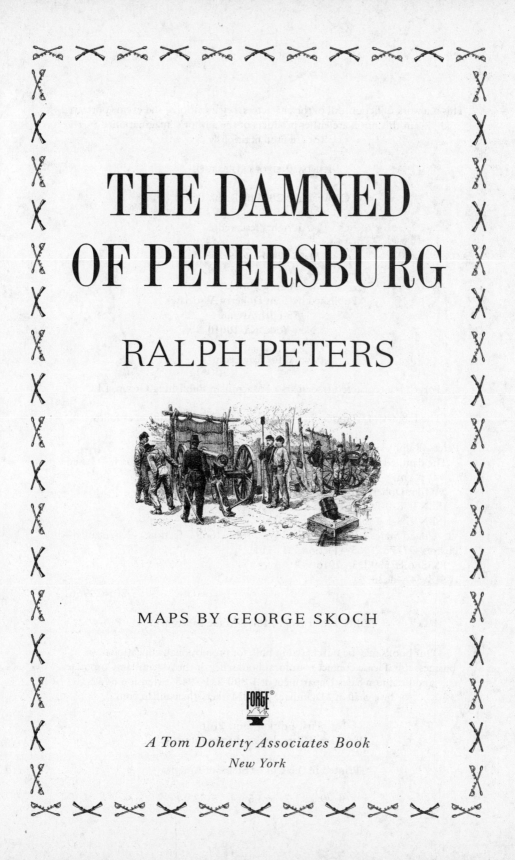

MAPS BY GEORGE SKOCH

FORGE®

A Tom Doherty Associates Book
New York

THE DAMNED OF PETERSBURG

Copyright © 2016 by Ralph Peters

Maps by George Skoch

A Forge Book
Published by Tom Doherty Associates
175 Fifth Avenue
New York, NY 10010

www.tor-forge.com

Forge® is a registered trademark of Macmillan Publishing Group, LLC.

The Library of Congress has cataloged the hardcover edition as follows:

Peters, Ralph, 1952– author.
   The damned of Petersburg / Ralph Peters ; maps by George Skoch.—1st ed.
      p. cm.
   "A Tom Doherty Associates book."
   ISBN 978-0-7653-7406-6 (hardcover)
   ISBN 978-1-4668-3982-3 (e-book)
   1. United States—History—Civil War, 1861–1865—Fiction.   2. Virginia—
History—1775–1865—Fiction.   I. Title.
   PS3566.E7559 D36 2016
   813'.54—dc23

                                                                    2016299661

ISBN 978-0-7653-7407-3 (trade paperback)

Our books may be purchased in bulk for promotional, educational, or
business use. Please contact your local bookseller or the Macmillan Corporate
and Premium Sales Department at 1-800-221-7945, extension 5442,
or by e-mail at MacmillanSpecialMarkets@macmillan.com.

First Edition: June 2016
First Trade Paperback Edition: July 2017

Printed in the United States of America

0 9 8 7 6 5 4 3 2 1

In honor of
Joseph Stanley Pennell
1903–1963
whose splendid novel of our Civil War,
The History of Rome Hanks and Kindred Matters,
must not be forgotten

Rebuke and dread correction wait on us,
And they shall do their office.

—WILLIAM SHAKESPEARE,
First Part of King Henry IV,
Act 5, Scene 1

PART
I

THE MINE

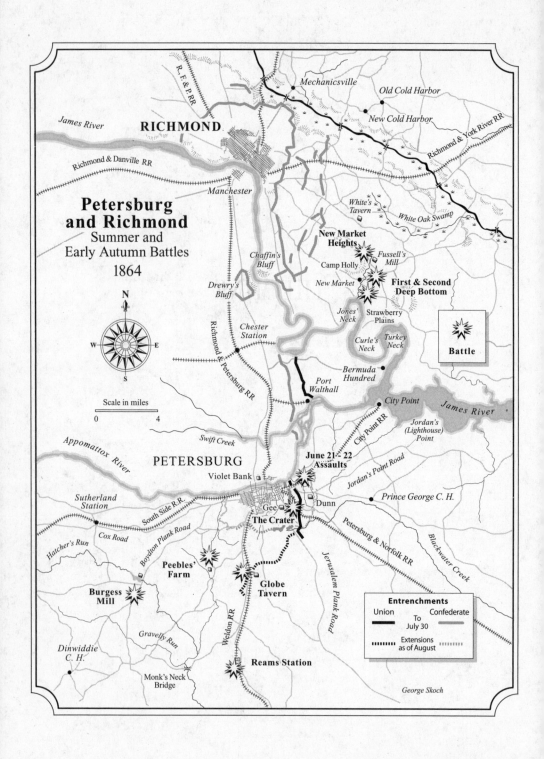

**Petersburg
and Richmond**
Summer and
Early Autumn Battles
1864

N
W   E
S

Scale in miles
0   4

Battle

James River

R. F. & P. RR

Mechanicsville

Old Cold Harbor

New Cold Harbor

RICHMOND

Richmond & York River RR

Richmond & Danville RR

Manchester

White's
Tavern

White Oak Swamp

**New Market
Heights**

Chaffin's
Bluff

Fussell's
Mill

Camp Holly

Drewry's
Bluff

New Market

**First & Second
Deep Bottom**

Jones'
Neck

Strawberry
Plains

Chester
Station

Curle's
Neck

Turkey
Neck

Richmond & Petersburg RR

Bermuda
Hundred

Port
Walthall

City Point

James River

Jordan's
(Lighthouse)
Point

Swift Creek

City Point RR

Appomattox River

PETERSBURG

**June 21–22
Assaults**

Jordan's Point Road

Prince George C. H.

Violet Bank

Sutherland
Station

Gee

Dunn

South Side R.R.

The Crater

Petersburg & Norfolk RR

Cox Road

Boydton Plank Road

Blackwater Creek

Hatcher's Run

**Peebles'
Farm**

**Burgess
Mill**

**Globe
Tavern**

Jerusalem Plank Road

Weldon RR

Gravelly Run

Entrenchments

Union   Confederate

To
July 30

Dinwiddie
C. H.

Reams Station

Extensions
as of August

Monk's Neck
Bridge

George Skoch

ONE

Early evening, July 28, 1864
Deep Bottom, Virginia

In heat as thick as syrup, skirmishers pecked. The crack of the rifles seemed dulled, the sparse commands reluctant. And the usual catcalls were missing, the hard teasing. Too hot even for insult. Suffocating.

Between the shots, flies hummed. Vermin, at least, could be relied upon. Loyal to the army to the end.

Dust marred the light. The stench of men and stink of powder had weight. Scorched air scraped lungs. Bewildered, random casualties drifted rearward. Others, shattered, rode litters toward their pain.

The romance of war, Barlow mused.

Flies surrounded him. Unable to figure out how to reach the shit encrusting his drawers. Just as Grant and Meade couldn't get at Lee, stymied by the forts and trenches at Petersburg. Or here, in front of Richmond. The black flies and the brown couldn't pierce his sweat-hardened shirt or fouled britches, and the behemoth Union Army of the Potomac, augmented by Butler's Army of the James, could not penetrate the Confederate lines. It was all of a piece, one grand incapability.

A rush of the dizzies unsettled him. His horse snorted and stepped. The day would never end.

"You all right, Frank?" Nellie asked, not lightly. Nelson Miles had not shone, but he'd still performed better than Barlow's other subordinates. As usual. A clerk before the war and newly a brigadier general, at his best Miles fought with spectacular savagery. But no man had been at his best the past few days.

"Hardly matters, does it?" Barlow soothed his fly-pricked horse. "Another grand absurdity. Poor plan, badly carried. Hancock doesn't know what to do, what with Grant and Meade and Humphreys dispensing 'advice.'" He looked away, unready to bear the features of any man, even one who almost passed as a friend. "We should've tried again today, at least properly *tried*. Now Lee knows the whole farrago's a bluff."

"The men are blown," Miles said. "I lost more to heatstroke on the march than I did to the Johnnies."

Barlow's eyebrows tightened. "Not sure that's an achievement to be proud of. Anyway, they're shirkers and slackers, the half of them. Bounty-jumpers. Dregs of the draft, what have you. You need to drive them hard."

"Frank, I think I know how to 'drive' men. They were falling in bunches before we crossed the James. Why anyone thought, in this weather . . ."

Barlow laughed. One low, unattractive syllable. "We're a *diversion*, you understand that? That's what galls me, Nellie. Winning wasn't ever in the cards." He lifted a hand. "I believe all this was only meant to draw off troops from Petersburg. In service to the great mine, the secret that's no secret." He laughed that lonely syllable again. "With Burnside behind it, that ass. . . ."

Miles' horse quivered in the heat. Barlow's gelding copied him.

"Frank"—Miles tried again—"you look seriously *ill*."

This time, Barlow's laugh was genuine. "Of course I'm ill. Everyone's ill. Virginia bears more plagues than Pharaoh's Egypt."

Shitting blood for a month. Feet worse than ever, itching infernally. Hard not to scratch the flesh right down to the bone. And the toothache back. Along with the stab of old wounds. A fine specimen of humanity he was, at the venerable age of twenty-nine.

Long way from Harvard Yard. Or Brook Farm. Or his Manhattan law office.

And Hancock, the sorry bugger, had it worse. It was obvious

that he lived with constant pain from the Gettysburg wound. There had been stretches earlier in July when Hancock could not get up from his cot. And conditions behind the ever-expanding trenches had grown so grim, so torrid and filthy, that even Hancock's English valet—a distinctly unsavory character—couldn't keep the corps commander in clean collars.

A pair of litter bearers passed, lugging a panting boy with his eyes rolled back. Barlow couldn't see blood and it got his temper up: If he could face the heat, so could the men.

Behind the scrap of shade that Barlow and Miles had commandeered, and beyond the herd of staff men keeping their distance, distempered ranks of troops waited in a tree line, allowed to kneel or lie down to wait, all of them measuring shadows that grew too slowly, hoping that no order would come to advance. It was far from the splendid division Barlow had led just three months earlier, before they plunged across the Rapidan. *That* division had been squandered in mindless fights for worthless plots of land, in grinding slaughters. By the time they'd reached Cold Harbor, Barlow had *almost* sympathized with the shirkers. The best men had fallen at the forefront of repeated attacks, leaving the cautious and cowardly to crawl back. His ruined division had been replenished with scum.

The sole hint of grace in all of it, in the long, blood-sodden summer, in the murderous heat and lung-tormenting dust, had been his Belle. When she took sick, he had been shocked at the depth of his emotion, finding himself less the stoic than he'd believed. She'd been stricken with typhus, caught from a soldier nursed at the City Point hospital, infected because she had given herself to the horror of wards and surgeries to remain near to her husband.

They had married at the outbreak of the war, their affinity more one of minds than of crude passions, a match of congenial spirits. Arabella stood ten years his senior, which philistines found odd, but the marriage had been logical enough. She *was* the cleverest woman he'd ever known: well-read, of strong opinion, unafraid. It had seemed quite a good arrangement, and so it proved.

When he'd thought her lost, he'd been astonished at his desolation. Alone in his tent, he had wept.

Now she was mending, under good care in Washington. Magnificent, marvelous Belle.

When the war ended, he'd keep his promise immediately. He'd take her to Europe, to Rome. She wished to sit where Gibbon had paused in the Forum. *His Arabella.* The flesh of his lip brushed a crooked tooth and approximated a smile. *His Belle.* A woman more excited about the history of Rome than the latest Paris fashions, a serious woman.

His mother, whom Barlow adored, always took pains with her *toilette,* had even done so when they'd lived on pennies, blue-blooded beggars. Of course, she had rather disliked Arabella at first. That was in the natural order of things. But Barlow felt the breach had been repaired.

Yet, he remembered: his mother, at her most regal, saying, "Francis, she never *laughs.*" And then, with a moment's reflection, adding, "But neither do you. . . ."

Unfair and untrue. He still felt the slap of her words.

To Europe, though. To Rome. Perhaps some foreign doctor could heal his feet.

"What's that?" Barlow demanded.

An assault? By Gibbon's men?

"Cavalry at it again," Miles responded. "Not much to it, but they do go on." He patted his mount. "Hard on the horses."

Of course. The firing was well to the north. Where Sheridan, fierce and foul, was back in action. If "action" described the feckless cavalry fighting.

It troubled him that he hadn't placed things properly.

Dizziness. Flies. Heat. His own stink engulfed him. Suspenders off his shoulders and dropped to his flanks, checkered shirt clinging, saber a dead weight, Barlow felt hollow and top-heavy. Was he, in fact, capable?

Capable or not, he would not give up his command until they carried him off. The man who quit in war was no man at all.

"Nellie, I don't mind a fight . . . ," Barlow began.

It was Miles' turn to laugh.

"I don't mind a fight," Barlow repeated. "But the pointlessness, the blundering . . ." He straightened in the saddle and the flies tracked his change of posture. "I'd like, just once, to see a plan of quality, a scheme with some least forethought. Something beyond 'Go out there, bleed, and come back.' I have no more confidence in Grant—or Meade—than I would in a howling madman."

His father. Gone mad, God-infected. Lost. A man of the cloth who had torn the cloth asunder, deserting kith and kin, driven by demons. Barlow had not seen his face since childhood. And he did not wish to see it now.

Yet, at times, he wondered what had become of that fallen star.

Shooing off his personal escort of flies, Miles said, "I don't know. Wastage aplenty, I give you. But Grant did fight Lee all the way to Richmond. And over the James."

"And now we're stuck. Butler was stuck, now we're all stuck. Wait and see, Nellie. Burnside's affair will be another cock-up. Everyone's out of ideas." His guts churned. "If ever any man in this army had one."

"Lee's stuck, too," Miles said.

"And it just goes on."

Miles declined to argue the point further. Too hot for speech. Out of sight, on the edge of the skirmish line, the firing quickened. Only to swoon again.

Sweat burned Barlow's eyes.

This, he told himself, *is life's reality.* Immeasurably removed from the Harvard classrooms where, as an undergraduate, he had played at thought and preened. The experiments of the great Professor Agassiz on viscosity couldn't begin to measure this fetid air, nor had the lectures on aesthetics foreseen this blighted landscape. Except for Arabella, all of the things he had valued seemed a fraud now, as empty as the boasts of an Irish drunkard.

Harvard valedictorian? What had come of that? The truth was that he had not cared for the honor, had striven to come in first only to deny the place to Teddy Lyman, who had wanted it so much. He had scored a hollow triumph out of meanness—was that the quality, above all others, that equipped Francis Channing Barlow to be a general? Smirking again, he recalled those awful hours of German philosophy, the imagined importance of the "latest ideas" to cross the Atlantic. What had *they* amounted to? *Die Welt als Wille und Vorstellung?* Will certainly mattered, but reality was more than the mind's concoction. The world wasn't some figment. It was blood and shit and bone. And a witless sky.

Poor Teddy Lyman. A good chum, despite all. Forgiving. Volunteer aide to that old crab Meade and always good for the latest gossip from Boston.

Barlow gulped bitter water from his canteen, wondering if he should try to eat a cracker to calm his insides. The skirmishers, his recalcitrants and the Johnnies, had fallen silent, too drained to do more.

"Might want to stir things up a bit," he told Miles. "At least, make sure those scoundrels of yours are awake."

With his sunburned, freckled face revealing annoyance, Miles nodded. No man, colonel or corporal, wanted to move, to do anything. The heat was an animal pinning you down and slobbering all over you.

Before Miles nudged his horse into motion, Charlie Morgan appeared. Back where a primitive road parted the trees. Hancock's chief of staff rode at a pace that defied the heat, kicking up dust and drawing curses from soldiers.

"Oh, Christ," Miles said. "We're going back in after all."

Barlow shook his head. Warily. "Doesn't make sense, at this point."

They waited for Morgan to close the distance. Barlow's feet itched monstrously.

Hancock's chief of staff reined up. Dust swelled and Barlow snapped, "I doubt you bear glad tidings, Charlie. Shall I take a guess?"

A noted cynic and famously profane, Morgan looked oddly

somber. He was so discolored by dust that a skirmisher might have taken him for a Johnny.

Uncharacteristically, Morgan paused before speaking. As if he brought orders for a suicide charge.

"General Barlow . . . ," Morgan began. Then he stopped.

What the devil? Barlow wondered. A shiver went through him. Good God. He wasn't being relieved, was he? For what cause? He'd followed his worthless orders as best he could. They couldn't have marched any faster, there was no reason—

"General Barlow"—Morgan tried again—"Frank . . . perhaps you'd like to dismount?"

"For God's sake, Charlie. I'm glued to the saddle with shit."

"If you'd dismount, though . . ."

"Oh, bugger it. Fine." He swung out of the saddle, long-legged, fanning his own fumes, smelling his reek. Aware of slime, grit, itch.

He stood on firm ground, but was hardly firm himself.

Miles, too, had dismounted. Morgan eyed him, as if weighing whether or not to ask for privacy.

"Whatever you've got to say, Nellie can hear it," Barlow told him. "Nothing in this army stays a secret."

"General Barlow, I regret—"

"You've conveyed your demure reluctance. Just get on with it."

It struck Barlow that Morgan had yet to utter a single obscenity. *That* was queer, indeed.

Surely, Hancock wouldn't let Meade or Grant relieve him? They'd had their disagreements, but Win had seemed to be grooming him. To take over the corps, should Hancock's wound continue to suppurate.

Morgan stepped closer, immune to the scents of humankind. His whore-weathered, war-hardened face, so fierce, all but trembled.

"General Barlow . . . we've just gotten word. Frank, your wife is dead."

Barlow stared through the man.

"I'm sorry," Morgan went on. "You have my condolences. Hancock's, of course. . . ."

"When?"

"Yesterday. We just got the news. From Teddy Lyman, the message went through Meade's headquarters."

Barlow nodded.

"Hancock's ordered a tug up to the landing. To take you to City Point, to the steamers. We're just waiting for Meade's authorization. For your leave. There's the usual nonsense. Miles will take the division while you're away."

"Yes."

"I'm so sorry, Frank," Miles put in.

"It doesn't matter," Barlow said. He placed a hand atop his saddle to steady himself. Feeling his bowels about to betray him again. One more death. Why should it matter? Amid all this? Why should it matter? Why should it matter at all?

Tears raced from his eyes, a humiliation.

"Did you say something, Frank?" Morgan asked. "Are you all right?"

Afternoon, July 29
Camp Holly, eastern defenses of Richmond

*W*atermelons. Two wagonloads. The boys did spark when the drivers turned into camp. Oates was glad he had done it, gone into Richmond and dug into his own pockets. Which were hardly deep.

No time at all and his men—these men who were his consolation after the great wrong done him—were at the melons with buck knives and bayonets, or just busting them open on the ground, revealing and reveling in that woman-pink fruit, wet pulp, eager as children, made children again by war. His boys, his men. The 48th Alabama, "Fortykins" to their brethren, since so many of these hill men had blood relations in the regiment, usually in the same company. Strong, willing, able men, if rubbed thin by poor rations and hard marching. Men as good as a cheated colonel could ask.

Just weren't his old 15th. The regiment he had led up that hill at Gettysburg, a hill nameless then, where he left his brother John dying, left him to the Yankees, because he had his duty, and later he learned that the hill was called "Little Round Top," though it had been plenty big enough for a slaughter. He had *led* that regiment, his 15th, that many-footed, many-headed beast he had loved more than any woman he recollected. *His* men. He had led them until he was wounded in the autumn and then he had come back to lead them again, limping, hip grinding bone on bone, pestle and mortar. He'd led their falling numbers through the Wilderness and Spotsylvania, each killing ground worse than the last, and then through the one-sided butchery at Cold Harbor, that day no more than a massacre, the killing so easy and terrible that his own men, unscathed, had vomited.

The 15th had been *his, his, his,* until Major Lowther, a shirker in a fight, had come back from Richmond with the rank of colonel, granted by the Senate of the Confederacy, and bearing along with his undeserved patent the news that Oates wasn't really a colonel after all, his commission had never been signed, and maybe he wasn't a lieutenant colonel, either. Gloating, Lowther had offered to let Oates stay on as the regiment's major.

He would not, did not.

He had gone to Lee himself to plead his case, and Lee had passed him along to Jefferson Davis, both men full of useless sympathy, unwilling to fuss with legislators. Davis had acknowledged his right to his colonelcy, though, and given him the 48th to salve the wound, since Oates already knew the regiment, had led it along with his own back in the bloody, bloody, bloody days of May, when it had not had one field officer left standing. Even now, it wasn't truly a regiment, but a remnant.

He had clutched the command, gnawed by the injustice done him, reminded of it each day because Law's Brigade was held in reserve and his 48th tented right beside the dastardly Lowther and his 15th Alabama. His days were as bitter as wormwood.

His mother did love that expression: "My days are as bitter as wormwood." She would shake her head and speak in the glory voice, though not at the volume, of a circuit preacher, the sort who rode a mule, not a horse, and had mastered the cadence of the Holy Bible, of speech impregnable. His mother and her chore-burnished faith in the Lord. On a swept-clean porch, she would mouth those words with a lean sort of affection, as if complaint were a thing to be nursed and cherished.

Complaint, that ready delight of hard-used folk, song of his blood.

Oates stood with folded arms, watching the men devour the watermelons, their cheeks shining with drip. His back was to the river in the distance, turned resolutely to the Yankee gunboats, inured to their occasional puffs of devilment, the range too long for the shells to do him one-tenth the evil Lowther had done unto him.

Washington had encamped on this very spot, so it was said, with his army triumphant. Just after Yorktown. The echo was pleasant, but Oates wasn't blithe about another such victory, here, with his people pressed against Richmond by the Yankees. Who kept coming on again and again, drab devils.

Oates didn't take to feeling cornered.

Well, you just had to face it one fight at a time. And not over-ponder.

Still, it had been a queer sort of relief when, two days before, they had been ordered down the New Market Road, where the Yankees had stirred up a fuss. And then they had marched back again, after the scrap went quits. Nothing to it but the heat and dust.

He watched, bemused, as a first few men strayed over from the camp of the 15th, slavering, enticed. As if by Eve herself. By watermelons as tempting as Delilah, as plain a come-hither as a lifted skirt. Oates understood desire. And he watched them come, watched them edge their way in, watched them take the offered fruit in hand, intruders teased but tolerated. His men, new and old.

More of the boys from the 15th brisked their way over, hound dogs on the scent. Just too many, and it would not do. They had to learn that this fruit, this gift, was for his new men now. Let Lowther, the tightfisted bastard, scour his own purse. Let *him* buy a treat for the men he'd stolen away. Let *him* burn.

Oates strode forward, hip not much of a bother this ripe day, maybe heat-soothed, and he said, "You men there. Cates, Jones, Kirby. Rest of you. Those melons are for the Forty-eighth, and they won't stretch. Y'all get back to your camp." He could not help but add, "I'm sure Colonel Lowther's got watermelons coming."

"Aw, Colonel. There's plenty enough."

Oates shook his head. "I don't see it, and don't you sass me, Farley. You get along now. Take what you have in hand and go your way. Hear?"

And go they did, in sorrow. Cut down to sulking children. War made a man a creature of dependencies, waiting, helpless, for rations, garments, orders. Independent fellows who would have beaten and perhaps slain the man who took a tone of command with them back in low-country Alabama, his realm, or in the hills that spat out the 48th, these hill men who had brethren of Yankee leanings and no love for the Confederacy, men without niggers who couldn't see fighting to keep niggers where they belonged, men from hills where only white faces showed themselves and lived, particular people who wished to be left alone, yet here they were, almost three hundred still, now that he had drained the Richmond hospitals.

He had taken over this rump of a regiment, men who had strayed from discipline, and he had let them know that the days of slumped shoulders were over. He'd drilled them hard, hardest on his captains and lieutenants, and they had not troubled him much, for they knew his reputation for knocking down any man who needed knocking down, and he had led them in battle and well, and for all the groggy, sun-ain't-up-yet murmurings, the truth was that they wanted a firm hand, desired it as a woman desired things she could not admit.

He had taken on Richmond, menacing clerks not only with requisition forms, but with generous hints of violence, and he had gotten his new men better rations—such as they were—and new uniforms and even replacement rifles for the worst his inspections discovered. His little regiment was the best-looking outfit in Law's Brigade these days, and he had done that in a matter of weeks, let Lowther get down on his knees and lick his ass.

He burned with hellfire each time he saw that man.

Joe Hardwick, a lieutenant of some grip, stepped up to Oates. He held out a cut of watermelon. "You'll join the men, sir? Have yourself a piece?"

Oates remembered Billy Hardwick, young Joe's elder brother, from the brigade's old days. Two blinks after his promotion to lieutenant colonel, Billy had been captured by the Yankees and not heard of since.

Thick-bearded and dark of mien, a purposeful man and let every last soul know it, the new commanding officer of the 48th Alabama, William C. Oates, Colonel, CSA, pending confirmation by the august powers, shook his head as if declining to buy a fine hog cheap.

"You eat that up," he told the lieutenant. "Never cared for watermelon myself." A lie, a gargantuan lie! But the men had to know that the melons were for them, not purchased to satiate a colonel's craving.

Oates had satisfied a deeper craving on one foray into Richmond. He had asked after a house where the girls were clean and had taken his chances with pink, quivering flesh, that other rich and immemorial pulp. And he seemed to have come through unscathed. Despite the odds.

He might have lingered, but he'd been repulsed by the unclean sheets he'd only noticed when done with his doings. Even a whore had no cause to be a slattern.

Different standard for colored gals, of course, and he'd always been fond of them, of their engulfing scent and merry laughter. But a man didn't dare touch that sort around here, given all the contagion. He'd lost good men that way. So the best on offer had been that bored, too-costly white woman, a creature of painted nails and dirty toes, a slut who hardly bothered to lace her gown up between callers: a full month's pay in worthless money for a damned poor ride. Well, that about summed up the entire Confederacy, did it not?

Things hadn't worked out quite the way they'd reckoned.

Oates' eyes tracked Captain Wiggenton and waved him over through the shimmering air.

Passing a rind to his left hand, J.W. saluted with his right. "Yes, sir?"

"You let your brother officers know that I want the entire regiment turned out. Soon as the heat breaks. Get in an hour of drill before dark settles."

"Sir, I don't know as I'd say this heat ever breaks."

"Well, then you turn 'em out when you think I think it breaks." Oates refolded his arms, letting his hard face harden even more. "And don't you ever back-talk me again, not even a hint. Hear?"

"Sir, I—"

"You go on now. Do just what I told you."

"Yes, sir."

Before the younger man could flick a salute and move along, the captain's eyes jumped to another target. Behind Oates.

Oates turned and found Colonel Lowther striding up, dressed in every last inch of braid a colonel commanding was authorized. Too damned hot for that kind of fuss, but Lowther did enjoy his one-man parades.

"You go on now," Oates told the captain. "Git."

Lowther drew up a few feet away, as if he preferred not to smell Oates up too close. Or, perhaps, get his jaw broken.

"Oates, I'm told you've been luring my men with watermelons. Without asking my permission. As an officer and a gentleman, I must ask you—"

"Lowther," Oates said, "you clear out of my camp. And keep your boys out of my camp. *If* they'll listen to you." He narrowed his eyes. "As for watermelons, you sonofabitch, I look at you and know just where one'd fit."

Think that mine'll work?" Sergeant Eckert asked in his don't-trust-one-thing voice. "Think she'll go up?"

"Be quiet, Levi," Brown said. "Let Sam call the roll."

"Nobody's missing." Eckert scratched inside his shirt. " 'Least, not yet."

"Quiet."

First Sergeant Losch read the too-brief list of names. Unable to stand in ranks, the men of Company C sat on the firing stoop or squatted along the trench walls, tanned by dust and darkened with sweat but sheltered from the Johnnies a shout away, just up the slope. Johnnies who took a mind to shoot now and then. Levi was right, of course. Brevet Lieutenant Charles Brown knew the whereabouts of every man he led: fifty-four in all. And only that many because of returned convalescents. The only time a man left the baking trench was to lug the slops buckets back through the traverses—a duty some men sought for a break in the boredom—or to fill canteens or bring up hot eats or mail. Or for Brown to report back to regiment that nothing much had changed. Or for orders that only warned of more orders to come.

Today's orders had been unwelcome.

A few months before, men told they'd attack in the morning would have grown agitated, flaring at little things and scribbling letters. Dulled now, like knives used badly, they cleaned their rifles by rote and tried not to think. But men who had once slept soundly would shout in the dark.

Brown hoped he wasn't one of those who cried out. If he was, no one ever told him. But his dreams, too, were unsettled.

He needed to be steady, to remain sound.

Peering down the trench as the men responded to rasped-out

names, Brown knew the faces, the habits, the man-by-man smells, of those left on the roster. Most were friends or acquaintances from home, canal boatmen just as he'd been and hoped to be again. With his own boat, bought clear. A man of property.

The roll call echoed unspoken names, as well.

So many, so terribly many, had died, not least his brother Benjamin, dead of a fever at Vicksburg, on the banks of a river grander than the Schuylkill, sweating out his life atop bluffs that belonged to a different world. Since May, though, the pace of the killing had passed all decency. In April, Brown had been a corporal, in May a sergeant and then first sergeant. In June, with the last of the officers dead or wounded, he had been anointed an "acting" lieutenant, waiting for orders to make the rank real and leading the survivors of Company C of the 50th Pennsylvania Veteran Volunteer Infantry. Even the regiment's former colonel, lifted up to brigade command, had been wounded in one of the useless assaults made after the army snuggled up to Petersburg. The tally of dead, wounded, or missing exceeded the number of voices that answered, "Here!"

All the dead friends, the comrades. Others suffered captivity, like the Israelites in a sermon. Jake Guertler had died in one of the last assaults, just a month after Jake's brother Bill had been captured at Spotsylvania. Taken, along with a dozen other men from Company C. Poor Johnny Doudle, who had dreaded becoming a prisoner, had been collared by scarecrow Rebs. As Brown looked on, helpless, across a swale.

He did hope Doudle was faring all right, that he was still alive.

And his own best friend, Henry Hill, who had made a madman's stand back in the Wilderness, had been wounded the day the others had been captured. Henry, at least, would return. To endure an unsought and unwanted promotion to sergeant. Brown missed Henry, couldn't wait to see him again. Sometimes, Brown feared he missed him more than his brother.

A terrible time it had been, all senselessness. Hard to say which day had been the worst since they waded the Rapidan, but that charge at Spotsylvania was up for the prize.

First Sergeant Losch crabbed along the trench, waving off swarming flies. "All men present, Lieutenant. All those fit for duty. *In dieser Schweinerei.*"

Lieutenant. The rank still sat uneasily, but the men had taken his promotion well. And that was the hardest thing: These men whose kin he knew by first names all, they trusted him now. Even as Brown had to struggle to trust himself. By the magic of rank alone he'd become their father. But a father destined to kill at least a few of them, Isaacs to his Abraham, with no hope of an angel's hand to rescue them.

What would Pastor Colley say to that?

"The two days' rations? For the men to carry?"

"*Verdammt noch mal.* They're coming. The boys try, but the commissary comes late."

The commissary sergeants were all squeezers, heartless as missies raised up in brick houses. In the army, you were always at the mercy of someone or something. They got fresh rations now, but mess chums couldn't cook them in the trench line, and the company had to slop its vittles together in the rear. Then the eats had to come up through the traverses. The day past, a boy had been wounded scurrying up and the stew got spilled.

Of course, there had been times aplenty when they all would have been thrilled by the thought of beef fresh and free of maggots, no matter how late it might have been served or the risk involved in the carrying. But memories never helped an angry belly.

Losch shook his big Dutch head. "Since I am first sergeant, I think I hate sergeants more."

Brown smiled. Losch was the best choice left for his position, since his Dutch-talk helped with the boys who struggled with English. Brown glanced from Losch to Levi Eckert, the latter a sharp-dealing man even with his relatives, a conniver who had once tried to cheat a cousin out of a new-gotten pair of socks. But Levi was a fury in a fight, the men respected that. And his stripes seemed to have changed him, at least tolerably. Levi would never have sewn on those stripes but for the frightful losses, but, Brown knew full

well, neither would he have had a flea's chance of wearing a second
lieutenant's shoulder strap.

"Anybody sick yet?" Brown asked. "From that pie?"

"They will be," Levi put in.

Losch grunted and said, "I call up more shit pails. Such *Dreck*
a man puts in his mouth."

Brown smiled without merriment. "Would've gobbled it down
our gullets at Knoxville."

"This ain't Knoxville," Levi said.

"I don't know which *ist mir lieber*," Losch said. "Here or
there."

"Take the heat over the cold myself," Levi told him. "Keeps off
the rheumatism."

Losch shook his head. *"Mag die Hitze nicht."*

"Sam, the boys got you talking all Dutch again," Brown teased.
Reaching for better spirits.

The young first sergeant shrugged. "My mother is speaking
nothing else, you know. I write to her and confuse myself with
words." Losch smiled, sighed. *"Ach, die Mutti."*

And they pondered the bloody-footed winter past. Then they
thought on the molasses pie Jack Fritz's mother had sent him
through the mails, a mad thing to do. The pie had arrived broken
into mold-coated crumbs. But Jack—over howls of disgust—had
scraped off the filth and shared the remains with his butties.

Well, if a man didn't sicken from one thing, he would from another. Hard enough it was, even now, for Brown to drink water all
wiggling. Or to squat over a slops bucket teeming with worms.

Although he'd lived poor as a child and always worked with his
hands, Brown was a fastidious man. That was how Frances put it.
"Fas*tid*ious." He had needed to figure out what she meant the first
time she used the word. But she did claim she liked cleanliness in
a caller. And he'd always swabbed down the deck of his boat at day's
end and kept his ropes properly coiled. In another world.

Frances. His betrothed. He imagined her at her piano, in her
mother's parlor. His Frances, kind-eyed and soft. In his big, bruised

hand, her fingers had looked so delicate that he hesitated to grasp them. *He* was the one who refused to marry until the war was done. Too many widows in Schuylkill Haven already. She deserved more.

Brown sought to be a good man, to get through the war without turning bad forever, to be deserving of the things he wanted. But there were times when he sensed a beast inside, sharp-clawed, on a chain that might break at a tug.

Even in this world of beards and whiskers, Brown shaved close. As if a clean face promised a clean life. He longed to wash himself white again, to scrub off the filth of war, afraid that the dirt had already gone too deep.

The endless heat. At times, it seemed worst in the evenings. Heavier. Stale. He pushed back his cap and wiped the sweat from his forehead and eyes. Fit to cook a man, it was, even under a strip of canvas.

Even the longed-for rain days back had seemed to fall at a boil. And the mud that swamped the trenches had tortured them all before turning to dust again.

Brown wasn't fond of Virginia. Or of much else, at present.

He slapped at the flies and Levi aped his gesture. Sam Losch grunted again, too hot to bother.

"Well?" Levi said. "Seeing as how the company business is done for the next ten minutes, let me ask the opinion of the high-and-mighty Lieutenant Charles Brown. Before old Useless Grant himself sends down for his advice." Levi fussed at the dirt with a sliver splintered from a crate. "Think those pit-boys from north of the mountain can make their damned mine work? Blow our Confederate brethren to Hell for breakfast?"

Brown wasn't minded to think on that too hard, given the prospects. Rumors had blazed down the trenches all day. The 50th and the rest of Willcox's division—even the reserves held back by the railroad—had received abrupt orders to support an assault planned for the morning. Company C would be relieved just after dark so it could pull back and form with the rest of the regiment.

So they could go forward again. After the "secret" mine was blown, the mine that was known to every skulker and sutler.

And if the mine failed? They'd probably go forward anyway. Once the army started in to doing something, it was hard to stop the doing, even after it stopped making any sense. Until enough blood had been spilled for the generals to show they'd made an effort.

Be careful, Brown warned himself. He daren't speak so. Not one word about his doubts, his ugly mistrust of things. The men were discouraged and blue as it was, with little left but a grudging sense of duty.

"Well?" Levi demanded.

"Good men in the Forty-eighth," Brown said. "Miners, most of them. They know what they're doing."

"But does anybody *else* know what they're doing? There's the question."

"Pleasants is a good man," Sam Losch put in. "*Ein guter Kerl. Doch wild.* Maybe our colonel he should have been, but he takes the Forty-eighth."

Pleasants had been a mine engineer back home, with something a touch dark and foreign about him, a fellow with a brain in his head but calluses on his hands. The kind of man you respected before you could say why. Brown had known him, just slightly. Their relationship had been limited to talk about re-siting a coal chute outside Port Carbon, the better to feed the loads into the boats. Brown had been pleased to be asked for his opinion by such a man. Not that his advice had any effect. The coal company did what it wanted, and it had not wanted to pay to move the chute.

It was said of Pleasants that his wife died young, months after their marriage, and that he chased death but could not get himself killed.

"If Colonel Pleasants says that mine will work, it's going to work," Brown declared.

"Hark to the voice of Solomon!" Levi flicked an ant from the back of his hand. "Little buggers bite. All right. The mine works. Boom, up she goes. But you heard everything I heard. More, no doubt. Seeing as you're a high-and-mighty lieutenant." He scraped the barren earth again. "Them coons was set to go in? Do some fighting for once? All trained up and ready to go? And they call them off when the circus comes to town? You tell me why. You just tell me. Here we are, fighting so Old Abe can free the Children of Ham to take a white man's job, and he won't even let them fight. No, sir. Send in more white men to die."

When Brown didn't answer, Levi continued. "And I blame Grant. Old Meade don't do nothing without his say-so."

"That a fact?" Brown said in the sharper voice he was mastering. "I guess when they make you a general, you can fix it."

"What's chapping you?" Levi asked, surprised at Brown's sudden harshness.

Down along the trench, the newest men worried their knapsacks and tightened their leathers, as they'd been told. The older hands played cards or picked lice from their garments.

Brown could hardly say why he'd turned sour. It struck a man like a cramp.

Corporal Oswald scuttled up the trench, hog-dirty and pleasant-faced.

"Supper coming up," he announced. "Fresh beef, all right, and plenty more to carry."

The Reb sharpshooters started in. Just like them.

First Sergeant Losch rose to see to his duties, but Levi Eckert tarried. "You know which division's set to lead the attack?" he asked, barely whispering.

Brown nodded. Yes. They'd all heard the rumors haunting the lines since noon.

"Worst division in the corps," Levi continued. "Garrison men. Useless."

Brown wanted to say, "Just be glad that *we* won't be out front," but officers could not say such things. Officers had to show confidence. Even if they didn't feel it, not a lick. He felt terribly old at twenty-three.

"There any point behind your pestering, Levi?"

The sergeant grew earnest. "Tell you the truth, I wouldn't mind seeing this fizzle. Right at the start. Can't go in on the flank, if there ain't no flank to go in on. And I can't say I'm much minded to go in, that's just the truth. It's been one mess after another since we got here. *Before* we got here."

Brown considered the man in front of him: an unlikely survivor, given the risks he took during a fight. Levi Eckert, for all his faults, had never been one to show fear. And while Brown wasn't given to profane talk—Frances didn't like it—he saw Levi as one hard-made sonofabitch. But all of a sudden Levi looked like a ghost of the man he'd been.

"We'll go in," Brown said.

Eight thirty p.m., July 29
Mahone's Division
Confederate lines, Petersburg

Still got your cow, I see," Doc Brewer said. He set down his cake plate.

Brigadier General William Mahone nodded mildly, not quite looking at his white-haired visitor. He tilted his chair another few degrees, relishing the risk, the calculation.

The shack's porch creaked. Not much of a headquarters, but it served. Beyond a low ridge, heat-whipped pickets annoyed each other. Nothing to that firing, just obligation.

"Chickens, too," Mahone replied. His sharp voice of command had soothed to a gentlemanly languor. "Wouldn't need to fuss so, if you medical fellows paid more attention to what's inside a man's carcass than to what's left in his purse." He smoothed his billy-goat beard.

The old man tapped the whiskey bottle he'd brought out from the city. "You won't join me, then? In a draught of this pleasing elixir? In return for that fine cake?"

Mahone shook his head. "Blessing in disguise, my dyspepsia. So Otelia tells me. No fear of taking to drink, burn my insides out."

The old doctor nodded with seasoned gentility. "Take it over the gout, though. That's a plague on a man." He splashed more whiskey into his tin cup, drawing envious looks from lurking staff men. "Mrs. Brewer paid a call. Wife of yours is a firecracker, Billy."

Mahone snorted. "Stick of dynamite, more like."

Otelia, pure spunk. Mahone enjoyed the pleasant sparring between them, brisk exchanges that never rose to a spat. When he'd completed the Norfolk line, after laying tracks right through that endless swamp and doing what his fellow engineers thought impossible, he and Otelia had delighted in labeling the newly created stations, drawing their names from the novels of Walter Scott. There had been one water stop they could not agree on, though. Until Otelia laughed that you-look-out trill, halfway between a lady and a hoyden, and said, "We'll call it 'Disputanta.'" And they did.

A detail of soldiers, thin as famine, loped toward the rear. Pretty marching wasn't called for, but Mahone almost rose from his chair: He liked a degree of crispness in a soldier, heat or no heat. Hard times wanted hard men.

Doc Brewer sipped his whiskey, maybe reading his mind. "Infernal weather. Not sure I've seen worse."

Hot it was, indeed. But Mahone was a Southside man, born and bred, and the heat was just a bad neighbor a man got used to. Did like the ocean breezes they'd had in Norfolk, though. Hadn't liked the yellow fever much. Fifty-five, that was. It had seemed a muchness of death back then, but war had taught him a higher mathematics.

"Never could get too riled," Mahone said, "over things I couldn't change." He gazed into the mellowing light, felt the still-hard air. The passing soldiers had faded to ghosts of dust. Settling his chair's front legs on the porch, he called, *"Hannibal."*

"Same cow, same nigger," Doc Brewer mused.

"Different cow."

The servant appeared. "Suh?"

"Any more buttermilk?"

"You done drunk it, Marse Billy. Git you the plain ole, though."

Mahone turned to his guest. "Glass for you, Doctor? About all I can offer, I'm afraid."

The old man held up his whiskey. "Wouldn't dare start drinking cow's milk now. After all these years of specimen health."

"One glass, Hannibal."

"Suh."

When the servant had gone, Doc Brewer shook his head. "Billy, what's to become of those poor people? If the Yankees have their way? They could never take care of themselves. . . ."

"They take care of us," Mahone teased, just to be contrary.

The old man drank and sighed. "Give a simple man a simple task. Give him time, and he'll master it. But the notion—"

"We haven't lost the war yet," Mahone said, a tad sharply.

"No, no. Of course not. I only meant—"

"You meant 'What if?' That's all right, no offense taken. Many a man must be asking himself that question." A half-smile lifted one side of his mouth. "Just won't admit it. That's all."

"And you? What do you foresee? Between old friends."

"I'm an engineer. I deal with the problem at hand."

Doc Brewer shook his head. "First dishonest thing I've heard you say, Billy. You were always a far-thinking man, 'long as I've known you. How you made your fortune." The old man seemed to fade into the shadows. "Saw what this war would bring, better than most folks."

"Well, the Yankees have a bloody business ahead before they lick anybody. That's what I think."

Downcast, the old man repeated, "A bloody business."

"You know, I'd like to find Otelia better lodgings," Mahone declared. Eager to change the subject. "Better than that sty she's boarding in. If you should hear of anything . . ."

Doc Brewer nodded. "I'll ask about."

"I'd take that as a kindness."

The servant delivered a glass of milk streaked pink. Mahone drank deep. To soothe his belly, his soul.

His guest leaned closer, seeking intimacy. "Billy, you and I do go back . . . otherwise, I would not presume to ask . . ."

"That's a worrisome preliminary."

"All this business about a mine now. Is there . . . I mean, people are saying the Yankees are tunneling right under the city."

Mahone's smirk lived and died in a brace of seconds. He shook his head. "Fool nonsense. Far as the city goes. You tell people that. The good citizens of Petersburg need to worry about what's on top of the ground, not what's beneath it." He scratched the side of his neck. Even undone, the collar itched in the heat. Southside man or not. "As for a *military* mine, that's another matter. Alexander was convinced a month ago they were at it, tunneling somewhere up around Elliott's stretch."

"And you think . . ."

"The Yankees would be damned fools not to try it." Which was why he had his men waking at two thirty every morning and standing to by three. Their prospects were especially worrisome now, with Lee stripping the lines so thin to shift troops north of the James, responding to more Federal shenanigans.

"I see. And might they . . ."

"Succeed? Devil only knows. But one thing those boys over there do have is anthracite miners, deep miners. And mining engineers. In their position, I'd certainly try it myself." Cocking one short limb against the banister, he pushed the front legs of his chair off the floor again.

"And . . . might we expect this soon? A detonation?"

"All depends on the engineering difficulties. I'm a railroad man, not a miner. But they'll have soil issues, ventilation issues. More than that, I can't say."

He almost wanted the Yankees to do it, to get it over with, if they planned such a thing at all. Rumors ran madcap, the men were unsettled. Heat-hammered. Rendered indolent of flesh and mad-dog hot of temper. Waiting.

And things along the line had gotten a bit too quiet for his taste. The Yankees were up to *something*, no least doubt.

Mahone had known his guest for years and liked him mightily. But he wasn't minded to discuss military matters any further. His old friend seemed to sense it, if belatedly.

"We'd take Otelia in ourselves, if—"

"Wouldn't want that," Mahone said firmly. "Didn't mean that at all." He smiled and added, "You'd live to regret it."

Otelia. With her sense of humor that could peel a rattlesnake. His wife was a filly who needed a fair stretch of pasture.

That sense of humor had only failed as the infants died, one after another.

Don't think on that now.

Having reached the right application of tonic from his bottle, the doctor cast off his last formality. "Speaking of your missus, got to ask you . . . meant to for a time now . . ."

"How I came to be married to so fine a woman, and her the taller of us by a good two inches?" Otelia. No flawless beauty, truth be told, but a rose who wore her thorns proudly. His wife: an ornery comfort, indispensable.

"About Second Manassas. What she told that courier."

Softened by remembrance, Mahone grinned. "You mean when they told her I'd only suffered a flesh wound—"

"And she said, 'Then I know it's serious. For William has no flesh, whatsoever.'" The old doctor cackled.

"Yes, sir, that's about right," Mahone agreed. His soldiers joked that he was every inch a soldier, there just weren't many inches of him. "Little Billy" Mahone, survivor of Nat Turner's rebellion as a child and a graduate of the Virginia Military Institute, at just shy of five feet five inches tall, had been forced to look up *at* many a man, but there were a good sight fewer he looked up *to*.

"Might want to get back home. Before full dark," he told his friend from the years of peace and prosperity.

Doc Brewer nodded. "Leave the whiskey?"

Mahone shook his head in the gloaming. His long beard dusted his shirt. "Some fool'd just drink it up. You take it along."

The old man rose from his chair with a reserve of vigor. "My congratulations, by the way. Hear you're set to get promoted, soon as President Davis finds his pen." He slapped off the dust that had settled on his clothing. "*Major* General Mahone. Won't that be fine?"

"Reckon we'll see," Mahone told him.

Eight thirty p.m., July 29
Dunn house, headquarters, Union Ninth Corps
Petersburg lines

Oh, dear, Burnside thought. Dear, dear.

He feared he had made an error.

Absently chewing a cuticle, Burnside looked down at Ledlie. Ledlie looked up at him. The corps commander lowered his eyes and began to pace again, still gnawing his finger.

"Nothing for it," he said with a sudden shake of his head, as if warding off a chill in the awful heat. "Nothing for it."

"What?" Ledlie asked. Burnside feared the fellow smelled of alcohol.

Nothing for it.

His other division commanders had left him, Potter in a huff, Willcox uncertain, Ferrero still aggrieved. Only Ledlie remained behind. As if stunned by what had befallen him.

Staff officers shied away. Busy enough they were, busy enough. So much to do, all the changes to the plan . . .

Burnside rued missing his dinner.

Meade, Meade! Terrible man. How could he, how could he do it? U.S. Colored Troops, all about the Negroes. Ferrero had them prepared, all prepared. Then Meade interfered. Bags under his eyes, the insistent nose. George Meade. Telling him, only the day before, that Ferrero's U.S. Colored Troops could not lead the assault. Politically dangerous, Lincoln already in trouble. If things went wrong and the Negroes suffered a massacre, all the abolitionists would howl, claiming the darkies were used as cannon fodder. Cannon fodder! Politics! Lincoln! Meade! He had appealed to

Grant, but got no relief. Meade was only Grant's henchman now-adays. And here they were. With the mine set to go up in seven hours. Less.

Burnside wiped a palm over his bald crown, skimming off sweat. Horrid weather, horrid. And now this . . . this upheaval. The best-laid plans . . .

And he'd made things worse, made them worse himself. Why had he done what he did? Meade had told him to lead with his best division. But that would have been Potter's. Or Willcox's, in a pinch. But all of their men were tired, tired. Didn't have the heart. Straws, he'd had them draw straws. It had seemed the only fair way to go about it, with Ferrero's darkies held back to go in last.

If they went in at all.

It had seemed like a good idea, even gallant. Then Ledlie drew the short straw. Ledlie! Didn't deserve a division, terrible man. But he couldn't be relieved. Far too well connected in New York, in Albany. Political man himself. Of sorts, of sorts. And any man who wished to have a future in Rhode Island politics—as Ambrose Burnside did—couldn't afford to have enemies in New York.

Now here they were, here they were! Ledlie to lead the attack. Dear, dear. Ledlie. Of all people. Bad enough behavior on the North Anna.

Dropping his hand from his mouth, Burnside said, "You *must* be ready, Ledlie." He stopped pacing and skimmed away sweat again. "*Will* your men be ready?"

"They'll be ready."

"Perhaps . . . you should see to them?"

"Have their orders," Ledlie muttered. Was his voice slurred? Well, he only had to be sober by the morning.

"You *must* clear the lanes through the obstacles. You *must* see to it. After dark, right after dark. Quietly, of course. But no obstacles, no obstacles. Clear the lanes in front of the covered ways. Plenty of lanes, wide lanes."

"Thy will be done."

"What? What?"

"Been seen to."

"And your officers . . . they understand? They understand everything?"

"Everything."

A staff major passing between them appeared doubtful.

"Right out of the covered ways and forward! No hesitation," Burnside continued. "Every subordinate officer must understand. Speed is *everything*. Point of detonation isn't the goal. Only the means, the means. They *must* get past the mine's effects, get on to the second ridge, that cemetery. Get to the second ridge . . . and we have Petersburg, Petersburg shall be ours!"

"Ours," Ledlie repeated.

"One regiment, only one, moves to either flank to provide security. Everyone else goes through the breach and on to the second ridge."

"Security," Ledlie said. He perked up. "I thought Grant's orders were to forget about flank security, just go head-on. In every attack. Not slow down, just go on."

"That's right, that's right. Just one regiment, that's all. Out on either flank. The rest go straight ahead." Burnside hesitated, then asked, "Really, Ledlie, don't you think you're needed at your division?"

The New Yorker frumped his chin. "Staff can see to everything, what they're for." But he rose. *Did* he smell of alcohol? Burnside couldn't be sure, couldn't be sure. Everything else smelled so awfully. But Ledlie's reputation . . .

Straightening his sword belt to go out, Ledlie paused and looked at him imploringly.

"Really think that mine is going to work?"

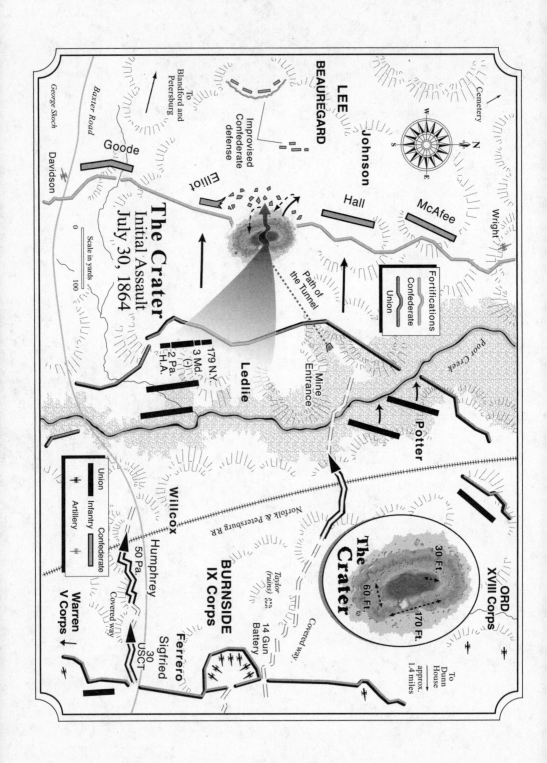

The Crater
Initial Assault
July 30, 1864

LEE
BEAUREGARD

Johnson

Improvised
Confederate
defense

Elliot

Hall

McAfee

Cemetery

Wright

To
Blandford and
Petersburg

Goode

George Skoch

Baxter Road

Davidson

Path of
the Tunnel

Scale in yards
0
100

Fortifications
Confederate
Union

Mine
Entrance

179 N.Y.
3 Md. (c)
2 Pa.
H.A.

Ledlie

Poor Creek

Potter

Willcox

Norfolk & Petersburg RR

50 Pa.

Humphrey

Covered way

30
USCT

Warren
V Corps

BURNSIDE
IX Corps

Ferrero

Sigfried

Taylor
(ruins)

14 Gun
Battery

Covered way

The
Crater

30 Ft.

60 Ft.

170 Ft.

ORD
XVIII Corps

To
Dunn
House
approx.
1.4 miles

Union
Infantry
Artillery
Confederate

TWO

Four a.m., July 30, 1864
Entrance to the Union mine

Colonel Henry Pleasants looked down from his perch on the earthworks.

"Let them wait," he said.

All of them. In their thousands. Sweating in the darkness, in the never-abated heat. Ledlie's division had deployed just behind the forward line, the massed soldiers slowly taking form as the night retreated. And the three divisions ordered to follow stood packed in the covered ways or squeezed together down in the ravine at Pleasants' back. Waiting. And waiting. Ten thousand men at the ready, with more filling in behind and additional corps alerted to support. All waiting, the generals doubtless impatient, quarrels suspended as they watched their timepieces. Pleasants sensed them all fidgeting, fearing, praying, and growing more worried about the great scheme by the minute.

Let them wait. He meant to do things right.

"Look you, Colonel," Reese whispered, trying him one more time, "the light will have its way and the Johnnies will see."

Pleasants considered the man down in the trench. The night had paled enough to detail his face, and his dirty shirt shone. Harry Reese. Tall for a Welshman, redheaded by daylight. With shoulders that spanned the gallery of a mine, almost too big a fellow to work underground. But Reese was the perfect beast to serve as a sergeant, rough but fair.

"Not yet," Pleasants said.

He gazed up the slope, past the clustered shadows slowly

becoming men, to the Reb entrenchments just atop the ridge. The outlines of the opposing earthworks showed black against the ruins of the night.

"Damned fuse," Douty muttered. Another man with mining in his blood, stripped to his undergarment from the waist up, Lieutenant Douty's whisper reeked of hate.

Yes, the "damned fuse." Pleasants had requested the reliable sort of fuse he knew from the anthracite fields. Just as he had asked for a new theodolite, which Meade's chief engineer had failed to provide. His men had not even been issued the requisitioned miners' pickaxes, but had filed down their too-large Army tools. And the fuse, old-fashioned and crude, was delivered late in ten-foot strips that had to be bound together. To a length passing five hundred feet. Leaving over fifty splices where a fuse could fizzle.

And fizzled it had. Burnside had ordered the mine blown at three thirty. Pleasants had lit the fuse at three fifteen.

And nothing happened.

Now it was after four.

Reese and Douty had volunteered to reenter the mine at once. But Pleasants had refused his men permission. As he continued to refuse them now. With the entire Ninth Corps gathered around him, waiting to go forward, striving still to be quiet but growing restless. And with all the rest of the Army of the Potomac and Army of the James cocking their ears for the blast that refused to come.

The darkness grew ever thinner.

Reese and Douty had as much heart stuck in that mine as he did. More, perhaps, for Reese had been his tireless foreman, a skilled man ready to show what he could do and unusually bitter toward the Rebs. For his part, Pleasants wanted to prove that he had been right and the Army's pompous engineers dead wrong when they insisted the mine he conceived was impossible, rolling their eyes and claiming it could not be ventilated. Men, those were, who had briefly studied the use of mines in a classroom at West Point, while he had been down in the darkness year after year, down in that netherworld between daylight and firedamp, that deathly, deadly place, an anthracite mine.

Because of that experience, because of the horrors he had witnessed before the war taught other men the grotesquerie of wounds and Death's resourcefulness, he had seen mutilations down the pits to make hard men vomit, wounds suffered not for a cause but for a pittance.

So Henry Pleasants knew what happened when a fuse appeared to have gone out and men rushed into the mine to reignite it. Only to have the fuse leap back to life and blow them to shreds. Or bury them alive.

A bad fuse was a widow-maker. And his 48th Pennsylvania had widows enough.

This would be a day of deaths, he knew. But he would not sacrifice Douty and Reese unnecessarily, not after all they'd given to get this far. Call it stubbornness, Pleasants thought, or call it what you will. But the pit-head rule was to wait one hour before permitting reentry. And he meant to wait that hour.

Soon, too soon, the Rebs would be able to see all that waited to strike them. Each minute counted, he knew, and the knowing had weight. It did not matter that the troops, once past their own defenses, faced barely a hundred yards of open ground. Even with the Reb battery straight ahead blown to hell, enfilading guns could sweep the slope.

If, indeed, the Johnnies were blown to hell. Pleasants had reckoned carefully and asked for six tons of powder for the mine's chambers. Grudgingly, the engineers of the Army of the Potomac had authorized four tons, telling him that their calculations differed.

Calculations done by men who couldn't believe he could do what he had done.

Soon enough, there would be light for a slaughter, a butcher's light. The light that distinguished men, that marked them as targets.

In the morning dusk and stubborn heat, Pleasants drew out his watch and brought it close to his face, a gesture he had repeated countless times since the fuse was lit. He struggled to read the slender black hands truly.

Abruptly, he slid from the parapet, landing flat-footed in the last clear space left amid the mass of soldiers: the roped-off hollow at the head of the mine.

"All right," he told Reese and Douty. "Relight the damned thing."

Four fifteen a.m.
Dunn house
Ninth Corps headquarters

Grant came in.

"What's the matter with the mine?" he asked George Meade, who had shifted to Burnside's headquarters for the attack.

To Meade's relief, Grant didn't seem much perturbed. One fine thing about Grant was that he rather expected things to go wrong and took setbacks calmly.

"I don't know," Meade admitted. Around him, staff men with little to do for the present sought to appear to be doing a great deal. "I'd guess the fuse has gone out."

Grant nodded. "Burnside working on it?" He took out a cigar.

"I've sent two men forward to get a proper answer. Burnside's at Fourteen Gun Battery. Where he can watch the attack."

Lighting his smoke, Grant said, "Think I'll go forward myself. You stay here, look to the rest of the army. If things prove satisfactory, I want a general attack."

Meade nodded.

Grant puffed, exhaled. "Colored Troops, too, if Burnside thinks he can use them. Let them follow, once the worst is past. Give them some experience." He smacked his lips around the black cigar. "Just not up front, you were right."

Again, Meade nodded. Over four months, he'd learned to read Grant's speech. For all the lieutenant general's subdued manner, his utterances had more nuance than a Philadelphia society dinner. Today, Grant's tone did not invite contradiction.

A sergeant approached, a rough-cut man feigning respect and not quite bringing it off. He touched two fingers to an eyebrow, glanced at Grant, and told Meade, "General, the telegraph's up, she's ready."

Meade looked at Grant, then turned—sharply—to General Humphreys, his chief of staff.

"Humph, send Burnside a message. Ask him what the devil's holding things up."

A man with the eyes of a wolf and a bite to match, Humphreys said, "Already written. They're sending it right now."

Smartly timed, the telegraph key clicked in the depths of the farmhouse.

"If he doesn't reply immediately," Meade said, "send another message. Keep after him."

"Don't need to be told," Humphreys responded, as gruff as ever. "I've known Ambrose Burnside long enough."

For a stretch of silence, everyone waited for the promised blast. Grant consumed his cigar at a rate that belied his outward calm.

Papers rustled. The telegraph tapped again.

"Tried a mine at Vicksburg," Grant remarked. "Two, in fact. Hoped this might go better."

At first, neither of them had thought much of Burnside's scheme. But that colonel of his, Pleasants, had been convincing. And of late, after inspecting the progress of the work—and looking hard for flaws, as Meade realized—even Duane, the Army of the Potomac's chief engineer and a prideful man, had come around to believing in the business. They all had. Despite the prevailing distrust of Ambrose Burnside.

The man's notion of leading with U.S. Colored Troops, greener than they were black, had begged catastrophe, practical and political. Letting them follow to consummate a victory was one thing—Grant was right about that—but the abolitionist papers would have made bloody hay out of any appearance of squandering their pet Negroes. They'd gone absolutely mad about the Fort Pillow mess out west.

Still no explosion. Perhaps nobody would go in at all. Perhaps it would be just another of Burnside's infamous failures. Meade thought it criminal that the fellow remained in command of a corps. But politics ruled.

Teddy Lyman delivered tin cups of coffee. Meade was enormously fond of his volunteer aide, a sound Bostonian. The coffee, on the other hand, was foul.

"The mine may still go up," Meade told Grant, warring to keep the nerves out of his voice. "Even Duane's convinced it's been properly done." He gestured at the oilcloth windows. "Concerned about the light, though. It has to blow soon. Or we'll have to call it off."

Grant's face hardened. It was a phenomenon Meade had seen again and again since May. Grant's features didn't alter, except for the faintest tightening of the eyebrows. But his flesh seemed to turn to stone and his eyes to glass.

"I want the attack to go forward," he said. "Whether the mine blows or not."

Four twenty a.m.
Head of the mine

Snapper Reese burst from the mouth of the mine.

Gulping fresh air, he said, "She hardly burned forty feet in, sir. Powder we laid in the trough might as well have been pissed on. Didn't get past the third buggering splice."

Pleasants got smell close to the man, restraining himself from gripping the sergeant's arm. "Can you relight it? Is the fuse itself dry enough?"

Reese nodded: *Yes.* "I need twine. And a knife, a good knife." He didn't wait on further words but scrambled for the scraps that remained from assembling the fuse the evening before.

Pleasants turned to his nearest soldiers, the handful that had not yet been dispersed for provost duty. In thanks for their month of labor, the men of the 48th had been relieved from the attacking force, while he himself would serve as a special aide to General Potter, his division commander, for the day.

"*A knife.* Damn it, who has a sharp knife? Or a bayonet, a sharp one?"

The men knew what Pleasants was like when he was angry. A knife appeared promptly in a dirty paw.

Reese had stepped back beside Pleasants. He seized the knife and scuttled into the gallery.

Around them, the army rustled.

Damn it all, Pleasants thought. Forty feet! That meant almost five hundred feet and fifty splices to go. That came out to roughly fourteen minutes. *If* there wasn't another break.

It was already light enough to see fear in faces.

Four thirty-five a.m.
Fourteen Gun Battery, Ninth Corps

Frightful weather. A fellow sweated himself right through his woolens. Frightful. Burnside wiped his forehead with a handkerchief.

Major Van Buren approached him. Again.

"Sir, it's another message from General Humphreys."

Humphreys, Meade. Meade, Humphreys. Mightn't they leave him alone to see this through? No one liked a delay, but Pleasants would fix it. Surely he would. Pleasants. Fine fellow. Mercurial, though, mercurial. That was the word. Fine engineer, though. Brilliant. Burnside hadn't seen fit to pester the fellow, but now Meade was on him, as Grant would be on Meade. Wretched business, command. Fredericksburg. Ghosts.

A man had to know his limits, Burnside decided, that was the thing.

"Shall I reply, sir?" Van Buren asked.

"Not yet, not yet." Burnside peered into the predawn twilight. Able to see his men by the dark thousands, mere silhouettes still, but visible, too visible. Packed in like tinned oysters, like oysters in a great tin. Down the covered ways and into the creekbed, then spread across the opposing slope on their bellies. Crowding almost to the Rebel entrenchments. Waiting, waiting.

He didn't want to be a bother to Pleasants, but . . .

Turning to an aide, Burnside said, "Pell, do go down and see what the problem is. With my compliments to Colonel Pleasants."

It was only a delay, no more, the Ninth Corps commander assured himself. The rest was bound to go splendidly. It had to, he'd staked his all on it.

Major General Ambrose Burnside, commander of the Ninth Union Corps, Army of the Potomac, fully intended to eat his dinner in Petersburg.

Then they'd see.

Four thirty-five a.m.
50th Pennsylvania Veteran Volunteer Infantry

Mine's a bust," Levi Eckert said, disgusted but not disappointed. "And to hell with all that, too."

Lieutenant Charles Brown withheld his judgment. The truth was that he was no more enthusiastic about the attack than Levi, but he felt a certain kinship with the men of the 48th, the miners from back home, even if most hailed from north of the mountain. He hated to see other Schuylkill County men fail.

"Just another damned bust," Levi continued.

In a low voice, Brown told him, "Sergeant Eckert, shut up."

Did feel like a bust, though. Levi was right. If the mine was going to go up at all, even the worst of the generals must see it had to blow before dawn. Before the Rebs woke up to themselves and readied a warm reception.

Wouldn't be long before the sky took color now. And the sun would strike that far slope where the first troops lay. Going forward would be as mad as those assaults back in June, when so many had died for nothing.

One of the newer privates turned and bent over, vomiting into a connecting trench. Other men leapt aside to avoid the splash. Filthy as they all were, a fellow still felt disgust at certain things.

One blessing was that his regiment and the rest of the brigade had been held a good ways back, near the big battery. With Ledlie's bunch in the lead and Potter's boys ahead, too, the 50th Pennsylvania wouldn't face the worst of it. Even if the mine went up, their day might come to nothing but a long wait, lucky as those coons mustered to the rear.

Levi had been right about that, too. The U.S. Colored Troops would go in last, if they went in at all. And white men resented it. How could a fellow not? When Ethiops were coddled while white men died?

Birds. Calling up the sun. Weren't as many as there should have been. Most had fled a time back, dislodged by the general ruckus of the war that had come to visit.

Some of the men whispered prayers in the spooking light. Brown knew he needed to read more of the Bible, and he did try. Frances would be so pleased, if he took on the sayings and had them handy. Anyway, it couldn't hurt to figure his way through the strangeness of the Lord. Brown wondered time and again over how what was written down could be so different from what Christian men went preaching. Lately, he had read in Judges about a woman's wicked misuse by a mob while her husband hid. He had never heard that preached on, not one word, but Brown could not imagine behaving that way, were any man to lay a finger on Frances. But, then, he never understood about the meek inheriting the earth, either. In his experience, the meek didn't fare too well.

As tense as anyone now, he slapped at a fly. What had gone wrong this time? *Would* the attack be canceled? A man just wanted to *know.*

And a leader had to know. Or pretend to. So much of leading men, he had learned, was fakery.

"Verdammt noch mal," First Sergeant Losch complained.

Yes, Brown thought. Damn it all.

And the peculiar stench that lay on the land like a blanket. The thousands of men waiting to attack had taken on a queer smell, a reek that differed from their routine stink, like piss and ashes packed up in your nostrils.

Over by the big battery, officers came and went. No one had told Brown or his men exactly when the attack was meant to begin, but something had gone wrong, there was no doubt. Old soldiers knew.

Maybe Levi was right and it was a bust. And he wouldn't mind that a bit.

Don't think like that, he warned himself. You're an officer now. Don't think like that.

Brown wasn't afraid. He'd stopped being afraid a fair time back. But when he'd stopped being afraid, when he'd lost that sour-stomach dread, he'd lost the passion for a good fight, too. Now he just did his duty, no less and no more.

He reached inside his blouse and scratched. Hoping he hadn't picked up the camp itch again.

"Why don't they do something?" Billy Tyson called, too loudly.

Brown turned on them all, more disturbed than he'd realized. Perhaps fearful, after all.

"I don't want to hear another word out of one man in this company."

The ground began to rumble.

Four forty-four a.m.
Head of the mine

Pleasants looked down at his pocket watch and realized his hand was shaking. He snapped the case shut again and sucked in air.

Up the slope, in light that grew paler each moment, Reb sentinels stood atop their fortifications, braving the risk of bullets as they sought to make out what was happening. Something was wrong, they felt it. But the curve of the hill worked against them, hiding the blue waves about to rush toward them.

A bit more light and they'd spot the foremost ranks, though. And probably see the divisions massed to the rear, their numbers too many to fit in the covered ways.

What if the fuse failed again?

He clicked open the watch, mere seconds after he had last read the time.

Four forty-four a.m.

Beneath him, the earth throbbed, a giant disturbed in his sleep.

Rumbling. Growing louder.

The ridgetop swelled like a sore.

He gripped the parapet.

The crest above him erupted. Slowly, hugely. A great mass of earth rose skyward, propelled by hellfire.

The roar hit his ears with fists.

The great clot of earth rose and rose. Then it stopped, suspended, a hundred feet skyward.

It broke apart.

In those raw seconds, Pleasants saw things infernal in the air: twisted men, torn limbs, flying cannon, splintered logs, and disintegrating crates.

Everything dropped, thumped back down, crashed. Smoke fumed and billowed. The cloud spit dirt and stones in every direction. At the first eye-narrowing sting, instinct yanked Pleasants down into the trench.

He pressed himself against the earthen wall as the heavens fell, with the earth still trembling under him and the first shouts and screams grown audible.

Debris hammered the earth. Blown powder burned his nostrils.

The cannonade began, with dozens of batteries pounding the Rebel lines. As soon as he sensed that the rain of scraps and clay and stone was done, Pleasants leapt back up to watch the attack go forward.

And he saw a thing that he had not expected: men in blue,

running. Not toward the enemy, but back toward the ravine, racing back through their own lines, terrified by what Pleasants had wrought.

Four forty-seven a.m.
50th Pennsylvania Veteran Volunteer Infantry

Jesus Christ almighty," Levi Eckert said.

Four fifty a.m.
Ninth Corps forward lines

Goddamn you, get back up that hill!" Colonel Elisha G. Marshall barked.

Around him, staff and line officers collared soldiers or threatened them with revolvers. Dozens, then hundreds, of soldiers from Marshall's brigade had panicked, fleeing headlong into the ravine, down toward Poor Creek, plunging through troops formed up to their rear, and disordering those formations.

Where the hell's Ledlie? Marshall wondered. He did not think much of his division commander, but he expected the man to be present, drunk or sober.

Dust obscured the Reb entrenchments above, but Marshall had seen enough to know that the mine had done its job. And more. The explosion had knocked him off his feet, panicking soldiers around him who thought he'd been killed.

With grit annoying his teeth and eyes, Marshall herded his soldiers back up the slope, snapping at them to get into formation, shouting at the officers, "Gentlemen, take command of your lines!"

He could read his men: They were regaining their composure, but needed a firm hand now.

Christ, though, that mine had been something.

Artillery rounds screamed overhead, plunging through the smoke in search of targets.

It took nearly fifteen minutes for Marshall to get his men back in good order and ready to storm the breach on the ridge above them. Given the general skittishness, he decided he would personally lead the 2nd Pennsylvania, heavy artillerymen lately recast as infantry.

"Second Pennsylvania! Rise up! Forward, march! By the right flank, march!"

But much remained a shambles. No one had opened the broad lanes promised through the defensive barriers, leaving only a narrow bridge of sandbags for the brigade. And not one ladder in sight. Sword raised and taking care of his footing, Marshall led the way, shouting, *"Forward! Forward!"* Leading not a compact assault force, but a double file of human ants streaming uphill through the smoke.

At least the Johnnies, stunned, weren't shooting yet.

Five ten a.m.
Mahone's Division, Confederate lines

A little man on a big horse, Mahone ignored the Yankee cannonade and rode up to Brigadier General Weisiger, commanding his Virginians.

"Davey," Mahone called, "we're going to be needed, might as well get a start on things. Alabama boys will spread out, cover your line. Pull your men out of the trenches. Do it by ones and twos, you keep 'em quiet. Don't invite the Yankees to make a fuss. Form up back by that orchard, ready to march."

"Any news?" Weisiger asked.

Mahone shook his head, imperturbable in the face of shell bursts: The Federal artillery was in a shooting temper, but mostly shooting long. "Reckon the boys up there are a mite too busy to send out circulars. You just get ready. I expect to hear from Hill any moment now. If not from higher powers. Reckon on marching fast, hard fighting after. Full canteens, extra cartridges. Split open some crates and let the men help themselves."

Jaw tightened, Weisiger saluted. Mahone rode on, heading for his Georgia brigade, calculating that with a good bluff, his Alabama brigade alone could hold his line. The earthquake that had passed underfoot and the tower of smoke three miles or thereabouts distant did suggest a mine hadn't been just talk. And the Federals would strike where their mine went up, that much was as plain as a chin-less schoolmarm.

Nor would the Yankees come lightly.

A man couldn't be certain, what for the poor light and smoke, but the explosion looked to have come just where Alexander had predicted, up around Pegram's salient, Elliott's stretch.

Bad ground, that. On a good day.

And they'd picked a sultry morning for it. Hot work for all concerned. He'd have to march his men roundabout, take the road down along Lieutenant Run, and keep them out of sight. Add at least two miles to the march, so call it five in all.

Davey Weisiger needed to be certain canteens were full.

Things couldn't happen instantly, Mahone knew. Matters had to be sorted out, decisions taken, and orders issued. But he did itch to get moving. The longer the delay, the higher and hotter the sun. And the more calls there'd be to speed the march along. He wanted his men to arrive in fighting trim, not falling-down heat-sick.

His horse shied from a near shell burst and Mahone brought the beast to order. Sharply.

Bound to be a devil of a business. He'd been about to order his men to stand down from their watch, concluding that another morning would pass unmolested as the dawn pinked up. Then he'd heard that faraway grump and seen the pillar of smoke smear up the sky. And he knew he'd be in the business, given that his division was all that was left to Beauregard and Lee to plug things up, what with most of the army sent north of the river. He'd given orders swiftly and, he hoped, clearly. To get two lean brigades—all the line could spare—ready to march.

He hoped it would be enough.

Mahone ached for news as much as Davey Weisiger did, but he suspected he'd get none for a time. Those close to the mine would be as stunned as a mule hit full face with a plank. Truth was that, for all he knew, the Yankees were already on their way into Petersburg.

Well, if he had to, he'd move without orders and face the consequences. And he meant to lead with his Virginia Brigade, his old command. Its regiments were filled with Southside and Tidewater men, from Petersburg and the down counties, from Norfolk and the land between the swamps. Fighting for their homes, they'd do all right. The Georgia Brigade would follow, and its men were sound enough.

Horse spurred half to death, a rider found him: Captain Starke, a staff man of A. P. Hill's.

Mahone didn't wait for the panting captain to speak. He declared, "I'll have two brigades march-ready in an hour. Just have to thin my lines without telling the Yankees."

But Starke could not contain himself, crying, "God-awful thing, god-*aw*fullest thing, god-awful. Whole battery lifted up in the air, all gone. Just *gone*. Hundreds of men, hundreds. . . ."

"Well," Mahone said in a voice of rail-yard iron, "we'll have to see to it."

Five twenty a.m.
The Crater

A forearm thrust from the earth. The fingers clenched and unclenched, striving to trap air for a buried mouth. One of many—so many—men buried alive. Legs kicked the air as Johnnies trapped under heavy clay struggled to free themselves, while disembodied heads cried, "Help me, Billy Yank! Help a fellow Christian. . . ."

And try to help his men did, ignoring orders to continue forward. Marshall pressed them, but only to a point. He felt a touch of bewilderment himself. More than a touch.

What stunned him wasn't the destruction and death, but that so many Confederates had survived, limbs broken, bodies smashed, but left alive. Some just sat there, mostly whole, coated with dirt and amazed, staring madly and muttering to themselves. Marshall's brigade had entered the crater at least ten minutes before, but his own men had grown as astonished as the Rebs. Mortified by what the blast had wrought.

If some Rebs survived, it seemed that hundreds of others had been killed. Limbs lay strewn on every side, and intestines draped the pit. A mustachioed, whiskered head lay about like a child's forgotten ball.

Some Johnnies had begun sniping from a distance. It was already dangerous for a man to raise his head above the high wall of clay at the rear of the hole.

Marshall and his staff attempted to bring the men to order, to detail a few to succor the Reb survivors while re-forming the confused regiments to push out and deepen the breakthrough. But conditions grew worse by the minute, with more troops piling into the hole instead of expanding the flanks and pushing forward.

"I seen it," a shaking Rebel prisoner cried, eyes flaring, "I done seen the seventh seal broke open, this here's the end of the world. . . ."

Crushed men cried for water. In a dawn gun-barrel hot.

The great hole did seem a foretaste of Hell, with all the torn bodies and great logs snapped like twigs, with the dust that refused to settle lit orange by the rising sun. Marshall judged the hole to stretch between one hundred fifty and two hundred feet along the entrenchments, with a width of maybe forty feet and a depth of twenty-five feet at the very bottom. It was two craters, really, one larger than the other. And that ugly, steep back wall of clay made it all but impossible for men to climb out the far side.

Will Bartlett, Marshall's fellow brigade commander, stomped up on his cork leg. Mad as a stepped-on rattler.

"Bugger the devil," the brigadier general snapped. He was a blue-blood Harvard sort, the kind who might have been hated had he not been so embarrassingly brave.

"Will, you can't pile any more men in here. We discussed—"

"That's shit for the birds now," Bartlett cut him off. "This hole's like honey to a swarm of flies. *You* try to stop them coming in."

"We've got to get the men out of here. *You* need to push north," Marshall told the newly minted brigadier, who outranked him now. "Give my men some space. I've sent Powell back to Ledlie, to report." He grimaced. "Not sure we can expect much help, though, if we don't fix things ourselves."

A miracle in the chaos, a runner found them. He held out a note, first toward Marshall and then, correcting himself, toward the man with the star on his strap.

"From General Ledlie."

Shots, groans, curses, the shriek of artillery. Flabbergasting Marshall, some of the soldiers had paused to serve themselves breakfast. As if reaching the crater was all they meant to do.

Bartlett passed the note on to Marshall: an order to press forward.

Marshall nodded. He told the runner, "Tell General Ledlie we're doing the best we can."

When the courier had gone, Bartlett grimaced and said, "Ledlie." He snorted. "Old Ask-and-He-Shall-Deceive ought to come up here himself. But he won't, that one." He looked at Marshall. "Did *you* understand his orders last night? I damned well didn't."

Marshall glanced around the pit. On the flank, Charlie Houghton and his defrocked heavy artillerymen had sorted out two Confederate fieldpieces, turning them against their former possessors. That much was encouraging. In the hole, regimental officers were doing all they could to re-form the men, cursing and cajoling them.

Now he had to do his part.

"All right," Marshall told his fellow brigade commander, "I'm going to push out the Second Pennsylvania, gain some room. And get out of this plague pit." He waved a hand toward the high rear wall. "See what actually lies beyond. But I need support on the right, sir. Quiet down the Rebs shooting from the traverses."

"Oh, well. Do what I can," Bartlett agreed. And he levered himself along on his cork leg.

Marshall shouldered his way through the blue-coated mob to the pit's edge where the 2nd Pennsylvania, his defrocked cannoneers, waited in a degree of martial order.

The men would have to work their way out from the side of the pit to make the attack. A few sharpshooters had managed to climb the back wall and cling to the parapet thrown up by the blast, but no regiment could advance over it. Too steep, too high. It would take an engineer company hours to make it passable.

The great hole had all the makings of a trap. They *had* to move forward.

Marshall explained to the regiment's officers what he wanted done. And the 2nd responded smartly enough to its orders, scuttling out of the crater and into an adjoining trench line, despite harassment from the Rebel marksmen. After sending back orders to the 179th New York and 3rd Maryland to prepare to follow on, Marshall clawed his own way out of the hole, gave the order to charge, and followed the Pennsylvanians at a distance, eager to see for himself what lay ahead.

His men went forward boldly, with a cheer. Then their flag fell. Here and there, the attackers halted abruptly, their advance blocked by unexpected trenches and traverses. The Reb position behind the pit was a crazy rabbit warren, a disorderly mess of bombproofs and ditches from which ragged men popped up to fire before disappearing again.

The delays, all the damned delays. . . .

Shocked they may have been at first, but the Johnnies were recovering their senses, aiming ragged-but-expert volleys at their approaching enemies. Marshall could see a low white house on the ridge ahead and, to the right, the cemetery Ledlie had mentioned vaguely. Petersburg lay just beyond.

But one regiment wasn't going to be enough. Repositioned Reb artillery opened on his men, buckling what remained of their lines and splashing the air with blood. Gore speckled Marshall's face, though he stood well to the rear. Nonetheless, the Pennsylvanians—already on their third color-bearer—pushed on, covering a hundred yards and more, before the attack became so disjointed it lost all its thrust.

Men sought cover in the nearest trench or edged to the rear.

Take at least a division to reach that ridge, Marshall decided, a division in good order. And the real obstacle—which had come as a shock—was the slovenly maze of trenches and ditches and bombproofs that would, by itself, break up advancing formations. There was an open stretch of ground to the north, rising from a swale, but it led nowhere. Every feature of the terrain seemed designed to confound an attacker, an incidental defensive work that would have made Vauban proud.

As his soldiers filtered back, rueful and bloodied, Marshall ordered their officers to put them in the northern end of a cavalier trench that had survived the blast, where his Maryland battalion was hard at work, trading shots with the Johnnies.

And Colonel Elisha G. Marshall, old frontier Regular, stiff and aching from his Fredericksburg wound and haunted by a frail wife and sickly daughter, sidled back into the crater to organize the remainder of his brigade and try to redeem an effort already faltering.

What he found shocked him: Another division—Potter's—was piling into the overcrowded hole.

Six fifteen a.m.
50th Pennsylvania

Thanks to clots of artillery smoke, Lieutenant Charles Brown could barely make out the heights across the ravine. But what he glimpsed discouraged him. Maybe a dozen Union flags waved in the hole the mine had left, packed too closely to make any sort of sense.

Still, more blue lines plunged forward, leaving the Union defenses to dash up a hillside raked by a masked battery. The open ground between the forward trenches and the damage the mine had done was dotted with the dead, the wounded, and the cowering.

"Make way, make way!" an officer called as he pushed up the covered way.

"Make way yourself," a hoarse voice told him.

"Going the wrong way, Cap'n."

"Where's your mule, sonny?"

The covered way into which the 50th Pennsylvania had descended admitted, at most, four men to pass abreast. Now those waiting to advance lined the sides of the trench, with wounded men, Reb prisoners, ammunition bearers, and any number of busybodies bumping along in the middle.

"Don't smell like any great success to me," Levi Eckert said. "Got the stink of trouble on it already."

Brown ignored him.

Stretcher bearers jostled a major rearward. A white edge of bone thrust from his blood-caked brow.

"What are we waiting for?" a young voice pleaded, a voice barely short of tears. "Why don't we go in?"

"Just be glad you're still waiting," Levi told him.

The order came down to move forward and form for a charge.

Six thirty a.m.
Fourteen Gun Battery

W here's Ledlie?" Burnside cried. "Can't *anyone* find Ledlie?"

None of the staff men responded.

Shaking his head, Burnside lurched back to the parapet, buffeted by the concussions off the guns. Earning their keep, he had to give the artillerymen that, they were earning their keep.

Burnside lifted his field glasses, peered through the smoke, saw nothing encouraging, and lowered the glasses again. He turned to Major Van Buren, who had grown ever more deliberate as the morning advanced and hopes retreated.

"Perhaps Ledlie went forward, into the pit?" Burnside said.

The major appeared less than confident of that.

"And Potter? Potter?"

"With his division, sir. In the forward trenches."

"Up in the pit?"

"No, sir. In the trenches. With the remainder of his division."

"Good, good. In the trenches. And Willcox, I've seen Willcox. Haven't I?"

"Yes, sir. He's moving forward."

"Good, excellent." Burnside turned full face to the aide, who had grown rather unkempt during his trips to the line and back. "We have to make something out of all this, Van Buren. The point of crisis approaches, a man can feel it. And crisis brings opportunity, does it not?"

The aide didn't answer.

Meade, George Meade. Burnside could hardly think about anything else. The fellow had just insulted him unspeakably! And by telegraphic message! And Humphreys, that crude and blasphemous man! Both of them pestered him endlessly. Why wasn't he doing this? Why hadn't he done that? As if any of this was easy!

Somehow, Meade had gotten his hands on a message not intended for his eyes, a message meant for Burnside himself, about conditions up there in the pit. And Meade had accused him—all but accused him—of dissembling in his reports.

Meade had pressed him, rudely, to seize the next ridge now or take his medicine. Advance, or call it all off.

And admit failure. Again.

They *wanted* him to fail, that was the thing.

Grant was behind it, of course, the bloody-mindedness. Throw men away, hurl them to their deaths, that was Grant's way. Worse than Fredericksburg. Spotsylvania, Cold Harbor. And the June assaults right here on the Petersburg line. Massacres, every one. Yet Grant was Lincoln's pet, while Burnside's peers spoke of Fredericksburg in snickers.

Now Grant was rumored to be prowling the lines. No good could come of that. Why couldn't they leave him alone to fight his battle?

Nothing going right. Ledlie. Where *was* the sot? Beastly fellow.

Politics, politics. Hadn't opened the lanes through the defenses, Ledlie had not. Despite a direct order. Bad behavior atop bad luck. And Humphreys, Meade's henchmen, snarling through the telegraph, never satisfied with any report.

Ferrero's men, the Colored Troops, were to be committed, after all. "If necessary." Leaving it on his shoulders, of course, to decide whether it was necessary.

Ambrose Burnside knew who would take the blame, if matters worsened. They all conspired against him, every one of them. And he'd tried to be a good fellow, a warm companion, to them all.

Of course, there was still hope things would turn around. Willcox about to go in. Might make the difference. Sheer weight of numbers.

Burnside turned to order Van Buren off again, but the poor fellow looked fagged out. He decided the major had earned himself a respite and glanced about for another trusted staff man.

"Pell? Find General Ferrero. Tell him to prepare the Colored Troops."

"Orders have gone out, sir. The brigade commanders have been alerted and we're searching for General Ferrero. No one knows where he is."

That surprised Burnside. It took him a moment to recall giving the order.

Too much on his mind. Not least, the despicable conduct of George Meade.

"Then *find* Ferrero and order him up immediately."

First Ledlie playing hide-and-go-seek. Now Ferrero.

Fighting a headache summoned by the guns, Ambrose Burnside reached into his pocket, felt the telegraphic message he had crumpled in his outrage minutes before, and decided to send George Meade a sharp rebuke. The army commander's message had been a personal affront, an unspeakable condescension, far beyond the prerogatives of a military superior. The tone was simply ungentlemanly.

And a gentleman had to comport himself as a gentleman, no matter the circumstances. Burnside could not let the insult pass.

The war could wait for the moments it would take to draft a protest.

Heading toward the field desk that had been positioned for his personal use, Burnside begged again, "Has *anyone* heard from Ledlie?"

Six forty a.m.
Field hospital, 20th Michigan, Union entrenchments

You'll be busy soon enough," Brigadier General James H. Ledlie told the surgeon. The ongoing cannonade sifted dirt between the planks that formed the bombproof's ceiling. "Get the saws ready, get the knives out," Ledlie went on, voice slurred. "Chop 'em all up."

Surgeon Orville P. Chubb did his best to ignore the man, general's star or not. He knew Ledlie by sight, of course, but did not answer to him. And he and his orderlies had to be prepared for casualties to arrive at any time. Their regiment and its parent brigade were formed up to attack.

"Trouble with you butchers," Ledlie continued from his bench by the wall, "is that you're lazy. You take the easy way out. Cut off a man's arm over a hangnail. Rather than take the time to sew him up."

Chubb said nothing. He feared that the general would flush him and his men back out of the dugout, the nearest place to the fighting that was safe enough to serve as a dressing station. A life could be saved by fifty yards, and Chubb had spent his best years saving lives.

Ledlie's staff men haunted the entrance, ducking in and out and looking sheepish.

"Wonder why I'm sitting here?" Ledlie asked the surgeon directly. "You wondering that? Why I'm not out with my men?"

Chubb shrugged and bent to help an orderly erect a collapsible operating table. The war's technical advances were a wonder, as were the advances in medical knowledge and care. The great field hospital at City Point would have been unthinkable even one year before.

"I'm *wounded,* that's the problem," Ledlie declared. He extended his left foreleg like a dance hall girl. "Right here. In the foot. Spent ball. Terrible pain, terrible. I couldn't possibly lead an attack."

"Have a look at it, if you like," Chubb told him. "See if anything's broken."

Beyond the entrance to the bombproof, men going forward cheered.

Ledlie smirked. "What do *they* have to cheer about? What does any man have to cheer about anymore?" He took out a silver flask, attempted to drink, then turned it upside down. "All gone," he said in a voice almost childlike.

"Keep the bandages covered, for God's sake," Chubb told a new assistant. "You've got dirt falling on them."

"Malaria, that's my problem," the general continued. "Had it for years. Only thing that helps is a proper drink. Chills, fever. You know the symptoms. Leaves a man incapacitated, sitting here shivering. Only whiskey helps."

An orderly laid out blades and saws in the order Chubb preferred. The cadaverous young man then covered them with a towel that would not remain unstained.

"I'll need more water than that," the surgeon told another of his helpers.

"I need a medicinal drink," the general said.

Chubb restrained himself.

"Doctor, prescribe me a drink," Ledlie said. His voice had acquired a new edge of menace. "I need fortification. So I can stand the pain and rejoin my men."

Chubb turned to a subordinate. "Clarke, fish out the rum."

"I said 'whiskey,'" Ledlie reminded him.

"Rum's what we've got. If you don't want it . . ."

"Rum will do." The general contorted his face. "Filthy drink, though. 'Nigger whiskey.'"

Another general appeared in the low doorway. Much to Chubb's chagrin.

"Ah, Ferrero!" Ledlie called. "Our coon-coddling dancing master! Come have a drink, man! Butcher-boy there's buying."

"Don't mind if I do," Ferrero said. He crossed the dugout and joined Ledlie on his bench.

"Unbelievable mess out there," the newcomer said.

An orderly handed each man a tin cup with a measure of rum, but Chubb withheld the bottle.

Ledlie touched his cup to Ferrero's and drank the rum straight down.

"Not enough," he complained. "Not enough for my malaria. Damned Jew sutler wouldn't be that stingy."

A sweat-caked officer plunged inside the bombproof, calling, "General Ferrero?"

Ferrero nodded and said, "Over here, Pell. Why the grand *furore*?"

"From General Burnside, sir." The latest intruder extended a slip of paper. "Orders for your division to attack. Immediately."

Ferrero snorted. "Preposterous! My division couldn't move an inch. Willcox has the covered ways jammed up. Potter's mob, too. I can't move an inch, tell that to Burnside."

With an expression that tipped into insolence, Pell withdrew.

"One more drink," Ledlie announced.

Seven a.m.
Company H, 30th United States Colored Troops,
Sigfried's brigade, Ferrero's division

While his white officers conferred and awaited orders to advance, First Sergeant John H. Offer exhorted his men.

"Going to be a great fight, this fight. Hear me? Greatest fight we seen yet. And the weight of all this war, it riding your backs. We take Petersburg, then old Richmond next. That be how we whip Lee's army, them bondage men, Egyptian and the Philistine."

Straightening his back and lifting his shoulders, Offer continued, "You *know* we ready. Show the world the braveness of the colored man. So pray now for a strong heart, a mighty heart, you pray to the Lord. Pray we rise to do our part at last. And every man think of the colored folk still in them chains, you think of your brothers and sisters. And think of all the great generals going to be watching you today, watching the Negro, see if he can fight, if he can hold himself upright like the white man." The first sergeant nodded and hardened his face. "You listen now, you all be listening close. Any skulkers going to feel my bay-net. Hear?"

He looked around at the earnest faces, at men he knew full well, from the earnest freedmen, some of whom could read newspapers and talk high-tone, to scooted-off slaves, with their fool expectations of freedom and the beat-in sloth that had to be shaken out of them . . . if the white man failed, these men would be given the long-delayed chance to prove their worth, after all their tribulations.

His will be done.

The first sergeant concluded, "You just remember Fort Pillow! Remember what been done to the colored man by those devil men yonder." He raised his voice to a pulpit pitch and cried, "Remember Fort Pillow!"

His men cheered and it had the feel of a hymn-sing rising to thunder. Other Negroes, not his, but who had eased in close to listen, men whose faces shone in the morning light, glistening with the day's first harvest of sweat, faces in black and maroon, coffee brown and bronze, high yellow and just shy of white . . . those men cheered, too, echoing his cry of, "Remember Fort Pillow!" and adding: "No quarter!"

"No prisoners, no prisoners!" men called gleefully.

Then the white officers reappeared, their faces pale and fixed with looks of destiny.

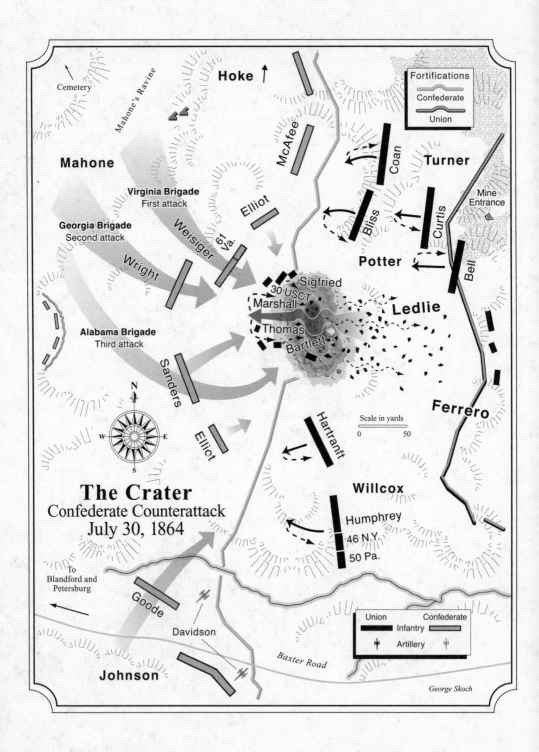

The Crater
Confederate Counterattack
July 30, 1864

George Skoch

THREE

Why don't they press the attack?" Lee demanded of those who rode beside him. To Lieutenant Colonel Walter Taylor, the old man sounded unnerved. This wasn't merely another bout of Lee's peevishness, fed by poor digestion and arthritis. Lee's senior aide, Taylor had not seen the commander of the Army of Northern Virginia so unsettled since Spotsylvania, on the day Hancock broke the line and word arrived from Richmond that Stuart lay dying.

Again, today, there was bountiful cause for alarm.

Battle thrashed on the high ground beyond the ridge that concealed the horsemen. Every man present knew that their re-formed line was barely holding, each moment of survival a marvel, a wonder.

Hooves clopped, keeping shy of a trot to spare hard-ridden mounts.

"Why don't those people come *on*?" Lee asked again.

Lee spoke to himself, above all, Taylor knew. The old man would be thinking that if *he* were in command on the other side, the Yankees would have reached the Petersburg depot an hour back. The Yankees had blown a massive hole in the line, only to fumble about and all but halt. And incompetence—on either side—outraged Robert E. Lee's professional pride.

Those opposing him had been his peers, his brothers-in-arms, before the war, and he seemed to feel that his former comrades let him down when they were defeated too easily. That said, Lee sought not just victory, but his foe's humiliation.

The Lee that Taylor knew, while admirable and inspiring, was far from the loving father the men supposed. Lee would sacrifice anyone to win. Behind that studied façade of immaculate manners, Lee was the hardest, proudest man Taylor knew.

Mahone needs to come up fast, Taylor thought, but he did not voice it. Lee's mood was best left untouched.

Artillery rounds shrilled overhead as Federal batteries overshot the battlefield. The shells plunged blindly into the city, a further outrage. For hours, every nearby soldier had been thrust into the line to struggle, against fantastic odds, to keep the Yankees out of the Cockade City. Yet all those efforts summed to a meager offering. Only the Federals' inexplicable fecklessness had delayed catastrophe.

Lee would be mad at himself, Taylor saw that, too. Irate at his error of sending so many divisions north of the James, falling for what now seemed to have been a ploy.

Indeed, why *didn't* the Yankees come on? The old man's question haunted every horseman, from Lee himself down to his color-bearer.

"Perhaps," Beauregard offered of a sudden, "our colleagues in blue had a limited purpose today. Could be the mine's effect surprised them, too." He cooed to his horse. "Spectacular, I must say."

Lee shook his head. "I don't believe it. I cannot believe that." He turned in the saddle and called back to Taylor, "Where's Venable? Venable should have returned. Where *is* the man?"

"He may have stayed with Mahone, sir. To guide him."

Lee was not to be appeased. He snapped, "His purpose isn't to 'guide' General Mahone. His duty is to this staff."

Everyone pulled back an invisible inch.

"*Why* don't they press their advantage?" Lee asked again, spurring Traveller lightly.

Squandering hours, the Federals had done no more than push out a hundred yards or so to either flank of the pit. Yet they had the strength to smash forward, if they summoned the will, and Bushrod Johnson's men would be overwhelmed. From the ridgetop, a man could tally over a dozen regimental and brigade flags in the ruptured space they'd seized. It was almost as if the Yankees were staging yet another ruse, a thought that pestered Taylor. The Virginia Military Institute had taught him the trick that Marlborough played with his banners at Ramillies.

He did not dare suggest such a thing to Lee, not when the old man was seething.

Instead, to cheer up Lee, he said, "The Carolinians have been making it hot for them, General. Came right back to themselves, got down to business. McMaster has—"

"*They* can't hold them," Lee said sharply. "They're far too few, should those people show resolve."

"Might have just made a shambles of things, our Yankee inter-locutors," General Beauregard tried again. "Been known to hap-pen. If so, *tant mieux.*"

"I simply cannot believe that they haven't come on," Lee said stubbornly, ignoring his subordinate and old rival. "They have the numbers, they have every advantage."

Affecting an easy heart on the worst of days, Beauregard leaned into his pommel, pointing the way ahead with a repertoire smile. "House I mentioned is just up there. Gee family manse. Hardly re-nowned for elegance, but the view's superb. Five hundred yards from *le place de combat.*"

"Good," Lee mumbled.

They turned their horses up the hillside, back toward the rid-dles of the battle.

Charlie Venable galloped up, man and beast splashing sweat.

"At last," Lee said.

The party halted.

Lee called out, "Colonel Venable? Where are Mahone's bri-gades?"

"Following, sir. Quick as the men can march. Had to go round-about, hide from the Yankees." Panting, Venable reached for his canteen, then thought better of it. "General Mahone's leading them personally. Said he couldn't just send off those brigades, preferred to take them into the fight himself."

Lee almost smiled. "Which brigade's to the fore?"

"Virginia Brigade, sir."

Lee nodded. "I *knew* it. I *knew* Mahone would lead with the Virginians."

For a too-brief moment, Lee's spirits appeared to rise. Then, above them, the crash and crackle of battle swelled again.

"He's needed *now*," Lee said.

Seven fifteen a.m.
50th Pennsylvania

Brown didn't like it. Things just lurched and stopped again, with even less sense of a guiding hand than usual. Leaving the covered way and crossing the creek, the brigade had formed ahead of the old defenses, divided into two wings, both facing left of the mayhem around the pit. Preparing to charge, they had fixed bayonets, nerves high. Then they waited uselessly, just standing there in ranks. As men fell dead and wounded, the soldiers were ordered to their knees and finally onto their bellies. They'd waited like that for nigh on an hour now.

Deployed on the far left flank, the 50th was shielded by the roll of the slope, but the Michiganders over on the brigade's far right were getting punished. And stray bullets found an occasional Pennsylvanian. One solid shot from a Union gun fell short, tearing a corporal from Company D to pieces.

They hadn't slept. The wait seemed endless. Brown's put-on calm wore thin.

He couldn't see the pit anymore, thanks to the roll of the hill, but it sounded like the fight was stuck in one place, not going anywhere.

What worried Brown directly, though, was that the 46th New York had been put in the front line for the assault, immediately to the right of his own men. Brown didn't trust the 46th or the captain leading them. Those men were city Germans, recent immigrants, all jabber, sour tobacco, and reluctance. They were different beasts from the Dutchie farmers and sturdy canal boatmen, old stock all, who speckled the ranks of Company C and the 50th. Brown had nothing against Germans as such—not if they'd fight—but he'd seen the 46th New York behave badly too many times.

Who had put the 46th in the front line? Were any of the damned officers using their brains?

Then he remembered that he was an officer, too.

"Some general needs to shit or get off the pot," Sergeant Eckert said.

This time, Brown didn't shush him.

Want to waste a unit's ration of spunk, this was how to do it. As they'd rushed from the covered way to form up, they'd seen the slope that led up to the pit. A Reb gun section concealed on the right spewed canister. The slaughter every man witnessed didn't lift hearts, and giving men time to ponder it was a cruelty.

The 50th had been mostly spared so far, but Brown reckoned they'd get no more than thirty yards up the slope before the roll of the ground served them up like beefsteaks.

"*Alles doch Wahnsinn,*" First Sergeant Losch complained. "What do they wait for?"

Even Losch, a Dutchman as hard as anthracite, sounded unsteady.

Just get up the damned hill, Brown coaxed himself. Just get your men up the hill and into those trenches. Just do that. Then see what comes next.

The heat, fierce and early, stuffed his mouth with dirty cotton. He'd warned the newer men to ration the water in their canteens. But they'd waited so long, through darkness and light, that his own canteen sloshed hollow.

"What the bejeezus?" Levi Eckert asked. He'd raised his head to stare northward.

Brown looked, too: The brigade's right wing was up and

moving forward. Part of it, anyway. The movement seemed out of joint.

He heard no orders from anyone, but hard on the flank of the 50th, the New York Germans scrambled to their feet. A moment later, they, too, plunged uphill, in disordered lines.

With Major Schwenk still recovering from his wound, Captain Brumm was the regiment's senior officer. He dashed along the 50th's front.

"On your feet, men!" he ordered. *"Dress the line, dress your lines!"* But the captain didn't—couldn't—wait: The assault had taken on a life of its own. Brumm pointed uphill with his sword. *"Forward, Pennsylvania!"*

"Led into battle by a damned watchmaker," Levi grumbled. Not meanly, though. Brumm was one of their own, a Company C man, and he'd risen by merit.

With his own sword still an oddity in his hand, Brown called orders to Company C, pulling the others along by his example.

Up that slope. Calves burning from the first steps. Brown about-faced and briefly marched with his back turned to the enemy, inspecting the ranks that followed, bidding them close on him.

A soldier staggered and dropped. Not from Company C.

Brown faced the ridgeline and the great ruckus again. A few more yards and they'd be in butcher's range.

Off to the right, men cheered.

Smoke drifted downward, speckled with points of light.

"Auf! Auf!" a burly German officer called. He sounded like a barking dog to Brown.

Captain Brumm shouted, *"Charge!"*

The 50th gave a dry-throated hurrah. Brown rushed uphill, comrades running beside him. Men panted and growled, leaning into the steepness.

The trench line's parapet loomed through the smoke. Those speckles of light came from rifles thrust beneath head logs. Brown judged that his men could cover the open ground before most of the Johnnies up there had time to reload.

An enfilading artillery round struck the front rank of the New York Germans, spraying blood across the slope to the 50th. Some Dutch bastard wailed, *"Verloren! Alles verloren!"*

The New Yorkers turned and ran.

Didn't go straight back down the hill, either. They bolted to the left, away from the Reb crossfire, stampeding through the ranks of the Pennsylvanians.

Brown swung the flat of his sword at the closest runaways, threatening them with his pistol, and Levi went at them with his rifle butt, cursing to fright the devil out of his doings. But the New Yorkers wouldn't be stopped.

Some men from the 50th joined the rout.

Not Company C, though.

Not yet.

Reb shells found the range and added to the chaos. The left wing of the brigade's attack collapsed.

Captain Brumm manhandled men with no regard for their regiment, shoving and punching and kicking them back up the hill. But for every man arrested, a dozen more fled.

The captain's eyes met Brown's.

Brown shook his head: Plain hopeless.

"Fiftieth Pennsylvania!" the captain shouted, raw-throated, fighting the uproar. "Fiftieth to the ground! Lie down, down where you are! Officers, see to your companies."

Brumm didn't lie down himself, though. And somewhat to his surprise, Brown didn't go to ground, either. He paced the broken ranks, counting heads and trying to rally those good men gripping the hillside.

"Oh, cripes, Brownie," Billy Wagner said, "get down yourself and don't be no damned fool."

"That's 'Lieutenant Brown' to you," Adam Burket corrected him. Then he added, *"Lieutenant* Brown, get the hell down, would you? God knows who they'd make a lieutenant next."

Men lying nearby cackled and catcalled, possessed by the soldier's humor amid death.

Brown dropped to his knees. But he didn't join the merriment. He felt sickened.

Just another colossal, useless waste. All of it. Only good that he could see in the business was that, for once, Company C had not suffered a single loss. That made the failed assault almost worth celebrating, he supposed.

Brown wondered if anyone's heart had been in the attack. Soldiers handled badly behaved badly. Men would risk their lives, even give their lives. Plenty had done so since they crossed the Rapidan. But they wanted to see a point to it. There had just been too many head-on, headlong, headstrong attacks that amounted to nothing but dead and wounded comrades. Especially here, in this godforsaken place, a landscape so forlorn it was nature's poorhouse.

Captain Brumm ordered a withdrawal by companies. Their fight was over.

Seven forty a.m.
30th U.S. Colored Troops

His men had a chance to fight at last, and Colonel Delavan Bates led them with all the vigor of his twenty-four years. His regiment of U.S. Colored Troops long had been consigned to minding the rear and guarding supply trains, to chasing wayward beeves or digging trenches. But not today.

Even the vague orders passed down through Colonel Sigfried, that terse command to "Go forward at once," had not daunted him, nor had the apparent stalemate up on the ridge. He believed in the men he led, believed in them deeply, and intended to prove their worth for all to see.

"Fix bayonets!" he shouted, a command echoed quickly by the company officers.

Steel scraped steel.

"Trail arms. By the right flank . . . march!"

And this was it, their moment. He led the way, scrambling over the sandbag bridge to pass the old lines, and his men funneled after him in a double file. It surprised him that the way forward had not been cleared in the hours of struggle, but excitement beat down a momentary doubt.

The slope ahead crawled with wounded men struggling down through the corpses. Fired from a flanking Rebel battery, canister and solid shot scraped the ground, playing rag doll with living and dead alike.

Turning, Bates called, *"Thirtieth, forward! Forward!"* He stepped on the paw of a wounded man, who cried out.

Don't falter, he warned himself. Do this for *them*.

A fan of canister found the regiment, slaying half his color guard. Blood hosed the survivors and a head flew past, chased by other bits of meat and bone. Bates saw a first man turn and run, only to be beaten by his sergeant, clubbed back into the ranks.

The colors rose again.

"Lieutenant Bowley," Bates shouted, "align your company."

Bowley, in turn, bawled orders at his line-closers.

Many a black face was ashen now. But jaws were fixed and eyes narrowed.

"Company officers! Look to your alignment!"

Not enough to be brave. Bates wanted his men to show *better* than those who had gone before and faltered. Better than those who jeered at the notion of the Negro in uniform.

More men fell. Some cowered. Sergeants raged. The majority tramped onward. Up the slope. In what passed for good order on this day.

Bates had not been in a battle since Gettysburg, where he had led white men, and he had forgotten how the singular roar broke down into parts as you entered it, separating into the crumping of distinct blasts, the rip and hiss of shot, the queer singsong of bullets that missed their mark, and, not least, the myriad sounds men made in fury and suffering.

He lofted his sword again, pointing to the right flank of the pit, where he believed Colonel Sigfried wanted the regiment. He wished his orders had been a bit more detailed.

As Bates closed on the crater, debris and bodies challenged the regiment's order. Men surged forward, sensing protection amid the jagged walls raised by the blast.

Bates leapt over a shelf of earth and nearly tumbled forward, blundering into soldiers bursting with curses. His own men pushed from the rear.

"Good Lord, Bates!" an almost familiar voice called. He recognized General Bartlett, of the famed cork leg. Another brigade commander, Colonel Marshall, stood beside him, uniform filthy. "Get your Abyssinians out of here! There's chaos enough!"

"Del, go to the right," Marshall told him more calmly but as firmly. "Your men can help out there, clear out more trenches. You're worse than useless here."

When he turned to his soldiers he felt their lust to kill. And nearly anyone would suffice for an enemy.

He shouted his voice to a ruin, pushing back through the tumult to master his men, pulling them out of the flank of the pit, confusing them with no time to explain. Feeling his way as best he could, he led them to the right, northward, along a trench line so crowded the regiment barely could pass Indian file. By turns, white soldiers cajoled his men or mocked them, making way grudgingly.

He tried a traverse, but found it packed with troops milling without purpose. Dead men lay trampled underfoot, their uniforms blue or a vague and ragged gray.

It was impossible to make an attack from those trenches.

Bates ordered his men to face about again. He led them in a scramble back over shattered head logs and ruptured parapets, back into the treacherous freedom of the killing ground between the former lines. Bellowing until he choked, he warned his officers to control their men.

Deprived of other courses of action, he tugged his dwindling regiment northward again, paralleling the trench line and braving a storm of fire. No longer pausing to look back to see if men followed, he dashed ahead, sword held aloft, until he judged he had passed the final traverse in Federal hands.

When he turned about at last, most of his men were still with him. Their order was barely discernible, but it would do. Pivoting toward the Reb abatis, he raised his cap on the tip of his sword and shouted, *"Forward, Thirtieth! Charge!"*

His voice was so raw and the racket so great, he realized few men heard him. Cap lofted high on the tip of his blade, he waved his men on with his left hand and began to weave his own way through the obstacles. Blessedly, the artillery had blown gaps in the defenses.

Busy sniping at Federals in the traverses, the spread-thin defenders were shocked not only by blue-clad soldiers leaping the parapet, but by their black faces.

His soldiers went at the Rebs with the fury of madmen. Some Johnnies just ran. Others fought back in a rage and were shot, bayoneted, and clubbed. Quick contests of man against man collapsed into mob killings. Waving his soldiers on to the next traverse, Bates saw a Reb pop out of a bombproof and fire his rifle against a corporal's chest.

"Nigger sonofabitch," were the Reb's last words

One man after another put bullets in him. When he dropped, Bates' men beat him with their rifle butts and bayoneted his corpse.

The sight appalled Bates, but there was no time to chasten those soldiers or anyone. And he could not help but feel he understood. To the degree any white man might.

A black sergeant brought a Reb battle flag to show him. The fellow was bloody and beaming.

The close-quarters fighting pressed to its end, the ugliest business Bates had seen in the war. The remaining Johnnies ran hightail or surrendered, and Bates' next challenge was to come to the aid of a captain shielding a half dozen disarmed Confederates from his own soldiers.

"Don't let them niggers kill us," a cracker voice pleaded.

Bates shoved the leveled rifles aside and snapped, *"Stop it. That's enough."*

The command met bulging eyes and flaring nostrils, curled

mouths and heaving chests. Men in blood-christened uniforms, with bayonets ready to plunge. For a brazen moment, Bates was uncertain whether he'd be obeyed.

"The next man who harms a prisoner will hang," he said in a voice he hoped was sufficiently firm. "Move on, if you want to fight. There's work aplenty."

His soldiers grunted and went along, trailing a mood of grievance.

"Good Lord, Del," a white voice said.

Bates turned and found Seymour Hall, colonel of the 43rd U.S. Colored Troops, heading a file of his soldiers.

"Followed you in," Hall explained. "Only thing that seemed to make any sense."

First, Bates spoke to his captain. Pointing at the prisoners, he said, "Get these men out of here. Fast. Hand them over to the first white soldiers you find." Then he asked Hall, "Morrie, can you shift to the right? Can you push over to the right?"

Hall nodded. "Do what I can. Ain't this the damnedest, though?"

Shouts and screams sounded a few traverses off.

"Have to keep them in hand," Bates said. He shook his head. "And the high and mighty insisted these men wouldn't fight. . . ."

Hall nodded and set off.

Bates followed a blood trail past mutilated corpses. When he reached the ditch where the thrust had finally stalled, he found his men silent and panting. The angriest of them leveled their rifles over the lip of dirt, enthralled by the prospect of killing men who once might have been their masters. Others sat inspecting their wounds, more amazed than distraught. The rest reloaded their weapons, ramrods clanking, or wiped gore from bayonets. One man vomited hugely.

A hard-eyed soldier asked Bates, "We done good for you, Colonel?"

Before Bates could answer, a tap on his shoulder made him jump embarrassingly.

Major Van Buren, one of Burnside's staff men.

"You're a long way from home, Van Buren," Bates said.

"Where's Colonel Sigfried?"

The question surprised Bates, although he couldn't say why. He, too, had been caught in the frenzy, if less brutally.

"Haven't seen him," Bates told the major, "since we left the line."

"Why have your men stopped?"

That question, too, startled Bates. "This is as far as my orders go. If they went this far." He glanced about. "And these men . . . these men have done splendidly."

"But you've stopped."

"Good Lord, man, we just broke through the Rebs and took dozens of prisoners. More than dozens. And a battle flag." He grimaced and gestured toward the next Reb position. "Listen to that volume of fire. How much do you expect of a single regiment?"

"Doesn't matter what I expect. General Burnside wants Sigfried's brigade to take the cemetery, up on the next ridge. And you're closest." He took off his cap and wiped away sweat with his sleeve. "Look, Colonel, it can't be far. You need to go forward *now*. By order of the corps commander."

Bates listened to the implacable rifle fire to his front.

"If you need to see a written order . . ." Van Buren reached into his blouse.

Bates waved him off. "If you wouldn't mind asking Colonel Hall to support us? On our right?"

"Where's Hall?"

Bates gestured down a traverse. "Over there somewhere."

"That's not much help," the major said. But he did head off in what seemed like the right direction.

Bates considered his men, their evident combination of shock and exalted exhaustion, of bloody ecstasy and lingering doubts. They needed to be reorganized, made back into soldiers again. But if they had to resume the attack, well, the sooner the better. Every moment allowed the Rebs to organize their next line.

Walking the trench and addressing the men, he said, "One more bit to do, boys. One more stretch of line out there needs taking." Trying to read these faces made suddenly strange, one, then the next, and the next, faces that he had believed he knew, he declared, "I'm *proud* of you. I could not be more proud. You showed them what you can do. Now I need you to follow me again. And to behave like soldiers, *disciplined* soldiers."

They understood. "Fort Pillow," a man muttered.

Bates turned on the fellow. "*Damn* Fort Pillow. You need to be *better* than them. Can't you see that?" He stopped himself. No time for sermons. Words wasted lives.

"Officers! Get your men up. . . ."

Perhaps two hundred soldiers remained within range of his voice. Forgoing the formal orders of the drill field, he simply shouted, "*Come on!*" And he led the way over the parapet.

A shocking volley struck them as soon as they left the ditch. As if the Johnnies had known they were coming and waited. Men tumbled back into the trench or doubled over, gut-shot.

"*Come on!*" Bates sliced the air with his sword.

It wasn't far to the Rebs, not far at all. A man could throw a stone and hit them square.

But his men fell too fast. The barely formed line staggered.

"Come over here, you black-ass sonsofbitches, see what you get," a Reb yelled out.

Another called, "Shoot their goddamned nigger-loving officers. . . ."

It was the last thing Bates heard before something struck him powerfully in the cheek, snapping back his head and almost dropping him. He stumbled and clutched his face, discovering a bloody slop on the side of his head, a mess of flesh and bone. Maybe teeth, as well.

Blinded, he thrust out his other hand, grabbing the air and fighting to keep his balance.

A second bullet struck him and spun him around.

He fell into someone's arms. He believed he could see again—

light filtered through blood—but he could not focus. Letting himself be all but carried rearward, he tried to speak, to order his men to withdraw, but his jaw wouldn't help.

"What's happening?" he tried to say. And failed.

Blurred forms manhandled him back into the ditch.

"What happened?" he struggled to ask. He knew, but he didn't know. Flashes of memory dizzied him, the blow repeating itself.

Someone poured water over his face.

"The men . . . ," he said.

"You shush now, Colonel," a startlingly tender voice told him. "Just shush. You all be fixed right up."

He could see. But not well. So many faces. Black giving way to white. The devil's own bang-up racket. All around him. Inside his head.

The hurt started up, abrupt and overwhelming.

He groaned, slipped. Strong arms braced him up.

Men hoisted him over a parapet. He understood they were taking him back to the Union lines. They were carrying him, strong arms in lieu of a litter. And as they left the trenches he had entered less than half an hour before, a flinty Northern voice remarked, "Well, so much for the coons."

Eight thirty a.m.
Confederate lines below the cemetery

Billy Mahone was sorry he hadn't had time for his eggs and milk. Made for an angry belly, burning hot, as if he'd drunk acid. But if his guts were in a temper, he supposed it was fitting enough. The rest of him was in a temper, too.

Yankees were using nigger troops against white men. Stunned him, when he heard it. The mine was bestial enough, but arming darkies and turning them loose on white men . . . the swine who would do such a thing would loose them on white women, too.

Mahone had possessed seven slaves, accidents of inheritance

and dowry, and found they were more trouble than they were worth. Didn't care to have them too near, either, crowding a house. He'd sold off five, including a truculent cook and her brats, and reckoned he was stuck with his wife's fuss-gal and his body servant, a boy who never failed to find his appetite. Times were when Mahone was uncertain as to who was tending who, given the Negro's genius for intractability and general not-doing. And when you got to railroad work, fact was that paid men, black or white, worked harder. Better to hire those you needed, cooks or gandy dancers. As long as a fellow wasn't afraid to sweat, he'd take on a Chinaman.

He considered himself a practical-minded, modern man, an engineer, a builder of railroads. Privately, he'd long believed that slavery was a rickety undertaking, pitiful for everyone involved. But the men who held his railway bonds didn't know how to get out from under it. Take his slaves, and the rich man was a bankrupt, cracker-poor.

And Mahone remembered his father rowing his family out on the river, fleeing Nat Turner's marauders. The notion that Negroes and whites should commingle in society was as repugnant as it was damn-fool. That was the nut of the problem, and the Yankees just ignored it. Be a different story, though, once free darkies niggered up their cities and pawed their womenfolk.

Squatting at the drain end of a shallow ravine, Mahone fumed and listened as Lieutenant Colonel McMaster, a South Carolina man who'd been fighting since dawn, sketched a map in the dust and explained the respective positions. McMaster was sound. Unlike old Bushrod Johnson and too many others.

Mahone had ridden ahead of his troops to gather information, but Johnson's headquarters had been little help and the general himself had been more concerned with his breakfast—while a line thinned to emaciation held back a feast of Yankees. The most Johnson offered was a lieutenant to guide Mahone up to the lines. Where he and McMaster had found each other, to their mutual relief.

"See here," the Carolinian said, "this here's the ravine and here's us." He traced southward. "That's as far as I took you, up where it shallows out." The stick moved eastward. "You saw them. Across that open stretch. Say three hundred, maybe three-fifty yards. Plenty of hogs to hunt over in that hollow."

"Still can't believe they used niggers," Mahone said.

"Reckon they ran out of white men willing to go. Here now, General. They've got the pit and maybe a hundred and fifty yards of our entrenchments to the north. Less to the south, I'd judge. Can't say to a certainty."

Mahone shook his head. Noise, heat, bile. "That's a bit more than General Johnson claimed."

"Haven't seen him up here," McMaster noted, not without spleen.

"How many?"

McMaster shrugged. "Lord knows. Plenty. Thousands." Gaze drifting, he calculated. "Maybe five or six thousand. In the fight proper." He raised an eyebrow, skeptical of his own words. "I could be off a good lick. How many men you have, General?"

Mahone smiled, not happily. "Two brigades coming up now. Eight hundred Virginians, about six hundred Georgians."

Neither man remarked that numbers that low weren't truly brigades, but regiments with an extra ration of flags.

"My Alabama boys are set to follow," Mahone added, hoping it was true. "Be some hours, though. Have to make do, in the meantime."

After learning from Beauregard how desperate the crisis had grown, he had dispatched a note to his corps commander, asking that his Alabama Brigade be sent up, too. The detachment left back in the rifle pits would have to make do with bluff and paper dolls.

A man had to take action and bear the risks. He reckoned A. P. Hill would see that, too.

Mahone's aide, Girardey, emerged from the covered way behind the ravine. Mahone had worked him hard and the captain's uniform was dark as a Yankee's with sweat.

"Come on over here, Victor. Show you how I want the brigades set in."

Born French and raised Deep South, Girardey squatted down beside the two officers and studied the dirt map. Mahone explained it precisely as McMaster had done.

"Does seem a challenge, sir," the captain said. His face sharpened. "Wounded fellow back a ways claimed the Yankees put in their Negroes."

"That's a fact," McMaster said.

"I'll be damned."

"No," Mahone told the younger, taller man. "They'll be damned. You wait."

Eight forty-five a.m.
61st Virginia, Weisiger's Brigade, Mahone's Division

First Lieutenant John T. West led his company out of the covered way. General Mahone stood waiting at the foot of a swale. It sounded as though all the devils in Hell were at work.

West had pondered Hell. Born into the Methodist Church, he felt that he had only truly become a Methodist the past winter, when Man the Fallen's eternal prospects had revealed themselves to him at a camp revival. Since then, he had sought to live as properly as a soldier could, preparing himself to face the Judgment Seat.

First, he had to pass muster with Billy Mahone, a short man with a long beard and a manner that lit men up, parson or profane.

As the troops passed by, Mahone addressed them in a voice stripped raw: "Remember your homes, men, remember old Norfolk. Our fine city, under the Yankee boot. And you get angry, you get yourselves right angry. Because you're going to charge when I say 'Charge,' and you're going to whup the goddamned Yankees, and you're going to do it without stopping to shoot until you get to the trenches they stole this morning. And then you're going to give them the bayonet, hear?" The little man's eyes were molten. "One more thing now. Yankees sent in their coons. That's right, boys, niggers in soldier suits. Schooled to kill the white man." His voice didn't rise but tightened until it was narrow as a blade. "Show them no quarter. They raised the black flag and showed your brothers none. I'm not of a mind to bother about prisoners."

Mahone paused to let the words strike deep before repeating the speech to the next span of troops. West followed the regimental column up into the swale, where General Weisiger and Captain Girardey guided men into position.

Two small mortars had been positioned halfway up the depression, stumpy weapons hurling balls in a high arc, and powder-grimed men sprawled up on the rim of the swale, firing at the Yankees, but the Virginia brigade was ordered to hunker down and keep out of sight.

The news that Negro troops were in the fight riled up the men. They spoke of it with heathen spite, without the least Christian mercy. Nor did West feel merciful himself. *This* fight would not be one for gentlemen or for New Testament Christians. The lessons would be culled from Kings and Joshua.

"Officers of the Sixty-first!" Colonel Stewart called as he prowled their rear. "Company officers, in your turn! You slide on up and take a look at the ground we're going to cross. Don't make some damned show of it, stay down. Yankees don't need to know we're coming their way. But have yourselves a look, you take it in. Don't want my officers peeing their drawers when they're ordered to go forward."

Stewart's officers wouldn't pee their drawers. The colonel knew that, and so did those he commanded. Still, when West's turn came, he was appalled. What he could see of the Yankee position crawled like a kicked-up anthill. Rifles blazed forbiddingly from the busted-up ground, and so many flags poked the air he couldn't count them.

First Lieutenant John T. West commended his soul to Jesus Christ, his Savior, and regretted failing to bid his brothers farewell. He would've liked to see Norfolk County again, but it didn't seem likely.

Nine a.m.
Mahone's Division

General, they're coming!" Girardey hollered from the top of the bank.

At first, Mahone assumed his aide had spied his Georgia brigade, which had fallen behind unaccountably. But Girardey's attention was elsewhere.

The Yankees were getting ready to charge. Before he could charge them himself.

Mahone yelled, "Find Weisiger. Tell him to charge. We'll go it with the old brigade alone."

No damned choice.

Girardey dashed up the ravine, heading toward the shallow end, hunting the brigade's commander. Three hundred yards off, the Yankees piled out of the captured trenches, forming up where Mahone had meant to strike.

When he couldn't spot Weisiger, Girardey ran out in front of the brigade. Drawing his sword, he shouted, "Virginia! Forward!"

Nine a.m.
61st Virginia

As the Virginia brigade rose and burst from the swale, screaming like devils on fire, First Lieutenant West felt he wasn't so much running as flying toward the Yankees, hurled through the air by invigorating, unchristian, howling, shed-blood hatred.

The Rebel yell had never had such bite to it, the battle flag had never shone so mean-heart crimson, and it was no time or place for pretty ranks, just every last man aware that the trick was to get across that lonely eternity of open ground and leap in among the Yankees, black or white, just get on into those trenches and get to killing.

Glancing left and right, reveling in the splendor of the charge for one cut of a second, bedazzled by the martial beauty, West yipped and yelled along with the men beside him, sword in his right hand, pistol in his left, running straight for the blue caps and blue-clad shoulders—grown ever closer—and the orange-flame-spitting muzzles piercing the dust and smoke. They hadn't even got to the Yankees when they came up on the first stray darkies and, disdaining to waste bullets, clubbed and bayoneted them in passing, the joy of the deed transcendent, almost as rich as congress with a woman.

A Negro in blue rose up, then dropped to his knees in front of West, calling, "Let me come over, boss. I done, I done."

And West, despite himself, waved off a soldier about to kill the pitiful swine masquerading as a human, telling his fellow grayback, "Plenty ahead to shoot. Let that one go."

Then they were truly flying, leaping piled dirt and careening into the ditches held by the Yankees. Shrieking with blood-want and rapture, they shot, clubbed, swung, stabbed, punched, and ripped flesh, splashing the blood of white men and colored, daubing the air scarlet, spraying each other, slapped in the face by man-meat torn away, all amid profanity sublime and hate-sweat and guts ripped forth by withdrawn bayonets, man-belly caught on blades and dragged out like sausages.

Shouting mindless, meaningless orders, West rushed along a traverse. Where it bent back, he found a passel of white Yankees. Two of them lowered their muskets toward his middle.

Diving across another blue-belly, he leapt atop one rifle and batted the other away, too drunk with fury to marvel at himself. His soldiers were with him again, slaying Yankees mightily, and West beat both the Yankees who'd want to kill him over their heads with his pistol's butt and the hilt of his sword, Christian faith suspended, bashing them as a wicked child might crush a crippled rabbit with a rock.

Somebody said General Weisiger was belly-shot, but it meant little, for Colonel Stewart, a closer presence, rampaged wild among them, driving his men forward, an inspiration.

"West," Stewart called, "you clean out that next ditch." Then the colonel told a terrified, cowering Yankee officer, "You want to be spared, you git off to the rear, back thataway. I'm not about to coddle you sonsofbitches."

Billy Pate, who'd popped up for a look across the parapet, dropped back down, cackling, gleeful, and said, "Nigs is running like the hounds are on 'em."

Stewart, still near, said, "Well, they ain't *all* running. Look to it, boys."

West led. Men followed. And it was true: Not all of the coloreds had run. They collided with a fierce bunch. Billy Pate shoved his bayonet into a man so deeply that he couldn't pull it back out and a black soldier slugged him with the stock of his rifle. Pate reeled, but he wouldn't go down. The Negro hit him again.

West put his sword through the man's throat. On his right, Jere Tompkins clashed rifle against rifle with a big Negro, both men baring their teeth like dogs, until a bullet fired from inches away blew the Yankee's brains out the side of his skull. That just enraged Billy Pate, who screamed, "I got nigger mess all over me, there's nigger blood all over me."

The melee soon turned in favor of West's kind, with the last blue-clads beaten groundward, the trench a trough of blood and soldiers bashing and stabbing the wounded and dying as if the next step might be to devour their flesh.

A Reb West didn't recognize, a man addled in with the 61st in the course of the fighting, bayoneted a Negro over and over, stopped to puke on the man, gasped, wiped his maw, and bayoneted him some more, telling the corpse, "Git up, you nigger sonofabitch, git up." He was still tormenting the body as West moved on.

A fellow Johnny waved a captured Union flag and was shot in the back for his troubles. Then West found himself suddenly alone, fending off two taunting blacks with his sword, parrying their bayonets, forced backward until he stumbled over a corpse.

"We got 'em for you, Lieutenant," a familiar voice assured him. Prematurely.

In the ensuing brawl, one of his own men stabbed West in the shoulder.

It hurt like mortal sin. With an instant, burning hurt. Dropping his empty pistol and clutching the wound, West toppled onto a writhing, blood-bubbling Negro. The darkey tried to bite him, going at his neck right through the collar, and got a bayonet through the eye as his reward.

West hoped he hadn't got Negro blood in his wound.

Nine twenty a.m.
30th U.S. Colored Troops

Rally, rally!" Sergeant Offer cried. Enraged and shamed, he clubbed a fleeing soldier with his rifle, then grabbed a molasses-toned coward by his sleeve. "Washington, turn your behind around, you stand right here and fight."

But the lad, who had battled bravely minutes before, had been rendered meek and fearful by the turn of things. When the Rebs descended mercilessly upon them, the best men had fought and fallen, unleashing a panic that ran through the rest like cholera through a plantation.

When Offer released his grip, the private shriveled like a forgotten apple. Then he skedaddled.

Not all of the 30th ran, though. Even now, men fought. Offer gave up his attempt at rallying others and, face bleeding and uniform torn, rejoined those with the deep-down strength to fight on. A few of the white officers had run, too, but most had either died or stayed with their charges. They tried to give orders but could do no more than hold some survivors in place, bitter-hearted, disappointed black men firing and reloading and firing again, shooting toward wicked enemies yards away, unwilling to be made less than they had come to believe they deserved to be, their embarrassment as fierce as the mark of Cain.

Enemies? Despite his share of trials and tribulations over the years, despite a lifetime of seeing in men's eyes and hearing in their voices how little they valued him, John Offer had never grasped how many lurking enemies he faced. All because of the color of his skin, a curious, incidental, indelible thing. He had known the Rebs for his foe-men, but the shock of his life had come as the 30th first fell back, fighting sharply as it withdrew, only to meet volleys from the rear as men in the same blue uniforms shot down Colored Troops and cursed them, even bayoneted them, driving them off in slack-jawed, wide-eyed mortification and damning them for their nigger-ness.

Should-have-been comrades had shot them down like dogs. And the Rebs to their front had murdered them like varmints. All a man could do was run or fight.

Sergeant Offer chose to fight. But the stripes on his sleeves burned his flesh. Confidence gone, he clung to heathen rage.

The rump of the 30th was pushed from the last trench. The stalwarts broke into two parts. Most of them—Offer among them—withdrew down the slope toward the old lines, attempting to show some last discipline, some ragged display of pride, while the remainder were forced toward the boiling pit, where no man was welcome.

When Offer reached what passed for safety that day, tears scorched his face. He was embarrassed until he saw his captain, a white man, bawling like a child. The sight dried his tears instantly, enraging him worse than the Reb savagery had done, worse than the treachery of his fellow Yankees.

He would have liked to slap that boy, to redden his smooth white flesh with a hard hand, to tell him, "You don't know one thing, not one thing how it's like, how a man been lifelong kept. down, valued less than a rich man's dog, skills honed high and honest, and *still* judged less than those of a white-skinned drunkard or a thief, you don't know what it's like, no you don't, 'cause for you this here's a high and noble cause, way you go talking, but you're *still* white, and you're *still* the master, but unto y'all comes the day—and maybe soon—when none of us niggers let it be that way, not anymore."

He seethed and sat down as white provost men drove his brethren back to their ranks, prodding them with bayonets and gloat words, all of it unneeded but satisfying to those white men in blue who had not even fought.

Smearing away tears with the back of a paw, Offer's captain came over to him, squatted down, and laid a hand on his shoulder.

"You did your best, Sergeant Offer."

Offer would have liked to strangle the boy, to mash his skull. Instead, he answered:

"Do better next time, Cap'n."

Nine forty-five a.m.
The Crater

A first mortar round arced and dropped amid the disorder. Shreds of carcass flew. The wounded shrieked, the untouched howled. The Rebs had not reached the pit itself, but they'd launched a second attack, determined to close the wound gouged in their line. More and more soldiers were pressed back into the twin holes, where it was all but impossible to move. White additions had grown as unwelcome as black.

"An inordinate disgrace," General Bartlett declared.

"Any disgrace in particular in mind?" Colonel Marshall asked him. "I see a bushel of 'em."

Bartlett snorted. "Rather a few, I should think. Ledlie. Burnside. Myself, not least. And the way those blackamoors bolted." His blue-blooded smirk returned. "Abolition's a splendid topic for lectures, but Phillips and Garrison seem to be absent today. . . ."

Marshall had witnessed the wretched spectacle, too. The mad flight of the Colored Troops to the rear had given hundreds of other men all the excuse they needed to run for their lives. But not all the Negroes had run, and credit was due. A portion had fought as well as the white men that morning.

Bartlett was an odd duck, though. Marshall wondered what the Apaches he'd trailed would have made of him. And those God-ridden Mormons would have eaten him whole.

Another mortar round plummeted into the mob. A body flew up like a boy tossed on a blanket.

"Don't know what *you're* waiting for," Bartlett told Marshall. "Best get out. I told Hartranft the same thing."

"Not yet."

"Doubt there'll be time later. You know how fast these things go, once they start going."

"I still have men in here. And wounded."

"Won't do them one spot of good, you lingering. I'll be trophy enough for our noble antagonists." He shook his head. "Never saw such a godforsaken mess. You'd think it was masterminded by a Yale man."

Up on the crust of the pit, the best soldiers had burrowed in to pick off the Rebs. With unsettling regularity, men sprawled backward, shot in the head. Yet, another man always took the casualty's place and resumed the duel. If some men just milled like cattle, others would not quit until they were killed: A contingent of Indians from the 1st Michigan Sharpshooters had strayed in from Willcox's bunch. They manned a stretch of the rim with handsome tenacity and chanted dirges over fallen comrades.

Such men deserved far better than they'd gotten, Marshall knew. And the fault was his as well. He should have demanded better, clearer orders. They all should have done so. But every brigade commander in the division had shrugged it off, tired men accustomed to working things out despite their superior. This day, their negligence had cost other men dearly.

"I'd best see to the flanks again," Marshall rasped, trying to be heard above the din. "What flanks we have left."

Throat all dust and burrs, he yearned for nothing so much as a drink of water. But none was to be had. The wounded that hadn't been trampled thirsted terribly.

"You take the right. I'll see to the left," Bartlett told him.

Marshall nodded and turned to push his way through the roiling herd. More men would have fled, he knew, but the slope between the lines had become too deadly. Now they wouldn't fight and wouldn't leave. And he was alone, his staff depleted, its members all sent off on useless missions, first in search of Ledlie, then directly to Burnside. None had returned, nor had he received one reply.

Still, he hoped to maintain defensible lines, to just hold on.

Until when? Dark? That would take a damned miracle. And for what? The pit was worthless in itself, its possession as unsustainable as it was pointless.

A sergeant caught up with him, breathless.

"Colonel Marshall, Colonel, sir . . ."

"What is it, man?"

"It's General Bartlett, sir. The general's killed. A mortar . . ."

Oh, Christ. Appalled, plain sickened by all of it, Marshall followed the fellow back through the press and push and stench, rough-shouldering any man who got in the way.

He found Bartlett propped against the clay, waving off would-be helpers.

"Leg blown off . . . ," the shocked sergeant explained. "I saw him fall . . . I thought . . ."

Bartlett spotted Marshall and grinned ruefully.

When Marshall had come sufficiently close for Bartlett to be heard, the general said, "Absolutely destroyed my new cork leg. Have you any idea what a proper one costs, the number of fittings?" He slapped away another helping hand. "Well, I suppose I'm well and truly stuck."

Fresh Rebel yells cut the morning.

FOUR

Grant came in dirty and sweat-glossed, trailed by Horace Porter, a tattletale aide Meade considered less than a gentleman.

Any other creature would have been glad to get out of the sun, but Grant made a tiny gesture and told Meade, "Talk. In private." He led the way back outdoors.

In the distance, fighting thrashed. The sun burdened Meade's shoulders. Distasteful Virginia.

"Hot, all right," Grant said. He stopped in a patch of shade by tethered horses, their smells rich. Rarely one to raise his voice or let others read his face, Grant showed plain disgust around his mouth.

"Burnside," Meade began, "has been—"

"He's finished," Grant said. "Attack's a bust."

"He insists he can still make progress."

"Believe that?"

"No."

"I told him to end it, pull back."

"He's desperate, Sam. He knows what this will mean."

Grant's ginger beard shone with sweat.

"He's been impossible all morning," Meade continued. "His reporting has been . . . dishonest, to be frank. And consistently late. I only learned how bad things were when a message meant for him came to me instead."

Grant stroked a horse's neck, then drew a burr from its mane. Meade often suspected that Grant preferred horses to men.

Turning abruptly back to Meade, the general in chief let his anger flash. His voice remained low, but his tone grew fierce:

"I have never seen . . . *never* saw such an opportunity to carry a fortified line. Right there for the taking. And I never expect to see such a chance again." He petted the horse. "A lieutenant could have carried that position."

Meade let the words fade against the racket of war.

Grant wasn't finished. "The mine *worked*. That's the bitter nut." He shook his head, a great display of emotion by his measure. "Had I been a division commander, I would've led my men up there myself." Brown eyes hardened, he added, "Couldn't find a one of them. Went beyond the parapets myself. And I could not find one division commander forward. Just a peck of colonels and brigadiers wondering what to do next." He half smiled. "Young Porter had him a fit. Convinced the Rebs were going to scoop me up."

"Glad they didn't."

Grant wiped wet from his cheek and beard. "Fine opportunity wasted. Unforgivable. Just unforgivable." He fixed his eyes on Meade. "Court of inquiry's called for, I think."

"He's given adequate cause." Meade hesitated. "But the politics . . ."

"Seeing Lincoln tomorrow. At Fortress Monroe. I'll tend to it."

Artillery boomed. Both men glanced toward it.

"Unforgivable waste," Grant repeated. He stepped off toward the house. "Any water hereabouts fit to drink?"

With the mood suddenly eased, Meade said, "I can't vouch for the taste."

"Going back to City Point. Settle things up, George. Nothing I can do here but get angry. And that never helped."

Teddy Lyman, who was a gentleman, stepped from the house to meet them. He was followed by Porter the sneak, Grant's crawling spy.

"General Meade," Lyman said with that Boston reed in his voice, "I thought you might care to know, sir. Telegraph message. General Burnside's riding back here to see you. With General Ord."

"Christ," Meade snapped. "The fellow won't give up."

Waving his aide toward their mounts, Grant said, "He gave up all that mattered."

Ten thirty a.m.
Confederate lines

Billy Mahone watched another string of frightened Negroes in blue stumbling to the rear. By the time he had gotten into the trenches himself, the slaughter had grown cruel enough to ruin good soldiers. The traverses retaken by the Virginia brigade were carpeted with corpses, most of them niggers extravagantly mutilated. His men had outrun restraint, beyond Mahone's fit of temper and taste for revenge. He had put a stop to the worst of it, more or less, ordering regimental commanders to accept attempts to surrender from white men or black.

Still, he smoldered to ponder the Yankee viciousness. Creating Nat Turners by the tens of thousands. He did not regret his initial "no quarter" command. But enough was enough. Matter of discipline.

When a soldier whumped a black man with a rifle butt, Mahone accepted that as a flash of temper. And a Negro shot for sassing his white captor deserved what he got. But now that his outrage had been tamped down to method, Mahone chose not to condone a further massacre. Didn't want Otelia reading in the papers that he was a butcher.

Still, he didn't expect all the Negro captives to make it to Petersburg. Nor was he minded to look into matters too deeply. Just had to keep things within a certain tolerance.

Had enough on his hands, anyway, without fixing on the coons. Matt Hall and his Georgians hadn't exactly covered themselves in glory. Mahone had sent them forward to build upon the gains made by the Virginians, but the Yankees still in the pit had organized themselves well enough to sting. Ordered to attack and extend the right flank of the Virginians, the Georgians had started off well enough, only to break under successive volleys and stray left, piling in atop some unhappy Virginians.

And the fighting had settled into a grim back-and-forth, with Mahone awaiting the arrival of his Alabama Brigade, his last punch left to throw.

Nor had that gone smoothly. Perplexing and riling Mahone, A. P. Hill had approved the dispatch of the Alabamians, but had sent the order back to Mahone, instead of straight down the line to Johnny Sanders. For all the haste impressed upon his courier, he didn't believe he could expect the Alabamians to get started on their march before eleven.

Bushrod Johnson appeared out of the hollow, guided by Mc-Master.

About time, Mahone reckoned.

"Nice piece of work, I hear," his fellow general said by way of greeting.

"Not nice enough," Mahone told him. "Yankees are still in there. Stubborn as mules."

Another herd of bloodied-up Negroes came by, shoved on by gaunt captors. Bushrod Johnson spit in the column's direction. "Big Mandingo there would've brought twelve hundred before the war."

Mahone asked, "What can I do for you, General?" He could not quell the image of Johnson gobbling his breakfast in the rear. When the man should have been forward with his troops.

"Well," Johnson said, "I reckon it's more a matter of what I can do for you. Or what we can do together. Beauregard says we're to 'cooperate.' Push 'em all at once, lance this carbuncle."

Mahone felt the urge to say, "Well, hallelujah! Glad you can join the hymn-sing at long last." Instead, he told his fellow division commander, "Makes sense to me."

"How soon you think we should go?"

"Not till my Alabamians come up. I'd say one o'clock."

"I do believe Beauregard had something sooner in mind."

Mahone held back his temper.

McMaster had seen enough of Mahone to take warning. Intervening, the colonel said, "Heat'll be hard on your men coming up, sir. But they surely will be welcome."

Perhaps Johnson sensed something, too. He said, "Well, one o'clock will suit, I suppose. Take me time to get to my right flank, anyway. Damned Yankees hit the middle of my division."

"If you," Mahone said, "can close the trap, my boys will deal with the pit."

"I can work down from the left," McMaster told them.

"Right shouldn't be no problem," Johnson added. "Not once I get there, tie things back together."

"Good," Mahone told them. "Come one o'clock, we hit those sonsofbitches from three sides. Meantime, I suggest shifting the artillery."

He suspected, though, that bayonets would decide things.

Ten thirty a.m.
Dunn house

Lieutenant Colonel Theodore Lyman, Harvard class of 1855 and student of nature, felt sorry for Ambrose Burnside. But not sufficiently so to defend the fellow.

If Burnside had committed one military blunder after another, his behavior toward Meade had been sheer folly. The Ninth Corps commander had even paused in midbattle to pen a note to Meade all but demanding satisfaction on the field of honor. Not least, he had accused Meade of falling short of the standards of a gentleman, a charge that was guaranteed to raise Meade's ire. Old Philadelphia was harsher about some matters than Boston, although Lyman rather supposed Pennsylvanians had to try harder.

Atop all the rest, Burnside had absented himself from the front to plead a case he lacked the wit to make. He had not even paused for privacy, but launched into justifications in front of dozens of officers and men, including two beribboned Frenchmen who had attached themselves to the Army as observers—although Lyman had begun to suspect that free victuals attracted them as much as did any martial revelations.

Now Burnside was *pleading* in front of everyone, a sorry business.

"George, really . . . the battle's not lost, it's *not*. If Warren supported me, if Hancock—"

"The order stands. Withdraw as soon as practicable." Meade's voice gave Lyman a chill, but at least the Army commander kept his temper better than often had been the case.

Burnside turned to his companion. "Ord, tell him, tell him! It's not lost yet. One more division . . ."

Meade turned his raptor's stare on Ord, who simply shook his head.

"One more push," Burnside pleaded.

Meade exploded. It had been bound to come.

"*Where*? For the love of God, man? *Where*? *Where* would this magical 'push' be delivered? Into the pit? Where, as nearly as I can ascertain, you've squandered four divisions?" Except for the gray bags under his eyes, Meade's face was raw-meat red. "Including your damned minstrel show." He turned away. "I *never* should have permitted that, never should have let you send them in."

"But—"

"Do you even *know* where your subordinates are? *Do you*?"

"George, I—"

"Hadn't you better be back with *them*?"

"We could reach Petersburg, I swear to you, I swear it. . . ."

Meade opened his mouth as if to shout the man down. But he only turned his back on Ambrose Burnside. A few steps short of a battered door, he paused to repeat, "Withdraw. As soon as practicable. That's an order. Not only from me—from Grant."

When Meade had gone, Humphreys approached the broken corps commander.

"Burnside," he said, "*can* you withdraw? No nonsense now."

Damp-eyed and sweating, the corps commander said, "I think it would be best done after dark."

Noon
The Crater

Raw of crotch and weaving through spells of dizziness, Marshall had managed to contract and connect the defenses to the right of the pit. As a consequence, the Rebs could no more inch forward than could his own men. But the casualties grew ever worse, mostly men shot through the head when they rose to fire, or men made delirious by the heat, shivering out their lives at a temperature that must have passed one hundred degrees in the hole.

He remembered feeling downcast at West Point, convinced that, having missed the Mexican War, he would never witness such great events himself.

Now this hell. A far cry from the plods of the Utah War or chasing Navajo renegades in Arizona. He'd gotten his war, all right.

Would he ever see his wife and daughter again?

The Johnnies had brought up more guns on the flanks, sweeping the hillside between the lines and making it impossible to send back any more wounded. A few brave officers and sergeants made trips for more ammunition, with many falling, but the Reb sharpshooters had their best sport shooting down every man laden with canteens.

Back in the pit itself, the men had divided themselves into those who meant to fight and those who only wanted to survive. Of the latter, the white soldiers had gathered densely in the larger side of the pit, with blacks in the shallower depression to the north and the wounded everywhere. Marshall judged that as many as two thousand men were stranded in a space that would have been tight for a quarter their number.

When a staff man brought forward the order to hold out until dark and then withdraw, Marshall read it as a sentence of death.

Twelve fifty-five p.m.
Confederate lines, Mahone's Division, Alabama brigade

At twenty-four, Brigadier General John Caldwell Calhoun Sanders had seen enough of war to know his chances. And the single chance he saw was for his paltry offering of six hundred men to hit the Yankees so damn hard that they'd swear they'd faced six thousand.

In more of a mood to drink blood than the milk from that cow of his, Billy Mahone had suggested, with an ungentlemanly degree of clarity, that the battle was in Sanders' hands and his return would be superfluous should he fail.

Sanders looked at his watch again. Five more minutes. Of "rest" for men held under a sun that was downright equatorial. He long had claimed that Virginians didn't know summer heat from hog meat, that Alabama summers beat them all, but this day was a trial. He'd lost a dozen men on the march, lashed on by frequent messages from Mahone. Now his soldiers crouched in a scorched ravine, man-flesh offered up to the sun like a sacrifice, rifle barrels yet unused and already hot enough to blister calluses.

He liked a good fight, but this looked to be a bad one. Fated, though he never let on that he credited such notions. Put him darkly in mind of that rowdy night with his university brethren, just on the edge of secession, when sodden with drink they'd visited a wisewoman outside town, a creature who let her two daughters do one thing while she did another, gold welcome, silver accepted. Twixt friendly trips to the tumbledown barn, the boys had had their fortunes told for a lark, drawing a string of unlikely promises from the old woman's lips, though not one word of a coming war and the scythe it would swing among them. Her talk had been of wealth and wondrous brides, of young men's ambitions cut to fit the company. But when Johnny Sanders' turn had come, the old witch had stiffened, rejecting his palm and claiming—after a spell of discomfiture—that she'd used herself up and couldn't see one more thing.

His luck had held, though. With half his friends forced to beg treatment of a doctor renowned for discretion, Sanders had gone unafflicted. Generally, he had done his best to live by his pap's admonition: Gals, but not too many; drink, but not too much; and leave when the cards come out.

He had liked the university, but he loved the war. And as for the unwelcome memory of that prophesying crone, he reckoned that his wound at Frayser's Farm had answered her vision.

Anyway, he doubted that any creature up on two legs, even a poor-white sorceress, could have foreseen the desolation of the battlefield spread before him.

Across those few hundred corpse-strewn yards, the penned-in Yankees waited. Niggers armed and uniformed among them. Sanders reckoned his men would just see about that.

One thing he had never done was to lay with a black woman. Couldn't imagine a gentleman doing such.

He studied his watch again: just under two minutes to one.

Mahone had described the tricks of the ground, pointing to where Sanders' regiments were to strike the Yankee position. Rags sweated through, the men had panted and listened as the little Virginian explained to all that this was not a day for indifferent measures. And war-roughened men from up and down Alabama, wearied to ruination by that march, turned snake-mean again. In front of a crowd whose members towered over him, Mahone's effect on men was just uncanny: If witchery there was, he had more of it in him than any red-clay gypsy who whored her daughters.

But Billy Mahone's gift for mesmerizing soldiers still lacked the magic to transport Sanders' Alabamians and Carolina strays safely across that deadly space to the blue-rimmed volcano where Yankee bullets served for Pompeii's lava.

Sanders only hoped that *The Last Days of Pompeii*, which had enthralled him, wouldn't give way to the last days of the Confederacy.

He looked at his watch a last time and raised his sword. His men scrambled to their feet.

"Alabama!" Sanders shouted. "Forward!"

And off they went, with orders repeated along the whittled-down lines and last fears smothered by exhilaration.

Mahone had warned Sanders—forcefully—not to veer to the left at the Yankee volleys, as Matt Hall had allowed his Georgians to do. He needed to strike the pit walls smack in the center and on the right, and there would be no excuses. So he kept up a stream of commands—harsher than his habit—as the first Yankee riflery took its toll.

The lines buckled at a volley but rebounded.

The men wanted to charge, to cover that ground, Sanders understood. But he'd be damned if he'd give Mahone the least cause for complaint. His men were going to hit the Yankees where they were meant to hit them. Or leave a trail of bodies in that direction.

More men fell. Yet the volume of fire was less than Sanders expected.

His regiments on the right struck deep traverses and fell behind. The pace of the others quickened, but remained short of a run. As bullet-pierced men flung out their arms, officers corrected the ranks with profanity and swords extended sideward.

Ahead, Sanders saw Yankee rifles hastily laid below bobbing caps, faces pressed against rifle stocks, small bursts of flame, and shoulders turning to disappear again.

The firing bit through the Alabamian ranks. A color-bearer fell, but not the colors.

When Sanders judged that their course was fixed and the Yankees could not deflect them, he shouted:

"Charge! Alabama! Charge!"

Blue-bellies popped from the ground like Lazarus multiplied. Most ran. Others, fear-faced, showed themselves with raised hands. Sanders' men dropped into traverses too wide to jump, while those still aboveground dashed for the high wall.

But the Yankees outside the pit who hadn't surrendered were fighting now.

Throughout the war, men had shied from using bayonets. That

had changed at the Mule Shoe, Sanders had been a witness. Now his men took the Yankees with cold steel.

No, *hot* steel. Nothing cold in the whole, wide world this day. Men gasped like beasts and thrust blades into bellies. Cursing and swinging rifles, the toughest Yankees tried to stand their ground. Sanders scrambled over piled dirt and slid into a trench, shooting twice with his pistol before he was again flanked by men in gray.

He had yet to see a black face among the Yankees.

"Push on! Clear 'em out! Close forward!"

Blood burst from a man's shoulder inches from Sanders. He paused to clear gore from his eyes. A Yankee crawled from a bomb-proof. Sanders shot him in the face before grasping that the fellow meant to surrender.

Fortunes of war. He pressed on. Thrusting his sword into the back of a bluecoat who'd gotten turned around in a clinch.

His foremost soldiers tried to scale the high wall, to get at the Yankees, only to slip and fall or be shot in their faces.

But the fight had become a challenge for the Yankees. To shoot down at his men, they had to expose their torsos, to lean over their parapets. Soon dead and bleeding Yankees hung over the wall.

Then, as if by mutual agreement, the firing sputtered on both sides. Neither Sanders' men nor the bluecoats above them could get at each other without dying themselves.

Off to the left, the division's other brigades were doing their part again, the Virginians and Georgians renewing their assault. He even believed he heard cries that the Yankees were running.

Well, they weren't running yet from the Alabama brigade.

A delighted soldier scrambled past, crying, "Got me a nigger! I got me a nigger!"

But the fight had all but halted. His men couldn't get up over the wall and live, while the bluecoats couldn't lean out to shoot and survive.

Sanders didn't want to be the one left behind in the victory. They *had* to break into the pit.

His soldiers began hurling clumps of clay and rocks over the wall. Then a sergeant called, "Pick up the rifles, gather up the rifles! Throw *them*. Harpoon the damn sumbitches, spear the bastards."

In moments, abandoned Yankee rifles, bayonets fixed, began sailing over the wall. Howls and curses rose from the other side.

A lieutenant staggered past. He was a good boy from Clinton, the town Sanders claimed as his own. Now an eyeball lolled down his cheek and his scalp flapped. He made a noise like a cow that needed milking.

Harpoon rifles flew back toward Sanders' men.

He turned to his adjutant. "George, work over to the right, far as you can. See if there isn't a spot we can push through over that way."

The two men dodged a rifle that came down butt first. Soldiers laughed.

"This won't do," Sanders said. "Find a way into that pit."

The captain scurried off.

More hurled rifles. Catcalls. Occasional shots. The atmosphere was as playful as it was murderous, turning into a deadly county fair.

Before he could give orders—angry ones—a division staff man found him.

"General Mahone wants to know why you aren't in the pit."

"Yanks aren't inclined to admit us. *You* tell me how to get in there, and we'll go."

"The general wants your men to jump over the wall. Just jump."

Sanders stared at the fellow. "You are aware there's a passel of Yankees in there?"

The battle noise increased. Close by.

"The Federals have been retreating," the staff major said. "The Virginians could see them running."

"Then who's doing all that shooting?"

Freshly smeared with blood and dirt, Sanders' adjutant returned and ended the argument.

"Good God," Sanders said. "Are you—"

"We're inside," the captain panted. "We're in the pit."

One thirty p.m.
The Crater

Brigadier General William Francis Bartlett of Haverhill, Massachusetts, aged twenty-four, son of Charles Leonard Bartlett and Harriet Dorothy Plummer Bartlett, graduate of the Phillips Academy and Harvard (class of '62), was immeasurably annoyed. Condemned to sit against a stump of clay, cork leg gone and pistol emptied, he watched the brawl he could no longer influence. Bartlett commanded a wealth of obscenities worthy of a divinity faculty, but he no longer commanded any troops.

What he saw before him was mayhem, a small apocalypse.

The noise was infernal, the heat monstrous, the very air bloodstained, and the pit so packed with striving men that he could not even have crawled off, had he wished.

A shock-faced sergeant blundered by, trailing gray intestines. Men screamed, a thing unusual. Flesh separated and flew. Hard men who would have killed for a swig of water sloshed through blood.

More Rebs dropped over the walls, the newcomers screaming their barbarous *kee-yip-yee-hee* before crashing onto the backs of their fellow Johnnies. Unwitting men stabbed their own kind, while others were packed too close to bring weapons to bear, fighting instead with fists, claws, and teeth.

Men vomited over each other, fainted, were trampled. A Massachusetts soldier Bartlett recognized—despite the grime and gore—fell atop him, thumping an elbow into his ribs. Unaware now that Bartlett even existed, the man rebounded and rejoined the melee.

Wounded on two more occasions after losing his leg at Yorktown—with his last Harvard course work fit to his recuperation—Bartlett had to ask himself whether his last race was run. He found the prospect of death disappointing, although the irony of such an end brought a morbid smile to his lips. Perhaps he should've taken religion more seriously.

No gallant ends this day, no answered prayers.

A rifle stock missed his nose by an inch.

Suddenly furious, Bartlett threw his empty pistol toward the nearest Reb. No one paid him attention.

He drew himself up as best he could. To be shot was one thing, stomped to death another.

When the last Reb attack exploded over them, Hartranft had gotten off with as many men as would brave the slope below. Marshall, damn the thick sod, had refused to go and was still somewhere in the mayhem. If still alive. For his part, Bartlett had not been about to leave: He would not order sound men to risk their lives by bearing him away, and he would have found it ignoble, in any case, to abandon the last of his Massachusetts men.

It wasn't done.

But Marshall should have gone. Really, the man would be worthless in a Reb prison. Better at the head of his broken brigade. And the man had a wife and child, twin plagues that had not yet afflicted Bartlett. And, he judged, likely never would.

He could have wept from outrage and frustration, but that wasn't done, either.

The Rebs beat back the last good men through raw numbers and viciousness, dragging away prisoners. They were almost atop Bartlett.

And Bartlett saw a thing that appalled him as no other had done. His own men had turned on the Colored Troops mingled with them, shooting, stabbing, and beating them to death.

Other men fought on, though.

Such a waste.

The day's cause was lost irretrievably, and it had been lost for hours. What remained was pointless savagery. Had Bartlett had two good legs, he would have stood and ordered an end to the slaughter.

Instead, a Reb bellowed, "Why don't you damned fools surrender?"

And a Northern voice responded, "Why won't *you* damned fools let us?"

By mutual, inexplicable understanding, the fighting all but

ceased. A few Rebs could not master themselves immediately, nor could a few last Yankees. But it only took moments for the butchery in the main pit to end. Bartlett's men and the others mixed in with them threw down their arms.

"Oh, hell," Bartlett muttered.

The fighting on the right, in the smaller pit, dragged on for a few minutes. More Colored Troops over there, Bartlett knew. It was impossible to see what was happening, but the curses and begging hinted at great cruelties.

"Lookee what we got here," a Reb declared. "Got us a blue-belly general."

A mocking voice said, "Don't look like much to me, the hook-faced sumbitch."

"You git up," a Confederate sergeant ordered him.

Bartlett glared at him.

"I told you to git *up*. Boys, git that sumbitch up."

A pair of Johnnies grabbed him and lifted. Roughly.

Then they eased. Still holding him up.

"Got him but one leg. Yankees are down to using peg-leg generals."

"Ewell got but one leg."

"Ought to shoot the sumbitch. Leading nigger troops. He's got it coming more than those damned coons."

Bartlett declined to tell them that he did not command Colored Troops. His impulse was quite the opposite.

After a brief staring match, Bartlett said, "Well, gentlemen, shoot me, or let me sit down."

Three p.m.
Dunn house

It's over," Humphreys said. "Even Burnside admits it."

The chief of staff wore a look of general disgust on the best of days, but on that afternoon Andrew Atkinson Humphreys' features were etched in acid.

Meade opened his mouth to speak, then thought better of it. The worst of his rage had passed, leaving a sorrow best not revealed to any man. It had been Burnside's failure. But it had been his failure, too. Since the army botched its June arrival at Petersburg, so little had gone right.

In fact, nothing had gone right. Heat, squalor, and failed assaults, with his best subordinates sick and morale far lower than Grant could be brought to admit. The fine army that had crossed the Rapidan the first week in May no longer existed, replaced by a dull, immovable machine.

"Come outside, Humph," Meade said.

They walked through walls of heat. Without a conscious decision, Meade led his old comrade toward the spot that Grant had chosen earlier. It had not been the right day to press Grant, but Meade had hoped the decision had been made to send him to the Valley to deal with Early. He longed to return to an independent command, even a lesser one, to be his own man again. But Grant had said nothing.

Across the fields, stubborn cannoneers kept at their work. But the attack was over. Finished. For all but the wounded left between the lines.

And the prisoners. It appeared that a number—an appalling number—of prisoners had been taken.

In the miserly shade, Meade stopped and said, low-voiced, "I should have known better. Trusting Burnside with a main attack. And a damnably complex one."

"Burnside couldn't find a whore's hole with a lamp," Humphreys said. His family, like Meade's, was sufficiently rooted in Old Philadelphia to license speech forbidden to common society. Nor had frontier service restrained his vocabulary.

Meade fingered sweat from his temples. "I blinded myself. I made too much of the Colored Troops business. And lost sight of a fiasco in the making."

"We've all let him go too long," Humphreys said. "Everybody *likes* Ambrose, it's not just the politics. Even I like the worthless sonofabitch. I just don't want him commanding so much as a company. So there's your problem."

Meade recognized a sigh where strangers would have heard a snort.

"But now he's got to go, George," Humphreys continued. "That corps needs a firm hand, it's gone all to seed."

"There'll be a board of inquiry. Grant's for it."

"Board or not, I think you should put him on leave. And not call him back. Soften the politics of it."

Meade looked at the chief of staff, who had surprised him. Humphreys was a soldier down to the marrow.

"Unlike you, Humph. To consider politics."

"Fuck the whole business, as far as I'm concerned. But if Lincoln doesn't win . . ."

"As he isn't like to do."

Humphreys waved a paw at the day's debacle. "Then all of this isn't waste in a cause, to a purpose. It's just a waste." This time it was a snort and not a sigh. "Can't bear the damned thought, I must be going soft."

A parade of beaten, slump-shouldered soldiers passed rearward.

"Sometimes," Humphreys went on, "I can't understand why they don't turn their rifles on us."

Three p.m.
Petersburg

Bartlett stumped along, using two rifles as crutches. The path to the rear had been littered with Negro corpses, and beginning with the first houses—Southern and ramshackle—women emerged to deride the captives, often in language he would not have expected from women of the streets. The vigorous among the fairer sex hurled the contents of slops buckets and chamber pots toward them. They found Bartlett and his missing leg a particular source of amusement.

He believed he'd spotted Marshall some distance ahead, herded by men so thin they might have been specters. Cackling the guards all were, showing the teeth of ancients above the beards of the Patriarchs. They had robbed Bartlett of all that he had been unable to thrust in his boot. They robbed everyone.

"Oughta lock 'em in with their niggers and let them eat each other, they want to eat," a sag-bosomed, bonneted matron called.

Another simply asked him, "See what you get?"

Bartlett would have liked to respond, "I do, indeed," but thought it wiser to hobble along in silence.

Three p.m.
Gee house

The mood among Lee's staff and attendants was jubilant.

"*General Mahone did it,*" Lee repeated. As if the prospect of victory strained credulity. "Mahone, the Virginians . . ."

"Alabamians and Georgians, too," Colonel Marshall reminded him.

"And Johnson's Carolina boys," Venable added.

"Yes, yes," Lee said. "Of course. Them, as well."

But they all understood. With Beauregard's departure, every officer remaining was Virginia born.

Walter Taylor came back in, mustache weighted with sweat.

"Well?" Lee asked. His smile, so rare these days, had faded again.

The colonel stepped closer to Lee and the two other intimates. "I believe the worst of the abuses . . . has passed."

"All the abuses must *stop*." Lee's tone was categorical.

"Yes, sir. But the men didn't take things well, the Negro troops . . ."

Lee's eyes grew arctic. "I would not blame the dog that was trained to bite me, Colonel Taylor. I would blame the animal's master."

"Yes, sir. We're registering their officers, all the ones who led darkies."

Lee shook his head. Slowly, arthritically, majestically. "That is not what I *meant*. My point, gentlemen, is that the dog only does what it is bidden to do. Beyond satisfying its appetites. The problem here is far greater."

"Yes, sir."

Shots sounded from the rear. No man present would have been surprised had those bullets slain black prisoners. The orders had been issued to shun atrocity, and military honor had been answered. But each of them knew that orders had their limits.

Of a sudden, Lee's face took on an expression of sorrow touched with dread that none of them had seen him wear since he'd learned of Stuart's fate.

"Slavery has been a terrible curse," Lee said.

Startled that such a thing had been uttered openly, Marshall responded hastily. "But . . . the African left behind only pagan barbarism, his exposure to Christianity alone would—"

Lee cut him off.

"I did not speak of a curse upon the Negro."

FIVE

The vessel's cabin was as ornate as its occupant was plain. As he went in, Grant thought: Neither of us has been accused of beauty.

"Mr. President," he said. He touched his fingers to his right eyebrow, but didn't make a show of the salute.

Lincoln nodded. "General." He shifted as if to rise but did not. "Sit down, sit down."

Grant sat.

"Coffee?" Lincoln asked. "Afraid I've et up the breakfast."

"Too much already, thanks."

The steamer rocked mildly.

"Well," the president said, "I suppose the affairs of the day won't be put off, then?"

"No, sir." The man before him, all arms, legs, and exhaustion, looked a year older every time they met.

"I understand . . . that yesterday's matter encountered difficulties."

"We lost," Grant said. "Badly."

Lincoln nodded, briefly closing his eyes.

"Fine opportunity," Grant went on. "Threw it away. Miserable affair."

"The casualties?"

"High."

"High?"

"Between three and four thousand, I make it. Final numbers aren't tallied."

Lincoln scratched the side of his head and set loose a flurry of dandruff. "I regret that we haven't had . . . haven't experienced more success. I'll be frank, General Grant. I covet the sort of success the newspapers crave. I'm a politician, you know."

Grant took the plunge. "Burnside has to go, Mr. President. Yesterday was the last straw. Men won't fight under him, discipline's gone to the devil."

"Burnside . . ."

"If you agree, there'll be a court of inquiry. All done properly. But he has to go."

Lincoln leaned back against candy-striped cushions and rested a hand on the gleaming frame of the couch. "Inconvenient. But you're the judge of his soldiering."

"He has to go, Mr. President."

Again, Lincoln nodded. "Hold your inquiry. With my imprimatur. But keep me informed." He slapped his hands on his thighs. "Now. What do you think of Sherman? His progress?"

"He'll take Atlanta."

"When?"

Grant understood. "Before the election. Well before."

"You're confident? Might it not prove as . . . as much of a challenge as Petersburg?"

"No, sir. President Davis gave us a gift. Relieving Joe Johnston. Hood just brawls. Scrap at Peachtree Creek? Cost him more than he can afford to pay. Hood can snap, but he can't bite deep. Sherman's cut the last rail line and the telegraph. He'll fix Hood."

Lincoln took a fingernail to the side of his nose, making war on an itch. "I see the design. I do see it, you understand." He crossed his legs and folded his hands over a knee braced high. "But I find myself in the trying position of the farmer who craved a chicken dinner and had everybody crying for eggs with the bird already stewing. Grant, I've got to put some eggs on the table soon."

He uncrossed his legs, appeared about to push himself to his feet, then stopped again. "My own party wants me to step away from abolition. In the interests of peace." He nodded faintly to himself. "I won't."

"No, sir. Wouldn't help now, anyway."

Lincoln's lips twisted anew. "Others think I should step aside for you, General. They believe you'd have a better chance at the polls."

"I don't see it," Grant said.

"No. I suppose not." The president sighed. "We both have our jobs to do. To the end. Which brings us to the Shenandoah business. Grant, I cannot have another Chambersburg, can't have any more burnings in the north, no more incursions. I need you to stop the raids, put a stop to all of it. Settle things with Early."

"Yes, Mr. President."

"And?"

"Meade wants the command. But I like him where he is. Suffers like Job, with me looking over his shoulder. But he does good work. Good span, Meade and Humphreys." Grant longed for a cigar, but would not reach for one without Lincoln's encouragement. "I was George Meade, I'd light out for the Territories. Just to get shut of me."

"I'd hesitate about Meade myself," Lincoln said. "It might look like a demotion, and ill-timed. There's the Philadelphia faction to consider." Lincoln brushed his hand down over his beard. "And if you mean to relieve Burnside, sending Meade to a lesser command as well might signal defeatism. To the gentlemen of the press. Make them think that things aren't going well."

"They're not. But they'll go better. Not Meade, then."

He knew that Lincoln had been convinced by the Washington generals and politicians that Meade wasn't aggressive enough for the work. It was a lie. But that was Washington. And why Grant kept his headquarters in the field.

"And not McClellan, of course."

"No, Mr. President. Not McClellan."

"There would be an advantage . . ."

"He didn't follow your orders then and wouldn't follow mine now. Mr. President, the man I'd like to put forward is General Sheridan."

Lincoln's brows tightened. "Not too young?"

"Problem isn't the young generals," Grant said. "Problem is the old ones, set in their ways. Sheridan could do it, run Early to ground. But, whoever you choose, we have to combine the departments, make a single command responsible for the Valley. Too many behind-the-desk generals have a finger in the pie now. One command, and full authority for the man in the field."

The president nodded, but said, "Let me think on Sheridan. I won't keep you waiting. Just need to count the wolves that are bound to howl."

"Yes, sir."

"And you, General? What will *you* do next?"

"Hold fast to Lee. Not let him slip off. Cut his railroads. Force him to come out and fight in the open. Or starve." Grant really would have liked a good cigar. "Let Sherman finish with Atlanta and see what makes sense for his army after that. End the threat from the Valley. And count on the Navy to tighten the blockade, close their last ports."

Lincoln's face looked woeful even when he smiled. And he was not smiling.

"How long?" the president asked abruptly, voice uncharacteristically petulant. "How long before this ends, Grant?"

The upcoming election fouled the air.

"Can't say," Grant admitted. "But we'll end it."

Then Lincoln, ever admirable to Grant, allowed him a glimpse of broken teeth.

"Well, then," the president said. "I surmise it's time to let the others come in and convince us to do the things we've just decided on doing. Live long enough, I might get the hang of government."

Eleven a.m., July 31
Somerville, New Jersey

The mourners annoyed Barlow. Funerals had always seemed travesties to him, opportunities for vulgar display and for paeans better delivered while the deceased remained with the living. And Belle had been intolerant of platitudes.

Belle.

The day was growing hot, though it hardly compared to Virginia's miasmas. Men and women, dutifully somber, sweated through black dresses and coats better suited to winter. Black-gloved hands held up black satin parasols, funereal fripperies. Barlow even found his own black armband an affectation.

"Ashes to ashes . . ."

He wanted them all to *leave.* So that he might stand by the grave side without the need to concentrate on keeping the smirk off his lips, that bitter, bemused smile so sharpened by war. And his guts churned terribly. He had starved himself since noon of the day before, trying to empty his belly so that his sickness would not embarrass him—and Arabella's memory—by soiling his uniform trousers before a throng.

Dress trousers not worn for months, drilled through by a moth behind the knee. His war had not been one of splendid uniforms, but the military representatives from the New Jersey governor's office stood there garbed to perfection, the stuff of portraiture, not the field of battle.

He despised them all. And his feet itched.

Belle! Belle, Belle, Belle! The rite concluded, men and women took his hand and lavished condolences on him. His brothers, who knew him better, said nothing at all, just grasped his paw. His mother hung back.

Belle's family mourned truly, he understood that much. But he wanted them to go, too.

Really, it all was spectacle enough. Half the town had turned out for the burial, and he knew they had come to gawk at him more than they felt bereaved of Arabella. Strange children were encouraged to shake his hand.

He had not seen her face a final time. The iron coffin had been sealed, out of fear of contagion. The cruelty of that, of thinking of such a vivid woman so used, made him want to scream at a delinquent God and the empty heavens.

A challenging woman, Belle had been, but smooth of mind with him. They had *belonged* together.

He caught himself: The smirk, that bitter smile, had crept onto his face.

The night before, when he had arrived at the inn, sick and impossibly filthy, his mother had embraced him with her usual mix of love and theatricality. She ordered up a bath "at once," in her most imperious voice.

Before leaving him to his soak, she had admonished him: "Francis, you *must* dispense with that smile of yours, it's grotesquely Unitarian. You can't be seen smirking through your own wife's funeral." An actress born with the world her stage, she rolled her eyes and declared, "*I* know it's just your way, of course. But those who don't know you well won't understand. Do promise me you won't smile like that tomorrow."

His mother. A splendid woman still, with more than a trace remaining of her beauty, even if she was more substantial in form than she had been in those airy Brook Farm days.

Barlow said: "You know, Mother . . . this is rather a turnabout. When I told you I meant to marry, you claimed I never smiled."

His mother took a moment to recollect. Then she donned a superior smirk of her own.

"Really, Francis. I *never* said you don't smile. I said you never *laugh*."

She was correct. He had been wrong. Again.

Leaving him to his bath, she added, "I simply cannot bear that look of yours. It reminds me of your father."

Their sorrow expressed, the mourners drifted off. The merely curious sauntered away as well. His mother shooed his brothers along and measured off a respectful distance herself, leaving him by the grave side, leaving him briefly to his grief, with the only other two-legged creatures present a laborer of medieval aspect and the young woman who, surprisingly, had accompanied his mother this morning, a handsome creature Barlow couldn't quite place. Another of his mother's mysteries: Why on earth bring along a stranger—or near stranger—to this supremely intimate affair?

A frustrated suitor had labeled his mother "the piece that passeth all understanding." And Barlow had fought a boy who repeated the quip, even though neither of them had grasped its import.

"Belle," he whispered.

He could have fallen to his knees and wept. He might have wept beyond all reason, insanely. He could have let go of everything, his pride, his discipline, his dignity, his surly bowels. Instead, he stood slump-shouldered at the grave side.

"Belle," he repeated.

Then he said, "Arabella. Bella. Belle."

He found it intolerable, if predictable, that his mother stood there watching him, "respectful distance" or not. Did she imagine he'd blow out his brains from grief? When it was his duty to live and clutch her memory? Not for the first time, he felt that his mother consumed more earth and air than was her due.

But she loved him. He knew that. And she'd made her peculiar sacrifices to keep a genteel face on what, too often, had been true poverty. Their rooms had always had books, but not always bread.

On the verge of pity, he caught himself. It was beastly of her, the way she managed to make herself the center of his attention even now. Instead of leaving him to thoughts of Arabella, she intruded. At least the young woman she'd dragged along had the sense of decency to turn in another direction.

Belle.

Phrases he'd mocked with youthful wisdom assailed him, taking revenge: How *could* he live without her? She had no equal, and she never would.

Damn the war. Did it need to kill her, too? Hadn't he delivered slaughter enough to that altar? Was Death such a glutton?

Furious at the wide world—at the wartime wealth of the town and at himself—he wiped a renegade tear from the edge of an eye. He wanted to stay right there, to take root in the soil, in that raw earth under which Belle lay imprisoned, bound in iron.

How could it be that he'd never see her again? Never hear her slightly too-loud laugh? Or merely sense her warmth beside him at dusk?

She had nursed him back to life and he'd led her to death.

Mourning. Bereavement. Despair. The words did not begin to express the catastrophe of her loss.

Abruptly, Barlow turned from the grave. A cramp had warned him to hasten back to the inn. The dizzies were sneaking up, too. Rude needs had taken command, the ruffian flesh with its treacheries.

He straightened himself, replaced his hat, and prepared to run the gauntlet of his mother and her companion. He needed to consult proper doctors in New York during his leave, even if doing so scraped against mourning's etiquette. Belle would forgive him that. Meanwhile, he just needed to escape.

"Mother," he said.

"Oh, Francis, dear."

The honey-haired young woman remained a few steps off, the only sign of her unease a slight twirl of her parasol. She was very simply and very expensively dressed in well-cut mourning.

His mother took his arm and led him toward her.

The girl's expression was duly somber, but her eyes were pert. And arrestingly blue.

"Francis, you *must* remember Ellen Shaw? Nellie? Poor Robert's sister?"

His features tightened. "You're the little girl," he said. "You always sat on the stairs."

The young woman raised an eyebrow. "I was a *very* serious woman of twelve, I'll have you know." Then she remembered herself. "General Barlow . . . I'm sorry. Truly. The loss must be devastating."

Devastating? As good a word as any, he supposed.

His guts warned him again of a betrayal.

"And I'm sorry for your loss, Miss Shaw," he said, speaking too rapidly. "Bob was a splendid young man."

"You didn't seem to think so when you tutored him." But she smiled.

She was right, of course. He'd thought Bob Shaw a dullard—dreadful at maths, impossible at languages—and a mama's boy. Poor Bob. He'd made it through Harvard, barely, only to die with his darkies at Battery Wagner. When Bob had been killed the summer before, Barlow had been struggling back from his Gettysburg wound.

"I regret missing his memorial service."

His mother intruded. "Nellie's been simply splendid, Francis. I don't know what I would have done without her. She's been so gracious, coming along to sustain me."

"I was back in New York when I heard," Ellen Shaw explained.

"And she sought me out," his mother added. "So good of her."

Another cramp struck Barlow's gut, compelling urgency.

"I *must* excuse myself, I'm sorry. Mother. Miss Shaw."

He strutted off at a battlefield pace, hoping that if he could not reach the inn, he might at least last until out of their sight.

The girl called, *"Au revoir."*

Saturday, August 6
Richmond front

Oates enjoyed the hanging, which he judged salutary. Hadn't meant to attend, but a pow-wow for brigade and regimental commanders back at division headquarters had made the stroll over convenient. Wasn't a great fuss, just one regiment drawn up to witness the doings, but the condemned deserved his fate, a two-time deserter who had insulted a country woman's person, a scoundrel not even worthy of the customary bullets, gone to his end cussing all the world in language hot with vice. When the sergeant who had the run of things kicked the stool away—before the chaplain had quite finished up or the presiding officer gave the order—the fellow danced like a Baptist with the hallelujah shakes.

Took over a minute for him to still.

Handsome day for the business, that was sure. First break in the heat since May, a day of pleasant temper, when a man wasn't likely to drop down dead just walking. With fat clouds playing at bumps above and the fields ripe all around, it was one of those days that reminded a man of life's fineness, of the joy of drawing breath, and an extra punishment for the deserter who'd danced his final jig, sent out of this world just when a man wished to stay in it.

Oates regretted not marching his regiment up to witness the hanging. The unspoken admonition would have served. Not that he'd had a deserter since taking command. Not yet. But it was not a matter of unconcern. Letters from home, from Alabama, were half the problem. Human nature supplied the other prod.

Oates turned and walked back toward his camp, buoyant despite the grinding in his hip. Down on the unseen river, gunboats fussed. Not much to it, just nagging. The air wrapped around a man like fine-spun cotton.

Those letters. Men waited for them as impatient Christians waited on salvation, wanting it right now, thank you, and damn the rest. Oh, proper letters were a joy, letters scrawled when things at home were sound. A man could march for weeks on one sweat-stained page. But the tone of many a letter had changed of late, leaving the recipient crestfallen, sorrowful, sulking. No money back home, or what money there was didn't reach, its value fallen. Nothing to eat, or not much. Children sickly. *Come home now John you done enuf come home theres no one to plow I just caint stand it no more I feel so awful not knowing and lefft alone,* all misspelled and desperate, that reaching out so raw it could make a man howl, and then came the letters that spoke of things better unspoken, of men's wives gone astray or prone to do so, with rumors of troublesome comings and goings, sometimes in broad daylight, right there on a man's holdings, and report of the misdeeds of men who had avoided the war through some chicanery, men who, in their soft-hand way, did worse than that deserter with his neck stretched.

Men wanted to bust out for home, men young or old, married or interrupted in their courting, men desiring what all men wanted and near crazy for the lack of it. Another man this week had been consigned to a ward for the shamefully diseased, leaving Oates unable to figure out where the wretch had caught it, for no man short of an officer with a purpose had been allowed to take himself off to Richmond. But men found ways, of course. And so did women. It was the wonder of the human animal, that propensity for coupling. Oates himself felt a longing for woman-flesh that burned right through him, maddening, so that he had to take himself off to the privacy of the woods, thinking greedily, nearly insanely, on damp, resilient flesh, of hips well met, and of the laughing duskies he couldn't help favoring, their demands not matrimonial but immediate. Like his.

Lust, desire. Back in the 15th Alabama—early on, that was—they'd caught two fellows behaving unspeakably with one another. After beating them half to death, their comrades had made certain that the two of them marched in the front rank in every attack until lead used them up. Oates had let the sergeants see to the fuss, but he found the behavior a source of prime bewilderment. Always had.

How could a man not want a woman? He throbbed with longing even as he walked.

Hadn't had a letter himself for a time. Not that he had a woman obliged to write him. The sort he preferred didn't have their ABCs.

White women thought too much, that was their problem. Loving someone up was about the impulse, the right-now blaze of flesh, the grasping and gasping and the burst that took you next to dying. Worries were the enemies of pleasure, of every pleasure but drink, which wasn't his vice. He longed to rampage over a merry woman.

In that rich day, he could not hear one rifle shot. But the Yankees were out there, he knew, eyeing Richmond the way a lecher ogled a chaste girl. They'd come on soon.

No, he had not had a letter. His mother wrote less often now, for his father had made up his mind that Oates had played Cain to Abel with his brother. He had told them honestly, sorrowfully, in his own letters how he had been obliged to leave John behind, dying bait for the Yankees, while he saved the remnants of his regiment that bad day at Gettysburg, and his father, a man who never changed his mind once that mind was made up, had decided that William C. Oates was a wayward son who had wronged his brother and family beyond atonement.

When he got his Chattanooga wound, Oates had not gone home to recover but had taken up a planter's invitation.

His mother, who had held him, young, with the same fierce love with which she clutched her Bible, a Christian woman: She was caught between father and son, Oates knew, with loyalty turned one way and love another. His father was a hard and upright man, God-honoring and merciless, with the sense of justice of an Israelite, callused inside and out.

Well, Oates supposed, the war was his home now. As he passed between quivering fields, rain touched his shoulders.

Eleven thirty a.m., August 8
New York City

It's a lot of money, Frank," Ed Barlow remarked to his brother. The amber light in the study left deep shadows.

Frank Barlow nodded. With the profits Ed was making from their investments in wartime cargoes, he could have taken Belle to Europe in style.

Belle.

"Don't you want to inspect the books?" his elder brother asked.

"If I can't trust my brother . . ."

Ed donned a skeptic's smile. "Plenty of brothers are cheats. You were a lawyer long enough to know."

"Ed, I *choose* to trust you. Regard it as a quirk."

The elder brother's smile became a grin. "No quirks in *this* family, no sirree. Frank, you should see the bills that Mother's run up at the dressmaker's. Since the money began coming in. She'll bankrupt us all."

Feeling the ghost of a tooth yanked the day before, Barlow said, "Take the money from my share. She's dreamed of this day. Let her enjoy it."

"At some point, she'll need restraint, though. She thinks she's the Empress Eugenie."

"Not yet," Barlow told him. It was a curious thing: Although Ed was the elder by three years and a few months, the war had reversed their roles, leaving him, the warrior, to play the paterfamilias.

"So . . . how did today's visit with the doctor go?" Ed asked.

"Same as the others. Every one of them tells me that my feet need regular sea baths, that my drainage problems stem from 'insalubrious atmospheres' to which I've been exposed, and that, in short, they're stumped." Barlow reviewed the disappointments of the past few days. "I'll credit one fellow, though. He admitted his ignorance and suggested I travel to Europe. To seek out 'specialists.' To Europe, for God's sake."

Beyond rattling windows, the city strained and groaned, obese with wealth. The war was good to those who didn't fight.

"Why don't you?" Ed asked.

"What?"

"Go to Europe."

"Ed . . . I'm a general. Haven't you heard? With a division to command."

"You're not even in command of your bowels. You could die of that sort of thing, you know. And you look a wreck."

"Thank you, Doctor Barlow."

"Really, Frank. You've done your part. How many wounds is it now? Resign your commission. Take care of yourself. Enjoy your new prosperity." He paused. "Belle doesn't need company in the grave."

" 'Ask for me tomorrow, and you shall find me a grave man.' Oh, come. I'm not as far gone as all that."

"How many doctors have you seen? Since the funeral? Resign, Frank. You're already a hero. And we don't need any more dead ones. Just last night you were railing against your fellow generals, telling me none of them has the sense of Ned. That you're disgusted with all of them and with the whole damned war."

"I *am* disgusted. But that doesn't cancel my duty." He did not add that with Belle gone, the war was all he had.

"Frank, you're impossible."

Neither of his brothers had shown much interest in uniforms, despite Barlow's offer to find them good positions. On the other hand, they had served the family well.

"As a matter of fact," Barlow said, "I've decided to cut my leave short. New York's no more 'salubrious' than my camp. And you've got things in hand here, with the family. For which I'm grateful." Earnest of mien but lighter of voice, he added, "Don't be too hard on Mother. Indulge her a bit."

Bemused, Ed shook his head. "Frank, she's got you bamboozled. As ever has been the case." An eyebrow lifted, a smile swelled. "Did she give you a firm date? Or shouldn't I ask?"

"A date for what?"

"When she expects you to marry Ellen Shaw."

Taken aback, Barlow managed to say, "That's absurd. And tasteless. Good Lord . . . Arabella's barely in the ground."

"How convenient for Mother."

Ten a.m. August 9
City Point, Virginia

Just look at that," John Maxwell said. "Just look."

His skittish companion, R. K. Dillard, did as bidden and peered between the trees concealing the pair.

"Ever see anything like that? Busiest wharf in the world, I'd bet ten dollars."

"Paper money or gold?" Dillard tried to joke.

Out on the broad, brown river, hundreds of schooners, steamers, riverboats, tugs, barges, lighters, and gunboats waited at anchor or tacked into line to take their turn at the docks, unloading supplies of an abundance unthinkable to the half-starved army Maxwell and Dillard served, if without uniforms. Of particular interest to Maxwell, a string of ammunition barges fought against the current to hold their places, riding low in the water and crowding each other.

But that wasn't half the spectacle. On the wharf itself, hundreds of darkies labored to empty hulls, supervised by arm-waving foremen and guarded by unenthused sentries. Pyramids of barrels and walls of crates stood between the berths and a bluff, awaiting furtherance. Up on the high ground, a locomotive of the military railroad shot steam between warehouses hammered together in haste. Beyond, acres of caissons, limbers, artillery pieces, wagons, shanties, tents, corrals, and still more warehouses stretched to the edge of a ramshackle hamlet overwhelmed by the ruckus. The Yankees had built a military city in just weeks, a sobering, even daunting, capability.

And just past the brash display of matériel, Grant's headquarters sat on the spit of land where the Appomattox flowed into the James.

The view and his knowledge filled Maxwell with resolve.

The two men crouched on either side of the wooden box containing Maxwell's invention, his horological torpedo, a device that could be set to explode when desired.

"You'll never get through," Dillard declared. "There's guards everywhere down there."

"Oh, I'll get through. It's a rare Yank picket can't be talked around. Lazy as they are stupid. You saw how easy we passed the lines. Just play the dunce and stand there like a clod. Nine times out of ten, they pass you through."

"This is different."

"Damned right. Fools down there are even less alert. They don't expect a thing."

"I don't like it," Dillard said.

"That's fine, R.K., that's fine. You stay here and wait for the fireworks." Enjoying his project mightily himself, Maxwell hoped his companion wouldn't bolt. Then he decided it didn't really matter. It was all on him now. And he meant to do some damage.

It had cheered him to see Grant himself debark from a steamer an hour before. Wouldn't it be fine if his blast killed Grant? Wouldn't that be something? He'd be a hero throughout the entire South. And even if Grant survived, the destruction might shock him so badly that he'd withdraw from Richmond and Petersburg.

"You wait here," he repeated. He took up the small crate.

No one challenged him. He made it to the edge of the wharf, then did what he could to sink into the bustle, just another laboring man with a purpose none too urgent. He watched as an emptied barge cast off and a full one came in and tied up. He waited for that one to be unloaded, too. Watching for the right chance.

And no one said so much as "Howdy-do!" The white men were preoccupied and the darkies kept to their work, singing like fools. Officers checked manifests, quarreling with old salts. Masters of obscenity, sergeants cursed. Up on the bluff, couplings chimed and railcars banged. Shouted orders carried over the water. On the river, whistles and horns demanded that others make way for their passage. The air smelled of hot tar, boiler smoke, and bread.

Maxwell saw his opportunity. The captain of a newly docked ordnance barge waved off a deckhand and leapt ashore as soon as the gangplank dropped. Maxwell held back until the man walked out of sight. Then he gave it five minutes more.

One sentry to pass. He stopped Maxwell, but without menace. "Where *you* going?"

Balancing the crate, Maxwell pointed. "Captain told me to take this box aboard." He shrugged. "Just doing like I'm told, same as every man."

The soldier grimaced and waved him through. A few paces along, Maxwell set down the box and arched his back as though it pained him. Even now, the spectacle on the river was mesmerizing, the riches piled up on land a marvel.

It was all about to end. With any luck, he'd be known as the man who turned the war around and made Grant run.

When he bent to pick up the box again, he pressed a hidden button to start the timer. He had thirty minutes. And had to hope the captain wouldn't return and lift the lid.

He approached the barge, its bow lettered *J. E. Kendrick*. A string of Negroes awaited the order to start unloading the cargo.

Maxwell started up the plank, but a deckhand stopped him.

"What do *you* want?"

Maxwell repeated his practiced shrug. "Ain't nothing *I* want. But your captain wants this box here. Told me to set it aboard."

The deckhand pondered the business.

"All the same beans to me," Maxwell told him. "But when he asks, you tell him I come down and did as told."

"Give me the box," the deckhand said. "And you go on your way."

Maxwell handed over the crate. He was enjoying his role and, for a moment, he just stood there. "No tip?" he asked.

"You want a goddamned tip, you can take your cracker backside somewheres else."

"No need to do man down," Maxwell told him. And he turned away, barely containing the smile that fought to spread across his face.

He took things gently until he'd put the wharf's hubbub behind him. Then, atop the bluff, he switched to a jaunty walk, touching his hat when officers passed and whistling "Camptown Races."

Cautious at the last, he rejoined Dillard.

"Just you watch now," Maxwell said. "You watch."

Eleven thirty a.m., August 9
Grant's headquarters, City Point

Grant had moved his chair out of the tent to enjoy the breeze. And that was about the only thing to enjoy. He'd been gone for just two days, off to Washington and Monocacy Junction to put things right for Sheridan, and the amount of work that had massed to attack him upon his return was a trial.

George Sharpe had reported that Confederate spies were lurking around City Point. Rawlins dismissed the idea and they'd argued. Requests, complaints, and petitions sat stacked up. The cavalry was going through horses at a stupendous pace. The sick rate had climbed in every marching army except Sherman's, where it already had been high. Sherman needed reinforcement, and a contingent had to be pried loose from Paducah. The Navy wanted to withdraw two ironclads from the James. The members of a New Hampshire delegation felt themselves slighted, as if the war should pause for their convenience, and a letter from the governor of New York all but demanded a favorite's promotion. Meade wanted to see him, "at your leisure." And the sanitary commissioner stood off to the side, tapping his foot and scowling, doubtless bearing another report that would crush him with details while adding nothing to his understanding.

And Julia had grown unsure again about the schools for the children.

He marveled to think of Lincoln, of his sturdy humor when faced with insulting demands, his forbearance when attacked by petty men, the curses of politics. Grant was glad he didn't bear those burdens.

The breeze died.

"All right," Grant said, "what's next?"

The blast was the loudest thing he'd ever heard.

A storm of hot air and debris swept over the bluff, tearing down tents and shaking those left standing, but the drama was down on the wharf.

The explosion was immense. Men, munitions, wagon wheels, boards, entire walls, the wreckage of boats and warehouses, all flew madly skyward, flung to all points of the compass. The power seemed greater—much greater—than the mine upheaval had been.

More explosions followed. Fires flared. Men shouted, screamed, fled. On the river, boats careened. The bright day turned ash gray. Blown powder reeked.

Another blast tore the morning. Followed, at last, by a stunned calm.

Babcock was bleeding, but it didn't look serious. An orderly lay dead, pierced. Others cradled wounds. Blown wild, papers floated. A saddle had dropped from the sky between Porter and Rawlins.

Grant's ears hurt.

The unscathed members of his staff dashed toward the wharf's remains, but Grant remained seated. He *knew* he should have insisted that work on the new ordnance pier be expedited. Accidents were bound to happen. Now one had.

Simmering within, he mastered his temper. Had to be taken in stride, nothing else to be done. Cost of war. Put an *X* through that page of the ledger.

Still, he couldn't but recall the pettiness that had plagued him in the Northwest, in the prewar Army, where he'd been condemned to a quartermaster's duties. Back then, a man was chastised for an inkblot in a log, a missing blanket required a formal inquiry, and a load of rations gone astray could end a man's career.

War did change things mightily.

Grant rose from his chair, dusted off his coat, turned to his chief of staff, and waited until Rawlins mastered his cough.

"Infernal mess," Grant said. "Negligence, nothing but." He drew out a cigar to replace one torn from his lips by the blast. "Get things cleaned up. I want the unloading going again by nightfall, river's too crowded already."

"Right, Sam."

"And I want reports from the quartermaster, chief of supply, engineers, and the provost marshal. Take a switch to whoever you think deserves it, but no hullabaloo."

Rawlins nodded.

And Grant walked into the telegraph tent, which had been shielded by the cabin the engineers were putting up for his use. He reckoned that Washington had best hear of the accident from him, before rumors started and the newspapers announced the end of the world.

His ears still hurt, but he figured they'd come around.

Seven thirty p.m., August 12
Petersburg, Union lines

Heard that mine turned out bad," Henry Hill said in his slow-running voice. He sat on a stump, sewing blue stripes on his sleeve.

Brown was glad to have him back from the hospital. They all were glad, all of the old veterans still with the company, men who remembered Hill from before the war, when so many had worked the same jobs on the canal, and from battles where he'd been stalwart. Henry Hill was a man who liked to set his own pace, though.

" 'Bad'?" Levi Eckert said. "Whole lot worse than bad. Worst bust-up I seen in the entire war. It was a . . . a degradation to see it."

"Wasn't too rough for us," Brown told his friend. He and Henry had not been close back on the canal, but war had made them brothers. "Not our best day, though."

"Shame never killed a man, far as I know," Levi said. "And I'd rather be shamed than dead."

It wasn't true, Brown understood. But Levi talked everything and everybody down, including himself. It was just his way.

"Lot of sourness afterward," Brown added.

"Lambs to the slaughter," Levi remarked.

Finished with one sleeve, Henry Hill, reluctant sergeant, said, "Seems quiet now."

"Quiet" meant that they weren't being shelled directly. War changed a man's view of things.

"Just you wait," Levi told him. "We'll be in it again. Before you know it. Grant won't rest till he's killed this army twice over. The man ain't got no quit in him."

First Sergeant Losch had been quiet, left uneasy by a letter from home. Brown didn't know the contents, but recognized the effect.

Now Losch said: "Second Corps packs up. They go to Washington. I hear it when I am making right the rations—*so eine Schweinerei.* Better, I think, if we are going instead."

"We'll be here till the cows come home," Levi told him. "Or till Bobby Lee comes for breakfast. Luck of the Ninth Corps." He shifted his backside on his crate. "My, how I love Virginia, though. Hot as Hell, but not one-half as pretty. Even the white folks don't quite seem to belong to the human race. Can't see fighting to take a place I'd give away soon as I could."

Stripped of trees and trampled by an army, the earth on all sides lacked appeal to the eye, that much was true. Still, a man had to be grateful for what he got, Brown believed, and the men—the sensible ones—were grateful enough for this day spent in the small paradise of the rear. All of them hoping that one day might turn into two, then three.

"Hot," Henry Hill agreed, brushing off a fly. He worked painstakingly with the needle and thread, as if a faulty stitch might spoil his life. Back in the Wilderness, Hill had got into a stubborn fit, just plain stopping when everyone else was running, standing there between two skinny trees, facing off with a flag-flying Rebel regiment. Calling himself a fool all the while, Brown had turned around and stood beside Hill, popping off shots as fast as the two of them could and making those befuddled ranks of Johnnies come to a stop and level out for a volley, as if faced with a regiment in blue and not just two crazy men. Unscathed through a miracle worthy of the Bible, he and Hill had then gone high-tail themselves, scooting back to the line where the regiment rallied, eluding the angry, git-after-'em Rebs to the cheers of their own brethren and laughing like men insane as they tumbled over the breastworks to something like safety.

Brown was glad that Hill was back, a brother of kind replacing the brother of kin buried at Vicksburg. It did seem wicked and selfish, though, to wish more of the war on any man.

"Burnside goes," Losch informed Hill. "They say that Parke comes in."

"Believe it when I see it," Levi said. "Army don't ever get rid of bad generals. It's a elementary principle."

Brown, too, had heard the rumors, but said nothing. What would come, would come.

Levi slapped a mosquito on his arm. Squashed it and smeared it. Then he drew out a can of sardines to follow up his supper.

"Diese verdammte Hitze," Losch said. "The heat, it never ends."

Shaking out his jacket and taking the measure of stripes he had not wanted, Hill said, "Hospital wasn't bad."

"Pretty girls everywhere," Levi said. It was a joke that wouldn't wear out. The women who came out as nurses wouldn't worry wives and sweethearts.

"But I kept on thinking . . . ," Hill went on.

"Wonders never cease," Levi said, tucking into the sardines.

"About Doudle. How they grabbed John Doudle."

"Not just him, either," Losch put in.

"He was always so afraid. Of being captured." Henry Hill had already spoken far more than was his habit. He clearly had much on his mind. "I wonder if he's all right."

Brown had thought on Corporal Doudle, too. Johnny was an odd duck, good-tempered and smart enough to help other men refine their letters home, but more afraid of becoming a prisoner than of death or wounds. The Rebs had grabbed him that bad day at Spotsylvania.

"Well, at least nobody's like to be shooting at him," Levi observed. "Which is something I can't say for present company."

Henry Hill stood and tried on his jacket, as if it might fit differently.

"You a sergeant, me a sergeant," Levi said. "And Brownie a brevet lieutenant. Jesus, when I think what this army's come to . . ." He slurped the last oil from the sardine tin and went to picking his teeth with an unclean nail.

Brown, for his part, tried his best to stay washed, if with spotty success. Frances valued cleanliness, and living up to her notions of how folks should be somehow made her seem closer.

Abruptly, Losch told Levi, "Come on. You are done with your fishes. We see now how good you are a sergeant. We go to work."

Brown understood that Losch meant to give him some time alone with Henry. Losch was a fine-feeling sort for a bucket-head Dutchman.

Left to the little privacy soldiering offered, Brown said, "It's really good to see you, Henry. That foot all right, though? Looked like you were limping. You really healed up?"

"Yes, sir."

Brown made a face. "You don't have to call me 'sir.' Cripes, Henry."

Hill looked at him steadily and calmly. "You're an officer now. I need to call you 'sir.'"

"In private, though . . ."

"You're an officer now," Hill repeated. Then he added, "I hate this war."

Ten p.m., August 13
Headquarters, Army of the Potomac

Well, Hancock's off and on his way," Humphreys said. The chief of staff looked more disgruntled than usual. In a lower, private voice he added, "Don't much like it, though."

"You don't? Or he doesn't?" Meade asked.

"Both, I suspect. I can speak for myself, anyway. And there's not a man in the Second Corps who's going to like it when he figures out he's not headed to Washington, after all." Humphreys drank from a tin cup and frowned. "Coffee's worse than usual, and that's a goddamned achievement."

Meade had his own doubts about the move under way, but he said, "Humph, you don't like any plan concocted by Grant's staff."

Humphreys grunted and sipped more wretched coffee. "'Concocted' is about right. Idiots, far as I'm concerned. And you don't trust them any more than I do, George, so don't pretend." He clapped the cup on a table and folded his arms. "Things go right, they take the credit. Turn out badly, we get blamed." He shook his head. "I'm just not convinced they know what they're doing with this. They're harking back to old successes out west. But the James isn't the Mississippi, not by a stretch."

"Hancock will make it work."

"George, he's ailing. And we both know it. That leg of his isn't healing, it's getting worse. Old Win can hardly get his rump up on a horse." He turned sharply. "You have business with us, Lyman? If not, you step away and stop listening in."

"Off with you, Teddy," Meade added. Then he told Humphreys, "I know. And I hate it. Win's the best of them."

"By a good measure."

"He's grooming Barlow to take over the corps." Meade knew that Humphreys wanted the corps himself, wanted to escape the staff and lead soldiers again. But Humph was the finest chief of staff on the continent, indispensable. And Barlow was savage enough to follow Hancock.

"Barlow's sick," Humphreys said. "He's back, by the way. Sorry affair with his wife."

Meade thought, briefly, of Margaret, of how the loss of his wife would be unendurable.

"Yes," Meade said. "Unfortunate. Orders go out to Warren?"

Humphreys nodded. "If Hancock works his half of the trick, Fifth Corps will tear up all the track Grant wants. And if Warren needs stimulation, I'll see to that."

The Fifth was Meade's old corps. He still viewed it with affection.

The chief of staff repeated, "Hancock's going to have some disgruntled soldiers, though. Officers, too. When they figure out they're getting dumped at Deep Bottom again." He added, "Christ, it's hot, though. Even at night. Bad as goddamned Florida—which I still deem the shithole by which all other shitholes will be measured for eternity."

"Sometimes it's hard to believe you're from a Quaker line."

"Wore out any Quakerness long ago." He took up the coffee

cup again and drank. Humphreys was the only man that Meade had ever encountered who could swallow and grunt simultaneously. "Here's to Hancock, to bloody, buggering Win." He slapped down the cup again. "I wish to hell we could've planned this ourselves. Not a man on Grant's staff who isn't a braggart, liar, and scoundrel. On his best day. And Grant lets them all run wild. That explosion last week, the carelessness . . . somebody ought to hang."

Meade was perturbed with Grant, too. Sheridan had gotten the Valley command. And now this ruse with Hancock's corps seemed too complex by half. But Meade's views hadn't been asked. What authority he retained had been usurped again.

At his low moments, he wondered if Ambrose Burnside, humbled and sent off on leave with no chance of recall, might not end the happier man.

Nonetheless, he said: "Grant hasn't done badly. He's got Lee pinned, you have to give him that. And he certainly doesn't spook." He thought of Joe Hooker, of Pope, and of Burnside again.

Humphreys snorted. "Want me to sum up Grant's policy in four words, his martial wisdom? 'Try, and try again.' No matter the cost. This army's so smashed up half the men won't fight."

Meade knew all that. And he couldn't help sympathizing at least a bit with the soldiers tricked onto those transports for a display, led to believe they were sailing to pleasanter duties, but soon to discover the vessels turning back up the James in the darkness. Fooling Lee was one thing, fooling your own hard-worn men was quite another. Morale was already low.

And yet, Meade had to admit, there was something to be said for "Try, and try again."

Midnight, August 13
Libby Prison, Richmond

Brigadier General William Francis Bartlett pondered, yet again, the challenge of being a one-legged man with the runs in a hot and pestilential prison cell overcrowded with fellow officers as verminous of temper as they were vermin-ridden, all trying to sleep on filthy straw and failing, and sharing a single unlidded bucket for waste. It did not resemble the vision of war that had enthralled Bartlett when he first volunteered.

And then there were the flies. . . .

"Sic transit gloria mundi," he muttered.

"Oh, shut up, Bartlett," a voice from the darkness told him.

PART
II

THE ROADS

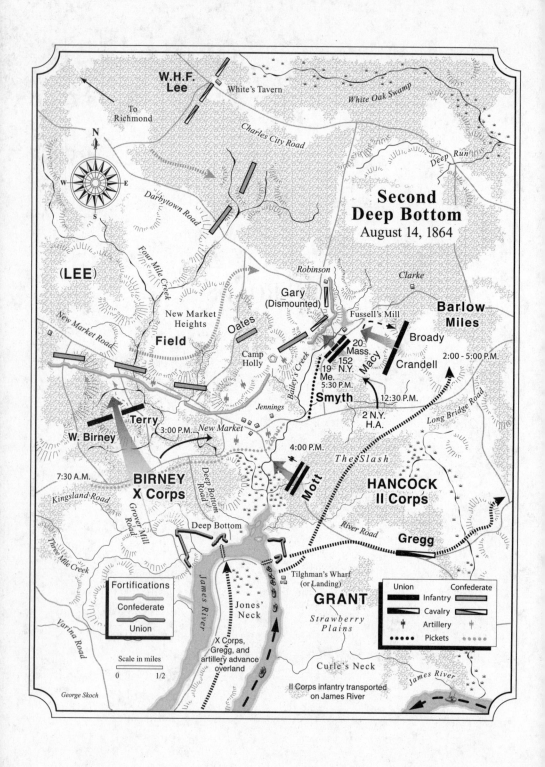

Second Deep Bottom
August 14, 1864

W.H.F. Lee

White's Tavern

White Oak Swamp

Charles City Road

Deep Run

To Richmond

N W E S

Darbytown Road

Four Mile Creek

(LEE)

Robinson

Clarke

Gary (Dismounted)

Fussell's Mill

Barlow Miles

New Market Heights

Oates

Field

Broady

Crandell

2:00 - 5:00 P.M.

Camp Holly

New Market Road

20 Mass.

152 N.Y.

Macy

19 Me.

5:30 P.M.

Smyth

12:30 P.M.

Jennings

2 N.Y. H.A.

Terry

W. Birney

3:00 P.M.

New Market

The Slash

Long Bridge Road

7:30 A.M.

BIRNEY
X Corps

Deep Bottom Road

4:00 P.M.

Mott

HANCOCK
II Corps

Kingsland Road

Grover Mill Road

Deep Bottom

River Road

Gregg

Three Mile Creek

Tilghman's Wharf (or Landing)

GRANT

Fortifications
Confederate
Union

James River

Jones' Neck

Strawberry Plains

Varina Road

Scale in miles
0   1/2

X Corps, Gregg, and artillery advance overland

Curle's Neck

James River

George Skoch

II Corps infantry transported on James River

Union	Confederate
Infantry	
Cavalry	
Artillery	
Pickets	

SIX

Brigadier General Nelson A. Miles saw Barlow riding back from Strawberry Plains at the head of his staff. The horses had been spurred to an impatient canter, just enough to tease out the flags a bit. Even Barlow understood that it was too hot to gallop if a mount was to last the day. Hot, and getting hotter.

Despite the distance, Barlow was easy to recognize, a lanky, imperfect rider in a calico shirt, saber and scabbard loose against his horse. In temporary division command while Barlow took the wing, Miles had begun losing men to the heat before they debarked from the steamers. Now, on the march at last, more dropped away. And the provost company's prodding bayonets didn't help at all, not against men collapsing and convulsing. It looked as if the brigades had been stricken with plague.

Off to the left, Birney's Tenth Corps scratched at the Rebs, but with lessened vigor. In command of the entire field, Hancock had planned to send the Second Corps into the fight along with Birney's dawn advance. But half the corps had still been out on the river, with the other half barely started on the march to its positions. The grand scheme imposed from above had collapsed immediately. Now they'd just slug it out again.

Miles had never seen a worse-planned, worse-run effort. Between the unyielding heat and the river mosquitoes, no one had slept in the overcrowded boats. And having been deceived, the men were disgruntled, to put it gently. Had anyone at Grant's headquarters thought of morale? The murmurs in the darkness had verged on mutiny.

Then things got worse. The James was a tidal river. And some fool, thinking only of darkness and concealment, had scheduled the debarkation at low water, when the larger transports couldn't maneuver close enough to the shore to lower gangplanks to reach the few wretched docks. Thousands of men had been forced to let themselves down, one after another, into rowboats and skiffs that could ferry them shoreward. Laden with packs, some had dropped into the water. Not all had been rescued.

And Miles had gotten word that the steamer carrying almost a full brigade from his temporary command—Barlow's division—had run aground. Those men still had not been put ashore and he'd had to order the column forward without them.

Then there was Barlow. . . .

Elevated to the command of the attack's right wing, Barlow seemed to Miles all but unhinged. Frank Barlow wasn't the sort to bellow and bluster, of course; instead, he grew cool and snide, grinding out words as if he'd been chewing bullets. But the man was off like old cheese.

On a horse gilded with sweat and drooling foam, Barlow reined up. Raising unwelcome dust, his staff wheeled around him.

"For God's sake, Nellie, you've got to *push* the men. We're hours behind."

"Frank, they're already dropping from the heat."

Barlow snorted. "Feigning, most of them. No stomach for a fight."

"That's unfair. And you know it."

"Get this division moving properly. Or I'll find someone who can."

"I've got seven dead of heatstroke. Dozens in fits. And those are just the ones I saw myself."

"Inferior breeding. Irish, I expect. Pick up the pace, Nellie, pick up the pace."

And Barlow rode off again, trailed by flags and a withered staff.

A few miles distant, on the Tenth Corps' front, the firing picked up again. Artillery joined in.

Captain Milligan, aide for the day, looked at Miles warily.

"Something on your mind, Milligan?"

"General Barlow's order to—"

"Maintain the current pace," Miles cut him off.

Someone had to save Barlow from his folly. And if Barlow wished to relieve him, then so be it. But Miles didn't intend to kill more of their own men than he could help. The march was already grueling, and canteens were empty. Even as he'd brought Milligan up short, he'd seen another man stumble from the ranks, dropping his rifle and flailing in a last, queer fit before falling down to foam at the mouth like a horse. When comrades tried to succor him, their officers drove them on, leaving the man behind for the medical orderlies.

They were marching under a baked-blue sky, in heat that rose from the ground and climbed a man's body. And it wasn't yet midmorning. The day promised to be monstrous.

Barlow was monstrous, too. Since his return from burying his wife, Barlow had kept that half-mad smirk on his face, lashing out now and then with insults he found amusing. And whether or not he had lost his mental poise, his physical state made him unfit to command. Frank Barlow was sick in body and soul.

Yes, a soldier had to do his duty. But Barlow's sense of duty was all awry. Duty demanded that a man be capable or give way to others. Frank might feel obliged to carry on, but Miles smelled pride and vainglory.

What had Hancock been thinking? It was common knowledge that Hancock wanted Barlow to take the corps when he couldn't bear the field any longer himself. But surely Hancock had to see Barlow's condition? Frank needed a rest. It was hardly the time to expand his responsibilities.

But Hancock was ill, too.

Perhaps Hancock had hoped to distract Barlow from his sorrow. If so, a great many men would pay the price.

Nelson Miles was grateful that his own worst complaints were insect bites and sunburn, the latter the price of fair skin and the red in his brown hair.

Barlow's staff disappeared into a copse.

Grown bitter, Miles consoled himself that if Barlow proved unfit to command, he'd no longer hear that haughty voice calling him "Nellie." He hated the nickname. And Frank knew he hated it. Which only encouraged him to use it.

Barlow was that sort of fellow, smirking with that snaggletooth, forever needling those he meant to befriend. On the few occasions another officer had tried to call Miles "Nellie," he'd brought the man up short. But Barlow existed in a world of Barlow.

And still, Miles reminded himself, Barlow had raised him up. The boy who'd clerked in a Boston crockery shop, devouring books on war and dreaming of glory, was now a general officer, with his twenty-fifth birthday less than a week behind him. And his rise had been due to Frank's tutelage and favor. Barlow had been the most ferocious officer in the army, a model of martial conduct for Miles to emulate. He'd been a brilliant teacher—far better than the quaint French colonel Miles had paid to teach him to drill back home—but class was at an end. Barlow wasn't just a danger to the enemy now.

Nelson Miles dreaded the hours ahead.

Eleven a.m.
New Market Heights

Oates said: "Isn't a question of whether we can hold. We can. Question is why the devil they don't attack in any force."

"I confess myself mystified," General Gregg said. Gregg had declared for Texas, but Oates still heard Alabama in his voice. "Given all their to-do."

In the dawn, the river below had been clogged with boats, steaming and whistling and coming about to disgorge tiny creatures in blue, the confusion even more pronounced when viewed through a set of field glasses.

Colonel Perry, who had the brigade, offered his opinion: "Well, if they were aiming at some sort of surprise, it didn't take. Knew they were coming last evening. Heard artillery crossing those bridges all night. Put down all the straw you want and burlap up the wheels, you can't keep an army quiet."

Lowering his glasses, Gregg said, "Can't accuse them of moving with alacrity, that's the truth. Heat's on our side. Yankees just aren't used to it."

Oates fought down the impulse to say, "This heat ain't on nobody's side." His men were completely exposed in their trenches and rifle pits, with only one poor tree in the regiment's stretch—the tree under which the three officers loitered.

His men had been ordered forward from Camp Holly the morning before. This was the second day they'd been left sweltering.

Waving a hand at the churned-up earth around them, Gregg said, "Yankee gunboats do throw a mighty shell." He looked at Oates. "Many casualties?"

"One dead. This morning. Had a lieutenant buried alive, but we got him out. A few wounded. Mostly, you can see the puff and take shelter."

"Colonel Lowther expressed a bit more concern," Colonel Perry noted.

And Oates wanted to answer, "Well, Lowther's a goddamned coward, a regiment-stealing, good-for-nothing sonofabitch." But he only said, "He's got his opinion. I'm more concerned about the Yankees in front of me."

"But you're confident you can hold?" Gregg asked again. His doubt was almost an insult.

Oates nodded. Heat or no heat, his men were primed to kill.

"Looks to me like they're shifting to our left," Perry said. "That column back a ways there, by the Slash."

"Their reinforcements been marching that way for hours," Oates explained. "But those blue-bellies down the hill aren't going anywhere. Plenty to go around."

"I make it at least a full corps," Gregg judged.

"More like two," Oates corrected him. Generals tried his patience.

"Grant does have a hankering after Richmond," Perry said. "Petersburg's the country cousin, Richmond's the belle of the ball."

A boat down on the river released a cloud of steam from a boiler. A soldier yelled, "Look out!"

The visiting officers threw themselves into the nearest pit, with the general landing indecorously on the colonel. A few other soldiers, caught unawares, leapt for cover, too. But most went about their business.

Oates just stood there. Furious. Hadn't been nothing but a puff of steam. And the soldier who'd cried out had known it, too. Having himself some fun with the high-up officers. Oates meant to see about that.

"Y'all can get up, gentlemen," he told his superiors. "Looks like the Yankees were aiming at somebody else."

"Oh, Jesus," Colonel Perry spit. "Jesus Christ."

The man couldn't stand on his leg. He eased himself back against the side of the hole.

"Ankle," Perry said. Raising a knee chestward and clutching said part.

Oates jumped into the hole and took the ankle in both hands.

"Christ, Oates!"

"Nothing broken," Oates told him. "Sprain, most like."

Perry tested the foot again. And grimaced. "Not even sure I'll be able to ride."

Oates truly did mean to have a reckoning with the play-the-fool soldier who'd called out the false warning. He'd find the man. One way or another. And there wouldn't be any more watermelons.

Captain Wiggenton sprang up from the main trench. "Here they come!" he shouted back to Oates.

"About time," General Gregg said. "Perry, I reckon we'd best get you out of here." With staff men rushing forward to help, the colonel soon had more assistance than any man required.

Oates gave an easy salute. "By your leave, gentlemen. Matters I need to tend to."

He was eager beyond common sense. First serious scrap since he'd taken the 48th Alabama. And with his old 15th on the right flank and the 4th Alabama—what remained of it—posted to his left, he meant to show what a difference a leader could make.

Let the Yankees come on. He'd give them a taste of salt and a dose of pepper.

But little came of the Federal probe. The blue-bellies gained a few rifle pits, then gave them up again. The only mortal loss Oates suffered was a fellow who went into fits and died of heat sickness.

What the devil were all those Yankees up to?

Noon
Bailey's Creek

Lynch," Barlow told the colonel standing before him, "dust away those skirmishers. On the quick. Take those fortifications beyond the creek. Before they can reinforce."

"Yes, sir," Lynch said. "I've got the New York Heavies in the lead. I just need to get them some water and—"

"You can get them water after they've taken that line."

Lynch looked worn, sleepless, stained, and sweat-caked. But they all were. It was everything Barlow could do to keep himself upright on his two pins, what with the dizzies ambushing him every few minutes. And his feet itched so horribly that he wanted to strip off his boots and scratch himself bloody. The last time he'd had his boots off, his skin had looked leprous.

"General Barlow," the colonel tried again, "I've already lost one man in five, and that's just a rough count. The heat—"

"We all feel the heat, Lynch. You'll lose more men if the Rebs fill in those trenches."

"I just—"

"We're not debating, Colonel. I gave you an order." He pointed.

"Send the Heavies straight down through that cornfield, get across the creek, and take those earthworks. No delays, no deviations. Don't waste time." Barlow inspected the man a final time. Lynch looked played out. But he'd have to play on. They all did. "Go on."

The colonel slumped away, shaking his head.

Barlow wanted to tell the man, "Damn it, I don't like it, either." But they'd fallen seven hours behind the plan, which was in shreds. As for the heat, if he could bear it, so could the dregs he commanded.

He just had to keep his mind clear. He had to show well today.

Charlie Morgan materialized. Riding a nag a peddler would have scorned.

Barlow smirked. "Where's your show horse, Morgan?" Hancock's chief of staff owned a coveted mount.

Morgan's face soured. "Damned heat. Not just hard on the men. Horses, too."

"Well, Cassandra . . . what doth thou foretell?"

"Hancock wants to know the reason why nothing's been undertaken. He's counting on you to punch through."

"For a start, my lead brigade's just coming up. Win may not have noticed, but we had some minor problems on the river. Or were you all napping?"

"Christ, Frank. I was hammering on those blasted docks all night. Literally. Hammer and nails, up to my stones in mud."

"Roaring success there. Bravo."

Morgan looked as though he wanted to throw a punch. Barlow's mood was no less foul.

Controlling himself, Morgan asked, "What shall I tell Hancock? He's just trying to pull this circus together, you know."

Barlow pointed to the right front, where Lynch's skirmishers stepped out from a tree line.

"Tell him I'm attacking."

Twelve fifteen p.m.
Long Bridge Road

As Miles rode past, a medical orderly struggled to pry apart the jaws of a man the heat had felled. Miles had lingered near the column's rear to herd the men, but hundreds had dropped away without a shot fired. Now the march had stalled again, leaving the troops to roast in open fields. Not yet loaded, rifles scalded hands. And the troops ahead had drunk the farm wells dry. Miles' own canteen had been empty for hours.

The only good news he'd had was that the regiments from the grounded ship had landed. Now they'd have another ordeal to face.

He'd only won Barlow's favor, he knew, because he was nearly as savage in battle himself. But he wasn't sure any soldiers on earth could give a good account of themselves in such a state of exhaustion, in such heat. And Frank did seem half-mad.

Rifle fire crackled ahead, perhaps a mile distant. It wasn't coming from Tenth Corps, either. Second Corps was in it, his own men.

He spurred his horse to a gallop, adding more dust to the misery of the march and hoping the animal wouldn't collapse too soon.

Twelve thirty p.m.
Bailey's Creek

Major George Hogg, commanding the 2nd New York Heavy Artillery, had never expected to find himself leading infantry attacks. Fond of mathematics, he'd signed up for the artillery and had spent his first years of service comfortably billeted in Washington's defenses.

Now here he was, with Jim Lynch telling him, only half in jest, "You can face the Johnnies, or you can face Barlow."

All of them had been shocked when, a few months before, they had been reassigned as infantry to make good the losses Grant had suffered in his first go at Lee. But after their initial dismay—that sense of having been cheated by heaven and earth—most of the soldiers he led had fought with a will, eager to prove themselves. And to his even greater surprise, Hogg had discovered the thrill of leading men.

If he wasn't the finest officer of infantry in the army, he was proud of not having done too terribly badly.

This was a bad day, though. A very bad day. None of the officers' horses had caught up with them and all had marched afoot, every man equally worn by heat and thirst. When he'd given the order to form for an attack, he had been almost surprised to be obeyed. Every man in the regiment was exhausted to dropping, with one in three peeled away during the march. He had been even more surprised when he'd ordered them to advance and the men had obeyed him.

Now it was one lone regiment—if a large one—sent to seize earthworks over a half mile distant.

No enemy fire met them as they progressed down the slope, colors centered on a rutted farm trail. But men dropped nonetheless. Hoarse officers and sergeants croaked commands, maintaining alignment. The heat seemed truly unbearable.

A man in the ranks cried, "Jaysus," his plaint worthy of a martyr.

Hundreds of footfalls crushed dry grass and weeds.

Still no firing.

The corn ahead looked stunted, the surrounding landscape parched, its greenery tiring too soon toward autumn.

One shot, then a few. Off to the right. Hogg guessed it was friendly skirmishers, not his own flankers. The firing tapered off.

Shooting at spooks in the heat. . . .

Going to be hard to maintain ranks in that corn. Wouldn't be surprised if some of the men grabbed the chance to hang back.

No matter. Just keep going. The heat burned through his uniform, hot irons pressing the cloth.

"Officers!" he croaked, gone dry. "Straighten your ranks, keep your intervals."

They entered the corn with a rasping, crashing sound. The ears, which should have been ripe, were browning off.

High season for corn back home in New York State. Hogg suspected there wasn't a man in the regiment who wouldn't have preferred to be back there today.

No matter. They had their work.

A cattle stampede through a canebrake could not have made more noise than they did in the corn. Any Rebs this side of Richmond had to hear them.

Still no firing, though.

A cross-trail cut through the cornfield. His diminished lines emerged briefly into the open before renewing their battle with the stalks. There were fewer men now.

Hogg paused to stand on tiptoes for a moment and thought that he spotted movement up the far slope, above the trees, in the Reb fortifications. Or it could have been the heat playing tricks.

Still at least a third of a mile to go.

Amid the thrashing and bashing, a mounted orderly found him.

"General Barlow says you've gone too far left. Your orders are to go straight for the entrenchments. Before they reinforce."

"I *am* going straight for their works. Unless there are positions I can't see."

He took off his hat, wiped the sweat from his eyes, and covered his scalp again.

"General Barlow says you're too far left," the man repeated.

As swiftly as he could, he called the commands he hoped would correct the trajectory of the attack, shifting to the right, more to the north. What Barlow wanted, he got.

Ranks disordered, his men broke free of the corn.

Reb sharpshooters opened up from the left.

Two men dropped.

Hogg could hardly see for the sweat in his eyes. Wiping them made it worse.

"Keep moving! Keep moving!"

A grove ahead, in the low ground, curled out to hug their flanks. As the regiment neared the trees, their crowns concealed the ridge, the object of the attack. It was all dead reckoning for the next stretch. Hogg wished someone had shown him his way on a map.

On the left, some of his men had paused to return fire at the Reb skirmishers.

A lieutenant collapsed. Shot, or stunned by the heat.

Another rider found Hogg. The horseman bent himself low as bullets sought him. His face was as red as raw meat.

"If you keep on this line of march," the messenger told him, "you're going to be enfiladed from the right. The Rebs have rifle pits all along there, over in those trees."

"I've been ordered to move to the right."

The orderly leaned down in the saddle as bullets snapped through the air.

"I wouldn't know about that, sir. I'm just telling you there's Rebs there on your right."

"You have orders for me?"

"Just that."

Not the best of days. . . .

Before he could overtake his advancing lines—shrunken by half or more—Johnnies did open up from the right as well. Hidden in a band of trees, they could only be detected by their rifle flames.

Struggling to be heard, Hogg called, "By battalion . . . right oblique . . . colors, guide on the right . . ."

The only thing he could do now was to clear out the Rebs from those woods. Couldn't advance and leave them behind on his flank.

Rasping out a succession of orders, he sent his rightmost companies into the trees. Men fell bleeding. Voices growled. Shots punched.

He turned back to his left and found the men had halted in the open. Unaccountably. Opening a gap of a hundred yards. Before he reached them, artillery shells crashed down among the companies, issuing from a battery masked from view.

"Get them into the trees!" he called to the officers. "Over there!" He needed his men together. One isolated regiment. Stranded without support in the heart of Dixie.

If Barlow had some magical gift of sight, where was the artillery support?

As his men moved, raggedly, into a right-wheel maneuver to join their comrades, a heavy volley hit them in the back.

What the hell was going on? The Rebs were everywhere. Whose idea had it been to send his men out alone?

Some of the soldiers caught in the field broke ranks and ran for the trees to join their comrades.

Hogg was surprised any man had the strength to run.

More artillery opened up, pounding the open field and splashing dirt. The last ranks dissolved amid the bursting shells.

Hogg gave up and followed them into the trees.

Dead Rebs lay in the thickets. It didn't appear that his men had deigned to take prisoners, with no man in sound mind or balanced temper. His own dead lay amid several blue-clad wounded. Those untouched by the scrap knelt and gagged on dust, or shivered with the unholy sweat of heatstroke, or simply panted like dogs run near to death. A few officers stood about, but everyone else lay sprawled or sat there slumped. And every face that turned toward him delivered the same message: "Don't ask me to do no more, I can't go on."

Hogg doubted he had a third of his men still with him.

Confederate guns began to shell the grove. Rounds burst in the treetops, and shrapnel hunted flesh. Limbs and branches dropped on men, breaking bones, and splinters pierced wool and meat. The noise threatened a man's last grip on sanity.

Hogg scrawled a note: "Have encountered enemy in force. Enfiladed by artillery, both flanks. Unable to advance."

He chose a sergeant who looked as though he still had a spark of life and told him, "Take this to Colonel Lynch."

One fifteen p.m.
Bailey's Creek

I don't need to see that coward's note," Barlow told Lynch. "I watched his abysmal effort. Hogg's utterly unfitted to command."

One thirty p.m.
Strawberry Plains

Grant listened in mild disappointment as Hancock described the day's actions. Hot even in the shade. Frightful for man and beast. But, in war, a man either drove or was driven. Grant did not mean to be driven.

Grant did note that Hancock's map was much better than the maps used a month before. The cartographers, at least, were making progress.

Win Hancock stood before him, plump and sweating. The landing and early attacks had not gone well, and Win was embarrassed, eyes as wilted as his starched white collar. The truth of it was, Grant understood, that few of the problems had been of Hancock's making, though he shouldered them like a soldier. Looking back, Grant saw that the plan had been all clever scheme and no common sense. That river business, especially.

Didn't do to dwell on it, though. Look forward. Think on what's next.

"I hear Birney took some guns," Grant noted. Trying to cheer up Win.

Win nodded. "Heavy howitzers. Rebs couldn't move them off. Got a flag, too." In the distance, lazy skirmishers picked and pecked. "Trouble is they've had so much time to entrench. Months now. Those lines on New Market Heights have become formidable."

Grant waved a fly from his cheek. "Plan was to flank the Heights."

"Barlow couldn't get up in time. The disembarkation mess. He marched the men as hard as they could be marched."

"I saw," Grant said. "Found one in the middle of the road."

"Day isn't over," Hancock tried to assure him. "I expect Barlow to attack in force. Once he's got everyone up."

Grant considered Hancock. Best field officer in the East. Or had been. Win couldn't hide the problem with his leg. Hardly tried to conceal it. And he was growing portly. Man who got fat on campaign wasn't moving much, wasn't active. Hancock often traveled in an ambulance, unable to bear the pressure of a saddle.

Many an officer had endured multiple wounds by now. But some wounds healed, and some didn't. Win would know when his time had come. Unlike Ambrose Burnside.

Two kinds of generals, in Grant's experience. Those who saw it when they were used up, and those who didn't. His job was to keep a watch out for the latter.

"Well," Grant said, prepared to leave, "do what you can today. Hit them again tomorrow. Keep at them, Win."

Glum faces all around, everyone suffering under the smack-a-man heat, torrid as Vicksburg. But Grant didn't take as bleak a view of the day as Hancock did. The failed assaults had revealed that Lee had not sent as many forces to Early as feared. Sheridan would be all right out in the Valley. And the presence of Hancock north of the James might even draw back a portion of Early's command. Meanwhile, Lee would have to stretch again, shifting troops from Petersburg to cover Richmond.

That was a help. Grant was already weighing his next move, another push westward beyond the Petersburg lines. Break up the Weldon Railroad, tighten the noose.

As Grant prepared to leave, Hancock stepped close and said, "Sam, I regret that we didn't do better today."

"Lick 'em tomorrow," Grant told him.

Three p.m.
Petersburg, headquarters of the Army of Northern Virginia

Marshall listened as the generals spoke.

"I fear we must take the risk," Lee told Beauregard. "I'll send two of Mahone's brigades north to Field. He's facing two Union corps and his flank's in the air."

"And if that's what Grant wants?" the Creole asked. "For us to thin our lines? So he can hit our other flank again?"

Lee's features revealed more doubt than was his wont. As his military secretary, Marshall had seen far more of the man than Lee revealed to others. That pinched look had been reserved for private hours.

"He may do precisely that. But we must protect Richmond above all, President Davis is adamant." Lee sighed, another indulgence. "Grant understands that, of course. He's far from the fool we'd been promised." Lee clasped his hands behind his back. Though his feet remained planted, he seemed to be pacing in spirit. "It's one matter to perceive that a thing needs doing, another to enjoy the means to do it. All we can do for now is to parry his thrusts and embarrass his efforts. Bleed him. Shame him. Deny him any victories before November."

Beauregard resurrected his pleasant smile. "Northern papers profess Lincoln's a dead man. Politically speaking. *Le roi est mort. . . .*"

"Our own newspapers assured us that those people wouldn't fight."

Enchanted by any discourse among social equals, Beauregard said, "Those were heady times, we all were foolish then. North or South, I believe we've sobered up."

"Have we?"

Deaf to Lee's tone—though Marshall was not—Beauregard pressed on. "The North's weary of this war, just sick to death of it."

Lee's expression asked, "And we are not?"

"Look how George McClellan's rallied the Democrats," Beauregard continued. "He'll bring them the Army vote, *vraiment*. And I know George, he'll see sense. Once he's elected, he'll give a fine speech to Congress and let us go."

Lee no longer looked at the man who wore the same rank on his collar. But he straightened his back and spirit. In a voice made brisk, Lee said, "Then we must make them wearier still of war." He turned. "Colonel Marshall? You may draft the order. General Mahone will detach two brigades, but he's to remain here himself."

Since the fight over the mine pit, Lee had begun to lean more on Mahone, Marshall had noted. And Lee had made certain that Davis signed his promotion. The old man was forever seeking another Jackson, another worker of wonders.

Well, Mahone was nearly as odd as Stonewall. The one with his cow, the other with his lemons.

"Yes, sir," Marshall said.

Beauregard exchanged glances with an aide. "And now I must receive a delegation of *les femmes héroïques*, the sturdy roses of Petersburg." With a smile, he added, "We'll see what November brings, *cher Général*."

And off he went, all bloody-handed vivacity.

Hours later, alone with Marshall, Lee broke a silence to say, "I fear McClellan will no more defeat Lincoln than he did me."

Five fifteen p.m.
Bailey's Creek

Miles got Barlow alone at last.

"Frank, this isn't working. You've been putting men in piecemeal all afternoon. It isn't like you."

A walking cadaver with fevered eyes, Barlow said, "The damned problem is that the swine don't want to fight. We're left with cowards. The good men are dead."

Earlier, Barlow had harangued all present about the failure of an attack by the patchwork remains of the Irish Brigade, so reduced that its battered regiments had been folded into Crandell's Consolidated Brigade, a collection of flags shot to pieces. There had been bad blood on both sides in the past, but it still was a shock to find Barlow gay in his mockery.

A subsequent effort by Broady's brigade had collapsed under shelling before achieving anything. Now Frank wanted to send in Macy's brigade farther to the right. Instead of one big push, it had been an afternoon of hapless pokes, with three failed attacks and three brigades broken in turn. The Barlow of mere weeks before would have cursed the general who made such naïve errors.

And Barlow, of all people, had grown obsessed with securing his flanks, stretching out his frontage instead of concentrating. It was as if Frank had determined to break every rule he'd set for himself.

"Frank," Miles tried again, "they're *not* cowards. They're used up. They haven't slept, they've had no water. They're dropping like leaves in a gale."

"We'll see what Macy can do." It was as if Barlow had not heard one word.

Five thirty p.m.
Fussell's Mill

No mercy to the day. After stumping fiery hot through a litter of sun-felled men and a wasteland of discarded knapsacks, haversacks, bedrolls, rations, playing cards, bayonets, a solitary Bible, and many an abandoned rifle and cartridge box—more like the leavings of a battle than its raw beginning—and after enduring the lung-gripping, break-a-man heat, that air like molten iron, here they were forming up in a let-go field behind a crest that hid the rest of the world and no man could doubt they were going to make an attack, waterless, worn, and witless as they were.

As artillery batteries pestered each other, Private Henry Roback wished himself back in New York. Sitting in the shade, by a deep, cool well.

As parched as their men, the officers limited their orders and exertions to those unavoidable. Colonel Macy rode past, inspecting them, saying nothing. A Massachusetts man himself, Macy got along fine with the New Yorkers and even seemed partial to the 152nd, though not so fond as he was of his own 20th Massachusetts. Macy on a white horse with his left hand lost at Gettysburg and barely back from his last wounding in the Wilderness, a decent man, mostly. Despite all the tribulations of the day, the colonel looked confident, cocksure as a farmer with his crop in. But that was how officers were supposed to look.

Roback doubted that any man present felt good about what was coming.

The brigade just wasn't the same anymore. Good units had gone bad. The 152nd New York still kept its pride, but all that got them today was a place in the first line.

Gawking rightward, trying to figure things out, Roback spied General Barlow, a demon made flesh, notorious. And just at that moment, a comrade said, "Cripes, there's goddamned Barlow. What's he doing here?"

They all knew Barlow on sight. And few wished to know him better. Some said he was a pet of the highest generals, but all Roback's comrades cared about was that he wasn't *their* general, that he led the First Division, not their own. But there he was, over by the sorry rump of the 1st Minnesota, slump-shouldered in the saddle, wearing his calico shirt, and scarecrow-gaunt. And, Roback feared, dispensing commands.

Had something changed? Was he their commander now? No one told them much. And all a man had been able to think about for hours was getting to the end of the march, to water, food, and sleep.

Now there was Barlow. . . .

A lieutenant called out Company D and led them forward as skirmishers. Roback was glad his company had not been chosen. Wasn't just that such duty had its dangers. Skirmishing work just took more spunk than Roback felt he had left.

Barlow trotted past, looking queer, with Colonel Macy seeing him along.

Roback knew the signs. They'd advance now.

To where? Couldn't see past that crest. Could be anything waiting for them. The artillery sure had found something to shoot at. He could spy black dots as shells arced toward the Johnnies, but couldn't see where they struck. Couldn't see where the Reb shots landed, either. Heard explosions aplenty, though.

Orders: *Attention. Carry* . . . arms. *Forward* . . . march.

The regiment's color guard remained in place and let the front line pass before stepping off. Asking a lot of his horse, Colonel Macy trotted out in front of the brigade. Pointing with his sword.

The heat was worse than a whipping. Damp wool chafed. A thousand strong, the brigade tromped crusted earth and brittle weeds. Heading for that crest.

Waiting officers let the first rank engulf them.

That crest. Blue sky beyond, hard blue, baked. Shells whistled near, but none found them.

Reckon they'll see us soon as we see them, Roback calculated.

"I'd sell my soul for one schooner of beer," a soldier panted.

"Devil don't pay for what he gets for free," another answered.

The skirmishers disappeared over the ridge.

Roback's head throbbed. It felt like mighty hands were pressing his skull. He wanted to sit down, to let the other men go on without him this one time.

He longed for water.

They struck the crest and marched over it. Mostly bare, a gentle slope dropped for a quarter mile, a soldier's nightmare. Patches of no-good cornstalks stood here and there, as if set up by the Rebs to break their ranks, but all the rest was exposed to the watching Johnnies.

At the bottom of the murderous slope, trees lined what must be a stream, if likely a dry one. High on the other side of the little valley, entrenchments and Rebel batteries were visible, connecting one grove to another.

The Confederate guns had stopped firing. Roback knew that the cannoneers were shifting the trails of their guns, repositioning them to fire on the wonderful target the brigade had just presented.

Anticipating the deluge of shot and shell, dry voices ordered men to close up and keep moving.

"Here it comes," a fellow muttered. No one had the grit left in him to shout.

One after another, four distant guns spit fire through wreaths of smoke. After an infernal wait, the shells dropped on the slope. Two fell short and splashed dirt. A third burst over by the 19th Maine, but Roback couldn't see the damage done. He had no idea where the fourth shell went, just heard its passing scream and final crump.

Roback had seen the elephant. More times than he cared to remember. The Rebs wouldn't even adjust the elevation on the guns that had fired short. They'd let the brigade come strolling into range, they had their marks.

Colonel Macy rode out in front again, white horse willing but too worn to prance. Roback had to credit the man, out there holding the reins wrapped around his left forearm, making up for that lost hand, and pointing forward with his sword as if crossing the remainder of the field, getting over that yet-to-be-measured stream, and climbing the hillside to the Reb positions was easy as spending money at the fair.

The next artillery salvo sailed toward them, puffs of smoke birthing little black specks that grew larger as they neared.

More Reb guns opened up.

Whump, whump, whump . . . whump . . .

The 19th Maine was getting its share, with Roback's regiment spared.

Colonel Macy's horse shrieked and recoiled, front legs lifting, rear legs buckling, blood bursting from its chest. The colonel leapt free as the beast fell, but his arm remained tethered. An aide rode forward, jumped from the saddle, and cut the reins with his sword.

The horse cried out like a soul in deepest Hell.

Then that all lay behind them.

Ahead, the skirmishers quickened. Some went to ground and fired into the tree line's beard of brambles. Others jogged forward, warily, bent as if resisting a nasty wind. Made small by distance, a soldier flung wide his arms and toppled backward.

A ball ripped through the New Yorkers, tearing a man in two a few yards from Roback. Men in the second rank shouted out, complaining of being drenched with the poor fellow's blood.

You didn't think about it. You couldn't care who it was. You learned to avert your eyes from fallen comrades, to just keep going forward, staring ahead.

Roback felt fainting sick. But he put one foot down, then the other. Keeping his place in the line.

The skirmishers had eased into the woods at the valley's bottom. Roback just wanted to make it to those trees, setting himself a goal that lay within reason.

Make it to those trees . . .

They entered a last patch of corn, raising a ruckus.

Rifle fire zipped over their heads and cut stalks around them. They emerged from the corn and saw tiny flames in the trees off to the flank, where the skirmish line hadn't reached.

Colonel Macy was back out front, riding a chestnut mount. Roback wished he'd just get out of the way. The men knew Macy, didn't want to have to learn the ways of another colonel.

A man screamed to high heaven. Unnerving. Few wounded men screamed at first. Too stunned. But this fellow screamed louder than a firehouse band.

Left him behind, too.

Colonel Macy's horse revolted, staggered, and fell on top of him.

Just keep going. Those woods. *Don't think.* Straight into those woods.

The artillery had shifted to the brigade's second line, Roback could hear the explosions to the rear.

Someone else's turn.

Just make those trees, those woods.

Bursts of light. Falling men. One fellow shouted church-voiced, calling on Jesus Christ to come and save him.

Officers and sergeants tidied the ranks. Splendidly, the colors remained untouched.

Those woods . . .

Reb fires. Heavy now. As if the Johnnies had captured repeating rifles.

Order was breaking down. Their lieutenant ordered them forward at the double-quick. Into the woods.

Briars and brush resisted the assault. Men bullied their way through, thorn-bitten, cursing. Roback heard the snap-scrape sound of a bullet striking bone, so different from the thud of a round hitting meat.

Who got it? Don't think. *Keep going.*

A voice called, "Help me . . ."

Keep going.

Heat-groggy, he couldn't recall if he'd capped his rifle.

The brambles pierced his uniform, tore his hands, clawed at his face. He nearly fell into a rifle pit concealed in the undergrowth. A Reb stared heavenward from its bottom, shot high in the throat. A woman's straw hat lay beside him, banded with grease.

Poison ivy, too. Just everywhere.

Movement. A fleeting form. Roback stopped. Cocked. Remembered to feel for the cap.

Too late. The phantom was gone.

Cheering from the right. Union huzzahs. They faded quickly.

"Push forward! Push on through! Don't dawdle, men. . . ."

He hated the unknown officer behind that voice. But he was too dry and drained to shout that he was doing the best he could, that all of them were. Stung by nettles and bloodied by thorns, he felt like he'd kicked a wasp's nest.

Comrades dropped into the creekbed ahead of him. There was still some feel of order to the business, if not much. More swamp than stream, the bottom tried to stop their advance. Men plodded through sucking mud, as worried for their shoes as for their lives. The Rebs had missed an opportunity, leaving the far bank's thickets undefended.

Keep going. Get through the mire. Just get to the far bank.

"*New York! Forward!*" some ninny called.

Roback wanted to tell that fool to shut up, to just shut up. But that would have taken more will than he had left.

He didn't want to pass out. Not here, in Rebel country. He didn't fancy seeing a Reb prison. Nor dying hereabouts, mad and untended.

The mud craved his shoes, triggering a sudden, delirious panic. But he fought back, mastering himself to stagger forward.

Shells burst in the treetops above the stream. Cutting branches. Splashing shrapnel. One man folded over like a clasp knife.

Roback made the far bank at last and joined a little band. Mostly New Yorkers, but with Maine boys mixed in. A sergeant took charge and led them up the hill. There was firing ahead, much more of it. Vines grabbed ankles.

The going grew steep, the brush thicker. They heard curses and blows. A man paused and fired at something. A stranger's voice demanded, "Lieutenant? Where are you?"

A Johnny cackled, unseen.

They reached a rifle pit that others had already passed, leaving two dead Rebs and a fellow Yankee with his face smashed in.

"Come on, come on!" another voice encouraged them. "The Reb line's just ahead."

Thunderstorm of musketry. Either they'd found the Reb line, or the Johnnies had found them.

"Wait," the sergeant cried. "Halt."

Roback knelt low. Nearby thrashing and crashing. More rifle fire just above. Mocking voices. And nothing but brush and drifting smoke to be seen amid the trees.

"Every man," the sergeant said, "see that you're loaded and capped. Get ready, get ready . . ."

Clang of ramrods, fumbling fingers.

"Load and stay low. Don't fire until I say so."

What did the sergeant know? Roback couldn't read the sounds at all, couldn't see anything. It was all too confused, and his thoughts wouldn't come clear. Bullets ripped the air from every direction. Heat cramped his guts.

Crashing through the brush above them. Coming on fast. Toward them.

"Just wait," the sergeant whispered. "Wait now."

It sounded like a herd of cows in a cornfield.

"Wait."

Footfalls. Cries.

"On your feet!" the sergeant bellowed.

They rose, raggedly. Leveling their muskets.

"Don't shoot! Don't shoot!"

Blessedly, no one fired. It was men from their own brigade, from the 7th Michigan.

"It's over," a man told them. "Too many Rebs. We got away. The rest are pinned down."

Two more soldiers joined them, breathless, and the Michiganders resumed their retreat. Roback waited. Looking to the sergeant. Waiting on an order, an excuse.

An officer stumbled into them. Bleeding heavily from the remains of an ear.

"Withdraw," he said in the too-loud caw of a deaf man.

Six thirty p.m.
Bailey's Creek

Barlow watched the litter go by, bearing George Macy rearward. Unconscious, the colonel struggled for breath. A pair of staff men brought up the rear. Slinking off.

Arms folded over his chest, Barlow nodded in Macy's direction.

At least Macy hadn't funked it half as badly as the others. The man had behaved like a soldier. But hadn't he anyone left who could do the job? The division he'd led in May had been irresistible. Now it was worthless, useless. . . .

Of a sudden, Barlow wanted to curl up and weep. It had nothing to do with Macy. Or with any man touched by the day. It was an overwhelming sense of not being commensurate with the universe, incapable of willing his way through. A sense of failure immeasurably profound.

But Barlow did *not* cry. Nor did he allow the dizziness to unman him. And if his rump was raw, he'd been through worse. Only his horrid feet would not be mastered.

He wished he possessed a Roman commander's authority to decimate units proven cowardly. Macy's first line had done its part, but the second line had stalled after his injury. It was more than an embarrassment. The brigade's performance was a humiliation.

Barlow found himself on the ground. Unsure of how he'd gotten there. Whirlwind dizzy. Sweat bursting from him.

When his eyes regained focus, he saw his staff clustered around him, afraid to touch him. As soon as he could, he willed himself to his feet.

"I tripped," he said. "All of you, back to your duties."

Slowly, they obeyed.

Refusing any assistance, Barlow made his way to the tent put up for him and chased off the lurking orderly. He drank nearly a full canteen of water, gulping until his throat hurt. Then he splashed a bit over his head. He felt emptier than he'd thought a man could feel.

"Belle," he said.

Ten p.m.
Deep Bottom

The heavy darkness gripped the men in their thousands, insisting that they fight for every breath. For the first time in weeks, thunder grumbled and lightning cut. Then the rain came, heavy as molasses, replacing one curse with another, the soldier's lot.

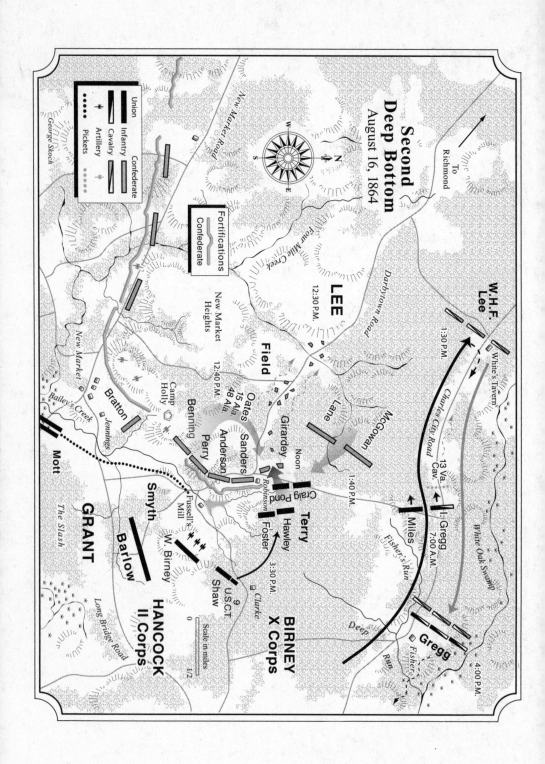

Second
Deep Bottom
August 16, 1864

Union
Infantry
Cavalry
Artillery
Pickets
Confederate

Fortifications
Confederate

George Skoch

To
Richmond

New Market Road

New Market Heights

Four Mile Creek

Darbytown Road

LEE
12:30 P.M.

W.H.F.
Lee
1:30 P.M.

White's Tavern

Field
12:40 P.M.

Camp
Holly

Oates
15 Ala.
48 Ala.
Sanders
Anderson
Perry
Benning

Girardey

Lane

McGowan

Noon

Charles City Road

13 Va.
Cav.

New Market

Bratton

Jennings

Bailey's Creek

Mott

Smyth

Fussell's
Mill

Robinson

Craig Pond

Terry

Hawley

Foster

1:40 P.M.

Miles

Gregg
7:00 A.M.

Fisher's Run

White Oak Swamp

GRANT

The Slash

Barlow

W. Birney

Shaw

U.S.C.T.
9

Clarke

3:30 P.M.

BIRNEY
X Corps

Deep

Run

Gregg

Fisher's

4:00 P.M.

HANCOCK
II Corps

Long Bridge Road

0   1/2
Scale in miles

SEVEN

Handsomely done, Gregg!" Nelson Miles told the cavalry colonel.

The two officers watched as horsemen charged along the road in a column of fours. Already flanked by Miles' infantrymen and dismounted cavalry, the last belt of Reb skirmishers collapsed. Small encounter though it was, the effort was the first perfectly executed maneuver Miles had seen since Barlow broke into the Mule Shoe at Spotsylvania. It let him hope that this day might go well.

"Rooney Lee's pack," Irvin Gregg said. "Him we can handle. But if Hampton's on the field, we'll feel some knuckles." He looked skyward. "Heat was bad enough, but this humidity . . ."

Miles rearranged his kerchief to shield his sunburned neck. He'd had enough and more of Virginia's summers.

Instead of launching a grand assault, Hancock had squandered the previous day in minor attacks and probes, every effort marred by delays and drawn out by countermarches. A deluge had drenched the ebbing afternoon, deepening the mire left on the roads by a night of rain, slowing all human efforts, and Miles had grown frustrated with the world. Barlow had held himself together, bodily, at least, but Miles had started to worry about Hancock, who had ordered the Tenth Corps to shift to the right, playing hopscotch with the Second Corps, still seeking the Reb flank.

No doubt it looked like a splendid plan on paper, but Birney's

Tenners had taken their turn at battling the heat on the march as they shifted northward, with men falling out in even greater numbers than the losses the Second Corps suffered the day before. The heat had grown so grim that men died resting under trees. With orders vague and routes confused, the Tenth Corps had passed behind the Second only at midnight.

Hancock had been in a constant grump, riding about to quibble with subordinates, a changed man and for the worse. Disappointed by Barlow—but still defending him—Hancock had reassumed direct command of his corps, as well as of the overall operation, with Barlow returned to division command and Miles to his brigade. It hadn't helped.

"First a muddle, now mud," a wag had commented.

Then, with Miles' soldiers resting at last, Hancock had reached past Barlow to order the brigade to support a cavalry movement, with Brigadier General David McMurtrie Gregg commanding and Miles paired off with Colonel Irvin Gregg, the general's cousin and junior member of one more family dynasty in blue. Despite the hurried night march required for his brigade to be in place by dawn, Miles had been so glad to leave Frank Barlow that he'd welcomed the orders detaching him.

Now he and Gregg the Lesser had pulled off their little trick, getting off to a fair start on their push down the road toward Richmond.

Let the Tenth Corps make its grand attack. Let others have the glory of the day, if that was their destiny. Supporting the cavalry's tussle with the Rebs, Miles felt like a prisoner newly freed.

A pair of troopers shepherded three unhorsed prisoners eastward. The Confederates looked a bit seedy, though not so unkempt as their infantry.

Miles called, "What's your regiment?"

A hard-eyed Reb with greasy ringlets answered, "Thirteenth Virginia, sonny. Kiss my ass."

Nine a.m.
New Market Heights

Oates was vexed. For two days, the Yankees hadn't done anything much, first parading around in the sun, then parading around in the rain, and now content to sit still while his soldiers baked for nothing. What action there was this morning banged away well to the left, up by the Darbytown Road somewhere, another fellow's problem. It did appear that the 48th Alabama would just swelter and suck eggs again, alongside his old 15th and that strutting scum-yellow peacock, Colonel Lowther, a man Oates still had a good mind to beat with his fists, even if it cost him his command.

Whip the Yankees first, he cautioned himself. *You don't know what's coming, you just think you do.*

The blue-bellies down in the lowlands did look fewer and listless, though.

"Get over here, Hardwick," he called to the nearest lieutenant. "You pass the word that I'm coming around to inspect the rifles myself. Don't want to see one speck of dust."

The lieutenant saluted and fled.

Hard to keep the boys in proper trim. Oh, their rifles would be fine. But they needed to keep occupied and not just squat in a ditch, thinking of Lorna or Joan and rubbing their piss pipes.

Damn, though, he needed to get into a fight, any fight. Show up that swine Lowther. Show how a true man did what needed doing.

The battle sounds in the distance ebbed, though a battery remained obstinate.

Another worthless day of nothing much.

Nine a.m.
Charles City Road

What do you make of that, Miles? Think it's a ruse?"

Miles considered the captured map spread across his saddle. "I doubt General Chambliss got himself killed to play us a trick."

"Classmate of mine at the Point, you know," David McMurtrie Gregg told his borrowed subordinate. "Always liked him. Decent man. Wish he'd had a better end. And a better cause."

Brigadier General John Chambliss, CSA, had galloped blindly into a Federal volley while searching for his own cavalrymen. The Johnnies were having a difficult morning, with Gregg's horsemen and Miles' infantry pushing up the road toward White's Tavern, threatening Richmond.

"I hope Irv keeps that hand," Gregg said of his cousin. Irvin Gregg, who had begun the day at Miles' side, had been struck by a ball just below the wrist, forcing him to the rear. "Well, best get on. I'll send the map to Hancock, see what he makes of it. Probably just pass it on to Sharpe and let him riddle over it."

The map taken from Chambliss' pocket laid out the Richmond defenses in detail. It did seem too good to be true.

Miles touched two fingers to his cap. "I'm going forward again. Heavies need watching."

"Join you shortly," Gregg told him. "Just want to see John's body handled properly. The devils had cut off his buttons and cleaned out his pockets before I got to him." He paused, then repeated, "Decent man. Courtly, in that easy way they have."

Miles was a bit surprised to find David Gregg so wistful. Gregg was a man who chewed iron.

Rifle fire broke out ahead and Miles spurred his horse forward. The breeze created by the canter was welcome, a respite, however slight. If Chambliss was dead, so was the air on this swollen corpse of a day.

The cavalry advanced so swiftly that Miles' men had to struggle to keep up. And the undergrowth flanking the road had claws and teeth. Miles' horse bled from his forays into the brush and his riding boots showed gouges. But he needed to stay close, since he didn't trust the 2nd New York Heavies. Not after their wretched showing two days before. If Gregg's troopers could work through those brambles dismounted, his men would do no less, the cost be damned.

Riding toward the spat and spit of rifles, he encouraged lagging soldiers to keep up and tore at any officers who failed to keep them in line.

The Rebs pulled back again before Miles could reach the latest encounter. They were buying time, not really fighting. Waiting for reinforcements. The attack had gained almost a mile from the spot where Chambliss fell, and Miles felt a growing concern that they might outdistance all support, only to see the fortunes of war turn against them. Birney's attack, the day's main affair, had gotten under way, he could hear the racket, and that would draw off most of the Rebs' reserves. Still, Miles would have preferred to be tied in with Tenth Corps, at least through flankers. In a crisis, Gregg's horsemen could withdraw a great deal faster than the infantry, leaving them stranded. And Miles knew all too well the back-and-forth gamesmanship of cavalry duels along roads.

Christ, he thought, you're winning for once, be glad of it. Don't go to bits like Barlow.

He caught up with his Michigan and New Hampshire regiments.

"Good work, good work," he called. "Stay after them, boys."

"And would there be any water, sir? I'm dry as Granny's gash."

"Take it from the Rebs," Miles told the man.

Barlow. The question of loyalty nagged Miles. He'd been unspeakably angry with Frank, vicious in private thoughts. Yet he owed Frank much, he knew it well. And he *liked* Frank, for all his quirks. Could it be resentment? Over all Frank had done for him? That common form of ingratitude? Or was it just temper strained by the monstrous heat?

What *was* true loyalty? Where did its limits lie? It sounded splendid in novels, with clansmen rallied around some Highland chieftain, fighting to the last. But what about the chieftain's debt to his clansmen? Did he owe his foremost loyalty to Barlow, like some feudal knight? If so, what did Barlow owe him? What code, what bonds of fealty, trumped all others? The modern age was hardly the age of chivalry, and yet . . .

Did he owe his first loyalty to the men he commanded? To duty itself? To the army? Or to a general cause? Had he betrayed Barlow in thought, if not in deed?

What did that say of him as a man, a friend, a subordinate? On the other hand, what did it help, if he excused Frank's incapacity and more men died for naught? The business wasn't as clean as in those books. . . .

Colonel Kerwin, who'd taken over Irvin Gregg's brigade, greeted Miles on a crest.

"How far back are your men, sir?"

"Not five minutes," Miles said. "The lead regiments."

"If they'd relieve my boys, I'd like to mount them again."

"A further advance?"

Kerwin shook his head. "I've orders to stop here. Until General Gregg comes up for a look."

"Well, my men will be glad enough to stop. Problem may be getting them going again."

The colonel grimaced. "Don't think I've ever been hotter in my life." He patted his horse. "I'm losing horses."

"I'm losing men," Miles told him. "Found any water?"

"None."

Eleven a.m.
Darbytown Road

Give it to them, pour it on!" Girardey shouted. Few men could hear for the uproar, but he couldn't help shouting encouragement.

The Yankees had turned back, but Brigadier General Victor Jean Baptiste Girardey, who'd been a captain thirteen days before, had something to prove. No other Confederate officer had ever made such a leap, but his actions at the mine made him the exception. And he intended to show Billy Mahone, A. P. Hill, and Robert E. Lee that their judgment had been sound.

"Aim right, boys! Clear away those blue hogs troubling Sanders!"

He was still in a bit of a daze about it all, proud and delighted. He had neither sought nor expected such a thing. But the country to which he had been brought as a child, this land he had come to love so, this American Southland, had honored him handsomely. His twenty-seven years had been good years, with only a few re-membered glimpses of France and many treasured memories of Georgia, of dear Augusta, and of New Orleans, which had given him a wife who wouldn't mind promenading on a general's arm. Her delectable Creole vanity would glow.

The last Yankees slipped out of range. Those that could be seen. It was ugly country, brambles, pines, and incised earth, murderous to an attacker, but confusing enough for those tasked to defend it.

The firing petered out.

"Officers," he called. "Tally your ammunition. Report by regi-ment."

His Georgia Brigade. *His* brigade.

They'd been able to ride the railcars north from Petersburg, sparing them much of the march. But the last miles in the rain and the blind-a-man darkness had been a trial, and water was scarcer than virgins in a fancy house. Thus far, he'd lost more men to the heat than to bullets.

The Yankees had made two assaults and both had failed, their efforts addled by the broken terrain and well-timed volleys. His Georgians had not been tested yet, not really. The hardest blows had gone in against Sanders' Alabama Brigade, with Sanders com-manding a slapped-together division.

Sanders. Brave man, good man. But Girardey had not missed the glints of jealousy. And not merely from Sanders. Many a man was piqued by his elevation.

The thing to do, of course, was to prove he deserved it.

"Think they'll come again, sir?" an officer asked.

"They'll come again," Girardey said. "And we'll knock them back again."

"Too damned hot for this," a soldier noted.

Eleven thirty a.m.
North of the Darbytown Road

Brigadier General Alfred Howe Terry disliked displays of temperament. So he had refused to blow up on anyone after his division's first advance ran into a pond none of Hancock's people had mentioned. Of old Connecticut blood, Terry preferred solutions to theatrics. And when his second probe went forward and found Rebels and ravines where none should have been, leading to a second repulse, he took that in stride, too. Nor did he offer excuses when his corps commander, Davey Birney, chided him to attack again at once. He quietly demurred and saw things done properly.

Birney wasn't a bad sort, but he wasn't a Yale man.

Terry grasped how to do the thing now, and that was all that mattered. He'd always taken pride in craftsmanship, whether carving scrimshaw as a boy, practicing law in New Haven, drilling militia, or in the throes of battle. A New England gentleman held his tongue and let his work speak for him. And he was about to strike a resounding blow, one that would satisfy Birney and deliver a gentlemanly retort to Hancock and his deified Second Corps.

The army's champion, "Hancock the Superb," had botched things three days running. The poor old fellow survived on reputation. Nor had his ever-lionized subordinates done well. Birney's Tenth Corps, by contrast, always seemed to be slighted. Now Terry meant to achieve what Hancock and his corps had failed to do: break the Confederate lines and send the Rebs reeling.

It was all a matter of paying attention, whether to points of law or to the details of the terrain. It had taken some hours and losses, but he understood the ground and the Reb dispositions. He believed he saw the weak point in their defense. This time, he'd hit them with three brigades, the two on the right echeloned for a double blow, with the Western Brigade leading, formed on a narrow front behind a copse, a surprise for the Johnnies.

It was largely mechanics, really. Move swiftly with maximum force over the shortest possible distance, converting volume to power through concentration. Calculation, not gush, that was the thing. And remember your men are human. Spare them from the heat as long as possible. Study what lay in front of you. Give clear orders and see that they're obeyed. Then hit a blow as hard as you can deliver. No need for any fuss.

As the last of his men formed up, the Rebs poured on shot and shell as if dreading the future, firing blindly and guessing at the range.

Terry strolled over to Hawley's brigade and told a covey of officers:

"No need to display yourselves, gentlemen. Everyone knows you're brave. Have your men lay down until we're ready. And take cover yourselves." He smiled as fully as heritage permitted. "Believe I'll take a tree myself. Bad form to fall on our side of the lines."

And there it was: the supporting cannonade he'd asked of Birney. The sound of guns well tended always inspirited Alfred Terry. He stepped out to have a proper look and found the cannoneers were doing splendidly. Barely exposed, a Reb breastwork nonetheless took a direct hit. Then it suffered another.

One had to feel for the fellows on the other side. But not too much.

He took off his hat and patted his face with a handkerchief doused with cologne water. Another sweltering day. Hard on the men's spirits. But he'd seen that they all had full canteens for the attack, and no excuses. Give them a taste of victory and they'd be fine.

Terry looked at his watch, waiting for word that his last brigade was ready.

Noon
Darbytown Road

The Yankees burst from the trees. More of them than Girardey had expected. His Georgia brigade was stretched thin and he felt a moment's alarm. But his men were intent and ready, steadying their rifles on berms and rails. And the ground was broken, a mess of felled trees, stumps, and stumble-holes, a trial for any attacker.

"Hold your fire," the new brigadier cautioned. "Officers, let them get close."

The first two Yankee advances had been halfhearted, barely annoying his section of the line. Their numbers were greater now, but he doubted that their resolve was much increased. The Federals wilted fast in the Southern heat.

"Let them get close," he repeated in a lower voice. Revolver in hand, he pressed closer to the earthworks thrown up in haste.

One good volley. And Victor Jean Baptiste Girardey believed the Yankees would fold their hand again.

Coming on fast, though. Pushing through the obstacles with a will. Hurrahing.

One good volley. And they'd shut their mouths.

Coming fast.

"Ready! Take aim! Fire!"

His line erupted in spurts of flame and smoke. He heard mad groans and cries. And the urgent clanking of his soldiers' ramrods.

The Yankees would give a volley. Then they'd run. Just how they behaved.

But as the smoke wisped off, Girardey was shocked. Hurrahing anew, the Yankees didn't pause to return the volley but ran hard for his line, bayonets fixed.

It all went too fast. The first Yankees leapt over the ragged parapet before his men could reload. Blue coats and caps plunged among them, thrusting bayonets. Rifles blasted chests and faces, bellies and groins.

His men hadn't fixed bayonets and tried to do so now. Girardey fired his pistol once, then paused, frustrated by the melee, fearing he'd hit his own men. As he watched, dumbstruck, a Georgian swung his rifle by the barrel and the stock hit a Yankee's jaw so hard it tore it from the man's face. Bayonets lifted the hellion off the ground as blue-bellies cursed him.

His men began to turn and run. Some threw down their weapons.

All this in seconds.

Girardey found his voice: "Stand, boys! Stand, for God's sake! We have to turn them back!"

A bullet struck the center of his forehead.

Twelve fifteen p.m.
Clarke house, Union Tenth Corps headquarters

The smarmy bastard had done it! Major General David B. Birney could only lower his field glasses and shake his head in wonder. Terry had broken the Confederate line in the blink of an eye. His troops, climbing the hillside, seemed unstoppable.

Terry. A fellow with no more swagger than a fence post. Impossible to befriend and imperturbable. The saltbox sonofabitch had really done it.

Now Terry wanted support. Birney turned to his nearest aide.

"Go to my brother. Tell him to advance his division immediately. He's to follow Terry's bunch. And keep on going."

To a nearby major he added, "Crandall, take down a message for General Hancock. Be quick, man. The slavers are running. He's got to bring his corps into the attack. Put it politely, but make it clear."

Birney intended to make his breakthrough stick.

Twelve twenty p.m.
Darbytown Road, Robinson farm

Ticks. Everywhere. Major General Charles Field disliked the fiendish creatures, but he'd grown weary past caring. Hardly snatched an hour of sleep in the night, at it like a field boss before dawn. He'd gotten the reinforcements set in right, though, Sanders' and Girardey's brigades, on loan from Billy Mahone. And they'd whupped the Yankees handily.

He dozed, but willed himself to stay in the shallows, war-trained not to let himself drift off. Alert to the snap of rifles and shouting down the hill, he ignored the rustle of staff men slipping into the cornfield on private business.

The shade was a seductress, though, a Jezebel. That hint, if nothing more, of coolness on a torrid day felt precious. He was a proud man, Charley Field, proud of his work this day, with the Yankees repulsed handily, and proud of the way he'd handled Hood's old division since he'd gained its command in the winter.

Yankees were at it again now, back for a third helping. He knew how to read the firing and not flare up like a fool at a few huzzahs. The position his men held was strong, much of it concealed. The Federals were hurling men away like a drunkard squandered silver.

A mosquito bit him on the back of the neck.

If men had any decency, Field concluded, they'd outlaw war in the months of July and August. The heat just took a man down. Thirty-six years old, hardly a Methuselah, he felt as though he'd been dancing all night with bobcats. And his wound from Second Manassas was in a temper.

Mahone's men on detachment had straggled in during the night, weary and parched. They did know how to fight, though. Sanders was strong, always had been, according to campfire lore. And the new fellow, Girardey. Well, they'd just have to see. Bound to be many a jealous colonel, with that boy jumped up from captain to brigadier general. He'd have to weather that. Pretty little fellow. French, though he didn't sound it. Well, Girardey had held his own so far.

Field spit a fly away from his lips and remembered. All the dead, the friends lost. Class of 1849 hadn't shamed West Point, but it hadn't been lucky.

A few more minutes and he'd need to rise. Have a look around, let the soldiers know he was watching over them. The Yankees were still at it down the hill, but more fool them. Hadn't made one gain stick in three days of trying.

He sighed. Wondering how many ticks he'd pull off that night.

His nephew and adjutant, Willie Jones, called out, *"General, they're breaking."*

Field blinked once, then shuttered his eyes anew against the brightness. "Damned right, they're running. What did you expect?"

"No, sir," Willie yelled, all hot. "It's *our* men. Our men are running."

Devil in a pickle jar . . . what the roaring hell? Field levered himself to his feet so fast it left him dizzy.

"Look!" Willie called.

His staff had rushed to the edge of the little plateau, where the road dropped toward the fighting. Field joined them.

And he saw a sight to make a man sick and bust his heart twice over. His own kind, soldiers under his command, came scampering up the hillside. More than a few had thrown away their rifles.

"Blind me, Jesus," Field gasped.

An aide exclaimed, "Yankees! Right down there!"

Field drew himself together. "Who's running? Can you tell?"

"It's those Georgians."

Mahone's bunch. Girardey's lot. That overpromoted captain would have some explaining to do.

"Well, *stop* them," Field said. "Corbin, take charge. Pistols out, gentlemen." Then he added, "Don't shoot, unless you have to. Just turn them around, form a line."

He called for his horse and barked orders at his couriers, sending three of them off to find reinforcements wherever they might be had. To a fourth man whose horse had been killed, he said, "Sergeant Powell, go right overland, go southward. Tell every ranking officer you meet that we need help, they're to strip the lines. Go, man, run!" And to his nephew he said, "Willie, Lee's on top of the hill. Go find him. Tell him the devil's got loose."

Then Field and his staff stepped into the roadway, revolvers drawn, calling on men—some by name—to halt and fight.

The soldiers ignored their words and their pistols alike.

Twelve thirty
Darbytown Road

Go back," Lee begged, "go back! We must drive those people, push them back. Rally, men, rally. Do not let your fellows down. Go back . . ."

Few heeded him.

Lee sat on his horse in the middle of the road. When men spotted him, they shied, easing out into the fields. But they continued to flee.

"Soldiers! Remember your pride, your homes . . . your country. Turn and fight, turn around. We must retake those works . . . remember yourselves . . ."

At the Wilderness and again at Spotsylvania, his appearance had been enough to staunch the flight of men shocked into panic. Instead of retreating farther, they had seized his bridle, insisting that they would fight if *he* went back.

This day . . . mortified him. Some soldiers turned about at his behest, but such were few, too few. He feared he had lost his gifts, perhaps his army.

The sounds of battle approached—those horrid Yankee cheers—and Lee's dismay became anger. He nudged Traveller into the path of a black-bearded man stumping dead-eyed toward the rear.

"You there!" Lee called, voice changed to one of command. "Where are you going? Aren't you ashamed, sir? Disgracing yourself . . ."

The dead eyes changed to doleful and the soldier lifted a much-tormented hat, grimacing in sudden pain as he did so.

The man's scalp was torn and hanging, the skull exposed.

He replaced his hat and walked on.

His men. These men. Such men . . .

Lee turned his horse and followed the wounded man. Overtaking him, he spoke in a voice soft enough for a lady's parlor:

"There's good water over there." The general pointed. "Behind the house. There's still water in the well. To clean your wound."

Twelve forty p.m.
South of the Darbytown Road

Those are legs you got, not candy canes," Oates snapped. "Y'all keep up."

Hot as a baker's oven, all right, and men were going down. But he was determined to trot them and get them into the fight with no time lost. Staff men had dashed by, wetting their drawers and wailing that the Yankees had broken through, that Oates' 48th Alabama and the 15th, the latter stolen by a human carbuncle, that oozing chancre, Lowther, were the only hope to stay the disaster up on the Darbytown Road.

Oates hadn't waited for Lowther to cite date of rank and try to take charge of both regiments. He got his boys going at the double-quick. Would've whipped them like mouthy coons, if he'd needed to. Wasn't a day for pity, not one ounce. His bad hip ground so wickedly he could almost hear it creak, bum leg arguing hard against the pace. But this was a day for dirt-fighting, not show-fighting. He'd sent his new horse to the rear, getting down with the men. Oates meant to remind everybody, from Bobby Lee down to the lowest skulker, what a man could bear, what a man could do.

But, damn, if Lowther didn't follow after, trotting hard and going afoot himself. Oates preferred to think that his old 15th followed after *him,* though, the way a hound still harked to an old master.

"I'm cooking right up," a man called, the strain of the day in his voice.

"Well, see you cook right through," Oates told him, all of them. "I'm hankering for side-meat, you can spare me the fixing up."

Going through a stretch of trees, he made sure no man slipped off. Every rifle mattered. And there was pride.

Lord, it was a hot one, though. With the gone rains haunting the air.

Battle noise kicking up and closing in. Yankee artillery delighting itself, spendthrift with ammunition.

Oates doubled back along the column, using himself hard, ever seeing to the things that needed seeing to. Another soldier began to stagger. Captain Wiggenton seized the man's rifle, lugging it for him, and insisted the man keep going.

Young Wiggenton was one fine officer.

Oates sprinted back to the head of his little column, hip a misery.

As soaked as if they'd been tipped in a creek, the lead company left the trees for the light of a field. Just ahead, the Darbytown Road was Lucifer's own chaos. Men ran every which way, but mostly the wrong way. Oates cast about for anyone who wore enough rank to give him orders, who might know where they were wanted.

It looked as though they were needed everywhere, but the worst of it, a crashing, howling mess, sounded down on the right, a roustabout brawl of thousands. Smoke struggled up through rotten air, chased by the roar of men turned into beasts.

Oates recognized General Anderson. Not in his chain of command, but it hardly mattered. Without giving Lowther time to catch up and assert his seniority—let the man's cowardice show to the whole world—Oates halted his shred of a regiment.

"Oates?" the general said. "Good God, man, you're welcome here."

"Got my Fortykins. Fifteenth's coming up. Where should I take them in?"

Anderson looked doubtful. Maybe reckoning how small a force trailed Oates. Maybe stunned out of good sense.

Oates waited. Impatiently.

With a troubled nod, Anderson told him, "Eighth Georgia's still holding on. Down there." The general pointed. "In that piece of woods somewhere." He smartened his carriage. "Oates, if you think you can do anything . . . go tearing into them."

Oates snapped a salute.

The Federal line below, glimpsed over low trees, had regrouped and looked set to parade. Near a mile's worth of them, stretched across a great field and into a grove. He did believe he saw where he needed to go, just on their flank.

"Alabama! Forward . . . right oblique . . . march!" Time to quick-march now. Let them catch a bit of breath, with the fight coming. Keep them together. When they were on their way into the cauldron, he added, "Time to earn your pork and pone, Alabama."

"Ain't seen no pork in a Bible age," a soldier called back.

Another man cackled, "Git me some Yankee bacon."

"And coffee," another called.

That deep-down thrill on the verge of a fight was in them now. They'd fall down dead before they'd skulk away.

To Oates' surprise—mixed pleasure and displeasure—Lowther made the 15th conform to the 48th's movement, trailing on the left. Lowther . . . was almost acting like a soldier.

A wide grove, not too deep. Treetops and branches cracked off and crashed down under Yankee artillery. Had to go through it. Get on that flank. Halfway onto it, anyhow. Overlap them.

"Come on, boys, keep your order and come on!"

He called out to his captains and lieutenants, telling them to deploy the regiment into two lines as soon as they left those trees. And to be quick about it.

The noise in the grove was stunning. Whole trees toppled. Men hurled themselves out of the way.

They stayed together now. Without the need for admonition or threat.

Leaving the trees, they faced a worn rail fence, a natural rallying point. His officers rushed the men into battle lines. Just as a passel of Yankees rose out of a swale.

Oates called orders to aim and fire as swiftly as he could spill the words from his mouth. The Yankees were hurrying, too. Halted barely fifty steps off, rifles raised, their thumbs cocked hammers.

Both sides fired in a flurry of moments. Men fell around Oates, some crying out. But blue-bellies dropped like bottles swept from a shelf.

"Give it to them," he shouted. "Pour it into the suckers."

Aided by a corporal, Lowther was making his way down the line to Oates. He was clutching his side, where his uniform was darkening under his hand. Lowther crouched as he walked, in immediate pain.

Got him a real wound this time, Oates told himself.

Lowther came near. Oates stepped toward him.

Gasping, Lowther said, "I'm forced to retire . . . Captain Hill has the Fifteenth." He closed his eyes, pressing his side, then resumed his speech. "You're senior man on the field, Oates. You have the command." Then, with a glint of humanity in his eyes that would trouble Oates, Lowther said, "Good luck."

Oates shrugged, uncertain. But when Lowther had gone, he felt a raw, child's urge to shout after him, "I don't need your luck, not one damn bit."

The rifle duel continued. But old Alabama was getting the better of it.

Word came from the 15th that Captain Hill was severely wounded and Captain Shaaff had the regiment.

All right, Oates told himself. Shaaff's good. He had always been Oates' choice to lead skirmishing parties, a brave and cunning young man.

Captain Strickland of the 48th sidled up and pointed. "Colonel, if we can get around their flank, right over—"

A round cut through Strickland's hand and wrist, then cut off half an ear. The captain went down in a welter of blood, clutching himself at one spot, then another.

He was right, though. Oates saw it. They didn't overlap the

Yankees much, but it just might be enough. And they wouldn't expect a charge.

He sent a man to tell Shaaff to hold the 15th in place and keep
up the fire. Then he line-walked his Fortykins, telling the men to
get ready, they were going to charge and go through the blue-
bellies like Paddy went through the whiskey.

Shot in the head, a soldier splashed blood on Oates' lips. Tasting another man's life, he shouted:

"Forty-eighth Alabama . . . *charge!*"

His men leapt over the fence or just knocked it down. Howling
their gritty twist on the Rebel yell. Hosts of insects rose with the
charging men.

The waiting Yankee line began to step back. The blue-bellies
kept good order at first, but Oates knew that he had them.

"Alabama!" he screamed. Running with his men, pointing
with his sword. Wouldn't be any repeat of Little Round Top this
fine day.

The Yankees broke and ran.

Nothing short of high times with a woman came anywhere
near the feeling of that charge. As if men were meant to fight as
surely as they were fixed to extend their bloodlines.

"Alabama!"

Oates kept his sense, despite himself. Reckoning just how far one
torn-down regiment dared go. Faced with a whole Yankee army.

They were nicely on the flank of the blue-bellies, though.

Oates waved surrendering Yankees—the slow, the slightly
wounded, and the quitters—to the rear.

"Git on, git along, damn you," he told the captives.

"Best listen," a soldier cautioned them.

They came up on a turn-water ditch gone dry. It cut diagonally
across the field, as if dug out to serve them.

"Halt! Alabama! Halt! Get down in that ditch!"

A few men who had rushed ahead turned around to rejoin the
mass. Shot in the back, one man toppled forward with a look of
astonishment.

They were near a branch bottom. Not a hundred yards off, the whupped-on Yankees had rallied on their supports, atop a low hill.

"Y'all stay down now. Use sense. And fire up those blue-bellies over yonder."

"Get down yourself, Colonel," a soldier called. "Don't be no show horse on us."

All the powers of earth and sky slammed into Oates' right arm. Spinning him around. The bone cracked loud as a shot. He staggered and cried, "Unhhh."

Staggering to an apple tree half-fallen into the ditch, he dropped to his knees. Feeling his gone-strange limb, fingering the wound in desperation. Pain hit him like a plank to the back of the head. Unbelievable. No wound he'd suffered, no beating he'd ever taken, had hurt like this. It made him want to roll on the ground and scream.

He closed his eyes and panted like a dog. Struggling to master himself.

Huge pain. Immeasurable.

Through the bloodied mess of his torn sleeve, he felt sharp edges of bone. It made him want to puke.

He knew at once that the arm was lost. The bone had been severed between elbow and shoulder, with the lower arm dangling queer and the bone above the break splintered.

Men gathered around him, more concerned for him than for themselves. Lieutenant Hardwick scurried up and Oates beckoned him closer.

"Tell Captain Wiggenton to take command. I want him to charge that hill, charge it. Right now. They'll break, they just need a push."

"Colonel—"

Oates flashed fury. "You go do as I told you, boy. . . ."

"Fetch my sword," he told another man. "Sheathe it for me. Then you go on, too."

Wiggenton got the men up finely and charged down through a ravine. Shaking with pain and rage, Oates watched them go.

Finely done, just handsome. His little 48th surged forward in a gray-brown line, uneven but bold, and swept up the other side of the low ground, storming the hill as if they numbered thousands, not weary hundreds.

Oates shouted after them wordlessly, bellowing out his pain and pride at once.

A disordered stream of blue-clad prisoners made their way toward Oates. It was a moment worth clutching for a lifetime.

And him useless. With his favored arm barely attached.

He had to grit his teeth and close his eyes. He'd thought himself a hard man, but the pain meant to defeat him, made him quake.

When he opened his eyes again, he saw Wiggenton fall, right atop that hill. The boy dropped the way a man did who died instantly, a sack of potatoes dropped off of a wagon. Other men went down, too. Madly outnumbered. With the Yankees figuring it out.

Artillery rounds began to strike around them. Grudgingly, his men began to retire. But they brought along their wounded. Despite their numbers, the Yankees only followed at a distance, unwilling to put their paws in that bag of cottonmouths.

When the pitiful remains of his regiment had gathered around him again—exhausted, feverish, panting, made-hard men—Oates told them, "You hold this ditch 'long as you can. Then fall back on the Fifteenth. Hear?"

Lieutenant Joe Hardwick, bleeding himself, said, "Yes, sir. I'll see to it." Hardwick was the only officer Oates spotted among the living.

"Just hold this ditch," Oates repeated. "Got to get this scratch of mine looked after. And I don't need help from any man."

He took himself back across the field, in the wake of the Yankee prisoners, with the 15th holding that fence line, firing sweetly into the flank of the blunted Yankee advance.

By God, we did it, Oates realized. We stopped their whole damned army.

He caught a foot in a varmint's hole and jarred his arm.

Oates howled like a gut-shot dog.

One forty p.m.
Darbytown Road, Union lines

Alfred Howe Terry said, "It's scandalous, Whitby."

Birney's aide sweated and stammered. Bullets punished the air.

Barely containing himself within the bounds permitted a gentleman, Terry spoke again, leaning toward Whitby's sweat-beleaguered face. "General Birney *must* send more supports. I've just been hit on the flank by two brigades. Two brigades, at least. Struck like a nor'easter. We're holding, but . . . oh, for God's sake, man! Here's the breakthrough everyone's pleaded for, crying for it like infants for a teat. Here it *is*, Whitby! But I can't hold this ground, let alone push any deeper. Not if I'm not reinforced. That counterattack was just the Rebs' first gambit, we know their methods. They'll be piling atop us soon."

"General Birney's trying, sir. He's asked Hancock either to make his attack on the left, or to send us reinforcements."

"Well, what's Hancock waiting for? Tell me that. The Johnnies are going to hit us with all they can muster. They must've stripped the lines in front of Second Corps, Hancock could *stroll* to Richmond."

He was being unfair, he knew. Venting his wrath on Whitby. A staff captain and dogsbody, Whitby couldn't force anyone to do anything, let alone kick Hancock in the rump. Terry always regretted his rare fits of pique, even as he indulged himself, but *this* day . . . it was the chance they'd all been waiting for. . . .

He heard more Rebel yells.

Two p.m.
Darbytown Road

It would be all right, Lee believed. Hard fighting lay ahead, but it would be all right. Tongues swollen and backs bent, soldiers clad in gray and brown surged past him, going in the proper direction now. The new arrivals eyed him with the old awe, quickening their pace when he spoke a few words to them, his presence a potent drug against their exhaustion.

How did such miracles happen?

An hour before, calamity had loomed. With Chambliss dead and young Girardey, too. Now there was hope reborn, another mercy. The Lord had not abandoned them.

A wave of Carolinians went down the slope at the double-quick, willing their ravaged bodies into battle.

It would be all right, it was going to be all right.

Lee's heart had troubled him during the day's misadventures, but the pain had faded.

Walter Taylor returned from pushing men forward. Lee sought to avoid showing favoritism between Taylor, Marshall, and Venable, his staff triumvirate, but Taylor had been with him longest and knew him best.

"Well, Colonel?" Lee asked, voice restored to confidence, even calm.

Taylor drew his mount closer. "We're awfully thin on the New Market Road now, sir."

"Yes," Lee said.

"If Hancock attacks in force . . ."

"We must repel him," Lee said. His horse snorted, shifted.

Taylor nodded. "Yes, sir."

Lee examined the younger man's tired face. "All war is risk, Colonel Taylor. And caution is failure's friend."

Somewhere below, his men cheered. Musketry crackled afresh.

Lee felt drained and old. "It's a curious business, their failures. Again and again, those people have broken our lines. On that unwelcome day at Spotsylvania. In the mine incident. Here, today. Yet, they falter in the midst of their success."

Purely military problems always interested Lee. War was mathematics with a cardinal number unknown.

"We've faltered, too," Lee continued. "Though perhaps not so often, or faced with such grand opportunities. It is as if they surprise themselves by winning. And lose confidence."

"I've always thought it a matter of control, sir," Taylor said. "On both sides. Once the men are well in it, controlling them is impossible. In terms of advanced maneuvers."

A half-smile graced Lee's lips as he thought of Mexico, of a lost world's gorgeous simplicity. "Armies have become too great for our bugles and drums, our flags, Colonel Taylor. Yours is a new and terrible age, I fear. . . ."

Lee yanked himself from his reverie.

"Come," he said. "Let us see how things progress."

"Oh," Taylor said. "Colonel Oates was wounded. Leading that charge."

"Yes," Lee said. "I've heard. I hope he's not hurt too badly."

Two p.m.
Darbytown Road

Jesus *Christ*, stop the horse."

The mount, spared him by General Field, was being led at a walk, but the movement lit man-breaking pain in Oates' shattered arm.

The orderly with the reins pulled up the horse.

"Help me down," Oates ordered.

"Best ride, sir. Looks like you've lost yourself a hog's worth of blood."

"Help me *down*, goddamn it. And go easy."

The orderly—a small man—did his best to guide him groundward while Oates did what he could to comfort his arm.

He hit the earth flat-footed. The burst of pain was spectacular.

Gasping and squeezing his eyes shut to hold back tears, he told the fellow, "You go on now. Take the horse back . . . my compliments to the general."

"He told me to stay with—"

"And I'm telling you to git."

Oates turned back into the flow of ambulatory wounded, skulkers pretending purposes, and couriers doing their best to pound the last muck into dust again.

Oates cradled his arm and walked. How could anything hurt so much? Just a paltry arm. It made no sense.

Walking was better than riding. Merely plumb miserable, rather than downright unbearable. He'd done his work, though. The 15th and 48th both had been all his again. One last time. And they'd busted a few Yankee noses.

As he'd answered General Field's questions, trying not to break out in yowls of pain, just gutting through it, Bratton's Brigade and then Benning's had rushed past, going down like Moses from the mountain to read God's law to the Golden Calf–licking Yankees.

The horizon seemed to have a mind of its own. Wouldn't hold still. Men looked like blurs and beasts. His head felt light as a butterfly, but his feet were encased in iron.

Arm. What would he do with one arm? Left one, at that? Learn to write all over again. Other things. Have to learn to balance himself one-armed over a gal. And make her like it.

He warned himself against false hope. Of saving the arm. It was gone. He knew it. Just hanging there a time longer.

His feet and legs rebelled against the journey.

For a moment, Oates went elsewhere. Thinking about plowing a woman one-armed. Swirling in rut smells remembered. An ammunition wagon almost ran him down.

So weak. He'd scorned men who complained of the pain of their wounds, men who wept over themselves. Now he knew.

Wouldn't shed one tear, though. Would not do it.

He stumbled. Pain-lightning seared him. He made an animal noise instead of words.

At least you can walk, you sorry excuse for a bearded male of the species. 'Least you can walk, you're not lying dead back there.

But he couldn't walk. He needed to rest. How far had he walked? He didn't know. One of so many, so many, on the road. . . .

Staggering into a poorly barbered orchard, he had the presence of mind to set his back against a tree trunk and ease himself down to the ground. But the pain was everything Satan could wish on a man. Made him want to tear off the shreds of his own arm, then and there.

He might have dozed. Wasn't sure. Hand on his good shoulder. A little fellow knelt by him. Georgia voiced, not Alabamian.

"I heard you groaning," he said.

How could he hear anything? With the roaring locomotives in his ears. Battle. Battle of locomotives. See the Yankees run . . .

"Drink this. You have to help me help you. It's for the pain."

Oates felt the tiny bottle against his lips. "No . . . laudanum . . ."

"Ain't laudanum. And you ain't no blushing belle. You drink this now."

Oates drank, sucking in the bitterness, and swallowed as best he could. A driblet traced his chin.

"I'm going to bind up that arm now," the little fellow said. "It's going to hurt a mite. Got to stop the blood, though."

"Who . . . are . . ."

"Assistant surgeon . . . Georgia . . ."

"What?"

"Hold still now."

An artillery shell struck nearby, insulting them with clods of dirt and grit. The assistant surgeon ran high-tail.

"Sumbitch," Oates muttered. He drifted for a time.

"That's Colonel Oates."

"Me . . . ," Oates said. But he gained lucidity.

Two members of the 15th Alabama's ambulance contingent stood before him, although there was no least sign of an ambulance. Still, it felt like the finest luck he'd had since a high-stepping filly of a girl had demonstrated her disdain for her lawful husband during a trip that had taken Oates to Montgomery and kept him there for several extra days.

Had two good arms then. What would a fine woman make of a one-armed man? Dusky Sallies wouldn't mind so much, he didn't think. Not if it was a white man took to gracing them.

"Colonel . . . we're out of everything. Litters, everything. We have to—"

"Good God!" the other man cried. "The Yankees are here!"

Oates snapped to. Clearheaded as could be now. And he saw Yankees, indeed. Hundreds of them. Disarmed and trudging rearward, guarded by a lone sergeant of his Fortykins.

"Help me up."

"You shouldn't—"

"Help me up."

Leaning on one of the men, he stepped toward the road and the parade of prisoners.

Just like to rip that arm right off, get rid of it. Hurt the pain. Take a sharp knife to it. Kill the pain . . .

"You cut me six strong Yankees out of that pack. And bring 'em here. Pick 'em from those still carrying their trappings."

The ambulance men did as told. The sergeant herding the prisoners just touched his hat and said, "Whupped 'em good for you, Cunnel."

Oates stiffened his back, his speech, his heart. "You," he told a Yankee. "Take down that blanket of yours and roll it out."

The Yankee didn't have a mind to argue. They all gawked at his arm.

Can't look any worse than it feels, Oates thought. Striving with all the gumption he still possessed to remain manly.

Fireworks of pain. A true phenomenon.

"Couple of you boys help me lay on out. Then you're going to carry me a ways."

To his surprise, the Yankees took an interest. Two of them edged the ambulance orderlies aside and, with help from a third, eased Oates down onto the blanket. The pain made him quiver like a man with malaria.

Before they helped him lie all the way flat, a Yankee knelt down and offered his canteen.

Expecting water, Oates was thrilled to find whiskey scorching his tongue and burning his throat. He took a serious draught. Best thing on the worst day of his life.

"Little more," he said, not impolitely. The Yankee held the canteen to his lips. Oates got down as much as he could. He nodded faintly, wanted to say, "Thank you," but could not get out the words.

They eased him down. Whiskey had many fine qualities, but Oates found that its usefulness against pain was overstated.

They carried him in that blanket, six Yankees superintended by two orderlies, a queer little party amid the tumult of the rescued road to Richmond. Twice, they paused. And the best Yankee who'd ever drawn breath—in Oates' opinion—gave him more whiskey.

It seemed as though they carried him for miles. Bearing him through a wilderness of misery.

At last, an ambulance came by. There was room on the floor for Oates.

That trip was another agony, a pitchfork-prodded journey down to Hell. Other men, all officers, bled on him from their litters and the bed of the wagon trickled a red stream. A dead hand fell across him. He let it be.

When the ambulance reached the field infirmary, clotted blood glued his hair to the planks beneath him.

Three p.m.
Headquarters, Barlow's division

Barlow couldn't get up. He gathered his will and tried to clench his body, but he could barely lift his head from the cot. It was even too much to roll off the bunk for the slops bucket.

He had meant to lie down for five minutes, to gather himself.

Barely able to swallow, he'd left his staff and stumbled into his tent. Without a single word to an aide or orderly. Now he lay helpless, revoltingly soiled, unable to rise or think clearly.

A few more minutes, he told himself. Just need rest. A couple of minutes.

Belle was coming. She was going to wash his feet.

Someone entered the tent without permission. Barlow was too weak to protest.

"Good Lord, Barlow," a man said.

Charlie Morgan's voice. Hancock's chief of staff. Not Belle.

For God's sake: Belle was dead. How could he have forgotten? It made him want to cry.

What did Hancock want?

"Charlie," Barlow muttered.

"You need to be in a hospital, Frank. Dear God. You can't command like this. We need to get you down to City Point."

Mustering all the strength his mind could drive into his limbs, Barlow levered himself to a sitting position, greased with his waste.

"All right," he said in a docile voice he hated bitterly. Then he added, "If you can . . . stand my stink . . . get me to my feet." He closed his eyes briefly to help the world make sense. "I won't be carried off. Help me get up."

Three thirty p.m.
Headquarters, Union Second Corps

He looked like a dying man," Morgan said, pawing sweat away.

"They'll fix him up," Hancock said, with more confidence in his voice than in his heart. The tent fly under which they stood drew insects like a corpse. Not that there weren't real corpses enough to feast on.

"He insisted on riding to the river himself. Wouldn't take an ambulance. Just rode off, with shit all over him and two terrified orderlies. I sent a rider ahead to ready a boat."

Hancock wondered if anything else could go wrong.

"I've recalled Miles," Morgan continued. "Sent a rider. I thought you would approve, sir."

Hancock smiled grimly. "If I had a choice, I'd bust you down to captain. But I don't, and you're safe. Oh, that's fine. You did the right thing. The pony-boys were just pissing on each other, more wasted effort. Miles would have been better used here today." He scratched a wicked bite behind his ear, a lump that felt big as a goiter. "Couldn't make any progress on the Heights, Lee must've called up over half his army. And Birney's breakthrough's been falling apart." Hancock sighed. "I sent him two brigades. Too little, too late." He considered the scorched landscape. The effects of the rain had vanished, leaving the earth as thirsty as before. "I hate this place, Charlie, I hate it like clap in a corporal."

Three thirty p.m.
Darbytown Road

Stand, men, stand!" Lieutenant Colonel Armstrong commanded, emulating his father's pulpit voice. It was uncanny to hear himself amid the chaos of battle: He really seemed to be his father's son. "Show them you're the bravest men on the field."

" 'Cept nobody here to see it," a soldier teased.

The men ranked nearby tittered. Samuel Chapman Armstrong didn't mind. If the men could laugh, they weren't about to break.

"They'll know, Private Washington," Armstrong said. "Those who matter will know."

"You keep a watch eye on Washington, Cunnel," another soldier kidded. "He run like a rabbit, give him the chance."

"They're coming again."

Armstrong wheeled about. He didn't feel terribly brave himself. But he put his trust in Christ and did his duty. By these good men and their cause.

"Volley by company. At fifty yards," he shouted.

The Rebs came howling and yipping through the brush, invisible at first, noisy ghosts. Then movement nudged the smoke. In an instant, dozens more forms plunged downward through the undergrowth and trees. Dozens, then hundreds.

"Steady . . . steady . . ."

Sweat and blown powder, excitement and fear. His breath quickened. Every sensation Armstrong felt seemed impossibly strong, as rich as the fruits of the tropics. Even the killing heat seemed to fill him with life.

How soft the breezes of childhood had been . . . but the storms, when they came, were ferocious.

"Fire."

Mock his Negroes as men might, none could deny that he'd taught them to shoot well. Rebs tumbled, some throwing wide their arms as if crucified. A missionary's son, come from the Kingdom of Hawaii by way of Williams College, Armstrong had set himself the goal of turning the 9th U.S. Colored Troops into the finest regiment in the army.

The Rebel host was legion, but his soldiers repulsed them again, holding their exposed position even as nearby regiments collapsed.

"Good work, men. Now fill up the first rank. Sergeants, you know what to do."

He'd taught them to shoot, and he'd taught them to read. As his father, armed with the Word of God, had brought the miracle of alphabets and books to benighted islanders. The man who could read could feel his soul expand.

Now he needed these men to hold a bit longer. With the Johnnies screeching that tribal chant of theirs, that warbling terror.

How could the Rebels fight so bravely to keep millions in bondage? How could they be so far from God—and yet invoke the Good Book for their cause? Armstrong cared little for the Union itself. He even felt the United States would have been best served by releasing the Southern states, with their pagan cruelty and their Judas-like betrayal of Jesus Christ. But slavery must not endure, and that made this war a crusade worth Christian blood.

The Lord's work lay in leading these men beside him. To help them free themselves. That was a cause worth a man's small mortal life.

As more of the Union line collapsed, the Johnnies pushed past on the left. Approaching Armstrong, Captain Meyers said in a back-of-church whisper, "Sir . . . hadn't we ought to pull back? To maintain contact?"

"We have no such orders, Captain. The Ninth will stand." He turned his attention to the ranks again. "Sergeant Devero, see that Private Tolly straightens his cap. He's not posing for the ladies."

These men, his men. Who wept to realize they could spell out the stenciling on a crate. Who read the Gospels aloud with a fervor lost by their race of abusers.

The Rebs soon tried another approach, working around his right, as well, and using the foliage to sneak up on them and snipe. Men fell, but their lines did not waver.

There was no balm in Gilead, and no protection on their right flank, either. The 9th was the end regiment, right flank of the brigade and of the division.

A color-bearer crumpled. Another man took up the flag while comrades bore the fellow struck down to the back of the second line. Instead of skulking off, the fellows who had carried him off rejoined the lines.

He wanted them all, every one of the generals and the colonels on this field, to see that his men were the equal of any white regiment.

"Steady, men."

Always "men." Never "boys."

The Rebs came screaming down a hundred yards to the regiment's left, widening their breakthrough, and the last formation beyond the 9th collapsed. White men ran in dread, as if chased by Satan himself. Even those who kept to their colors retreated in a hurry.

"Captain Curran! Companies D and F will refuse the flank."

Men shifted almost gracefully, nimble, quick, and proud. Once, a soldier on the drill field had called Armstrong a "slave-driver."

The other fellows had shushed the man, but the epithet had pierced him like a nail. Now they understood the point of his firmness.

Sharpshooters dropped more men. Men who trusted him.

Hadn't anyone the decency to order them back with the others? Did some still find satisfaction in leaving U.S. Colored Troops to perish? He'd heard the horrid tales told of the mine pit.

The refused companies fired at any Rebs who strayed too close to the regiment's left. But the right was being bloodied, without the chance to respond. The men stood their ground stoically, but soon the losses would become unbearable.

The smoke across the field faded to gossamer. Armstrong saw that they truly were alone now. A single regiment left behind to stand against a slavemongering army.

It was folly to push his demonstration too far. He did not wish to slay these men for vanity. But every minute they stood their ground commanded more respect.

He could hear Reb officers giving commands in the brush, in hidden ravines and ditches. Assembling their men to finish off his regiment.

Enough.

Armstrong strode along his line, calling, "Officers . . . prepare to withdraw . . . at a walk . . . prepare to withdraw . . . on my order . . ."

There was no laughter now, no teasing to ease the nerves. Faces were bloodless and set, as if men feared to twitch a muscle or blink.

"Regiment . . . from the right . . . by company . . . at five-pace intervals . . . *with*draw . . ."

The command wasn't strictly by the book. But only one Book mattered. The important thing was that they understood, all of them, what needed to be done.

Fearing their prize might escape, the Johnnies catcalled and their firing increased. But Armstrong's men withdrew handsomely, stepping over broken ground and fallen trees and stumps, through rifle pits and ditches, keeping their order remarkably well and stopping crisply when he wanted a volley.

"Cunnel, you git back here, too," a man called.

"Hush up," a sergeant corrected him. "That man know what he doing."

But Armstrong didn't know, that was the thing. And he didn't much like the bullets tearing past. But if he pretended to care nothing for danger, the men would bear up, too.

And they did.

A party of Rebs exploded from a swale, coming at his left companies with bayonets. A sharp brawl send the Johnnies reeling back.

Confederate artillery sought their range. Thirsty for Negro blood. Unwilling to let them escape.

"Let my people go," they'd sing in the twilight, by their fires, *"let my people go . . ."* In voices so rich with suffering, voices of such yearning, that even freedom would not meet their needs. Only the blood of Christ would quench that thirst.

Armstrong wondered if the blood of others he'd shed in battle, no matter the justice and virtue of the cause, could be forgiven. The Sermon on the Mount denied the sword.

Well, even damnation was a price he'd pay to free these men.

He got the regiment into the cover of a shot-up grove. The Rebel pestering, their persecution, fell off.

As his soldiers approached the safety of the bristling Tenth Corps lines, he made the regiment re-form and march the last yards properly, colors high. And a miracle happened.

White men in blue uniforms cheered the niggers.

Four thirty p.m.
Clarke house, Tenth Corps headquarters

Letting his subordinates rest their troops, Miles reported to Major General Birney. There was still a bit of firing, but not much.

"You look ready to bite," Birney said.

"Bad day. Again. The cavalry don't fight, they flirt with each other."

"Saith the noble officer of infantry!" Birney fingered his beard.

"Well, no one's had a good day, as far as I can tell. Except maybe Bobby Lee. We *did* break through. For all it turned out to be worth."

"I heard."

"Hancock just . . . Oh, let it go. We funked it, that's the thing. Another waste." An eyebrow rose. "You've heard about Barlow, of course?"

"Yes, sir."

"Off to City Point. Clean sheets and broth. You've got the division, Win confirmed it." Birney's mouth curled. "Really, Miles, at this rate you'll be taking over the entire Second Corps."

"Maybe not."

"Well, I've got your other brigades loafing to my rear. Hancock sent them over, but too late. Consider them released back to your division." Abruptly, his tone went from cynical to broken. "Miles, we had a *chance,* we had such a chance . . . Terry ripped a grand hole in their line. . . ."

Birney rambled on for a time about lost opportunities, but Miles couldn't think beyond Frank Barlow.

Five thirty p.m.
Field infirmary, Darbytown Road

Oates groaned as the orderlies laid him on the table. Three surgeons he knew—Hudson, Burton, and Watkins—gathered around him.

"Sorry to see this day," Burton said.

"Reckon I'm a mite sorrier," Oates told him. What little effect the canteen of whiskey had had on him had worn off, chased by the pain.

"Colonel Oates . . . ," Hudson said, voice cautious, as if Oates might rise from the table and knock him down, "we'll want to administer chloroform . . ."

"The thing is," Burton jumped back in, "we need to look inside the wound. While you're under and holding still. I won't say the outlook's good, but we won't really know until . . . The point is, would you like us to bring you back from under the chloroform? To decide what we should do? Before we proceed?"

Oates realized he was occupying three surgeons. While the wounded covered an acre outside the farmhouse.

"Just do what you deem best, gentlemen. I have every confidence in you."

Now give me the damned chloroform, Oates thought. He'd never had the drug, had bitten a leather strap and suffered through surgery in the past. But he welcomed it now, the prospect of pain subdued, all thoughts of manly suffering abandoned.

Nothing had ever hurt this bad. It was an authentically new experience and one Oates would have been downright pleased to miss.

"Do what you have to do," Oates said. "Just get on with it."

Hudson waved to an orderly, who approached with a brown bottle and a handkerchief.

Oates awoke at sunset, propped under a tree. He'd just climbed out of a nightmare. There had been no pain, yet he'd been aware of them sawing off his arm, had heard the scrape of the blade and sensed a dulled wrenching.

Old Jimmy Morris sat beside him now, hale and whole and weeping. Old Jimmy and he went back to their first company. Oates had moved on, Jimmy hadn't.

"What're . . . you . . ."

"You're awake! Oh, praise the Lord!"

"Had to wake sometime." His head still had a swirl to it, though. "Jimmy, you're bawling like a gal left at the altar."

"Didn't know if'n you—" He stopped himself.

"If I'd die? I'm a sight harder to kill." His arm hurt dully, but the pain behind his forehead grew knife-sharp. He figured the pains would swap places when they were ready.

"Colonel . . ."

"Might as well start calling me 'William' again. I do suspect my colonel-ing days may be over."

Around them, men moaned, dream-spoke, gargled death.

"Anything I can do, sir . . ."

Why was it that his head felt near to exploding and his arm—the place where his arm had been, where pain had held such unchallenged dominion—just felt like someone had given him a beating, no more than that?

"There *is* something. Go on in to Doc Hudson. Catch him between his cutting, don't interrupt him. Tell him I'd like a big, fine glass of whiskey, if he can spare it. Settle this head of mine."

Relieved to be in action, Jimmy went off. Oates closed his eyes, then opened them again. A little afraid. Something about that chloroform . . . he suspected death might not be too dissimilar, an endless, cloudy nightmare.

He didn't bother to shoo off the fly that teased him. Couldn't be bothered. He did feel properly whipped, heat-burdened and much reduced. Literally reduced, by the volume and weight of one arm. Yet . . . the twilight had a beauty to it that would not be denied, a sky the color of mackerel, crowned with purple.

Going to find out what it was to be a one-armed man. Bitter thought. Better than dying, but hard to say how much.

Ugly thing for a woman to see, a man's stump. Maybe have to keep his shirt on, hide it.

Jimmy returned with a disappointingly stingy dose of whiskey. Oates reached for it with the ghost of a hand. It was queer, unsettling. He'd thought he'd reached out, even though the arm was gone.

"Give it here," he said, accepting the glass in his left hand. "Doc Hudson does pour meager."

He drank gratefully.

After relishing the glorious burn, he said, "Jimmy? There's something else. I recall you write a fair hand. Set down a letter for me? To my mother and father. Fool things happen. . . ."

"Surely, Colonel. But I have to shift you. You're propped up on my knapsack."

As the two of them fussed, an orderly in a blood-mottled coat approached. He bore a wretched gift.

"Colonel Oates? This here's your arm. Doc Hudson said to ask you what you want done with it."

Staring at the ravaged limb, Oates seethed. "I don't give a good goddamn. Ain't no service to me."

But Jimmy Morris said, "Let me bury it, Colonel. He can help. We'll bury it right the other side of this tree, won't take us long."

"Won't make *me* feel better," Oates grumbled, rich with spite.

"Make me feel better, though," Jimmy insisted.

Oates looked away.

Ten p.m.
City Point

Got yourself whipped again, Genr'l?" Grant's manservant asked.

Grant smiled gently. "Took some whipping, did some whipping."

Brushing Grant's worn jacket, Bill went on, "I declare, times I think you been whipped more often than black folks sold downriver. That Genr'l Lee, he sure your cross to bear."

"And I suspect I'm his. Hand me some cigars."

"The good cigars? Or the really good cigars?"

"I figure I'll smoke what you haven't smoked up yourself."

Out on the river, the whistles and horns were unceasing. The damage from the blast had been made good in days. Grant heard familiar voices in the new dark, too low to be deciphered. Camp talk, not staff talk. He could tell that much by the tone.

After fussing with multiple locks, a chest, and a litter of boxes, Bill brought him a fistful of stogies.

"Miss Julia, when she come, bound to object. You smokes so many."

"I won't smoke as much when she's here. Won't need to."

But Bill wasn't done with the evening's commentary. "That Genr'l Lee now. I bet he cuss you all the day and night."

"Then you guess wrong. General Lee disdains immodest language."

"Meaning he don't cuss?"

"Never. Or so I'm told."

"Well, that makes two born deacons, you and him." Bill set down his brush and brightened, playing his role as long agreed between them. "Maybe that there the problem, why you comes short of Richmond all the time. Maybe you the wrong man for the job, maybe turn Genr'l Rawlins loose on the feller. Or that devil-man Sheridan. Cuss him right to death, have him all crying, 'Please, Genr'l Grant, I surrenders. Jus' make him stop that bad-talk.'"

"Sheridan's quite fond of you, you know. He thinks you're quite the philosopher."

Bill tut-tutted. "That little fellow mostly fond of hisself."

Grant laughed. "You don't get to be a general by doing yourself down."

By the light of a lamp struck by suicidal moths, Bill looked at him doubtfully. "Miss Julia always say how you do yourself down something terrible. Wonder how you ever got where you got to."

"I'm slower about some things than my wife prefers."

"Scare me right to death, that woman do."

"Her bark's worse than her bite."

"Well, I don't care for neither. I jus' stays on her good side." Bill scowled, features maroon and hands deep brown in the lamp-light.

Grant let the conversation drop, although he enjoyed his bantering with Bill. Many a day, it was his only pleasure.

Well, this day had not gone as well as he'd hoped, or as badly as it might have. The longed-for breakthrough had evaporated, but the range of prisoners taken made it clear that Lee had rushed every man he could up from Petersburg. And that made it all worthwhile.

That day, he'd written to Lincoln, Washburne, Halleck, Sherman, and Sheridan, reassuring each on one point or another. But the most important message had been to George Meade, directing him to ready Warren's Fifth Corps for a raid on the Weldon Railroad west of Petersburg, one of the last two rail links left to Lee. With Lee's army concentrated north of the James, something might be accomplished to the west. Tear up some track, at least.

Yes, there had been disappointments. There would be more. If there was one thing Ulysses S. Grant understood, it was disappointment. But he had learned this one thing: how to wage war. What he needed to do was to keep his grip on Lee's throat while Sherman and Sheridan cut the South to ribbons.

That was what he needed to do, and Grant intended to do it.

PART
III

THE RAILROAD

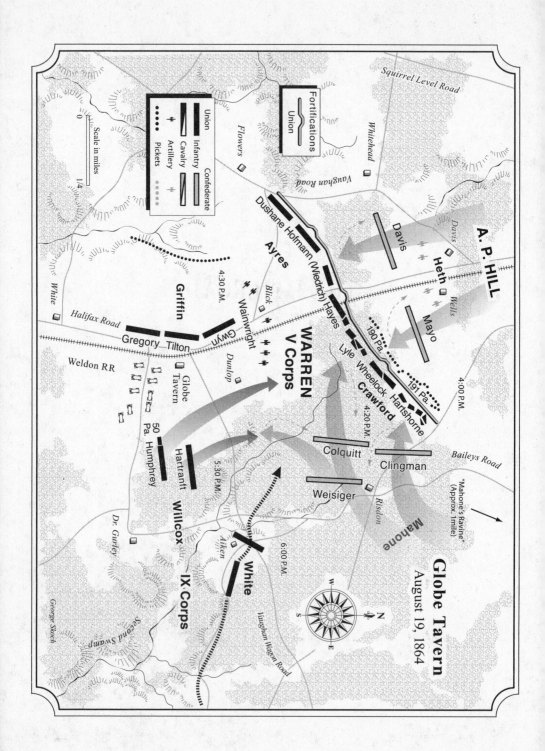

Globe Tavern
August 19, 1864

Squirrel Level Road

A. P. HILL

Vaughan Road

Whitehead

Davis

Davis

Heth

Wells

Mayo

4:00 P.M.

Baileys Road

"Mahone's Ravine" (Approx. 1mile)

Flowers

Fortifications
Union

Scale in miles
0   1/4

Union
Confederate
Infantry
Cavalry
Artillery
Pickets

Dushane

Hofmann (Wiedrich)

Hayes

Ayres

Griffin

4:30 P.M.

Blick

White

Halifax Road

Gregory Tilton

Wainwright

Gwyn

WARREN
V Corps

190 Pa.

Lyle Wheelock Hartshorne

Crawford

191 Pa.

4:20 P.M.

Weldon RR

Dunlop

Globe
Tavern

Colquitt

Clingman

50
Pa.
Humphrey

Hartranft

5:30 P.M.

Weisiger

Risdon

Mahone

Willcox

IX Corps

Dr. Gurley

Aiken

White

6:00 P.M.

Vaughan Road

George Shook

Second Swamp

Vaughan Wyson Road

EIGHT

Eight a.m., August 19, 1864
Globe Tavern

M ackerel?"

The regiment's commissary sergeant tossed another box of fish from the wagon. Rain slapped down. Shoes sank into the mud.

"You're issuing salted mackerel? Now?" Lieutenant Brown asked, bewildered at this fresh stupidity. Every time a man thought he'd seen the worst of the army's ways, he got himself surprised again.

"You get what I get. I don't like it none, neither." The sergeant hefted another crate, its top splintered off by his helper. "Come and get it, boys."

"Mackerel's only right," Sergeant Eckert allowed. "Been all but swimming these two days."

The men were disgusted and Brown was sour, but the distribution continued. The drenched soldiers slogged past, taking their rations. Few men liked the mackerel even when there was time to soak it and draw off some salt. Here, in the pelting rain and porridge of mud, when the Rebs might pop out of the gloom for spite, it was all but beyond the powers of Man to prepare the dry-packed fish and force it down.

Nothing to be done. Brown trailed his grumbling company back to the stretch of mud it had been allotted, amid the sodden remnants of the regiment. Across a field, a stripped rail bed ran past an abandoned building, its old paint yellow as jaundice. The open tract surrounding the ruin looked to be a square mile, fringed with woodlands and the usual undergrowth. The open plain was busy with artillerymen building embrasures for their guns, bogged ambulances and supply wagons, clots of bedraggled soldiers, mounted couriers splashing mud, and, as always, officers interfering with everyone's doings.

Under First Sergeant Losch's supervision, the company's veterans built cooking fires, working smoky miracles, while new men scavenged more wet wood, gleaning scraps passed over by previous tenants.

"*Viel Rauch,*" Losch snorted, "*doch keine Flammen. Gib Platz und schau mal, Jungs.*"

Yes, Brown agreed sourly, plenty of smoke, no fire. Well, maybe the rain would keep the Rebs away. But probably not. Didn't take a general to figure out that the Johnnies wouldn't take kindly to having their railroad snatched. Fifth Corps had grabbed the line the day before, just went out and took it and squatted down on it. Now the Ninth Corps had to lend a hand to back the claim. In weather that put a man in mind of Noah. Wasn't a fellow in the company who wasn't wet all through, and some were sickening. As for Brown himself, his thighs were raw on the inside, red as butchered beef, and his manly parts were annoyed.

"Can't cook this up nohow," Adam Burket complained. He stood up, grinned, and tossed a slab of mackerel into a puddle. "See if *that* gets rid of the damned salt."

Brown was about to call Burket to order. The men had to eat, to get something down their gullets, exhausted and hungry as every one of them was. But before he could act, a half dozen others tossed their fish into the brown water, too. Then everyone did. Laughing.

"Like fishing, only backwards," Billy Tyson said.

Brown had to let it go.

Sergeant Hill stepped close. "I don't like this, Lieutenant."

"Me, either, Henry," Brown agreed. "Salt-fish. Now, of all times."

"Not the fish," his old comrade corrected him. Hill gestured across the field to the line of trees.

Ten a.m., August 19
Headquarters of Lieutenant General A. P. Hill

At the first taste of the coffee, Beauregard made a face that deplored the decline of civilization. "We need a *major* victory over the Yankees," he declared. "Replenish our coffee holdings."

"Trifle weak," Hill admitted.

Boots squeaking, Beauregard walked to a map spread over a table. Rain smacked the roof of the house.

"Show me again."

The muffled commotion of staff work continued around them, though Beauregard was sure all ears were open. Gaunt and somber, Hill traced a finger over the heavy paper. "The ravine begins a few yards from Mahone's headquarters. Deep enough to hide a goodly force and wide enough for regimental columns. If something of a jungle. Runs behind the right flank of their Fifth Corps, just where they've left us a gap. Nigh on perfect."

"Warren hasn't been reinforced?" Beauregard asked skeptically. "You're certain?"

"Not that we've seen."

"Hard to see much in this weather. Common sense . . ."

"Had my scouts out. All night long and this morning. Didn't spot any movement." Hill tapped a finger east of the captive rail line, near the old tavern. "Mahone knows that ground. Better than any other man in this army. Surveyed every inch of it, back in his railroad days. And he doesn't mind telling you."

Beauregard smiled at the thought of Billy Mahone. Queer little fellow. A few degrees short of a gentleman, by Louisiana standards. Hellcat fighter, though.

"He knows that ravine, he used it before," Hill continued. "Back in June, when we gave Hancock a thrashing. Yankees still have no idea it's there, haven't figured it out. Not a picket near it."

Despite a heavy greasing, Beauregard's boots had not kept out the wet, and his stockings bunched. Dreadful weather, dreadful times. And that wretched excuse for coffee . . . a man did miss New Orleans.

Yankees were drinking coffee down there now.

"And then, *cher Général*?" Beauregard asked.

"Mahone strikes their flank with three brigades. He'll want more, of course, but—"

"There are no more," Beauregard finished the sentence.

"Soon as he hears the firing kick up from Mahone, Heth advances his division, right down the railroad line, straight for Globe Tavern. Heth hits them in front, once Mahone's called their attention to the rear. We catch them in a vise."

"*If* Mahone's successful." Beauregard rubbed a hand over his forehead. "I do wish we could've pushed them off the line yesterday. Before they entrenched."

"We tried."

"I know."

"Couldn't muster the force, sir. Not in time. Did what we could."

Beauregard nodded. "Mahone's composition?"

"Virginia brigade from his own division, all he's got left. Rest are still loaned out north of the James. I'm giving him Colquitt and Clingman from Hoke, best I can do." Hill took a turn at smiling. Powell Hill's smiles always looked pained. Beauregard assumed it had to do with the Virginian's private affliction, the rotten fruit of a youthful indiscretion.

"Little Billy kicked," Hill went on. "Insisting men fight best under their own generals, men they know. He thinks Bob Hoke should lead the flank attack. Given that two of the brigades going in are his."

"Doesn't sound like Mahone. Billy likes a scrap."

Hill shook his head. "I never can predict what that man will come up with before a fight. Once he's in it, though . . ."

"Well, *I* want Mahone in command. So that's settled." Beauregard crossed his arms in front of his chest, his carefully studied posture of contemplation. "How rich do you think he really is, Powell? Pastry cook he keeps makes the finest *gateaux* this side of the Quarter." He shook his head. "And that cow . . ."

"Rich enough, I'd wager. All those railroad men are Croesus incarnate."

Beauregard smiled again, with a tinge of rue. "Wish I'd invested in railroad shares myself. Rather than land, which has the unpleasant habit of just sitting there. *Je regrette . . .*" He waved away the past with considered elegance.

"Wish I'd had the *money* to invest," Hill said. "When's General Lee expected back?"

"Uncertain. Hancock's still rumbling up there. And President Davis has been . . . difficult. Regarding the safety of Richmond." He sighed. "Now this. Lose the Weldon and we only have the South Side. Hard to supply this army with one railway."

Beauregard caught a hint of condescension in his tone and arrested it promptly. Powell Hill was one of those impossibly proud Virginians, sensitive to the mere ghost of a slight. Not that any Virginian ever proved humble, in Beauregard's view. Pride was a powerful sentiment that had to be wrapped in grace—a quality only Lee and some few from the Old Dominion possessed. Came naturally to well-bred Louisianans, of course.

"But you know all that, Hill," Beauregard concluded. "Tell Mahone and Heth to go ahead." He paused, tightening his eyes, his voice, his heart. "Teach the Yankees a lesson they're apt to remember."

Eleven a.m.
Globe Tavern

Sitting astride his horse in the steady rain, Major General Gouverneur K. Warren cataloged his frustrations with his superiors. He'd taken the railroad the day before. Marched out in the rain and took it, succeeding where the army had failed in June. The

Confederates had tried, immediately, to retake it. And he'd driven them off. They'd try again today, even harder, and he'd see that they failed again. *He* knew what he was doing.

But did anyone *else* know what they were doing? Grant, Meade, even Humphreys—the latter rather a disappointment at times—had to be led to see sense. Ordered to raid the railroad and tear up the tracks, Warren had seized a solid position astride the line and promptly begun the work of destruction with all of his engineer's diligence. Days of rain had soaked the ties, making them hard to burn, but he'd managed that, too, then heated the rails and bent them. Meade, cranky and sneezing, had finally seen that a mere raid counted for little. The railroad had to be *held*.

Despite early scolds that the Fifth Corps would have to go it alone, Meade had belatedly promised more support. At Humph's urging, Warren suspected. He remembered Humphreys as a stern but benevolent captain helping a striving lieutenant make his way in the peacetime Army. Now the situation was reversed. Humphreys might be taught a thing or two. . . .

Grant had come around as well, only to make a muck of things in his uniquely benighted way. Meade, at least, had the discipline and mind of an engineer to balance his outbursts. But Grant? The fellow understood no more of tactics than a child. His order to push out toward the Rebel lines as far as possible and defend those forward positions put half Warren's men in a woodland so thick with brush they could barely move, while the other half were exposed for all to see.

Had Warren had his way, he believed he could have made his position impregnable. The lines of fire from the tavern across that open tract were perfect for Wainwright's guns. But too many of the troops had been forced to occupy ground the artillery couldn't support. And Wainwright could hardly roll his guns into the undergrowth.

A rivulet of water found its way between Warren's hat brim and his rain cape.

Nor did he think much of the promised reinforcements. Burnside was gone, good riddance, but Parke had yet to prove himself in his stead. And the Ninth Corps was still the Ninth Corps, no one's notion of reliability, appearing on the field in bits and pieces. Warren had chosen to hold the new arrivals in reserve, rather than send them up to relieve his own troops, weary as his splendid fellows were. Couldn't have the Ninth Corps breaking at some critical moment. His Fifth Corps would have to see to any real fighting.

He was surprised at the Rebs' tardiness. He'd expected them to attack early in the morning.

Perhaps the rain had addled their plans, as well? Lord knew, the Ninth Corps was barely straggling in, mud-caked and griping, with White's division nowhere to be seen.

At least Ledlie was gone. Ledlie and Burnside both. Had it been left to him, though, Warren would have swept out even more officers.

He turned to his aide and brother-in-law, Wash Roebling. If not a military man by profession, the major at least was a fellow engineer from a bridge-building family, with handsome prospects should he survive the war. Warren's sister, Emily, had been well served by the match, although the romance had rather startled Warren. But he'd married his own beloved Emily, his Baltimore belle, on the eve of Gettysburg. Gain an Emily, lose an Emily. Fair enough, he supposed.

"Roebling, I'm uneasy about the right. I'm not convinced Crawford understands where I want that skirmish line. He can be a bit thick." Crawford, a Pennsylvanian, had been a surgeon in the prewar Army, which Warren hardly viewed as a recommendation.

"I've seen to it myself," Roebling said. "His skirmish line's tied in with the rest of the army."

"It's not enough to be 'tied in.' Crawford has to get the geometry right, or that flank's an open door."

"It's been explained to him, sir."

Warren shook his head. "I'd countermarch a Ninth Corps division over to the flank, if I thought one trustworthy. I do not like that gap, Roebling. And Meade's no help. Or Humphreys. . . ." He felt sweat pooling under his rubber cape. "Damnable rain . . . I hope the men are keeping their cartridges dry."

"I'm sure they're trying, sir."

"Well, off with you. Press the rest of the Ninth Corps to stop dawdling and come up. They're better than nothing. Find White, wherever he's lolling, and give him a push."

Roebling saluted and clopped off, going slowly at first to avoid flinging mud. Warren decided to ride to his left to visit Charlie Griffin, the one subordinate he largely trusted. Griffin had been charged with refusing the corps' left flank with his division, in case the Confederates tried a deep envelopment. Charlie was an old soldier and something of a bear, but a positive Turk in a fight.

Making his way along, with his corps flag and national colors sodden rags, Warren marked the wretched look of his reinforcements again: The Ninth Corps seemed composed more of mud than of men. Of course, the roads were difficult, the wet earth of Virginia all but bottomless, but the more a man looked like a soldier, the more the fellow felt like one.

These blue-coated vagabonds looked a sorry lot, shoulders hunched around their dreary fires.

Unprompted, he thought of the Black Hills, their beauty austere and forbidding, and the wary, doomed Sioux. Ah, how hard they'd tried to keep him out, the scrofulous lot of them. But he'd bluffed them cold without firing a shot, and he'd mapped their sacred lands because they had to be mapped. Those had been exhilarating days, a time of singular purpose and clean accomplishment. Unlike all this.

A courier found him before he reached Griffin's entrenchments.

Saluting, the spattered fellow said, "General Meade's compliments, sir. He'll inspect the position at noon."

No, he won't, Warren thought. He'll be late by an hour, at least. With the roads churned into morasses. Even the quick-footed Johnnies were slow today.

"How's the general's cold?" Warren asked.

"I wouldn't know, sir. Will there be a reply?" The man's horse nickered.

"I think not."

Deciding to show his benevolence, Warren added, "If you're hungry, see one of the commissary officers. I believe the men are enjoying a treat of mackerel."

Twelve forty p.m.
Mahone's Ravine

Just keep moving," Davey Weisiger chided his struggling soldiers. "I'll have no slackers. Get along, keep moving."

Hard to keep up spirits in the rain, Mahone understood. But he could count on Weisiger and his Virginians. As for Colquitt and Clingman, he'd have to see. Their brigades had reputations as good scrappers, but Billy Mahone would have liked to have his own Alabamians and Georgians for this fight—not least to redeem their reputations after his soldiers had been misused by others in front of Richmond. He just wished everybody, including Robert E. Lee, would keep their hands off his men.

Weisiger forced his way through rain-whipped brambles to Mahone's side.

"Slow going," Weisiger said.

"Yankees will still be there," Mahone told him.

Around them, men complained but kept their voices low.

The going was severe, Mahone had to allow. The undergrowth in the ravine had outdone itself since he'd led men through it in June, and the tangles had been sufficiently wicked then.

The rain beat down harder. No thunder or lightning, though. Just an old Virginia downpour, Nature's vengeance on those who'd despoiled her chastity. He'd taken her on in swamps and on dry land, and he'd put her flat on her back. Now she was having her petty revenge of eye-slapping squalls and thorns to leave a fine uniform in tatters.

Well, he was going to bend her to his will, make her do service. If he knew the Yankees, Nature's pranks would go much harder on them, keep their heads down low. Yankees just never saw that men don't rust.

Mahone did like his comforts and liked to ride. Enjoyed the way a saddle gave him stature. But this was a day to go afoot, to march along with his men. Show them what a tough-made man could do. Aides could bring on the horses after the soldiers had trampled a path.

Men had to think he was proof against common feelings, that was the thing. They *wanted* to believe their leaders were forged by a higher order of blacksmith and out of different iron. So Mahone bluffed shamelessly, another one of his duties. Only frailty he couldn't hide was the acid that plagued his belly, but that was only a trouble to himself.

The men snatched wild berries as they went, gobbling them down. Lucky devils. He could only digest berries baked in a sugar cake, sometimes in a pie. With a glass of milk for the soothing. Wife teased him to a fret about his diet, calling him her "little ninny baby" to get his temper up. Otelia liked a man fiery and provoked.

He loved that woman like a bear loved a dripping honeycomb, and the stings just went along with her. When she got too obstreperous, he'd put her over his knee and spank her rump. She'd laugh like a brazen thing and grow accommodating.

Shoving a clot of branches out of the way, Davey Weisiger asked, "Have much to do with building the Weldon, sir?"

Mahone just about spit. "Not likely. Or it would've been built a sight better. Damn fools had nothing but a straight line to survey and lay, and they couldn't do that right. Bought unseasoned ties and rails a dog could chew." It made Mahone angry to ponder the business: He hated shoddy work. But he added, "Going to take it back, though. Poor-built or not. Going to do as much killing as it takes."

A thorn scratched his cheek and drew blood. That just made him madder.

Two p.m.
Globe Tavern

Lieutenant Colonel Theodore Lyman knelt on the rain-beaten roof, striving not to slip and envious of the poise of the upright signalmen. Volunteer aide to General Meade, promising scientist, man of wealth, and eternal captive to his curiosity, whether regarding the quirks of starfish or the Boston gossip, Lyman found army culture as exotic as the Echinodermata he'd researched under the peerless Professor Agassiz. Indeed, the Army of the Potomac seemed able to regenerate itself as readily as Asteroidea renewed its limbs. Both were splendid oddities.

Speaking of odd, he'd been thinking about Frank Barlow, his Harvard classmate. Barlow was back at City Point, frightfully ill, according to Ned Dalton. And that atop the tragedy with his wife. Lyman could sense all too sharply the blow such a loss might strike a man. If he were to lose Mimi . . .

Down in the mud, before the ruined tavern, an artillery sergeant bellowed at his charges, his profanity a wonder of locution. The cannoneers struggled to free a caisson from a trough of mire. When the vehicle resisted, the sergeant put his own shoulder to a muddy wheel—rather to his credit, Lyman thought. Wet and sullen, infantrymen looked on, uninterested in offering assistance.

Lyman did wish Barlow well, although he never could say why he liked the fellow. Frank was the awkward sort old breeding sometimes produced by accident, impossible to befriend in a civilized sense. At Harvard, Barlow had been respected, even somewhat feared, but little liked. Men sought his company, only to be rebuffed. It was as if an antimagnetic ring surrounded the man.

Lyman remembered him back in June, during the march to Petersburg: Barlow perched up in a tree, picking cherries and hailing his classmate to join him, a boy of nearly thirty years granted godlike powers over a multitude.

Barlow was quite the natural soldier, of course. Everyone

thought so. Almost everyone. Jealousy abounded in the army, and Frank did have his critics. But they were generally the baser sort.

As for himself, he cringed a bit when Frank turned that smirk toward him, communicating silently, "You're only playing, Teddy, and late to the game."

Ever the plunger, Barlow had joined the war at the beginning, while he and Mimi had only returned from Europe the year before, after Gettysburg, laden with paintings bought in Rome and a bit ashamed of themselves. And Barlow had made his way by merit, while his own status as aide-de-camp and his rank were a gent's allowances, the first a courtesy of grand old Meade, whom he had befriended in Florida, where the Philadelphian had been erecting lighthouses, and the latter courtesy of the governor, who was ever a good egg with the better families—the fellow simply groveled before the Lowells. Thus, Teddy Lyman refrained from critiquing military matters to the professionals, saving his thoughts for his diary and letters home.

Which was why he had not said a word to Meade or Warren or anyone about the funny gap on the right flank: He didn't want to seem asinine or boorish. Yet, what he had seen as he trotted about on errands from Meade and Humphreys nagged him more than a bit. He'd had to scramble up to the roof to escape the parleying generals below, just to avoid saying something untoward.

He'd been told that Humphreys, who could be a bit of an ogre, had remarked, "Lyman may be bald up top, but he has a brain underneath." A single foolish remark might dissolve that opinion.

He wasn't a courageous fellow, he didn't think. It had even unnerved him to clamber over the beams where floorboards were missing, and his perch on the roof left him queasy. So it hardly seemed proper to fault Warren's dispositions. And Warren's recent tiff with Meade had been ugly. He didn't want to start that up again.

Instead, Lyman studied the scene before him, a phenomenon

reminiscent of an ant colony, as a muddle of Fifth and Ninth Corps units engaged in that ordered confusion unique to an army. Charlie Wainwright's artillery had settled nicely into its embrasures, commanding a field a bit larger than Boston Commons, and Griffin's division looked to have the left flank well secured. Ninth Corps was arriving, bit by bit.

No doubt things would be fine. Warren was capable, if eager to put himself forward. A New Yorker whose breeding came of the artisan class and a "West Point gentleman," Warren was the sort welcomed on the north side of Beacon Hill, now that the better families were leaving, but who'd meet closed doors if he sought entrée on the south side. Still, whatever Warren's social position, Lyman hardly dared second-guess a veteran corps commander.

It simply wasn't done. Not by an amateur and supernumerary.

And yet . . . that right flank gnawed him. Earlier, he'd ridden to Ju White's headquarters in search of Potter and had found the two Ninth Corps division commanders together and ready to march to Warren's support as soon as Willcox's soldiers cleared the road. Message delivered and mission fulfilled, he'd cut across the fields to catch up with Meade, passing behind a skirmish line that seemed not only badly placed, but dangerously thin—the only connection between Warren's corps and the army's fortified line. The generals seemed untroubled, but Lyman feared that a nasty gap lay open—a gap of just the sort the Confederates fancied.

Down below, the caisson lurched from the mire, squirting mud and chased by still more curses. The weather really was beastly. Hot and dry, then wet and hot. Poor Meade had a cold so severe the old fellow could only hear when you shouted at him. Indeed, Lyman heard fond shouting down below, where a covey of generals and colonels had taken refuge.

Teddy Lyman felt yet another impulse to descend and warn them about that feeble skirmish line, that all-but-naked flank. But a fellow mustn't become a pest or make himself an ass.

Barlow's braying laugh rang in his memory.

Four p.m.
Fifth Corps right flank

Mahone wrung the water from his long beard. Look like a damn billygoat, he figured. Nothing for it. Did like to look his best on a battlefield, though.

Three brigadiers stood before him, rain-smacked.

"Look here," Mahone said. "Damned fools let us in, and they'll have a peck of trouble getting us out." He'd been nicely surprised, if not astonished, at the scanty nature of the Yankee picket line. Couldn't even call it a line, just soggy boys left cowering under trees. Swept right over them, with only one or two Federals getting off shots, their powder soaked and not even up to a fizzle when their caps sparked.

"What do you want us to do with those Indiana boys?" Colquitt asked.

Mahone went sour-mouthed. "Had rope, I'd just tie 'em up and leave 'em. Hate to lose a single rifle running them. Tell you what. Pick out the two worst soldiers you got. Should be plenty to herd those boys, they aren't in a fighting mood."

Colquitt nodded.

"Listen now," Mahone told them. "Tell you how we're going to do this, gentlemen. General Clingman, you'll advance on the right." He gestured with both hands. "Want you facing just this way. Understand?"

The old politician turned general nodded.

"Just that way," Mahone repeated. "And you keep going that way. Going to be confusing in the brush, but do your best to keep your bearings and drive them." He turned to Colquitt, another politician on whom rank had fallen. Pointing out his attack position, Mahone went on, "You're on the left, General. You'll align on Clingman's Brigade and guide on his left initially."

He regarded both men, judging each rain-flinch, each tic. "General Colquitt, you're going to bust out of those trees first, the way that grove runs. You'll see the old tavern ahead, tad to your left. Keep right of it and sweep across the rail line, take their left flank in the rear. General Clingman will be in the woods the while, so you may outdistance him once you reach open ground. As long as you're driving the Yankees, that's all right."

The rain grew louder, as if excited.

"General Weisiger, you'll follow in reserve, moving by column of regiments. We'll see how things develop, I'll be near you." He met each man's eyes in turn. "I don't want any slowing just because we roust up more pickets. Run right over them. We need to come up on their main line fast and roll it up, before they can get their hands out of their drawers. Surprise has to step in for numbers, so no early volleys. Hold off until you're sure it'll make a difference."

"If the rifles will even fire," Colquitt said. "This rain . . ."

"That's why the Good Lord made the bayonet. Now . . . General Heth will move as soon as we hit their main position. There'll be plenty of firing then, wet cartridges or not, and that's his signal. We'll be in their rear, he'll hit them head-on. Crack 'em open like a dried-up walnut."

Clingman, who'd been a senator once and seemed to retain his fondness for oration, shook an abundance of water from his hat.

"Well enough, sir," Clingman said. "Well enough. I do expect a proud day for North Carolina." He cleared his throat, the sound announcing: I got something for all of you to pay heed to now, so listen, 'cause I been a senator. "Given that we're in between their old lines and the new, we may come in behind them well enough . . . but it strikes me they might do the same to us shortly thereafter. If they've got reinforcements on the way. It could prove an embarrassment, sir. Were they to take *us* in the rear while we were engaged."

"General," Mahone told him, "that's my lookout. Your duty's in front. Now get your men formed quick, there's work to be done."

Four twenty p.m.
Union Fifth Corps lines

Brigadier General Samuel Wylie Crawford worked his way forward through the brush, alerted by a sprinkling of rifle fire off to the right. Didn't sound like much of a scrap, but he wasn't taking chances. The position assigned him was awkward, much of it stretching through woods so dense he had almost stumbled beyond his own forward line.

Rain cascaded from punished trees, and long thorns scratched like cats.

Followed by a party from his staff, Crawford scraped through the brush behind Lyle's brigade. Things looked to be in reasonable order, given the weather. Making his way on toward Coulter's line, he still heard bursts of firing, but the spark-up seemed to be easing. Probably skirmishers seeing spooks, he decided. Or straying pickets.

If Coulter hadn't gone sick . . .

In command of the brigade in Coulter's absence, Colonel Wheelock was a solid officer, but a brigade was a different beast from a single regiment. Crawford had questions for Wheelock, the military equivalent of an ear pressed to a suspected consumptive's back. Then he'd see to Hartshorne and that skirmish line.

Thrashing along, he passed men hunkered down, wet through, and resigned. He didn't need his medical training to tell him that the sick list was going to swell and that he'd lose good men to rotten feet. Strange life, his had been. He wondered at it still. A U.S. Army surgeon trained at the University of Pennsylvania— quite a rarity—he had spent his dusty outpost years mastering every ailment known to the frontier, clap to cholera, only to find himself in charge of a battery at Fort Sumter as South Carolina seceded. Then he'd become an infantry officer, with a better record than most in the recent bloodbaths. What might be next?

Crawford pressed on, with aides and orderlies struggling to keep up. The veterans on the line wore disgusted looks, but they took good care of their rifles.

The firing picked up again. It sounded closer.

A running soldier almost crashed into Crawford. As the fellow recoiled, his eyes flashed dread.

"What in the . . ."

That quick, the man was gone.

A few other skedaddlers crashed through the undergrowth.

Slapping brambles out of his way with his fists, Crawford increased his pace to a stumbling trot. How in the devil was he supposed to command a division he couldn't even see? What was going on?

More men bolted past. A winded captain found him.

"General . . . Rebs . . . thousands . . ."

"Stand up straight when you talk to me."

Flushed, the fellow bucked up his spine. "The One Ninetieth Pennsylvania . . . and the One Ninety-first . . ."

"What about the Pennsylvanians?"

"Surrendered. All of them . . . all . . ."

"Captain, consider yourself under arrest. And if you spread any more panic, you'll face a court-martial. For cowardice."

The boy didn't look as though he understood.

"Damn you," Crawford said, rushing on.

There was more firing now. Somewhere out in the bush. But it seemed to be moving away. Then another racket flared nearby. The burdened air played tricks.

More men ran past, scampering like rabbits. Many had thrown down their weapons. His aides couldn't stop a one of them.

Rebel yells. Ungodly close.

He stopped and waved up an aide. "Dash ahead. Find Wheelock. Tell him to leave the works by the left flank. He's to reestablish his line facing east. *Go.*"

Artillery shells began to splinter treetops. The shot patterns made no sense. It seemed as though both sides were shelling his soldiers, with as many or more rounds coming from Charlie Wainwright's guns in the rear.

How were the men supposed to hold up under that? Who on earth had given the order to fire?

He turned to summon another aide and found himself facing a band of delighted Confederates.

"Got us a general, ain't that the cake and the pie?"

A shell burst in the trees, flinch close.

"No tomfoolery from y'all. Jes' drop your belts and sidearms and go thataway. Plenty of company waiting. Hendricks, see them on their way a piece."

Itching to continue their attack, the Rebs looked to their sergeant. He paused to ask, "Where's your flags? You're a general. I want your damned flags, Yank."

"If you can find them, take them." He'd left them behind. They only hampered movement in the undergrowth.

"I'll do just that," the Reb assured him. "Come on, boys."

Larking children, they strode on with a yip.

"You git on now," the guard told Crawford and his officers. The Johnny lowered his rifle to his waist, pointing it at one belly, then another. A long, drenched beard flirted with the rifle's cocked hammer. "Git along."

In hardly a minute, they came upon a larger party of prisoners in blue.

"Y'all just go with them now," their captor told them, eager to rejoin his comrades.

The man had barely turned his back when Crawford ducked into the brush. He expected to hear commands to halt, followed by shots. But the Johnnies had more prisoners than they could oversee.

Crawford set off to rally his ruined division.

Four thirty p.m.
Globe Tavern field

Those can't be Rebs," Charlie Wainwright said. "They can't be."

But there they were, emerging from the woods in ragged lines, red flags hanging heavily in the rain.

"Shall I fire on them, sir?" the battery commander asked.

Along the line of guns, other officers and men stared in Wainwright's direction.

"Wait."

"They're within six hundred yards, sir."

"I can read the range, damn you. *Wait.*"

Several hundred, at least. More and more. Unmistakably Johnnies. Uncoiling from the woods like a big gray snake. But Crawford hadn't withdrawn. How had they gotten past him? If he fired on the Rebs, were Crawford's troops still in the trees behind them?

He remembered Warren saying something about forward troops withdrawing by the flank. Had Crawford pulled off to the left? To uncover his guns?

Where had the Rebs come from? Where was Crawford? Where was buggering Warren?

Four thirty p.m.
Globe Tavern

Fucked for beans," Charlie Griffin growled as he rode for the nearest artillery stand facing east. He all but jumped his horse over the gun line.

Pulling up amid the 9th Massachusetts Battery, he shouted, "Don't you see those Rebs? For God's sake, fire! Fire on them. Shell, case, solid shot, anything." The former artilleryman added, "Ricochet your shots in, blast those Rebs to wet shit."

"I have no orders from Colonel Wainwright, sir," the lieutenant told him.

Griffin fought down the impulse to thrash the boy.

"*I'm* giving you the order. And I outrank goddamned Wainwright. *Fire on them. Now.* Or I'll take over this battery myself."

The lieutenant made what Griffin judged to be a wise decision and began shouting orders for his one and two guns to load solid shot, with three and four ramming in canister. The redlegs jumped to the business.

What the devil was Wainwright waiting for? Griffin wondered. Made no sense, with the Rebs coming straight for his gun line, as perfect a target as any in the war. It just wasn't like him.

Griffin was riding hard for Wainwright, horse battling the mud, when he saw the corps artillery chief raise his arm and drop it.

A dozen guns tore apart the Rebel line.

Four forty p.m.
Globe Tavern clearing

Colquitt shouted orders, struggling to be heard above the clamor of Yankee artillery. Those guns had been positioned perfectly to receive him, as if the Federals had known just where he'd appear. And it was damnably clear that he wasn't going to get to the tavern, let alone over the rail line, by going it here in the open.

Damned shame, too. They'd made it into the Yankee rear, all right. Except for those guns, all before him was confusion.

But that gun line was too much.

He bullied the exposed flank of his brigade hard to the right, back into the trees, where there seemed to be plenty more Yankees set to surrender.

Four forty p.m.
Globe Tavern, south field, Ninth Corps reserve position

Men cheered as the gun line broke up the Reb attack and drove the Johnnies back into the trees. Brown didn't holler along, but he did feel the satisfaction of seeing the Rebs take a licking for once.

"Think we'll go in?" a new man asked, the inevitable question.

"Naw," Sergeant Eckert told him. "They just marched us out here to serve us that mackerel."

They'd go in all right. The 50th Pennsylvania Veteran Volunteers, the rest of the brigade, and, Brown was sure, the remainder of the division. Whatever was going on wasn't going well. Those Rebs who'd popped out of the trees up across the field might have been repulsed, but there weren't supposed to be any Rebs there at all. Some high-up general had a hole in his boat.

Anticipating orders, Captain Brumm trimmed the regiment for a fight. Brown got his men in formation, two short lines. Company C had forty-seven men present for duty, including himself. They'd marched with rifles loaded at dawn, and the day had been long and wet. He ordered the men to cap their weapons and aim high into the air, in the general direction of those Rebs.

"Get that barrel higher, Tyson. Shoot up at those clouds." Then Brown called, *"Fire."*

Of the forty-six rifles, perhaps a half dozen banged off.

The veterans understood what they were doing and reached for fresh percussion caps. The newer men looked befuddled.

"Cap your rifles again. Fire as soon as you're ready. Just make sure you're aiming high, pretend you're shooting pheasants that got a good start."

A few more rifles reported

"Again," Brown said. "Keep capping and firing. Sparks dry your powder. Once you've fired, don't reload till I tell you to."

"Look out, boys," Levi Eckert announced. "Lieutenant's in a rip-up mood, ain't had a letter all week."

That wasn't true. He'd had a letter from Frances the day before. But the men laughed, easing things, and Brown let it go. Since sewing on his stripes, Levi had shown an uncanny knack for keeping men in the right temper, tamping down fear with laughter. War changed men in unexpected ways, either brought out their best or their worst.

Captain Brumm hurried the regiment through the rifle-clearing trick. A supply sergeant made the rounds with extra caps. Every soldier tried to read the sounds of the battle up beyond the gun line, off in those woods.

The division's drummers began to beat the long roll.

Four forty p.m.
Coulter's brigade, Colonel Charles
Wheelock commanding

What was Crawford thinking? The order was madness. To execute it would show his flank to the Rebs while he was moving. They'd roll him up. And now he had artillery pounding his men from in front and behind.

Fuming, Wheelock crouched along the line, followed by his meager staff and ignoring the questioning faces of soldiers huddled in mud-soup entrenchments. With an oh-damn-it shock, it struck him that his 97th New York, on his left flank, had probably already gotten Crawford's order. They'd be gobbled up if they moved back on their own.

He grabbed a trusted courier by the arm. "Get over to the Ninety-seventh. Quick, man. Tell any officer you find that General Crawford's order doesn't stand. They're to hold their ground, prepared to fight in either direction. Until I send them orders. You understand?"

"Yes, sir."

The courier, a corporal, was a trusted, skillful man. Wheelock suspected he'd never see him again.

"Well, go!"

The corporal took off through the rain and murk.

More shelling. Heavier from the rear than from the north, where the Reb guns sat. Was Wainwright trying to kill them all? A chill thought struck him: Had the Rebs seized Wainwright's guns? He couldn't see anything much, and the tumult and clamor in the woods gave little away. More Rebel yells than Yankee voices, though.

A shell burst in nearby treetops. Branches crashed down, men screamed. Rifle shots zipped from what should have been the rear.

Wheelock strode along his entrenchments now, shouting orders for his men to climb over the berms fronting their ditches and shelter on the far side. His own corps' artillery was a greater threat than any Confederate gunnery from the north. And the worrisome Rebs were behind him, not in front.

Mud-slopped and nervous, the men cursed every officer who'd ever lived. But they obeyed him.

Just in time. A line of Rebs crashed through the woods toward them. Wheelock's regimental officers got their men up behind the earthen parapet and unleashed a volley. Startled, the Rebs halted. Some fired back. For all the racket, Wheelock couldn't make out what the gray-clad officers were shouting, but after another exchange of volleys the Johnnies drifted back into the trees.

In the wake of the Rebs, the courier dashed back toward the line, calling on his comrades not to shoot. The man was badly shaken.

"They're gone, sir. The Ninety-seventh's gone. Nothing out there but Rebs. And prisoners. They're herding them like cattle."

The Johnnies had pulled off another of their surprises. It just seemed that the generals never learned. Now the brigade—what remained of it—was cut off. Wheelock wanted to fight, to lash out, but he didn't like the odds or know which line of attack would serve a purpose. He'd lost one regiment thanks to that fool order, and he didn't intend to throw away the others.

With the battle sounds rolling westward, he decided to wait a few minutes more, then move out to the south to rejoin the corps. If it still existed.

Five p.m.
Globe Tavern, north field

Warren halted his party among strung-up, half-butchered beeves intended for dinner. The carcasses weren't what stopped him, though. Just ahead, Colonel Lyle emerged from the wood, unhorsed, hatless, and leading not his brigade, but a dozen men.

"Good God, man, where's your brigade?" Warren asked.

The colonel looked to the side. He opened his mouth to speak, but language defied him.

Warren felt sick. But he often shivered early in a fight, he knew the pattern. Just had to master himself.

He'd already ordered Griffin to send up two brigades to buttress the line. But that wouldn't be enough, he saw it now. Soldiers stumbled out of the trees by the hundreds, defeated, disarmed, and demoralized.

But if the Rebs had done significant damage, they had to be breaking up themselves by now. No advancing lines could hold together in that undergrowth. It was time to hit back, to deliver a counterblow.

He'd have to trust to the Ninth Corps. Parke, Burnside's replacement, hadn't reached the field, but Warren judged it might be for the best. He'd enjoy unity of command, no hesitation or quarrels.

God only knew if those fellows would fight or bolt, though. Burnside had been shooed away, but his spirit lingered.

At least Meade hadn't saddled him with Ferrero's Colored Troops. Either he or Humphreys had shown the sense to leave them behind to man the fortifications.

He waved up Wash Roebling.

"Ride back to General Willcox. Tell him to advance his division immediately. His lead brigade's to restore Crawford's line on the right, the second supports Ayres. I want the Rebs cleared out of those trees, and I'll tolerate no excuses."

Five fifteen p.m.
The Cauldron

Corporal Will Tanner had been captured, escaped, and been recaptured. But he did not want to test Reb hospitality, nor did he have a desire to see Andersonville, so when one of his fellow prisoners shouted, "Hell, boys, we got them outnumbered, don't be sheep," Tanner was one of the hundred or more captives who surged around their handful of guards.

It had almost become a game. The North Carolina boys did their reckoning fast enough and surrendered their arms. Another Yankee grabbed their flag, which the attacking Rebs had left behind.

"We's let you Yankees go," a gap-toothed Johnny tried, "so y'all ought to let us'n go on our way, too."

"Ain't the way it works, Johnny," a blue-coated sergeant told the man.

But somebody shouted, "More Rebs coming," and everybody, in blue or gray, scattered in the direction he thought best.

Five twenty p.m.
Coulter's brigade, Wheelock commanding

With artillery still blasting the grove from the front and rear, Wheelock made what he deemed to be the best of the bad decisions open to him: He ordered his diminished brigade back toward Globe Tavern. He'd hammered into the regimental officers to keep their ranks tight, maintain close contact, and be ready to fight their way out, but the brush made preserving order a slow business. All the while, treetop bursts added deadly shards to the steady rain.

The battle had moved west, about to the rail line by the sound of it. Might be action to the northwest, too, he couldn't be sure. And there still were minor exchanges to the east, at the skirmish level. But Wheelock found himself in a netherland, where stray graybacks and Federals alike wandered through the gloom, wounded, skulking, or lost. His men gathered up fifty or so bewildered Confederates, while freeing as many captives wearing blue—including men from his 97th New York. Twice, clusters of Rebs fired on Wheelock's lines, then disappeared. Discarded weapons lay everywhere, but Wheelock saw fewer corpses or wounded men than most fights produced. Things had gone too quickly to leave many casualties.

When he and his men broke from the trees into the Globe Tavern clearing, with wet flags waving to get everybody's attention, the artillery finally stopped firing in their direction.

Five thirty p.m.
Risdon house, Confederate second echelon

Mahone was pleased enough by the river of prisoners flowing past, but Colquitt had sent back so many that they interfered with Weisiger's Virginians as they unfolded into battle lines. And before he went down with a wound, Clingman had sent back word that he was herding at least a thousand Yankee captives northward toward Heth. The attack had certainly bagged its share of bluebellies.

It was evident, though, that command had broken down out in the trees, that success had brought a threat of disintegration. He'd lost communication with Clingman's command, and Colquitt had veered to the right after hitting artillery. So Colquitt hadn't taken the tavern field, hadn't made it deep into their rear. Nor was there any word from Harry Heth about his advance down the rail line, even though Mahone had sent a succession of couriers back to Hill. He had no idea whether the other half of the day's attack was succeeding or had fizzled.

And his belly burned like hellfire. He would've swapped a hundred Yankee prisoners for one glass of milk.

Plenty of fussing out there in those woods, the units mixed up and fighting all but blind. Reminded him of the Wilderness. Battle was ever attended by confusion, but there seemed to be an excess of it today. And the man who mastered the chaos best would win.

The Virginia regiments dressed their ranks under probing artillery fire, the Federals hunting an enemy they sensed but couldn't see. Trees concealed them from the Yankees and hid the Yankees from them, all playing a deadly game of blindman's bluff.

Weisiger splashed up. His horse had finally reached him.

"Orders, sir?" he asked Mahone.

"Colquitt didn't reach the tavern. Go and take it, Davey."

Five thirty p.m.
Globe Tavern, north field

Brown marched at the right of his company, ensuring the men didn't surge ahead of the colors. Rare was the Ninth Corps soldier who wasn't out for revenge, after the disaster at the Crater. The rest of the army looked on the corps as skunks, and Brown had even heard that Colonel Pleasants, who'd constructed the mine and did his part just fine, had gone a bit mad. So many a fellow had much to prove, and even Brown, a sober man, felt murderous.

On they plodded, slapped by rain, passing the arc of guns. Gone forward on the right, Hartranft's brigade had engaged the Rebs in a cornfield that edged the clearing, but the long line in which the 50th advanced had three hundred yards to cover to reach the trees. Then they'd see what came of things.

The company split to avoid an overturned wagon, one of its horses dead, the other quivering. Then they closed ranks again, rifles loaded with their driest cartridges and bayonets fixed.

Hartranft's boys had gotten themselves into a proper fracas. Brown had no doubt that his own brigade's turn was coming.

Captain Brumm pointed toward the trees with his sword, correcting the direction of the colors.

Dark, wet trees. Not tall, but smoked and ugly. Stray soldiers in blue stumbled out of the gloom.

"Steady up," Brown snapped. Emulating Brumm, he extended his sword. As if the men didn't know where they were going.

The sword still seemed a laughable thing to Brown. Not worth much in a brawl, that was dead certain. He wasn't some gentleman sword-fighter. And his pistol had been stolen the day before, while he was attending to private matters.

He missed the weight of a rifle in his hands.

When the front rank was less than two hundred yards from the trees, Rebs blundered out in a mob. The Johnnies hurried to sort themselves into a firing line, but this time Brown's side was quicker. Anticipating commands by seconds, the men halted, raised their rifles, and cocked the hammers.

"Fire."

A heap of Johnnies went down. But they got off a ragged volley of their own as Brown's men and a thousand others reloaded. The second Union volley sent the Rebs back into the trees at a scurry.

Good Yankee hurrahs trailed after the Johnnies.

Before Brown and his men could resume their advance, an officer in a rain cape galloped along the front of the line. Everything stopped, which made Brown seethe: The Rebs were running, it was plain Dutch stupid not to go after them while they had them spooked.

Instead, the entire brigade left-faced and marched west a hundred yards toward the rail bed. Then they right-faced back into battle lines. The order rang out to advance again.

The woods looked thinner here, the briars trampled, and a man could see a ways in. At the edge of the trees, the company trudged through a pool that reeked like a bad unit's latrine. For all Brown knew, it might have been just that.

Church men cursed their Creator.

Company C was among the first to pierce the uneven tree line. The battle noise on the right had grown stubborn and constant, and men were still killing each other off to the left. Yet things were so quiet to their front it was worrisome.

A line of Rebs rose from a trench. They fired, muzzles flickering through the rain. Brown was relieved that none of his men had fallen.

Captain Brumm dashed out in front of the regiment. He stumbled, then steadied himself and called, *"Pennsylvania! Charge!"*

No volley. Just charge them. The men responded with wolf howls and lowered bayonets.

They were on the Rebs before many of the Johnnies could reload. The Rebs had taken over a Union trench, and the parapet faced the wrong way to do them good. Brown's men leapt down into the ditch, firing close enough to chests to set wet wool to a smolder, then wielding their rifles as clubs, most of them shy of using their bayonets, a quirk Brown had learned to accept.

The Johnnies who could get away took off, fast as they could go. Brown grabbed one Reb man-child by the collar: The boy had just stayed too long and paid the price. Skinny as starvation itself, the lad was no match for Brown's left hand and the canal-man's strength behind it. He threw the lad to the bottom of the trench.

Brown didn't bother to threaten him with his sword, just kicked him lightly and said, "You stay there now, don't be no fool."

He scrambled out of the trench on the far side and topped the berm. Wasn't much shooting, but familiar voices were yelling, cursing, and grunting. He spotted Charlie Oswald and Joe Long going at it hand to hand with two Rebs just past the trench. It looked like Charlie and Joe had the advantage.

But in the hot-colored seconds that mark time in battle, Brown noticed something else. Amid the confused retreat of the Rebs, a color-bearer and two of his guards had lingered a hundred yards off, backs half-turned. Trying to rally their regiment, Brown figured.

He dropped his sword and picked up a discarded rifle, an old Belgian model. Then he ran hard for the Rebs, roaring as he surprised them from the side.

Startled, the Rebs whipped around to face him. But Brown had the rifle up, ready.

"Surrender," he said.

One of the color guards started to raise his rifle.

"Drop that." Brown held his muzzle five feet from the man's chest. "It's over, Johnny. See sense."

Both of the men with rifles threw them down, their faces as long as boys whose dogs had died. The sergeant with the colors stood there dumbstruck, jaw moving up and down but no words coming out.

Brown gestured with the musket. "Get on now. You know which way. Let's go." He was starting to worry that other Rebs nearby might take an interest.

He ran his prisoners back to the breastworks, with his entire regiment cheering him on and Rebs beginning to shout at him to come back, damning him to Satan's lowest caverns. Just short of the berm, with his comrades reaching to pull the Johnnies in, Brown grabbed the red flag from his prisoner.

He'd forgotten how heavy a wet flag could be.

He jumped atop the parapet, waving the banner defiantly, with men around him yelling like Saturday drunks and inviting the Johnnies to come back over and get it. He hadn't made a decision, didn't mean to act like that. He just did it. Some higher power had taken over and made him.

Robbed of their flag and insulted, the Rebs rallied well enough to send a nasty volley in Brown's direction. He staggered, almost fell, but felt nothing more. He just stood there, holding up the flag and wondering.

The heel of his shoe had been shot away. His hat flew off next. Still, he lingered an extra few seconds, aware now of his foolishness but stubborn, swinging the flagpole harder to unfurl his prize.

A sudden thrill of fear saw off his pride. Still clutching the Rebel banner, Brown leapt down in the trench.

His boys returned fire, relishing the chance, proud of themselves and of him. Charles Burket was struck dead. Billy Wagner fell. Charlie's cousin Adam had dropped earlier, a bullet through his brain. But Company C had taken a flag, proof of their worth.

The Rebs gave up and shifted off, leaving Brown with the colors and his three captives. Seated behind the berm, the mud-smeared Rebs wept bitterly. But Brown and his boys couldn't help rubbing it in. He and First Sergeant Losch spread out the flag, revealing more holes than a cheese got at by mice. It belonged to the 47th Virginia and had been "Presented by the Ladies of the City of Richmond."

Captain Brumm came up grinning to offer congratulations. "Lieutenant Brown . . . ," he began formally. Then his grin grew wider. "Brownie . . . damn all, I can't say whether you're the bravest man in this regiment or mule-kicked crazy, but that was a stunt I'll remember all my days."

The Reb sergeant buried his face in dirty hands.

Levi Eckert had slipped over the berm to retrieve the rifle Brown had used. He came back laughing in that high cackle of his, shoulders shaking in merriment. Tears squeezed out of his close-set eyes.

Levi looked at the dejected Rebs, at Brown, at the captain, and back at Brown again.

"This rifle here," Levi said. "Did you know it wasn't loaded?"

Six p.m.
Risdon house

Clingman was going to lose that leg, Mahone was certain. The brigade commander had been carried past on a litter dripping blood, with not just his jaw but his whole face locked up tight, fighting the pain and failing. As for Clingman's counterpart, Mahone had located Colquitt as he rallied his men in a clearing. He'd hoped to use Colquitt's Brigade to support Weisiger's Virginians, but Colquitt had fewer than two hundred men still with him. The rest were scattered over the battlefield, caught up in random encounters or just befuddled.

Matters had grown so uncertain that Mahone had led a miniature charge himself, to rescue part of his staff grabbed by stray Yankees. He'd watched the capture take place, startled at first, then lit up to a fury.

As for his Virginians, Weisiger had led them forward as ordered, but with more Yankees turning up where they shouldn't have been, he'd had to halt and position himself for defense. The Federals had brought up their Ninth Corps—most of it, anyway—and Mahone had heard men muttering to expect no quarter after the mine-pit slaughter. It wasn't the sort of scare-talk he liked to hear.

Now another blue-coated brigade, perhaps a full division, was tromping up the wagon road from the east, aimed at Weisiger's rear. And the Virginians were still a half mile short of the Weldon.

Had he had two more brigades . . .

It appeared that his men had captured almost a division's worth of Yankees, which would have been hailed as a triumph another day. But Lee wanted the railroad. And that meant Billy Mahone wanted it, too.

Six fifteen p.m.
50th Pennsylvania, Weldon Railroad

The Johnnies had come back at them three times. The first attack had been a screecher, fairly bold, with the braver graybacks almost reaching their line. The second gained less ground before it faltered. The third Reb advance spit a volley and melted away. There was still some fighting to the right and rear—Brown could hear rifles prickling—but it felt as though things had turned their way and weren't going to change back.

In the gloom, General Willcox, his division commander, came by to praise Brown's valor and promise that his brevet rank would be made permanent soon. All generals sounded the same when they talked to soldiers, as if selling patent medicines from a cart.

Brown was tempted to ask about that mackerel but decided it was wiser to be quiet.

Six thirty p.m.
Weisiger's Brigade

More Yankees out there than the Lord had ever needed to make. Yankees and more Yankees, just no end to them. Captain Hugh Ritchie Smith, General Weisiger's adjutant and a Petersburg man himself, was worried beyond his habit. He dashed along, slipping now and then in the grab-a-man mud.

Ahead, he saw the general, still up on his horse, a damned-fool thing.

The rain from above had eased a touch, but the rain of bullets seemed worse with each next minute. The Yanks had been working their way around both flanks, pushing the Virginia Brigade and a smattering of Georgians back on themselves, and the 12th Virginia had paid a hard tithe to Mars. On his last errand over to his old regiment, delivering an order to fold back a hundred yards, he'd found only two members of the color guard still on their feet—one of whom was his brother, Billy, a sergeant and a bit too gallant for sense.

Just wasn't a good day. Not a good day at all. Started off mighty and got stuck in the mud.

Smith reported back to the man he served. Weisiger hardly noticed. The general was occupied with Colonel Groner of the 61st, who was just back after his Spotsylvania wound and standing, brave and comical, on crutches turned upside down so the padded ends could help him through the slop. Groner had made the approach march on those crutches, every step of it, telling Weisiger and Smith that he'd missed enough of the war already and didn't have a mind to stay behind.

"It's my damned city they're after," he'd told anybody with an ear to hear.

Weisiger pointed. Groner saluted.

"Just push 'em back hard enough so they think twice," Weisiger added. And Groner levered himself back toward the 61st Virginia. Minutes later, the regiment rushed forward with a yell, knocking back a Yankee approach that had gotten a little too close. The 61st relied mostly on rifle butts to persuade the Yankees to remove themselves. Ammunition was getting alarmingly low.

"What's Mahone waiting for?" Weisiger said aloud, speaking to no one. "What the devil's he waiting for?"

Work done, the 61st limped back to the line to await the next surge of Federals. Mostly, though, the Yankees were fighting smart, closing to a hundred yards and pouring in fire, volley after volley, far more than their targets could return. Sometimes, when they felt full of themselves, a Federal regiment charged. But that rarely turned out happily for the blue-bellies. Instead, they inched forward, firing as if their ammunition was endless. Which it likely was, Smith reckoned.

"Sir?" Smith said. "You might get down off that horse. Do the men good, they're worried over you."

Weisiger gave a snort. "I'll get down, all right. But then you're getting up, Hugh." He smiled, not unkindly. "Ride back to Mahone. Tell him the Yankees have us all but surrounded. And they're determined to finish the job."

The general slipped from the saddle, splashing mud. His horse stood uneasy. Smith soothed it.

"Stay low. Don't need another dead hero like Girardey."

It jarred Smith to hear Girardey mentioned now. Not Weisiger's most attractive side. But, then, rare was the man devoid of jealousy. The adjutant knew how deeply the general had resented the credit lavished on Girardey over the mine-pit affair, when Weisiger's Brigade had done the work. And then that spectacular promotion, envied by all. Weisiger had not wept when word arrived of Girardey's death. He'd just said, "That's a shame," and gone back to business.

Plenty of death for all. Good men grew callous.

Heart banging, Smith put a foot in the left stirrup and rolled up into the saddle. Before he turned to ride off, Weisiger spoke once more, again to himself and to no one:

"Should've let me go in right behind Colquitt."

When he glimpsed Hugh Smith riding back too soon to have gotten to Mahone, Weisiger felt stricken. Had the Yankees already shut the gate behind them?

His men were falling fast.

Well, the Virginia Brigade was *not* going to surrender. Not while he commanded it.

The adjutant rode straight for him.

If the Yankees hadn't known where to aim before, they surely did now, Weisiger thought sourly.

As Smith splashed up, the adjutant looked brighter of face than expected. Horse was bleeding, though.

"Met Bobby Henry on the way back, sir. With orders from General Mahone. We're to withdraw behind the mill trace."

Handsomely timed, the Yankee fire eased.

"Hugh, get off that horse and handle the left. I'll see to the right. The brigade will pivot on the Twelfth Virginia, moving back by regiment, in echelon. Groner's got a piece of ground to travel, and the Sixty-first is already bloodied up. We'll need to help them get off."

They could whip the Yankees man for man, Weisiger never doubted it. Do it any time, day or night, rain or shine. But it never was man for man anymore. Not since Gettysburg, really. Kill one Yankee, a half dozen more sprang up like Hydra's heads or the spawn of dragon's teeth. And Grant, the beast, was no fool. Halting prisoner exchanges for all but a handful of well-connected officers. Good men rotted while the South bled white.

Reaching Groner just as the Yankees unleashed a hail of musketry, Weisiger said, "Virge, we're getting out of this mess. Sixty-first leads the pullback. Get 'em moving."

"None too soon for me."

Weisiger nodded. A round ripped past his ear. "Once you get the regiment back in those pines, you turn over command and take my horse. Get on back to Little Billy quick. Can't spare you again, you've had your holiday."

A soldier toppled beside them. Blood throbbed from his neck.

"Rather take my chances with the crutches," Groner said.

As Weisiger drew up his brigade anew to fend off the Yankees, Mahone appeared, horse prancing despite the slop.

Expression fixed in a meanness, Mahone said, "Got the prisoners off, great big horde of them. No more to be done now. Pull back your brigade sharp as you can, don't give the Yankees a chance to even the score."

"How far back this time?" Weisiger asked.

"Where we started this morning."

Ten p.m.
Headquarters, Army of Northern Virginia

Can't say what's keeping General Heth, sir," A. P. Hill told Lee.

Venable saw the look on Lee's face harden, but his tone remained measured:

"I suspect the day's requirements have detained him. Let us proceed."

Venable watched the tableau of generals form around the map: Lee solid and restrained, the dominant figure; Hill bent forward, scarecrow-lean and eager to explain; Beauregard keeping a calculated distance, suggesting that the day's disappointments had nothing to do with him; and Mahone, his finely cut uniform spoiled by mud, eyes burning like peat fires, mouth clamped tight.

"We gave them a proper licking, sir," Hill said. "We're still tallying the prisoners, but it looks to be near three thousand. General Mahone rolled their Fifth Corps up like a carpet."

"But," Lee said, "those people hold the railroad."

After a lead-heavy silence, Hill answered, "We came close, sir. I know that's not enough. But we came close. Their Ninth Corps had come up, behind the Fifth. Warren had two full corps to call on. We—"

"We failed to regain the Weldon line," Lee said. The old man's voice was clenched and cold, though still draped by civility.

Venable saw Hill's features weaken at Lee's change in tone. Powell Hill knew Lee better than any other corps commander. Better, Venable believed, than even Longstreet knew him. Hill saw others clearly enough, while Longstreet saw his reflection.

Nonetheless, Venable looked forward to the day when Longstreet's convalescence would end and he'd return. Lee needed Pete Longstreet, needed all of them.

Lee turned to Mahone. "General, I know your men fought bravely. I do not question that. But we fell short today. I would value your opinion as to why."

"Needed two more brigades," Mahone said.

Hill nodded in agreement. Beauregard watched for Lee's response.

The old man winced. He turned to Venable and his voice was searing, though not loud. "This lamp . . . the wick's improperly trimmed. It's smoking, it must be replaced."

Instead of calling an orderly, Venable leapt to the task. The wick was fine, he knew it. But Lee was not fine. The old man was struggling to remain the Robert E. Lee he wished the world to see.

Silence prevailed until Venable carried in a fresh lamp from the hall and keyed out the offending flame. The new lamp threw more smoke than had the old one.

Lee didn't notice.

"Always, always," the old man said, shaking his head slowly, "the complaint I hear is of insufficient numbers. But there will be no more men, not in the numbers you wish. We must make *do*, gentlemen, we must make do." He sighed, a rare occurrence. "Do I make myself clear?"

The others nodded, murmured.

"We did not regain the railroad today," Lee repeated. "So we must do so tomorrow, before those people can better their defenses. We cannot afford to attack fortified positions, not if it can be helped."

The old man touched a hand to his chest, but he quickly dropped it away.

"General Beauregard, General Hill . . . ready the strongest force you can assemble. At least two more brigades, beyond today's composition. Accept risk along the lines where you think it best. But we *must* reopen the Weldon, I cannot rely on a single line to support this army and the city." Quietly, dreadfully, he added, "I will not allow it."

After the generals left to pillage their lines of more brigades, Lee sat alone, pondering the map, while Venable scratched away in a corner, piling up papers that wanted the general's signature. Marshall was down with the bellyache, doubling Venable's load, and he never could make sense of the ordnance returns.

At last, the old man rose. "Have we other business, Colonel Venable?"

"Nothing that can't wait for morning, sir."

Lee truly did seem old. The change in hardly a year was painful to witness.

Hoping to lift Lee's spirits a bit, Venable said, "If we fell short today, sir, still . . . three thousand prisoners . . ."

Lee gave the entire world a withering look, sparing only Charles Venable.

"More prisoners to feed . . . and one less rail line to feed them. We must take back the Weldon road tomorrow."

But Robert E. Lee did not retake the railroad on August 20. The attack could not be organized in time. And when his subordinates struck with all the force they could muster on August 21, their valor failed in the face of entrenchments constructed with speed and mastery. In the course of multiple assaults, the Confederates suffered great losses among their officers, including Brigadier General John C. C. Sanders, savior of the Crater, who bled to death before his twenty-fifth birthday.

The field of Globe Tavern and its stretch of the Weldon line remained in the hands of the Army of the Potomac. Lee cut his soldiers' rations by one-quarter.

PART
IV

THE STATION

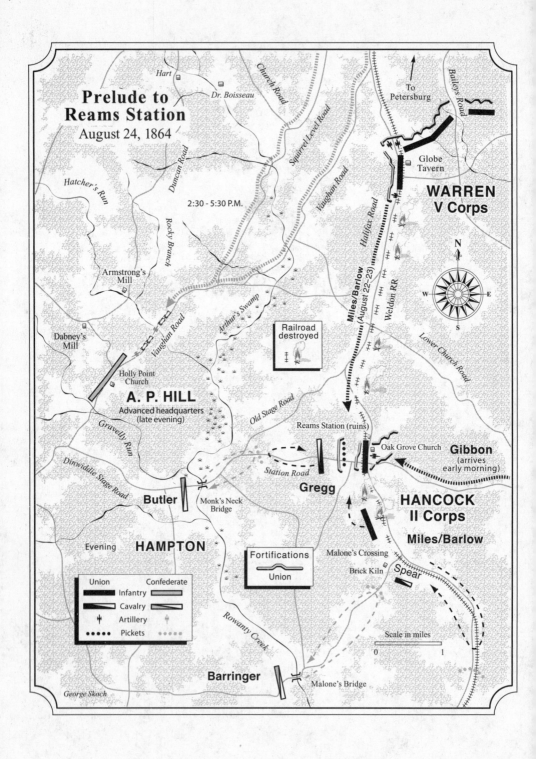

Prelude to Reams Station
August 24, 1864

Hart

Dr. Boisseau

Church Road

To Petersburg

Bailey's Road

Globe Tavern

Squirrel Level Road

WARREN
V Corps

Hatcher's Run

Duncan Road

2:30 - 5:30 P.M.

Rocky Branch

Vaughan Road

Halifax Road

N

Miles/Barlow
(August 22–23)

Weldon R.R.

Lower Church Road

Armstrong's
Mill

Arthur's Swamp

**Railroad
destroyed**

Dabney's
Mill

Vaughan Road

Holly Point
Church

A. P. HILL
Advanced headquarters
(late evening)

Gravelly Run

Old Stage Road

Reams Station (ruins)

Oak Grove Church

Gibbon
(arrives
early morning)

Station Road

Gregg

HANCOCK
II Corps

Dinwiddie Stage Road

Butler

Monk's Neck
Bridge

Miles/Barlow

Malone's Crossing

Brick Kiln

Spear

Evening **HAMPTON**

Fortifications
Union

Union	Confederate
Infantry	
Cavalry	
Artillery	
Pickets	

Rowanty Creek

Scale in miles

0   1

Barringer

Malone's Bridge

George Skoch

NINE

Eleven p.m., August 23
Armstrong's Mill

Father?"

The unexpected tenderness of the word ambushed Wade Hampton. Preston always addressed him properly as "sir" in the presence of others. Now, in the heavy dark, the softer term disarmed him.

A dying campfire teased wet uniforms.

"Yes, son?"

Testing his words before he spoke, Preston asked, "Do you worry? About General Hood? Atlanta?"

The words *our home* were left unsaid. Millwood in its grandeur. Sand Hills newer, beloved. South Carolina. Family.

"Best concern ourselves with the fight right here," Hampton said.

But he did trouble himself. About Sherman, relentless and hard and distant.

"If Atlanta falls, though?" Words spoken in a whisper.

Hampton almost replied that Atlanta was safe, the answer duty demanded. But if his position required him to defraud other men on such matters, he could not do that to his son, this fine young man in a drenched lieutenant's garb, his smell that of wet wool, young sweat, and, ever and always, the cradle.

"One city won't decide this war," Hampton answered, barely whispering. He felt refreshed conviction as he continued: "One great victory now, one more Yankee debacle . . . that's all we need. It's a matter of the election. Not of Atlanta."

"But *if* Atlanta falls . . . it boosts up Lincoln."

"He'll need a sight more of a boost than that."

He dreaded the prospect of the city in Billy Sherman's paws, though. If all of north Georgia fell—and he prayed it would not—South Carolina would be next. And his state could expect no mercy.

Poking the fire with a stick, he spoke more freely than usual. "I do regret the dismissal of General Johnston. Although it means your brother can come up. Now that Johnston has no further need of him." He interrupted his prodding of the embers. "General Johnston stands accused of not fighting to win, of being content to lose slowly. I fear that General Hood may lose too swiftly."

"So you do believe Atlanta—"

"Wait and see. Meanwhile, we have our own work."

Preston took after his mother, Hampton's first wife, although his face was fuller, the chin rounder. The boy was mustache-proud, eager for manhood, magnificently young. Hampton's eldest son, Wade IV, followed the male line, with a full frame and full beard, that commanding presence. Preston's carriage was upright, but eased by gentleness.

The boy wanted to speak further, Hampton could feel it. But Preston had been well brought up and preferred few words to many.

Major General Wade Hampton III, the newly appointed commander of the Cavalry Corps of the Army of Northern Virginia, sensed more of his son's yearnings than he dared say. Preston mooned about home things, Hampton knew. He recognized the sentiment because he bore it himself and indulged in domestic reveries. Many a man might sing, "There's no place like home," but not all meant it. Too many men of his class felt more at home in a Charleston bordello or a planters' club, drugged by whiskey and fables, dreading homes that meant carping wives and creditors. But Hampton loved "home" with a passion that even now, in middle age, could be hard to contain.

Preston felt the same way. Worried that the war might one day scorch the walls of Millwood, leaving his aunties homeless under the live oaks. Or that vandals in blue might set Sand Hills alight. Oh, Hampton understood. . . .

His stomach picked an argument, but Hampton chose not to rise and seek a bush. Not yet. It had been a long, hard day, with the prospect of worse on the morrow, and this repose with Preston was a treasure.

His stomach bit him again. The rough beans and pone his mess had cooked up were unfriendly to his innards. A big man, a bear in form, he could outride, outshoot, and outlast most anyone, familiar with the manly arts since childhood. But his belly was ever rebellious, his lust for refined cooking tantalizing. He'd not only kept a goodly table himself, back in those perfect days before the war, but he had been a dinner guest of the aged Duke of Wellington and of the Marlboroughs at Blenheim Palace, where the company was better than the cutlets. He'd savored the morsels of Paris, washed down by the best Champagne, and his cellar at Sand Hills had been almost as well stocked with claret and hock as his father's Millwood library had been with books, ten thousand volumes.

His life had been one of privilege and beauty . . . almost of nobility, if the plantation aristocracy counted as such. Interludes of joy had been punctured by the pall of early deaths and, once, ripped by a scandal undeserved—and, for his sisters, irreparable—but the thrust of his life had been forward, busy, full, his responsibilities impatient of his sorrows. Ever, he had done his best to maintain a life of grace, of hospitality among his kind and fair dealings with inferiors. He sought to employ his wealth worthily, even embracing the vulgar duty of elected office—the latter to please his father, who envisioned not just a family, but a dynasty.

And wealth there had been, or the long illusion of it. Reputed to be the richest man in the South, his father had died in 1858 a half-million dollars in debt, with first and second mortgages on plantations from South Carolina to Mississippi and his capital locked in his two thousand slaves.

Slavery. That *was* what this war was about, no honest man could deny it. States' rights, indeed: the right of a state to hold the Negro in bondage. Hampton granted the abolitionists that much. But it was all so much more complicated than the Yankees allowed. Hampton and not a few like-minded men had grasped that chattel slavery could not endure. But how were they to escape it? How to work their lands? How to retrieve their capital? All but the noisiest fools understood that slavery was a problem that had to be solved. But none of them could see a way to solve it.

At the special session of the legislature, back in December of '60, he'd taken the floor to oppose secession, knowing that his remarks would invite calumny. But that, too, had been his duty as a gentleman. He knew more of the world—not least of the North's resources—than the hotheads and firebrands pounding on their desks. And he'd harbored no romantic notions of war, no dreams of glory.

But war had come. And here they were in Virginia, far from Sand Hills, in a night as heavy as mourning. And Sherman was outside Atlanta, panting, vicious. With only a reckless brawler in his way, now that Johnston was gone.

His world lay under mortal threat, Millwood and his spinster sisters, Sand Hills and his cherished second wife, the hunting trips to Cashiers Valley, Virginia, and the private steamboat landing in Mississippi, the old, expected deference, the pride . . .

Yes, he was a proud man, but not a swaggering dandy like so many—not least these haughty Virginians, with their assumptions of superiority, their martial affectations and ignorance of the world beyond their counties. Hampton was a man who took pride in a tempered voice, in a well-tied cravat, in a bird brought down at a campfire-tall-tale distance, in shielding his kin against the storms of life.

He had taken pride even in his repute among Negroes, his people well treated and proud of their status in turn, given to bragging down at the gin that "I belongs to Marse Wade."

What would become of his slaves, if the Yankees won? Some, indeed, might manage decent lives, not all were ungifted. But the many? What awaited them, in their helpless millions? Lives of license and lawlessness, of promiscuity, poverty, and oblivion? They knew anger, but not ambition; lust, but not restraint. They sang like angels and had to be told it was time to wash their bedding.

What *would* become of the Children of Ham? Whichever side won the war? The Yankees imagined a heaven on earth, but Heaven was far away.

Preston said, "Can't wait to see my brother."

With the faintest quaver in his voice, Hampton answered, "Do look forward to seeing young Wade myself." A raindrop hissed off the embers. "See if we can't get some work out of that boy." Speaking over a belly growl, he added, "Why don't you get some sleep now, Pres? Like to be busy tomorrow."

"Think General Lee will take up your advice, sir?"

"And how would you know what advice I give General Lee? *If* I were to presume to offer any?"

"I'm on your staff, sir. Even lieutenants know—"

"Any lieutenant who hopes to be a captain knows when to keep his knowledge to himself." Hampton shifted his jacket, its fabric still weighted with rain. Gentling again, he said, "All I did was to point out an opportunity. If General Lee wished to send down a force of infantry, those Yankees by Reams Station could be plucked. If we showed a touch of alacrity." He ran a hand over damp hair. "Leave them unmolested, and I fear they'll not only keep on ripping up track, they'll reach for Dinwiddie Court House. And that would make the loss of the Weldon worse, a good sight worse, cut the wagon route, too." He gestured toward the darkness. "But it's up to General Lee."

"Folks say he likes you better now."

Taken a bit aback, Hampton replied, "He never disliked me, son. He just prefers Virginians." He was about to let the topic fade, but found himself musing aloud: "It was a hard thing for him to lose Stuart, Pres. They had that bond. Then to be faced with putting me over his nephew and his own son . . ."

"You wouldn't favor me. Or Wade."

What could he reply? It was true. He had delayed a longed-for promotion for Preston to avoid the look of favoritism. Pres had earned that rise in rank, but Hampton would not allow it. Perhaps in a few months . . .

"Point is . . . he did what he knew was right and gave me the cavalry. Just took him a little time to get used to the thought." Wistfully, he added, "General Lee loved Stuart like a son. And I'm too long in the tooth to fill that position."

"But you're a better cavalryman than Stuart was."

Hampton snorted. "Who says that?"

"The men. Most all of them. They say the cavalry never loses now."

"Well, bad luck to say it."

How stubborn, almost truculent, the Virginia brigades had been at his first touch. His manner seemed colorless after Stuart's theatrics, a comedown from the flashing cavalier. Worse, he made them fight dismounted, as infantry who moved fast, courtesy of horses—a lesson he'd learned from the Yankees, truth be told. And he'd proved his tactics worked, from Haw's Shop and Trevilian Station onward, until even Lee was forced to acknowledge his worth.

Pride, pride . . . beware of your pride, he warned himself.

Preston parted his lips to speak again, but Hampton was quicker.

"Go to bed, Lieutenant. That's an order."

Six a.m., August 24
Reams Station

Mother," Barlow muttered.

It was the first word Miles had understood since entering the tent. Frank lay on his cot, eyes closed, drool flowing from one corner of his mouth.

"Get a litter team," Miles told the orderly who'd fetched him. "And call up an ambulance."

White as a ghoul, Barlow began to shake.

"Frank, you damned fool," Miles said. Beyond canvas walls, the encampment bustled with work parties setting off to do more destruction and artillery pulling in at last after warring with swampy roads. "You horse's ass."

Barlow gave no sign that he heard anything.

He'd appeared without warning at Miles' side the morning before, looking as though he'd crawled out of a graveyard but swift to find fault and bark orders. Working their way down the railroad from Globe Tavern, the men of the division had done well despite their exhaustion, tearing up the line nearly to Reams Station. But that had not been good enough for Barlow, who'd ordered Miles to send out two regiments immediately to clear away any lurking Rebs, burn the station, and occupy the old fortifications, a crude set of earthworks thrown up in June, when Wright and his Sixth Corps had marched out to shield cavalrymen returning from a raid. Frank hadn't thought the men were giving their best—but then he never seemed to anymore.

Hancock, too, had been startled by Barlow's return. But Frank had put up a good front, not even trifling to offer assurances that he was fit to return to division command. He simply took over again.

Now here he was, laid out like a dying fish. All he needed was a club on the head.

Serve you right, if you died, Miles thought. Instantly, he regretted it.

The litter bearers arrived, two slumping bandsmen, followed by Barlow's adjutant. They recoiled at the sight before them.

"Well, take him up," Miles said. "And tell the driver to take the shortest route to the nearest railhead, no delays. General Barlow's to be rushed to City Point, with priority on transport."

"You might want to put that in writing, sir," Barlow's adjutant said.

"*You* put it in writing, it's your job. Just get him out of here."

Christ, I sound like Frank, Miles told himself. He pushed the canvas aside and left the tent.

He'd been disappointed at Frank's return, of course. He wanted to command the division himself, had assumed he would, that Frank would be out for a lengthy convalescence. Then Frank had pulled his latest stunt, not only upsetting the command arrangements, but instantly sparking resistance in the men. The surviving bits of the Irish Brigade had given them mutinous looks the evening before.

Now he had to resume command and rearrange things again, to see that the details from the other brigades were on their way, along with sufficient regiments to guard them. And the cavalry would ask for support again, he didn't doubt it. He already heard the pops of distant skirmishing. He could only hope they'd go another day without an attack—the men certainly weren't in shape for a fight.

Rebs couldn't let them continue wrecking the line, though. That was certain as snow in a Boston winter.

Well, there'd be no snow today. That was another certainty. It was high August at its fiercest, set to be another day of dueling sun and squalls. Hard on men given no time to recover after ten days of constant marching and fighting. To cap the exertion, they'd pushed so hard on their way back from the James that the infantrymen were calling themselves, not happily, "Hancock's cavalry." And they'd gone straight to work tearing up the railroad, extending the destruction Warren had wrought. The division was played out, used up, and morale in Gibbon's division seemed even worse. But the Second Corps was always Meade's and Humphreys' first choice for hard tasks.

Did they understand that it wasn't the corps it had been? How awfully it had been used up since May?

Miles began to wonder if Frank wasn't getting away at the right time. If matters went awry now, he'd be the goat, not Barlow. After all the damage Frank had done.

Well, you got what you wanted, he told himself. Now get yourself in hand. The men needed rest, but first they had to work. And to fight, if the Rebs came up. His job was to see it done, and no excuses.

First, though, he had to see Hancock, to inform him about Barlow. And Hancock wasn't in the best health himself.

They were becoming an army of invalids. Miles felt hearty himself, though. Almost jaunty, despite the lack of sleep.

Yes, he wanted to command the division. No matter how tired and worn the men might be. No matter the risks.

He strode through the interior of the entrenchments, an ugly, irregular horseshoe of mud walls, with hundreds of yards between one arm and the other. The brigades bivouacked outside the works were the lucky ones: The fort already stank of human presence. And it struck him again how poorly conceived the old defenses were. The shape of the lines, bent back on each other, invited bombardment by well-handled artillery.

Well, that wasn't his problem. Gibbon's division was taking over the works. Miles' men would spend the day in the open, to the south.

At least, his men could round out their rations down there. This countryside hadn't been picked over yet, still not denuded of crops like the Petersburg lines. The men had roasted green corn the evening before, and the most enterprising among them had "captured" chickens.

Still, he'd be glad to finish and rest the men. They needed sleep and shoes, new uniforms to replace their rags, and a few days with no duties beyond the commonplace.

Avoiding a mud-slathered limber and gun, he spotted Charlie Morgan ahead, standing in front of Hancock's tent and overseeing the circus. Morgan saw him, too.

Hancock's chief of staff waved.

When Miles got close, Morgan said, "We've heard. Dear Christ. Come into the tent, I have something to show you."

Miles followed him under the canvas. Hancock wasn't there.

Anticipating his question, Morgan said, "He's out back. Two men out of three have the bloody runs, but he has to grunt it out." The chief of staff fussed among the papers covering Hancock's field desk. At last, he extended a sheet to Miles.

"Typical Barlow," Morgan said. "Came within the half hour."

It was a surgeon's certificate of disability.

"Left the hospital on his own authority," Morgan went on. "In defiance of medical opinion. For what 'medical opinion' may be worth." Morgan's cynicism bordered on wonder. "He's ordered to take a convalescent leave—twenty days, Miles, twenty full days, for Christ's sake." He rolled his eyes. "No matter how sick I was, I'd turn the best whorehouse in Washington inside out in half that time. And what does Barlow do? Defies the order. He'd rather tear up railroad ties."

"He looked like a corpse just now."

"He'll be lucky if he *isn't* a corpse." Morgan reached out his hand to retrieve the paper. "I'll have to send it after the lunatic bastard. Like some coffee? It's wretched, but it's hot."

Miles waved it off. "I have to get back, straighten things out again." But he paused. "Does Hancock realize how worn out my men are? Seriously, Charlie . . ."

"Gibbon's janissaries are no better off. Maybe worse. Lucky Mott, back in the ditches." The chief of staff made a thoughtful face—by the measure of Charlie Morgan. "Do what you can today. I'll see that your men get a proper rest tomorrow. Gibbon's lot should be up to scratch by then, they can rip up the next stretch."

"Meanwhile, we're out here, splintered off from the rest of the army, with two gutted divisions and half our guns."

"Less than half, actually," Morgan said. "Hancock understands, of course. But what can the old bugger do?" In a moment of candor, he added, "He's beaten down himself, he's nearly as bad as Barlow."

As Miles turned to go, Morgan added, "And do what you can to divert the contrabands, would you? Point them somewhere else. I can't have them clogging the roads. And I damned well can't feed them."

"Like me to shoot them, Charlie?"

Miles went out into the steaming air. How could it rain so much and not cool down? He cursed Frank Barlow again, damning him beyond reason, beyond all justice. But as he passed through the clangor of Gibbon's division settling in, he had to admit he was awed by Barlow's will.

He wondered if he had such strength himself.

Five p.m., August 24
Reams Station

Henry Roback had stuffed his haversack full of ears of corn. The other members of the detail were equally laden and thus in tolerable spirits, despite tired arms and shoulders and backs, and feet that would be weary for days to come. They'd had to go deeper into the cornfield than anyone had liked, given the flurries of shots off in the distance. No one wanted to be scooped up by the Rebs. But the risk had been worth it, anything to get away from army rations. It was like folks back in Washington had made up a special office, with big desks and leather chairs, where they schemed to render vittles as awful as possible. Wilmer Dorrance called it a Rebel plot.

Uniforms steaming from an earlier downpour, the men passed a burned-out shanty with a charred loading platform where rails used to run. A water tank had been pulled down and lay smashed like Humpty-Dumpty in a storybook. A Negro family with bundles on their backs paused along the tree line, watching the soldiers go by, wary, the way deer stood stock-still before they bolted.

"Guess that's the station everyone's talking about," Elias McCammon said. "Can't say it looks worth the bother."

"Like everything else in this godforsaken place," Wilmer spit. "Them coons, too."

"What's got them frighted?" Roback wondered aloud. Negroes mystified him—he couldn't understand a word they said.

"Probably think you got romance in mind, Hank."

"First Division boys found chickens yesterday," Pete Buck said, thinking on more important matters. "So I heard tell."

"Won't be none for us," McCammon told him. He pulled out his pipe. "Count on it. Lucky they left us a cob or two."

The sound of halfhearted skirmishing just reached them. Roback hoped his teeth were up to the corn. They'd been a tad wobbly.

"Would be nice to have a pot of butter," he said. "I always was partial to butter on my corn."

"Rich man's habits," Wilmer warned, "never did a working man no good."

"*We* always had buttered corn," Elias McCammon put in, "and we weren't rich. I'm with Hank."

"Well, you come of farm people. Have all the butter you want. The rest of us have to pay for it. Salt's good enough for me."

"Just be happy we got all this corn," Sergeant Wetherall told them, closing the topic. Eyeing the entrenchments up ahead, he added, "Smarten up now. Don't want the officers thinking we're having a high time. Rifles up proper, boys."

"I was a kid," McCammon said, "we built us snow forts better than those lines. Looks to me like blind men and drunkards built them."

They passed soldiers stripped of half their garments, working with picks and shovels, if without a great deal of enthusiasm.

"Hurry up now," Buck teased the laboring men. "Rebs a-coming. We stole all their corn."

"I know where you can stick a cob," a brawny fellow with a pickax said.

"You boys happy now you joined the Army? Enjoying the easy life, all milk and honey?"

"Make that two cobs."

Entering through a gap where the rail line ran, Sergeant Wetherall commented, "Northern return isn't bad, but that's about it. Don't like that opening for the road, that's just where the Rebs ought to come. And why'd they put that wall other side of the rail bed, not this side? How're they going to get ammunition up for those guns?"

"Same way they got the guns up," McCammon told him, just being contrary.

Annoyed to have his soldierly judgment challenged, the sergeant said, "No room on that side for limbers or caissons. Care to carry powder over that berm? When the Johnnies start firing? Can't say I like this position at all, not one bit."

"Any luck, we won't be here that long," Roback suggested. He was never one for discord. "First Division already moved on."

"They're just ripping up track," Wilmer speculated. "They'll be back come nightfall, bet you a dollar."

Lord, it was stink-hot. All the heat crowded up late afternoons.

Roback felt the nip of a louse in his armpit. Hard to remember the last time he'd had a dousing that passed for a bath. Rain didn't count, just left a man feeling worse. Back on the North Anna? That long? Just scrubbing himself with water from a bucket since—when was it?—May. Old sweat clung.

"Smarten up. I mean it," Sergeant Wetherall told them. "There's Captain Burt and the adjutant. Don't go looking like the Oswego militia."

George Crimmons, who had been silent all day, laughed. "We *are* the Oswego militia. 'Least, I am."

"Lieutenant Quaiffe's all right, he don't mind so."

"Captain Burt's fair, too," Roback said, eager, as he always was, to see goodness. "He knows we been pressed."

"We'll see how long those two last," McCammon said, with months of weariness souring his voice. The 152nd New York had lost so many officers that it was now commanded by the captain. On the other hand, the regiment was barely the size of a company, with fewer than a hundred men present for duty. In a way, it balanced out, Roback supposed.

"Bad luck, talking so," Pete Buck told McCammon.

Seven p.m., August 24
Monk's Neck Bridge

Billy Mahone rode into Hampton's camp beside A. P. Hill. Had no real business being there, but he'd felt like coming out.

Rambunctious. A man could only sit still for so long when things were doing.

He saw a quizzical look pass over Hampton's slab of face. Just made him smile inside. Hampton was a man who couldn't bear not knowing what was what and who was who. No sense of humor, either. Big as the South Carolinian was, Otelia would've devoured him.

The party dismounted. Mahone followed Hill. Hampton's staff stood waiting. Every man present seemed dwarfed by the cavalry general.

Salutes rendered, Hampton held out his hand to Hill, then to Mahone. It was a quirk of Wade Hampton's that he always shook hands on meeting, unless in the midst of violence. Hampton's voice was soft and his handshake mild, as if that big paw whispered, "I don't need to impress you."

"Didn't know you were joining us tomorrow," Hampton told Mahone.

"Ain't. Just thought I'd take some air, come out and see how y'all plan to use my boys. While I'm back in the ditches playing solitaire."

Hampton nodded.

Hill put in: "Harry will be along. He's moving up his men."

"And holding up my two brigades behind," Mahone said, smiling. "With me left like a bridegroom at the altar."

"We'll have a potent force," Hill added. "Lee's all for it now, he wants Hancock crushed."

Hampton smiled down at the corps commander, then waved up a lieutenant, who approached with a hint of timidity. Mahone recognized the cavalryman's son, or believed he did. Didn't look much like him, though. Probably took after the mother.

"Your pardon, General Hill . . . General Mahone, I don't think you've met my son. . . ."

"Not formally. Know him to see."

"Then may I present Lieutenant Preston Hampton?"

The boy bent his shoulders forward an inch. He had fine, womanly eyes. "An honor, sir."

"I'm sure the honor's mine," Mahone said, thrusting out his hand. "Son of General Hampton's . . ."

The boy made a youthful effort to impress him with his grip. Mahone responded by clamping the offending paw hard enough to hurt, just short of cracking bone. Let the young buck learn that a small man wasn't necessarily a little man.

"Mighty fine handshake you got there, Lieutenant," Mahone said as he let go.

Boy would turn out fine, no doubt. If he didn't get himself killed, trying to live up to some notion of chivalry drawn out of a book. Mahone and his wife enjoyed the novels of Walter Scott no end, but never confused them with reality: Folks weren't really like that.

"My eldest son will be joining my staff, too. Young Wade." The cavalryman beamed out pride as he spoke, a rare display of emotion. "He's been serving with Joe Johnston."

"Army's bound to be better for it, gaining another Hampton," Mahone said. "I look forward to shaking his hand."

Turning, Hampton told his fellow generals, "I cannot offer a grand repast, but we did impound some splendid Yankee coffee. . . ."

A young man who knew his place, the lieutenant sauntered off. The ranking officers headed for the cooking fire.

Hampton was big, all right, but his gestures had an odd streak of the feminine. Passed for grace in Charleston, Mahone supposed. Yet Wade Hampton was said to have killed a bear—some claimed two—with just a hunting knife. And witnesses attested that he'd cloven at least one Yankee horseman from shoulder to waist with his saber.

It was also reputed that Hampton had been set against secession, that he'd predicted a war would be a disaster. Yet every day of that man's life, every privilege and every source of pride, had made this war inevitable. And he couldn't see it, none of them could. Mahone had read Carlyle at Otelia's prodding and could smell the *ancien régime* from a distance. Hampton seemed one of those doomed aristocrats, the kind who tried vainly to come to terms with a changing world and failed. Maybe more Dickens than Carlyle, from the book with that knitting harpy.

Tale of Two Cities. Could as well have been Washington and Richmond. And Hampton might be a brilliant cavalry officer, but he was a man of the past, no way around it.

Mahone didn't dote on such matters overly much. Didn't feel strongly, one way or the other. Just looked at things as they were, one more engineering problem. The stresses were such and such, the bridge bore so great a load and not an ounce more. No matter how the war ended, Billy Mahone believed that the bridge to the past that Hampton and his kind fought to preserve would collapse anyway.

The future belonged to the railroads, to steam, to gas lights and telegraphs, not to plantations built on nigger sweat.

Lee was that way, too, of course. Even Powell Hill was, if on a humbler scale. Beauregard might figure it out, but few of the others would. Aristocrats in a dying order never believed it was dying, couldn't imagine it. Wasted half their time squabbling amongst themselves, clinging to small advantages and exaggerating slights. Unable to see beyond their little fiefs.

Mahone was a proud Virginian, but not to the point of folly. He was well aware of Lee's mistreatment of Hampton the winter before, when Lee released his nephew's division and the other Virginians from line duty, sending them to unspoiled pastures to fatten up their horses, while Hampton's nags were ridden to death on outpost work along the Rapidan. Enchanted by his own name and all things Virginian, Lee had been unjust. All had seen it, none had said it. But, then, woe unto the Georgian who tried to enter an Alabamian hospital. Or to the starving Mississippian who tried to draw on North Carolina rations. . . .

There were times when the particularism and jealousies grew so hot that Mahone all but expected that, once they won the war, states would soon be seceding from the Confederacy.

A railroad man had to see past boundaries, though. However

the war ended, railroads would have to be rebuilt, and to turn a fair dollar they'd have to cross state lines, perhaps borders between nations, spanning a continent. The country may have broken apart and it might well stay divided, but empires waited for bold men to construct them.

Hampton and his kind relied on Negroes. Billy Mahone preferred surveying tools.

He wasn't fighting to preserve the past. Good riddance. He was fighting because that was what a man *did*. And because he didn't like being told off by Yankees any more than he bent a knee to the syphilitic sons of plantation masters. Or to their haughty daughters, who couldn't squat over a piss pot without a mammy's help.

Drinking his coffee and listening to Hampton and Hill patter on about horses, Mahone smiled to think of Otelia, who had more sense than any of them. When the war had begun and he'd moved to do his duty and place their little wealth in Confederate bonds, Otelia had put her foot down, telling him, "You and the other children can go play war, but you won't leave me poor, William Mahone. You can lay out this much, but not a cent more, and I'll hear no dispute. You're putting the rest in gold and you're going to hand it over to me to lay it by, not some hollowed-out bank. And when this war ends, whatever may come, you'll thank me. *If* you don't get your fool head shot off."

No, he wasn't rich the way rumors had it. But he wouldn't die poor. Hampton and his kind might prove bankrupts, though. Even if the South won, who'd cover their notes? The mills of England had already turned to India and Egypt for cotton. What did Hampton's puffed-up gentry offer a changing world?

With Billy Sherman clawing at Atlanta, things weren't looking happy for the old ways.

As for Mahone, he didn't hate Yankees particularly. Just found them obnoxious, self-righteous as driven-off preachers. The South knew how to live but couldn't afford it, while the North was rich but didn't know how to live. No, he didn't hate Yankees. But he didn't mind killing them, either. Or the coloreds they had no business stirring up. It was just in the nature of things. His nature, anyway.

He did enjoy the fighting, that he did. Be sorry when it ended. Finest thrill a man could have short of one other delight, and that act couldn't be performed in public. Sorry he wasn't included in this cotillion. But Hill wanted him in command of the lines because he trusted him to perform marvels, should the Yankees attack.

Still . . .

Otelia had foreseen so much, reminding him just the past winter, "Billy, it won't suffice for you to be the best railroad builder this side of the moon. Not if you don't have money enough to put up a front, so thank me. Comes time to rebuild, trick's going to be to get all the money other folks hid away to back your endeavors. And the best way to do that's going to be to put up just enough show to make them think you don't need them, that you're doing them a favor letting them in. There's nothing a rich man loves more than loaning money to a man who doesn't need it."

"Thought I married my little Otelia," he'd told her. "Here I find I'm wed to Becky Sharp."

"Sharper than you know, and you be glad of it, William Mahone. And don't you 'little' me till you've grown six inches."

As night wrapped around Hampton's camp and the talk eased to gossip, Mahone excused himself.

"Guess I'd better get on back. In case we got this whole thing upside down." He turned to Hampton. "Pleasure visiting."

"Always welcome, General," Hampton said.

"Y'all do good tomorrow," Mahone told them.

One a.m., August 25
Headquarters, Army of the Potomac

Another late night. Humphreys grimaced. Why bother to sleep at all?

Meade was still awake, too. He looked like an old hound past his last hunt.

Humphreys said, "Message went off to Hancock, all his questions answered. I'd feel better if he showed a touch more concern, though. Warren's convinced those Rebs are bound for Reams Station."

"We'll see," Meade said. His cold still clung to his voice. "Could be another go at Warren's position. Can't rule it out, not yet."

The chief of staff shook his head. "Doubt it. One thing you have to give G.K., he knows how to fortify. Lee would be mad to go at him now. Even I was impressed, when I went over there." He almost smiled, but didn't quite indulge. "Even old Dennis 'Heartless' Mahan would approve."

"Still . . . he's been wrong of late. And slow to correct himself. Size of his losses in the tavern fight, for one example. Grant first learned it from the Richmond papers. And he didn't like it."

"I didn't, either. But you know Warren, almost as well as I do. Damned good engineer, slow but thorough. If anything, he sees spooks, Confederates everywhere." Humphreys surprised himself with a yawn. "I expected a plea for reinforcements, but he's confident his position is secure. So Win needs to look out, I've tried to tell him. Those Johnnies are headed his way, I'd bet two squaws and a pony."

Meade caught the yawning contagion. "How many did Fisher count?"

"Eight to ten thousand on the march. Maybe more. All swinging around our left. And they're not working parties. Ambulance trains trailing them, supply wagons . . . they're coming out to fight."

"If Hancock needs help . . ."

"Could release two of Mott's brigades back to Hancock, I could make up the numbers. And we could pull a Ninth Corps division from Globe Tavern. Warren's got all he needs."

Meade nodded heavily. "Get out the orders early. Wait until Win asks, before you send anybody, though. He's been touchy. Don't want him to think we mistrust his judgment."

"He's tired," Humphreys said. "That mess north of the James. Second Corps needs a rest, George."

"Finish with the Weldon. Then they can rest."

"Might've been better to use another corps."

Meade's expression disbelieved that. "I trust Hancock."

"Win's not at his best, George. He's ailing. And look at Barlow . . ."

"Let's hope the medicos do their job this time." Meade's face tightened, thoughtful. "Remarkable officer, Barlow. For someone who never saw West Point."

Humphreys smiled, despite himself. "Your toady Lyman would set you straight on that point. Seems Harvard's the only institution of higher learning that counts for a monkey's fart."

"You're too hard on Teddy," Meade told him.

"Little coddler looks at me like I should be shining his shoes."

It was Meade's turn to smile. "Well, your credit's as good in Philadelphia as Teddy's is in Boston."

"I can't even bear the way those people talk."

Meade's expression grew milder, almost unguarded. "You know, Humph, I've always wondered about something. You . . . why West Point, not old Penn? And why did you stay in?"

"I could ask the same of you."

"No, it's different. My family had name. But no money. Lost it, that Spanish business, my father. So West Point was about it. But you . . . how far back does your family go? Almost sounds like they beat Willy Penn down the gangplank. And you're a wealthy man."

It was an unusually personal query from Meade, very un-Philadelphian. Humphreys ascribed it to the late hour, to their mutual exhaustion. But he answered.

"Didn't want to sit on the exchange, a third-rate Girard. Afternoons at the club, gout by forty, cow of a wife for company." He grunted at the horrors he'd evaded. "Wanted to *do* something. Make my own way, I suppose." He shrugged. "You know how it is, George, Army life. Like being an opium eater or a drunkard. Before you know it, you just can't give it up." He looked down at the floor, back through the years. "Been angry as the devil many a day, but I never regretted putting on this uniform."

In the background, the telegraph clicked: No sleep yet.

Before turning back to business, Humphreys said, "I suppose you're either an Army man, or you're not. Simple as that."

Two a.m., August 25
Mahone's headquarters, Petersburg

He dreamed of home, of his mother. His father was absent, the reason unclear. It was home, but not home. Bright summer. Hot. Mahone was grown, yet his mother was still young. They were on the river, hiding, fleeing. His mother sat pale and terrified in the boat. Nat Turner and his ruffians were after them, hunting them in particular. The river shone in the sunlight, golden and red as blood. At a bend, the banks were lined with uniformed Negroes: Nat Turner's men, hundreds, thousands, impossible. There was no way to get past them. They slipped into the water like alligators, coming for them. His father had left him and his mother, taking the others away, that was why he wasn't there. Leaving him to defend his mother against gaping black maws, uniforms, rifles . . .

He woke amid bedclothes poisoned by his sweat.

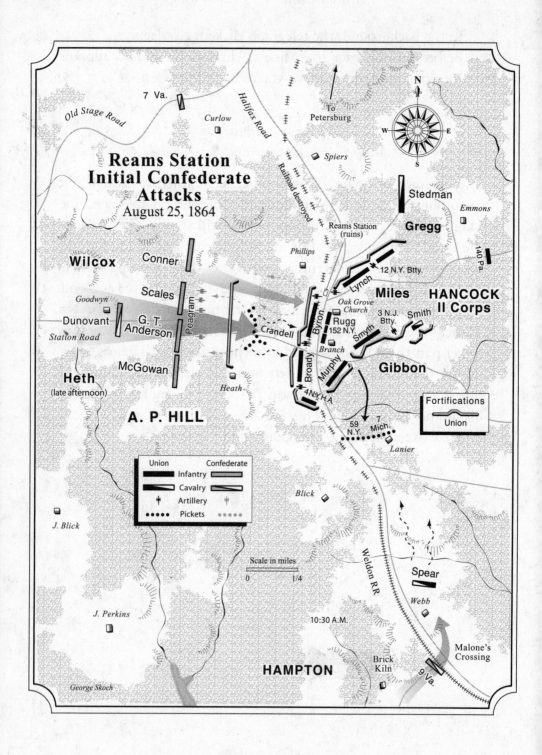

Reams Station Initial Confederate Attacks
August 25, 1864

7 Va.

Old Stage Road

Curlow

Halifax Road

To Petersburg

Railroad destroyed

Spiers

Stedman

Reams Station (ruins)

Gregg

Emmons

140 Pa.

Wilcox

Conner

Phillips

12 N.Y. Btty.

Lynch

Miles

HANCOCK II Corps

Scales

Goodwyn

Peagram

Oak Grove Church

3 N.J. Btty.

Smith

Rugg

152 N.Y.

Dunovant

G. T. Anderson

Crandell

Byron

Smyth

Station Road

McGowan

Branch

Broady

Murphy

Gibbon

Heth
(late afternoon)

Heath

4 N.Y. H.A.

59 N.Y.

7 Mich.

Fortifications

Union

A. P. HILL

Lanier

Union   Confederate

Infantry

Cavalry

Artillery

Pickets

J. Blick

Blick

Spear

Scale in miles

0   1/4

Webb

Weldon RR

J. Perkins

10:30 A.M.

HAMPTON

Brick Kiln

Malone's Crossing

9 Va.

George Skoch

TEN

Hancock limped toward the old frame church and the dismounting cavalryman. Miles followed, along with Gibbon, his fellow division commander, and Walker, Hancock's adjutant. Charlie Morgan was off, fists balled, stalking the quartermaster. Around the gathering of officers, Miles' soldiers worked to improve the defenses, sweating in the face-slap morning sun. Glad to watch others at work, the men of Gibbon's division lolled, waiting for orders to march out and take their turn at wrecking the railroad.

Brigadier General David McMurtrie Gregg handed off his horse. Face powdered with dust above a sweat-matted beard, he looked as though he hadn't slept an hour since the war began.

"No Reb infantry," Gregg reported, bloodshot eyes on Hancock. "Pushed two miles out, bit more. Just Hampton's pickets, up to their usual mischief. Rode off when they saw we were in force."

Miles sensed Hancock's relief.

"Good," the corps commander said. "That's good."

"He's still out there, though. Hampton. At least one mounted division, maybe two. He'll be prickly again today." Gregg smacked his hat against his thigh. Dust bloomed. "They don't want us crossing Rowanty Creek, they've made that clear enough. Spear thinks Hampton means to push up that bridge road, badger our work parties."

"I'm not concerned about Hampton. Just hold him at a distance," Hancock said. "I'll send you a brigade, if he gets ambitious." Hancock's expression tightened and he rubbed his close-shaven jaw. "Humphreys was all but certain we'd face infantry. The reports . . ."

"Probably extending their lines," Gibbon put in. "Making sure Warren can't flank them. The Weldon's gone, and they know it. Hampton's just ornery."

Hancock nodded. "Makes more sense than risking a fight this far out. Lee has to shield the Boydton Plank Road now. And the South Side. That's the game." Considering, he turned again to Gibbon: "Still . . . a bit of caution, John. Keep half your division under arms while you're out there."

"Everything else as planned?"

"As planned. Rip up all the track you can. Just keep an eye out. Wade Hampton would love to pull off a stunt." Hancock smiled his first smile of the day, perhaps of the month. "Such as scooping up a division commander and putting him on display in downtown Richmond."

The corps commander turned to Miles. "You look like something wants to come out of one end or the other."

"Rebs may just be late, sir," Miles suggested. "Hard march for their infantry, if they're looping around to come at us from the west." He scratched a mosquito bite on the back of his neck, a new plague atop his sunburn. "They attacked Warren late at Globe Tavern."

Hancock began to shake his head and stopped himself. "Well, we're not going to let our guard down." He considered his subordinates. "Are we, gentlemen? But the sooner we finish taking up that track, the sooner we can leave this shithole behind." His face had a lemon-suck look. "I won't mind going, myself."

"Men won't, either," Gibbon told him.

"All right, then. Every man to his duty. Walker, see if that damned telegraph's up. General Gregg, you keep Hampton amused."

"It's a vendetta now," the cavalry officer said. "Horses are tiring, though." He touched two fingers to the brim of his hat and turned to his mount.

Gibbon marched off, hard-faced and cold as ever, shouting

orders. His division staff rushed to overtake him. Walker headed toward the staff tents and an adjutant's endless concerns. Miles was about to step off himself when Hancock halted him by the lift of an eyebrow.

"You can ease up on the men. Since Gregg found nothing." Quickly, Hancock added, "I don't mean stop work entirely, of course. Christ Jesus, aren't these earthworks wretched? Just moderate the pace, don't work them to death." The big man's lips curled, wrestling his mustache. "I'd hoped to rest your men today, Morgan's been at me like Lucifer with a pitchfork."

"I'd like to strengthen the picket line, though. Bad enough that the guns can't support it properly, given those trees. If Reb infantry *do* turn up . . ."

"Damned trees," Hancock spit. "Can't very well cut down a whole damned forest, not with everything else I'm asked to do." He looked away, to the west. "Well, be grateful for the fields we've got. We've been worse off. Damned Wilderness, for one place."

The major general bent his swelling torso and rubbed his thigh. Miles doubted that Hancock knew he was doing it. Discipline and reserve were breaking down. Even among generals.

"Go ahead, Miles," Hancock finished up. "Run the skirmish line however you wish, it's your division now. But spare the men where you can." He took off his hat and sopped the sweat from his forehead with a handkerchief. Hancock looked older than his years, much older than he had the year before.

They parted. Hancock to take the weight off his bad leg, Miles suspected. As for himself, he felt uneasy, unsure if it was his sense that the Rebs would come, after all, or concern that he might falter in command.

Hancock was right, of course. The men shouldn't be driven beyond reason. He'd criticized Barlow for that very thing. But the entrenchments wanted more improving than a full day's work—a day of relentless labor—could achieve. They couldn't let up just yet.

That smaller grove to the north wanted slashing, for one thing.

The trees edged too close to the berm, there were no good lines of fire. The higher sections of parapet needed proper firing steps, and railroad ties might be put to use as head logs, though they'd need shoring. Not least, every rifle pit needed improvement.

He decided to work the men another hour or two before letting anyone rest. The temperature wasn't all that bad, not really. They could go until it got hotter, soldiers didn't melt.

Abruptly, he stopped. Amid the tumult of men at labor and Gibbon's mob preparing to march down the rail line.

"Barlow," he said.

It was grotesque. Frank wasn't even dead, but his ghost had possessed him. He'd been acting, thinking and sounding just like Barlow. Just the morning before, he'd pleaded with Morgan to give his soldiers a respite. Now he was driving them as hard as Frank would have done.

Was it just the difference between commanding a brigade and a division, between looking after soldiers and looking off toward a broader horizon? Had Frank's apparent selfishness, his seeming cruelty, been something else entirely? Had Frank been . . . right?

A soldier shoveled dirt against Miles' boot.

Ten thirty a.m.
Malone's bridge

Call that handsome, I do," Lu Davis said proudly.

"Fair start," Hampton replied.

They watched from the south side of the creek as the dismounted men of the 9th Virginia chased the last Yankee cavalrymen from the brick kiln. The bluecoats ran off on foot, more than a few throwing down their repeating rifles.

The Virginians hallooed after the scattering Federals, as if they were mounted again and hunting foxes.

"All right, Lu," Hampton told the colonel, "hold up about here. Until I have a better sense of things."

"We could drive the rest of them, sir."

"Don't doubt it. But hold up. Go rope your boys in."

Davis rode off, a touch disappointed but schooled to crisp obedience.

The grand attack on Hancock and his corps had not come off. Not yet. The last Hampton had heard from A. P. Hill, who was ailing again, was that he'd needed to rest the infantry, who'd taken longer to march down from Petersburg than expected. They were still miles short of Reams Station.

So Hampton had taken action on his own, making good use of the extra time. He hoped to lure as many Yankees southward, away from Hancock's position, as he could before Hill got Heth and Wilcox into line to strike the earthworks. Divide and conquer, Hampton told himself. Worked against many an enemy, not just those wearing uniforms.

Rifle fire pocked again to the east. His son galloped in.

As Preston drew up, Hampton spoke first: "Better have something important to tell me, Lieutenant. Important enough for you to risk spoiling that horse."

"Yes, sir." Preston. Breathless, eager, vivid. "Just like you reckoned. Yankee infantry, at least two brigades, coming down the Halifax Road at the double-quick."

"That your mathematics? Or Colonel Cheek's?"

"The colonel's, sir."

"Then you should have reported it that way."

He was being too severe, he knew. But he feared softness on a battlefield. Softness killed. And he feared paternal leniency. His sons had to be above reproach, like Caesar's wife.

Seeing the wound in Preston's eyes—his dead wife's eyes—Hampton added:

"Good work, Lieutenant. Now walk that horse and water him in the creek."

"Yes, sir."

Thanks be to the Lord and poor old Hancock. Sending his men out at the double-quick, in this heat. They'd be blown before they got into the fight.

His horse tapped one foot, then another. As if impatient for battle.

Hampton reached for his map bag and searched its innards for paper and a pencil. Before he began to write, he signaled that he needed two couriers.

Off toward the railroad, the skirmishing grew bolder.

Tearing off the first note, he told one rider, "Take this to General Barringer. Tell him there's no need for a reply, unless he's being pressed."

The courier, a man with a hawk's face and a Patriarch's beard, gee-upped his horse without the use of spurs: a poor man who'd never worn such before he put on a uniform. But the cracker rode like a demon, light on a horse's back.

Next, Hampton wrote to A. P. Hill, reporting the situation and promising to draw the Yankees southward for as long and as far as he could. Meanwhile, he'd threaten Hancock's communications back to the Jerusalem Plank Road and the Union rear. He'd keep Hancock worried, keep him looking south and east—while Hill advanced his men from the west and north. As politely as he could, he encouraged Hill to attack as soon as possible.

To the east, his horse artillery went into action.

Twelve thirty p.m.
Reams Station

Charlie," Hancock said to his chief of staff, "I'd like to punch that sonofabitch in the face."

"I don't know, sir," Charlie Morgan said, grinning near unto insolence with that rough, reassuring face, "I hear Hampton's a big one. Might not turn out jolly."

Hancock stopped amid the broad commotion, with heavy skirmishing on two sides of the earthworks.

"You don't think that I could whip Wade Hampton? In a fair fight?"

"Not from what I hear."

Hancock couldn't quite murder his smile. "Hell of a chief of staff you are. Where's your goddamned loyalty?"

"My job's to keep you out of trouble, sir. Which can be a challenge. I'm doing my best."

"Dog-fuck job of it this morning."

"I return the compliment, General."

A mad burst of hoofbeats announced that another detachment of cavalry was pounding in from the west, along the Station Road. Running like rabbits.

"Judging by their indelicate haste," Morgan said, "I suspect there may be more than a handful of Johnnies headed this way."

"Last of Gibbon's men back in?" Hancock asked.

"All but Smyth. The guns are in. Have to give Hampton credit. . . ."

"Bastard almost pulled it off. Damned near."

"Cavalry's good for something. Ours, I mean. Did find Hill."

"Late in the game."

"Not too late, though," Morgan said.

Leg paining him badly, the old wound oozing again, Hancock said, "Closer than I like. See to the left return, would you? How the digging's coming?" He didn't add that he preferred not to walk one unneeded step.

Hadn't it been sweet, though? Back when he was whole and hearty, all but worshipped as "Hancock the Superb"? He'd enjoyed the adulation, wasn't ashamed to admit it. And now? Who had he become? "Hancock the Lame"?

He longed for one more smashing victory. He knew he couldn't command much longer, his body wouldn't support it. But he wanted to win one more time, to go out with his plumage still intact. Maybe even with the colors brightened.

He'd done poorly that morning, though. He saw it all too clearly. Hampton had toyed with him like a saloon gambler tormenting a bumpkin. Had the cavalry not blundered into Hill's men at last . . .

Well, he'd managed to recall Gibbon and put the defense back together. The Rebs would have a time of it. As poor as the position was, the Rebs would have to charge earthworks. And that rarely turned out well for the attacker.

"Hancock the Disappointing"? he thought with a rueful smile. Until embarrassingly recently, he'd entertained the notion that he, not George McClellan, might be the Democratic Party's nominee in the election, the man to replace Lincoln. But McClellan it would be, after the convention.

His thigh felt as though the bone would snap in two. His fat leg. Not long before, he'd been the very specimen of an officer, physically splendid. Now there were times, at night, when he wept with pain, unwilling and unable to take remedies, refusing to turn to drink. His valet, an Englishman of remarkable skill and spectacular cowardice, recommended laudanum. Which, of course, was out of the question.

Nelson Miles came up to report. And Charlie Morgan strutted back at an angle, already finished inspecting the left return, no waster of time. Hancock longed to be as spry as his chief of staff again. Or Miles, with his loping, stride-a-league limbs.

"Well, Miles?"

"Retook the outposts. Won't be long, though. Before they come on in strength. They're massing out there."

"Goddamn those trees. I'm minded to ride out and have a look myself."

"Best not," Morgan said, stepping up to the huddle in time to overhear.

Annoyed with himself, his memory, his leg, Hancock had to ask, "Did I . . . I did order the surgery moved? Didn't I?"

"Yes, sir. To the church."

"Good." He caught the look that passed between Morgan and Miles.

"Oh, there's fucking Ivanhoe," Charlie said.

Hancock turned to see: Gregg was back. One hoped with better news.

"Goddamn it, Charlie," Hancock said, "I've warned you not to mock my fellow generals, not to my face. At least do it behind my back."

Putting a choirboy look on his pitted features, Morgan answered in a cherub's voice, "I tries, sir. But I looks at them and can't help myself, I can't."

The three men burst out laughing.

"You think I won't court-martial you, Morgan? You think you can't be replaced?" But Hancock couldn't overcome his mirth.

"What's the joke?" David Gregg said, drawing off his riding gloves. The fellow was as sweat-soaked as any horse.

"Morgan here was being an ass again."

Somber and stained, Gregg was in no mood for levity. Hancock had ripped into the cavalry general not an hour before, after Hampton's men had almost severed the road to the Union rear.

"Are we tolerably safe now?" Hancock asked, a ghost of anger, spawn of remembrance, returning to his voice.

"Yes, sir," Gregg answered stiffly. "I put two more of my Pennsylvania regiments back there." He looked at Miles. "General Miles' regiments have been released. I appreciate the loan, but the road's secure now."

"Well then," Hancock said, "let's see if Powell Hill's pisser is working today." He, too, turned to Miles. "Close off the *porte d'entrée* on the Station Road, get a barricade up. I think the last of the cavalry's back in."

Gregg did not demur.

Miles offered a field salute. "Best get back to business, in any case." A half mile off, on the skirmish line, the firing redoubled. "Does seem like the Johnnies mean to fight."

Just one more victory, Hancock thought. *Just one more.*

One forty p.m.
Field headquarters of Lieutenant General A. P. Hill, CSA

Major General Cadmus Wilcox found his superior flat on a bed of moss, red shirt half-unbuttoned and trousers loosened. Bejeweled with sweat, face clenched, and eyes unsteady, A. P. Hill looked as though he were suffering the torments of an early Christian martyr, an image at odds with the source of Hill's complaint. Everyone knew what ailed the man, although the word went unspoken. One unlucky night and lifelong penance. Wilcox imagined Hill's insides rotting from the crotch upward.

Forcing himself to acknowledge Wilcox, Hill said, "Heth isn't up. Need to wait for Harry. Do this right."

"Sir . . . we're late as it is. Hampton—"

"Hampton can hold his own," Hill gritted out.

"Yes, sir. But Hancock's all but trapped himself. It's a terrible position. I rode out and had a look. It's a big, broken horseshoe, but not big enough. Overshoot one of his flanks, you'll hit the rear of the other one. Hard to believe that Hancock would let it stand— it's a downright invitation to skin him alive."

"Harry will be up. He'll be up soon."

"Yes, sir. But our chance is *now*. Before Hancock comes to his senses and pulls out. I've got four good brigades . . ."

Hill's features tightened in a spasm of pain. He'd been indisposed that first day at Gettysburg, too, and urgently needed decisions had been delayed. Every officer who'd been there remembered it well.

"I don't know . . . I need to get up . . ." Hill made no effort to rise.

"General Hill, I beg you. Let me attack. Hit the northwest corner, I can take those works with the men I have on hand."

Hill didn't answer for a time. Wrestling with pain or demons. Or both.

At last, Hill said, "Go ahead, Cad. Bust Hancock."

Two fifteen p.m.
Reams Station

Miles rode to a spot where the parapet dipped, arriving just in time to see the last men from the picket line dash through the lanes in the abatis and fly over the rampart like drunken acrobats. Across the field, Reb skirmishers filtered out of the scrub pines, holding their rifles just below their shoulders.

Yes, they'd come on now. In strength. The wait was over.

He felt his muscles tighten, his pulse quicken. Nothing like it. Nothing like it on earth.

Dismounting, he tossed the reins to an orderly, then made his way along the wall behind his Consolidated Brigade. As he passed the pitiful remnants of the Irish Brigade, still clinging to their flags, if lacking numbers, he called out, "I'm told the Irish are a peaceable people, meek and mild. With no liking for a donnybrook. Is that so?"

He desperately wanted to repair the damage done by Frank and his accusations.

One Irishman called, "And pure enough for the choirs of Heaven, too, and fresh as roses, that we be."

Another blasphemed and responded, "Tell me who said it, Genr'l, and I'll thrash the deceiver meself."

The men laughed, ever a good thing with bullets probing, and a third voice called, "Don't worry, Genr'l, me boyo, for we'll hand 'em a crock of turds at the end of *this* rainbow."

Colonel Levin Crandell, commanding the Consolidated Brigade, had been running the picket line for hours. Soggy as a man caught by a thunderstorm, he came up gasping, saluting and not waiting for a return.

"Developed them as best we could, sir. Three brigades, maybe four. Wilcox's Division, took a few prisoners."

"Prisoners have anything else to say?"

"Don't know much, it seems. Marched hard yesterday and marched hard again today."

"No sign of Heth? Or Mahone? Anybody else?"

Crandell shook his head. "Not yet."

Men on the rampart and down in the rifle pits dueled with the skirmishers, who hadn't chosen to prowl far beyond the trees.

"Doesn't make sense," Miles said. "Feels like an attack. But I can't see them attacking with one division."

The colonel pointed southward. "They've got Hampton's cavalry, too. And he's a sonofabitch."

Miles wasn't convinced. If it was only one division out there . . . and under Wilcox, at that . . . hard to believe that Hill would like the odds. He considered the possibility that the Confederates were sweeping around a flank with the rest of their force, but Gregg's horsemen had both flanks picketed strongly, there'd be a warning . . .

"Here they come!" a soldier shouted.

Private Henry Roback couldn't see a single Reb. The 152nd New York and the rest of the brigade had been ordered by General Gibbon himself to march up and form a close reserve behind the left of the First Division—which now seemed to be led by General Miles, the young one with rusty hair. They'd covered the few hundred yards at the double-quick, only to halt near a rickety church and stand staring at the backs of their fellow Yankees, the earthworks and muzzle smoke hiding all beyond.

Plenty of racket, though: those tormented-animal shrieks of the Rebel yell, coming closer and closer, and the deep *whup* of cannon, accompanied by flash, recoil, and billow. Within the defenses, officers plunged about, shouting, the half of them getting in everybody's way. Up at the wall, the veterans were easy to spot, firing and calmly loading again, their actions aped with less steadiness by the new levies. Men shouted abruptly, letting off the terrible buildup inside them, and the artillery horses stamped but didn't stampede—veterans themselves.

General Miles rode the line, as calm as if the air wasn't peppered with bullets.

"Another fool general out to get himself killed," Elias McCammon said.

Roback just wanted to *see*. That was by far the worst part of waiting to go into a fight, the raw unknowing, the uncertainty about what the next minute would bring.

As he sometimes did, when the waiting dragged on, he began

to repent of his sins and transgressions, which suddenly loomed larger. Just that morning, he'd peeked at a little deck of picture cards a photographer had made of a shameless woman. The other men had hooted and whistled, speculating on vile possibilities, but he'd turned away after glimpsing a few poses, astonished and sickened that a woman would show herself like that . . . worrying that maybe all women were secretly that way, Jezebels, Delilahs. Temptress Eve. He'd been disgusted, too, by the way his flesh responded to the pictures.

Roback was far from the most religious fellow in the regiment, but as he stood waiting for war to take him in, listening to those Rebel howls, blue-mouthed curses, and soldiers firing as fast as they could reload, he asked of the Lord forgiveness.

Miles felt taller, stronger, lit ablaze. A few of the Rebs had gotten close, only to pay with blood or the need to choose between surrender and death. Now the rest of them hurried back across the strip of field, seeking the grove from which they'd come, leaving comrades on the ground to twitch, flail an arm, or lie still.

One thing baffled him, though: It looked like the Rebs had advanced just two brigades, not a full division. That had been plain folly, a waste of brave men.

Trees swallowed the last Rebs. The soldiers behind the parapet hurrahed.

This was the thrill of it. The fighting, yes, that was splendid. But this quick spasm of victory, the sudden release of a torrent of emotion, of submerged fears, bloodlust, desire, rage . . . *this* was the crowning glory of a battle, the brief, brilliant recognition that your flesh had conquered their flesh . . . a sensation too soon dissolved by the need to take stock, give orders, and wake the soldiers serving under you from their own spells.

"All right," Miles called. "Ammunition up! Litter bearers! Officers, restore your lines! I want a count!"

He was acting like a regimental adjutant and he promptly corrected himself, turning silent as he surveyed the slight carnage and inevitable confusion within the earthworks. He commanded a division now and had to act accordingly. Subordinates needed to see to the cartridges boxes and the maimed.

God, it was magnificent, though. He feared the end of the war, that it might come before he'd proved himself so thoroughly that, as the armies in blue were dismantled, he might be offered a place in the Regular Army. He dreaded a return to the crockery shop. Or a place in any other civilian profession.

He'd learned long since that the Army was his love, perhaps his only one. He enjoyed the camaraderie, the company of bold men, the order of camp life, and the thrill of gunfire. Nelson Miles had found his home, his brotherhood.

Three p.m.
Jerusalem Plank Road
Army of the Potomac rear

Lot more marching than thinking going on, it seems to me," Levi Eckert said.

"Always been true in your case," Lieutenant Brown told him. Putting one foot in front of the other, as hot and worn as any of them. The chafing along his inner thighs was maddening. When he went for a squat, the skin looked like bloody raw beef.

It was just a contrary, hard-to-get-through day, a shade worse than most. Not just from the heat and the strain of the march, it was more than that. The men—even good men—were tired in a way they had not been before. Soldiers fell by the wayside earlier and more readily, giving in to whims of incapability or just plain pretending. The thing was that they didn't want to fight, they'd had enough, at least for the present.

But it was Brown's job to make them fight. Without a first sergeant, too. Sam Losch had been left behind, sick with the bloody squirts. Losch and a dozen others. And the soldiers of Company C still fit to march were as filthy as any Johnnies you could collar, lousy, itching, and grimly in need of a chance to bathe and boil every item of clothing they possessed.

Brown was glad that Frances couldn't see him. Or smell him.

"Don't see how it's our place to rush off to help out Second Corps," Levi added. "I don't remember those high-steppers helping us."

"Just see to your men, Sergeant," Brown told his fellow veteran. "This company isn't going to go to pieces. Because you're not going to let it."

Other companies in the 50th Pennsylvania already had their share of shirkers, though. And Brown knew he'd lose a few of his own charges. Maybe more than a few. Hundreds of men already had fallen out from the shrunken division. Marching toward a battle still so far off that Brown could barely hear it, like listening to a thunderstorm on the other side of First Mountain back on the canal. They certainly weren't taking the most direct route.

The men muttered, shifted their packs, and trudged on.

"You! Schwab! Get back in your place." The voice rose from deep in Sergeant Henry Hill. It was not open to dispute.

Private Schwab caught up to the marching rank from which he'd drifted.

It was a hard thing to understand, the way men were. They'd been proud to roaring about their deeds at Globe Tavern, a week before. Now they were sour, unwilling, with one great, unspoken question hovering over them: *When is all this going to end?*

Brown found himself hoping what the others hoped, that the hot march would prove a mistake on the part of some general, that they wouldn't be needed, after all.

To the west, the growl of battle dropped to a murmur.

Three p.m.
Reams Station, Confederate lines

Wilcox gathered in his brigade commanders. Scales, Lane, Anderson, McGowan. Proud, rancorous men. Anderson and Scales stood there disheveled, displeased, tempers coiled, the failed attack not half an hour behind them. Lane and McGowan waited for Wilcox to speak, Lane was hot but steady, McGowan impatient.

Bad start. Got close, though.

"Going to do it right this time," Wilcox said. "More force. Hit that western rampart hard, make sure to overlap them on our left. That northwest corner, that's the place to break through."

Wilcox understood what they were thinking: *Why not wait? Until Heth comes up? Heth, at least, if not the brigades loaned out by Billy Mahone? Why not hold off until they could overwhelm them?*

Cadmus Wilcox did not intend to wait. This was his opportunity, the chance to emerge from Harry Heth's long shadow. And from the lengthening shadow of Billy Mahone, made a major general. He intended to break Hancock, to seize his flags and batteries. He'd already put his sharpshooters to work killing the horses harnessed to limbers and caissons. He wouldn't let Hancock save a single fieldpiece, if he could help it.

"When the guns stop, that's the signal to go forward," Wilcox told them.

Four fifteen p.m.
Reams Station

Hancock felt rejuvenated. His men had repelled not just one, but two Confederate assaults and had done so handsomely. Oh, it wasn't a grand victory to be feted down the ages. But it was a win and a clean one.

And if they came at him again, he'd be prepared. But he sensed the fighting was over for the day, with storm clouds gathering on the western horizon. The Rebs had been brave enough—bodies lay as close as fifteen feet from the earthworks. But it no longer paid to send men out to charge fortifications, even poor ones. The Rebs had played their hand and lost. The sharpshooting that continued was just spite.

He turned to Charlie Morgan and Frank Walker. "Telegraphic

message to Humphreys at headquarters. And to Meade, wherever he is."

The adjutant clutched his pencil.

"Two attacks repelled. No reinforcement required at present. Will call on reserve if needed. Intend to withdraw after dark, in accordance with commanding general's guidance. Too risky to abandon the works during daylight. Confederates remain present but inactive."

He slapped his growing belly. "That should do it. I miss anything, Charlie?"

"No, sir. I'll ask that the Ninth Corps division hold the road open. In case Hampton gets playful."

"All right, then. Frank, you get my message off. Before the telegraph line gets snapped again. Charlie, if Mitchell returns from his sybaritic sojourn at City Point, send him to me immediately. Could've used a proper aide today. And make sure somebody's bringing up replacement horses for the artillery teams. The Rebs seem intent on butchering horseflesh today."

Morgan summoned a cold-blooded face, far from the one he wore to tell whorehouse jokes. "Makes me wonder if they're really done. Shooting up the horses, that suggests to me they want the guns."

"Pure spite. Hill failed in those last attacks on Warren, failed badly. Now he's fizzled again. It's just him being spiteful, the horses are all his sharpshooters can hit."

Morgan looked doubtful, but Hancock found himself smiling. However small a triumph, the day counted as his first unblemished victory in months. His Second Corps, *his* corps, had regained its luster.

Even his bad leg seemed less of a bother.

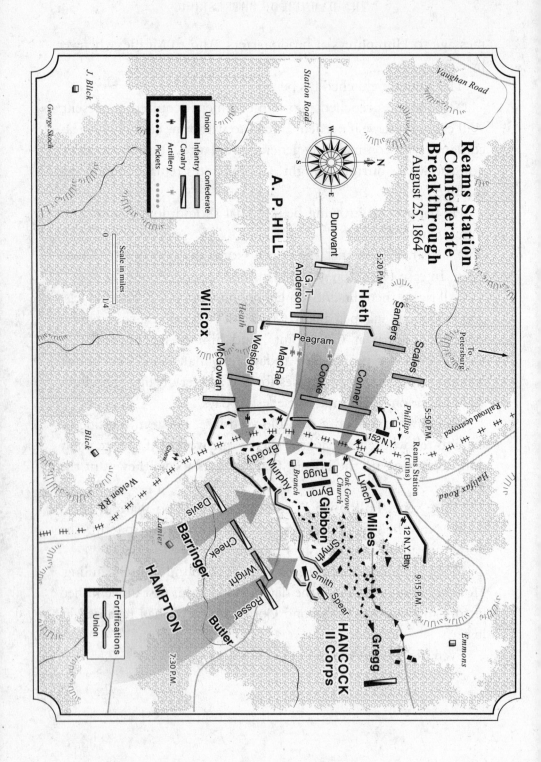

Reams Station Confederate Breakthrough
August 25, 1864

Legend:
- Union
- Confederate
- Infantry
- Cavalry
- Artillery
- Pickets

Scale in miles
0 — 1/4

Vaughan Road

Station Road

J. Blick

George Shook

A. P. HILL

Dunovant

5:20 P.M.

G. T. Anderson

Heth

Sanders

Scales

To Petersburg

Wilcox

Heath

Weisiger

Peagram

MacRae

McGowan

Cooke

Conner

5:50 P.M.

Phillips

152 N.Y.

Reams Station (ruins)

Railroad destroyed

Halifax Road

Blick

Weldon RR

Chew

Brody

Murphy

Branch

Rugg

Byron

Smyth

Gibbon

Oak Grove Church

Lynch

Miles

12 N.Y. Btty.

9:15 P.M.

Davis

Lanier

Barringer

Cheek

Wright

Rosser

HAMPTON

Butler

Smith

Spear

Gregg

HANCOCK II Corps

Emmons

Fortifications
Union

7:30 P.M.

ELEVEN

Give me the flag, son," Harry Heth said.

"General, I cain't do that," the private told him.

The cannonade Heth had ordered had fallen silent. Regiment after regiment, brigade upon brigade, the little army he led awaited his signal to advance through the pines, charge, and crush Win Hancock before the storm blew in.

With Hill flat on his back, Cad Wilcox had made a mess. Heth intended to fix it.

"Boy, you give me that flag."

"No, sir."

There they stood. In front of the men in their thousands. His division and Wilcox's, with two brigades of Mahone's bringing up the rear. While one private held up everything.

Tasked to send out a color-bearer, Lieutenant Waddell had chosen a goddamned mule. Heth almost tore into the boy—a soldier likely not twenty years old, but with lines cut in his face by blades of hardship.

The general checked himself.

"What's your name, Private?"

"Tom Minton, sir."

"Private Minton, I need to borrow your flag. To lead these men." Grandly, Heth swept an arm toward the regiments in plain view and those masked by greenery, adding, "It's the flag of the Twenty-sixth North Carolina, I can see that. Heroes of Gettysburg. I mean to honor it, son, carry it myself. Now let me have it."

"Cain't do that, General, sir. It's been trusted to me. You tell me where you want this flag to go, though, and I'll take it there, all right. But I won't surrender my colors."

The private was defiant beyond the outermost bounds of discipline. He needed a ride on a plank and a stretch of confinement.

Gripped by revelation, unasked and unexpected, Heth's heart changed. Pride overwhelmed him. Pride in a soldier so loyal to a torn cloth he'd defy a general, pride in an army so stubborn it would not give up.

"You won't give me your flag?"

The private shook his head.

Major General Henry Heth reached out and took the lad's arm.

"Come on, then. We'll carry the colors together, you and I. Let's wave your flag so every man can see."

In a moment, the two men, general and private, lofted the ragged red banner, flaunting it as a call to faith and a challenge to the faithless.

With a Rebel yell to rattle Creation, the shabby gray lines stepped forward.

Five twenty p.m.
Reams Station

The sound chilled Miles. The graybacks' yowling rolled across the too-narrow fields, as if Lee's entire army had arrived. Walking his line behind the Consolidated Brigade, he shifted quickly to wrath as he watched the first gray ranks burst from the trees.

Withdrawing pickets leapt over the breastworks, the old routine. Artillery pieces positioned to face the wood didn't wait for orders to open up. They fired case shot, then promptly switched to canister. At barked commands, the soldiers on the parapet opened fire—a crackle, then a roar.

Rebs fell everywhere, some dropping dully like sacks of meal, others broken apart by artillery blasts, scorching the air with blood. But they kept coming. Double-quick, flags high, rifles at the trail.

Keening that uncanny, ungodly screech. At last, they charged full out, defying their butchers.

His men kept up their fire. Miles shouted encouragement. The first Rebs reached the abatis and bullied their way through the sharpened branches.

"Shoot for their knees, shoot for their knees!" officers commanded.

The slaughter seemed immense. But the Johnnies weren't quitting this time.

Miles hastened to the right, to the 4th New York Heavies, shouting at them to concentrate on the graybacks slowed by the abatis, to fire obliquely.

When next he looked, it seemed the Rebs had been staggered. He spotted a few turning tail. Their formations were broken, moblike.

"Pour it into them!" he shouted. "Give it to them! Stand your ground and give it to them!"

It had been a near thing, but he felt he had them, that the Johnnies were ready to break. The carnage in the abatis was horrendous.

But when he looked left, the scene shocked him: *His* men were deserting the breastworks. Running.

Screaming, triumphant, gray-clad soldiers topped the parapet, followed by red flags.

Miles ran for the breakthrough, followed by aides and orderlies, with his horse-holder doing his best to follow along ten yards to the rear.

The Rebs were shouting, "Tarheels! Tarheels!"

Miles' line was folding inward from the flanks, with men on the right running, too. The Consolidated Brigade was collapsing, regiment by regiment, poisoned by draftees and new recruits.

Have to hold the shoulders. Hold the shoulders, close off the penetration.

As Miles paused at the edge of a railroad cut to take stock, a Reb color-bearer vaulted over the wall, landing in the ditch within touching distance, so close that Miles could read "North Carolina" on the banner.

Lane's Brigade, had to be. Tough buggers.

An orderly shot the Johnny. Miles called for his horse.

Hold the shoulders, seal off the penetration.

Rebs were everywhere.

Five forty p.m.

Harry Heth and Private Minton planted the flag of the 26th North Carolina atop the berm abandoned by the Yankees.

Five forty p.m.

Mounted, Miles could see that the Rebs who'd got through were disorganized. A shameful number of his men had panicked, but enough of his veterans still resisted to give the Johnnies pause. Confederate officers struggled to form up their companies and regiments, desperate to regain control and press the attack.

There still weren't that many of them in the works. They could be pushed out.

He rode the short distance back to Rugg's brigade, on loan from Gibbon and placed as a reserve. The men were still lying down from the bombardment. The one thing missing was Colonel Rugg himself.

"On your feet, men," Miles called, already hoarse. He pointed with his revolver. "That gap. Close that gap right there. Get up and give them a volley. Then charge."

The men rose, most of them. Instead of advancing, they turned and made for the rear. Not one fired a shot.

Five fifty p.m.

Things just felt plain wrong to Henry Roback. It wasn't the confusion, the smoke and noise. Not even the soldiers running for their lives. Something else just felt wrong.

They'd been detached from their brigade, and an unfamiliar

officer was screaming at them to change front and follow after him. Obedient, if doubtful, Roback and the rest of the 152nd New York scrambled over the berm of the northern return, with officers snapping at them to form back up and do it fast. At first, Roback couldn't understand what was being asked of them—they seemed to be leaving the fight, abandoning the defenses, rather than rushing to staunch the Rebel breakthrough.

Alarm gripped weary men, Roback felt it like a change in temperature.

As the officers hastily moved them forward again, at a left oblique, Roback grasped their purpose. They were being positioned to swing about and strike the Johnnies' flank, maybe their rear. And, sure enough, they soon were halted again and re-formed to enfilade the captured rifle pits, where Reb flags waved as graybacks muddled forward.

Before the regiment could fire a single volley, someone shouted, "They're behind us, the Rebs are behind us!"

And they were. A mass of them.

The 152nd New York broke ranks and fled. As he ran beside Roback, Elias McCammon's face exploded in a cloud of blood, launching bits of bone and an intact eyeball.

Roback ran faster.

Five fifty p.m.

Captain G. O. Holland, 28th North Carolina, Lane's Brigade, found himself at a social disadvantage. Waving his sword, he'd leapt atop the berm, only to discover that no one had followed. He looked down on a score of antagonized Yankees.

Mustering a confident look he hoped might appear genuine, Holland pointed his sword at his regiment's rear and announced, "Yanks, if y'all know what's best for you, you'd better make a blue streak towards sunset." When the Federals hesitated, he added, "Throw down your rifles and raise those hands, and I promise you won't be harmed."

To his relief and delight, the Yankees obeyed him, crawling over their parapet into captivity.

Five fifty p.m.

Miles rode for his Fourth Brigade, heedless of the danger. Broady's men still held their stretch of entrenchments, firing into the Rebs as fast as they could.

"Broady!" Miles hollered, gagging on the smoke. The colonel was occupied, back turned, deep in the fight.

Miles didn't want to dismount, there wasn't time. He reached out toward a soldier with an arm wound, halting him.

"First, you go and tell Colonel Broady I want him. Then you can go to the rear."

Bleeding like an opened-up hog, the soldier did as bidden.

Broady came up, smoke-blackened.

"Shift to the right." Miles pointed toward a line of abandoned rifle pits. "Hold there. Channel the Rebs. I'm going to counterattack."

And he meant to do just that. If he could find the men.

Broady looked hard-used, but he led a good brigade, if only a small one. The colonel said nothing, just nodded and turned back to his embattled soldiers, waving up his adjutant on his way back to the firing line.

Before Miles could ride off, the tenor of the commotion around him changed. Rebs flew over Broady's berm, landing amidst the 148th Pennsylvania. In seconds, a struggle of volleys became a chaos of man-on-man matches, with clubbed muskets, bayonets, fists, and even teeth the weapons of choice.

The Pennsylvanians, at least, were determined to hold.

Only a matter of time, Miles realized.

He shot a Reb with his revolver, then spurred his horse past the ambulatory wounded and other soldiers just sitting on the ground, as if having eggs on Sunday, past officers calling out the numbers of regiments that had dissolved and thieves looting discarded knapsacks. He rode toward Dauchy's battery, the 12th New York.

Dauchy had been hitting the Rebs still outside the parapet with canister, reloading as quickly as his cannoneers could.

Nearly riding down the lieutenant, Miles leaned over and shouted, "Forget the Rebs out there. Turn your guns. I need you to stop the Rebs who've gotten inside." He pointed through the smoke. "Shoot into that gap."

"Sir, our own men might—"

"*Fire into that gap.* My order, my responsibility."

A surviving orderly interrupted. "Sir, look over there. Off to the right."

Through earthbound clouds, Miles just made out another echelon of Rebel infantry. Heading for the extreme right of the line, an obvious attempt to roll him up. His flank pickets fled before them.

Christ. "Dauchy, you'll have to split your battery. And expose your guns, no choice. Work that gap. *And* the road up there."

All but sentenced to death, the lieutenant saluted.

Miles rode rearward again, hoping that, by some unholy magic, he'd find enough men to stage a counterattack.

Shells burst in the depths of the position, increasing the havoc. The Rebs had advanced their batteries.

But a miracle *did* happen. Where every other regiment seemed to have turned tail, Miles glimpsed the 61st New York changing front to meet the Rebel advance, pivoting off the earthworks, determined to hold their ground.

In the brimming chaos, the sight stopped him. The 61st was Barlow's old regiment and his own, its veterans men who once had bucked and kicked against Frank's discipline, only to proudly label themselves "Barlow's Regulars" after Frank led their charges on the Peninsula.

The New Yorkers were stalwart, refusing to give up an inch. But he needed more.

Damning the bullets that sought him, Miles called to small bands of soldiers and stray men who still had their rifles, "Look at the New Yorkers! Come on, men! Rally on the Sixty-first, we're going to win this fight!"

Some of the men upon whom he called just ran. Others stared, dazed. Some dozens followed him, though.

His division color-bearers found him again.

"Jaysus, General," a color sergeant exclaimed, "we thought you was dead twicet over."

More men rallied.

Taking personal command, he shifted the 61st across the northern berm—a low, halfhearted construction—and formed the shreds of other regiments on the New Yorkers' flanks. He judged his strength to be two hundred men.

The thing to do was attack.

Still mounted, with his division's banners following, Miles led his soldiers into the madness.

Six twenty p.m.

Pain forgotten, Hancock led another patchwork contingent forward to Miles, up where the brawling had spilled beyond the entrenchments and into the fields. He'd ordered Gibbon, who had two intact brigades, to organize a proper counterattack from the southern return, to try again to stem the flood of Johnnies. Meanwhile, Miles was all that stood in the way of a frightful defeat.

His men, *his* men, had never run like this before. He'd all but shamed himself, crying out, "Men! Will you leave your general? Men, will you leave me?"

They *had* to hold. The Second Corps had never been driven from a defensive position, not once in the war. If they could hang on for another hour, maybe a few minutes more, it might be all right. The sky was darkening prematurely, not only from the clinging smoke, but under gunmetal clouds that promised a downpour.

What had Wellington said? "Give me night, or give me Blücher"?

He caught up with Miles by three of Dauchy's guns. They'd been lost and, thanks to Miles, retaken.

"You shouldn't be this far forward, sir," Miles told him. Almost irritated. Bullets ripped the air.

"Then where the devil should I be?" Hancock turned his own wrath on Lieutenant Dauchy, who stood dumbly by a fieldpiece. "Well, Dauchy? Why aren't these guns in action? We took them back for you."

The lieutenant looked stricken. Unfair, Hancock told himself, you're being monstrously unfair. The artillerymen, all of them, were the bravest men on the field, standing to their guns until overrun.

"No lanyards," Miles spoke for Dauchy, shouting against the din.

"Fuck me bloody," Hancock said. Furious at the world, he turned on Dauchy again. "Well, *get* some buggering lanyards."

For the first time, he noticed the artillery sergeant sitting behind Dauchy, short jacket and breeches splayed open. Propped against the wheel of a gun, the fellow was holding up his own intestines, a string of bloody gray sausages, for inspection. The sergeant's face showed amazement, not the least suffering.

Hancock knew he owed Dauchy an apolgy. But apologies had to wait. Before releasing Miles back to his battle, the corps commander said, "Gibbon's arranging a counterattack. Any time now. Provost marshal and one of Gregg's regiments put up a screen in the rear, they'll bring back any runaways they can."

"Reinforcements?"

"Too late. Wouldn't get up before dark." His fault, his pride. He should have demanded that Mott's men as well as that Ninth Corps division come up the moment the Rebs were spotted in force. But he had wanted his corps' reputation restored. . . .

Pride.

Tugging his horse about, he told Miles, "You've got to hold them, Nel."

"To hell with 'hold,' " Miles said. "I'll whip these bastards."

The young brigadier looked as though he might do it, too. Ablaze and splendid. Urging his horse rearward, Hancock recalled the days when he'd been like that.

A round struck his mount in the neck and the beast toppled. Hancock barely rolled free. He struck the ground hard.

When he got to his feet, shocked and aching, an orderly informed him that his adjutant Frank Walker had just been captured.

Six twenty p.m.

Retake those works," John Gibbon told Tom Smyth, his favorite brigade commander. "Murphy can support you. Restore the line, Tom."

Smyth's mouth opened, but no words came out.

"Easier said than done, I know," Gibbon allowed. "But you can do it. You have to." He looked around. "Better than lying here taking it."

"Yes, sir. But Jesus . . ." He turned to pass on the order to his subordinates. Next to Gibbon, a color-bearer slapped his chest and fell bleeding onto his horse's neck, dropping the flag.

The men of Smyth's brigade had sparred with Hampton for much of the day. Then, exhausted, they'd found themselves being shelled from their rear as the Rebs attacked Miles' lines. Stray bullets had struck good men in the back. Things had gotten so bad that Smyth had ordered them to climb over their works and shelter on the outside. Compared to the artillery fire and the chaos within the entrenchments, Hampton's actions were little more than harassment.

Nerves were stretched, though. The men were aware—the veterans were—of how poorly things were going.

With his regimental commanders gathered hastily, Smyth explained what each man needed to do. As the group broke up again, he received word that he'd be supported by four more regiments, including two of Rugg's that had been pieced back together.

Smyth's confidence grew. He'd have a significant force under his command.

His attack dissolved within the first hundred yards.

Six fifty p.m.

Harry Heth was angry. He'd beaten the Yankees, fair and square, wrecking one brigade after another. And now his men had stumbled to a halt.

He stood just outside the entrenchments, receiving reports, issuing orders, and trying not to let his temper rule.

The Yankees couldn't push them back, but they couldn't push the Yankees any farther. And some damned bluecoat general was riding about as if on dress parade, a supernatural creature immune to lead. Bravest damned thing Heth had seen in a good age. He almost hoped a bullet wouldn't find the man.

The Yankees had rallied a desperate defense. Thanks to the general Heth couldn't quite recognize.

He'd done it, though. Shamed Win Hancock. The parade of prisoners heading rearward was set to rival the numbers taken from Warren at Globe Tavern. They were good men, too—the ones who'd stood and fought, not just skulkers and runaways.

Above the roar, a thunderclap boomed in the west, so powerful it shamed the human clamor.

He needed to finish this. Weisiger's Virginians, Mahone's bunch, had reached the field. They needed to go in and end the misery.

Turning to call for another courier, he was startled to see Powell Hill riding toward him, followed by his full retinue, flags lofting.

Hill certainly had a peculiar sense of timing. Heth would as soon have had him rest his innards a trifle longer.

"Thought they were whipped," Hill said.

Heth nodded. "They were. They are."

"Still making a ruckus."

"They're whipped. They just won't admit it."

Hill looked skyward: a breathing cadaver's face turned up to heaven. "Well, it's time they did." He spit. "Looks like we already took half of them prisoner."

"We'll take the other half, too. Or run them off. Sir, I'm told the Virginians have come up."

"Alabamians, too. Tired, but willing."

"I'd like to send them in. Close this thing down." Heth, too, glanced toward the lowering clouds. "Before the rain, before dark. Just make an end of it."

Hill nodded. "They're on their way."

Seven p.m.

Wade Hampton believed in the gentlemanly virtue of patience, when patience was asked for. But one of his black, keep-your-distance moods had settled on him as he watched and listened to the infantry get so far and then no farther.

His men had pressed the Federals all day. Even now, he kept their southern flank under light fire while probing to their rear back by the swamp. But it was the job of the infantry to storm earthworks, not a task for cavalry, mounted or dismounted.

What frustrated him the most was the sense he'd developed for the flow of battles, the sort of nose some men had for the where-abouts of game. Now he sensed—every long and broad inch of him—that the Yankees were ready to break for the final time, that his peers in gray just had to show resolve.

Blood told, of course. His grandfather had fought in the Rev-olution, part of the war of hatchets in the backwoods. And his father had served in the War of 1812. Perhaps some men were bred to fight, even if it wasn't their preferred path. Perhaps he had inherited something other men had not, instincts no acad-emy could teach.

"Time to get this over with," he said.

Standing near, his son turned fully toward him. Open-faced, eager.

"Sir?"

"Pencil and paper, Lieutenant. I have orders to write. Quick now."

If the infantry couldn't put a bow on this, he knew who would.

Seven fifteen p.m.

Mounted again—his horse had risen from the dead like Lazarus—Hancock met his chief of staff by the waiting headquarters wagons.

"What word, Charlie?"

"Two Eleventh Corps brigades are moving up. They'll hold the route open to the Jerusalem Plank Road. Scoop up the runaways, too. But Gregg needs to keep the road open that far back, say a mile and a half."

"Shameful. Goddamn it. *Shameful.*" Even if they held on until dark, they'd have to slip off like fugitives and give up the ground. It broke his heart to think it.

A few hundred yards to the west, the battle raged on, with Miles working wonders. And the artillery, bless them. He owed Dauchy and every redleg an apology. On bended knee.

Canting his rump from the saddle, Hancock reached over to Morgan and laid a hand on his shoulder.

"Colonel Morgan, I do not care to die. But I pray to God I may never leave this field."

Unmoved by his commander's display of sentiment, Morgan replied, "If we don't keep that road open, none of us leave."

Seven twenty p.m.

Here's what you need to do, Lynch," Miles said. He glanced again at the odd force the colonel had somehow assembled, a few hundred soldiers gathered up from the ruins of every regiment in the corps. Truly, a forlorn hope. "The guns have cleared them from that stretch ahead. You go right through, get back across the rail bed. Wheel left and hit them on the flank again."

The begrimed colonel wore an expression at once resigned to his fate and determined to fight. Nodding once, he turned to his motley force. In less than a minute, he had them on the move, their ranks uneven but willing, the men strangers to one another and led by officers they didn't recognize. They followed Lynch forward, their spirit a last glimpse of the old Second Corps.

Miles watched them go, peering through the smoke and filthy air as the little battalion crossed the rail bed and wheeled left as ordered, Lynch at the fore all the while. They halted, fired a volley, and rushed forward with a hurrah. He lost sight of them for a time, his view blocked by the parapet and a heavy drift of smoke.

When he glimpsed them again, minutes later, Lynch's informal command was in retreat, their numbers much reduced.

But they'd bought time. It was all about time now. Miles felt enraged, determined to sacrifice anything, any life—including his own—to assert the position, to hold until the Rebs had to break off. He was *not* going to fail the first time he had unfettered command of the First Division of the Second Corps, long considered the finest in the Army and now a wreck.

To his shock, he saw another brigade of Confederates advancing.

Seven thirty p.m.

Hampton's horse artillery fired a signal shot. He hoped the sound was distinct enough.

It was. In moments, his dismounted soldiers swept forward, some dashing through a cornfield, others breaking their way through tangled brush, and the remainder trotting across an open field. Screaming like devils loosed on a camp meeting.

"Sir? May I join the attack?"

Hampton looked at his son. "Lieutenant, your place is on my staff. Right here." Refusing to smile, refusing to show his pride, he added, "You've demonstrated your lack of judgment sufficiently often today."

By riding where the fighting was the thickest, stretching his orders into opportunities. A Hampton born, even with those gentle eyes.

Spurring his horse and raising a gloved hand, Hampton gestured for his colors and staff to follow him forward.

Seven forty p.m.

Gibbon was stunned. He'd turned the remnants of his division to fight the Johnnies advancing within the earthworks, fresh Reb blood pouring in. Now Hampton's troopers were coming at him like maniacs, striking the rear of his line, his former front.

All along the feeble line his officers and sergeants bellowed or pleaded. The best men fought for a time, but Hampton's dismounted savages swarmed over one section of works after another, firing in close, then swinging their rifles, howling like dervishes, crazed as Mamelukes.

As a second wave of Hampton's men—mounted this time— leapt their horses over the earthen walls, Gibbon's division broke fully and finally.

Seven forty p.m.

Lieutenant George Dauchy had managed to bring off three of his four guns, thanks to General Miles. But a fourth lay out there between the sides sparring on in the dying light.

He'd encountered Colonel Lynch withdrawing a battered force and had asked for help in rescuing the gun. Lynch had halted long enough to weigh the prospects, then told him it was folly. The colonel had orders to form a new line in the rear.

Dauchy didn't give up. It had been a dreadful day of shifting fortunes. He'd recovered those three guns and a fair share of his battery's limbers and caissons—dragging several off by hand— but he'd failed to provide any more support to Miles: The sergeant, a good man, sent to bring up more lanyards had never returned. And his best gunner had gone down, his belly a bloody hash. The fellow had managed to call out to Dauchy, then pass him his watch and $150, begging him to see that it reached his family. Dauchy had helped his men load the gunner atop a caisson headed rearward, but there was no doubt how the journey was going to end.

He had to give up on the gun, but a detail from the provost guard helped him draw off two last caissons by hand.

In all his wartime service, he had never felt so useless and so helpless.

"Best hurry on, Dauchy," Lieutenant Sweeney of the provost guard cautioned. "Rebs are all around us."

Eight p.m.

Wade Hampton rode along the captured works, shouting for his men to keep killing Yankees.

Eight p.m.

My cavalrymen are willing to try it, sir," Gregg told Hancock and Gibbon. "One more counterattack, everyone in it this time."

The three generals stood amid shredded regiments re-forming as best they could while remnants of others fended off their tormentors. Minutes before, the Rebs had seized what remained of the headquarters site and the telegraph station. Except for Miles' stand on the northern quadrant, all was a shambles.

From the side, Charlie Morgan put in, "Miles wants to fight it out."

Hancock looked at Gibbon. "John?"

"My men are blown, sir." He sent Morgan a bitter look. "I'm not going to indulge in false bravado. My division's in no condition for a counterattack."

Thunder boomed, humbling the last artillery pieces at work.

His subordinates waited on Hancock. Morgan feared that the corps commander was on the verge of weeping. Hancock's hands were trembling.

Instead of losing control of his emotions, the corps commander told them, "That's it, then. We withdraw at dark." He paused again, as if disappointed in his own comportment and pondering a retraction of his words. But he only said, "Charlie, send Conrad or someone to Miles. Don't go yourself, I need you. Tell him . . . tell Miles he's to serve as our rear guard. As soon as the field has been cleared, he's to march for the Jerusalem Plank Road, we'll see him there."

The clouds above them fired rain and hail.

Nine fifteen p.m.

Nelson Miles was the last Union officer to leave Reams Station. He personally led off the final detachment of the rear guard, the remains of Barlow's old 61st New York, which had convinced all pursuers that further harassment was a poor idea.

Ten p.m.

Lieutenant Charles Brown was soaked to the gizzard. But he'd been wet before. He was a canal-man, after all. Living wet was just a part of the calling. No, his dismay, his discouragement, had little to do with the downpour, vicious, even painful, though it was.

The 50th Pennsylvania had formed its line a few miles to the rear of the day's fighting. Instead of joining the battle, they'd been deployed across a country road, ordered at first to halt any stragglers, then ordered to let them through.

Brown could not recall seeing any men so thoroughly defeated. Even now, in the rain-swept, leaden dark, he could read their passing forms, their hunched-over shadows. They were mere ghosts of the soldiers they had been. Some seemed ashamed, some angry. Others just stalked rearward, glad to be shut of things. A fair number still had their weapons, while others went empty-handed. The officers hardly bothered to give commands.

At first, Brown's men had joked a bit too loudly, sneering at the condition of the ever-praised Second Corps, darling of the newspapers and weeklies, while the Ninth Corps was the butt of every report. But as the hours passed, the men grew sober. Wet and sober. Even the thickest of Dutchmen began to see that a terrible thing had occurred, that this shattering reached into their lives, too, that something incalculable had been lost this day.

Earlier, the mocking soldiers had spoken of the retreating men as "them." But Brown knew that a heart-gripping change had come over the last of his charges when Levi Eckert said plaintively, "Looks like the Johnnies really whipped us good."

TWELVE

Eight fifty p.m., September 4, 1864
City Point

Grant looked up from the telegraph message.

"Atlanta," he said.

Work ceased. Every staff man present turned toward him.

A grin stretched Grant's mouth.

The officers and men erupted in cheers. Papers flew. Porter and Babcock began a preposterous jig. All around Grant, war-hardened men howled with the glee of children.

When the tumult began to ease, Grant said, "Isn't Sherman the fellow? Three cheers for General Sherman."

They hurrahed Cump three times and three times more, their cries so loud he must have heard it in Georgia.

Every officer wanted to shake Grant's hand.

The newspaper fellow, Cadwallader—a vain, sly, useful man—declared that Champagne wine would arrive momentarily, compliments of the *New York Herald*. The journalist kept a stock of liquor and treats of seductive bounty.

Won't get any more work done tonight, Grant decided, feeling for a cigar. He'd been sitting in front of his tent, smoking quietly and already missing Julia and the children, who'd just ended their visit. And the sergeant from the telegraph station had run up big-hipped, a bear in a hurry, hastily saluting with a paw and thrusting out his message.

And there it was: *Atlanta*. Since early morning of the day before, rumors had crossed the lines and a tantalizing pair of telegrams had hinted that Sherman's troops had entered the city. Then nothing—the line running back to Nashville had been cut.

But here it was, confirmed, the splendid news that changed so many things. He wished John Rawlins present, missing his friend. Coughing blood, Rawlins had gone on leave at Grant's insistence, with Grant thinking on his own brother dead of consumption. John should have heard this news with the rest of the staff. Meade, as well. Meade was on a thankless leave, back in Washington for a few bad days, sorting out the endless accusations lodged against him by rivals who'd failed at war.

Thoughts of Washington, even fleeting, left Grant more convinced than ever that his wisest decision of the year had been to locate his command in the field, not in the poisoned halls of the War Department.

Hard on George Meade, though.

The Champagne wine arrived as promised, with Cadwallader taking over as master of ceremonies and Grant content to let him play the role.

He could not have felt prouder of Cump, or happier for Lincoln. Stanton and Halleck would have read the message, of course, and they would have rushed off to the President's House, presenting the news as though they, not Sherman, had taken the city.

That was all right. What mattered was that the splendid news would lift the president's spirits: Lincoln appeared more careworn each time Grant saw him. The president was up on firmer ground now, thanks to Sherman's success. And the Democrats had gotten a timely comeuppance, smack after their convention, leaving George McClellan in a bind.

Now Sheridan had to do his part and whip Early out in the Valley. If Phil didn't make a move in the next week or so, Grant intended to travel north and prod him. A man's first independent command was a heavy weight, he knew it well. Then Wilmington, they'd have to close the port for good, the Confederacy's last lifeline to the world. More could be done in Alabama, too. And, of course, there was the matter of where Sherman should aim next.

The fall of Atlanta had all but won the war, Grant was convinced. The question was how many months and how much more blood it would take for the Rebs to accept it.

Cadwallader approached him, extending a glass. Grant was more impressed by the gleaming crystal than by the beverage.

"Surely," the journalist said, "on so glorious an occasion . . ."

Grant held up a hand: No. "Rawlins left me under orders."

Denied a tale to add to his gossip portfolio, Cadwallader smiled nonetheless. Really, it was magnificent, wonderful news to every man present.

Grant realized that the ague and aches that had plagued him for weeks were gone.

Surrounded by the headquarters revelry, he followed the spread of the news by the rolling cheers. Impossibly swiftly, the outburst of joy had leapt beyond the depot and onto the river. Steamboats, tugs, and ironclads blew horns and whistles.

Leaving his officers to their merriment, Grant sat down at a deserted desk, took up a pencil, and wrote to one of the few men who had believed in him in the dark days:

> *I have just received your dispatch announcing the capture of Atlanta. In honor of your great victory I have ordered a salute to be fired with shotted guns from every battery bearing upon the enemy. The salute will be fired within an hour, amid great rejoicing.*

He waved over an enlisted orderly, a fellow who'd known that the fancy drink wasn't for him.

"Take this to the telegraph tent. It's to have priority over all other messages."

Adam Badeau, his military secretary, came up. Empty glass in hand.

"You'll pardon me, sir, for saying I told you so. I knew the rumors were true, they had to be. We all had faith in General Sherman. As you did."

Now they had faith. But scant years past they'd all called Cump a madman for stating that the war would last years and require an army in the hundreds of thousands.

"Couldn't let word go out," Grant said. "Not till we knew for certain. Too many premature declarations of victory."

Like the newspaper fellow who, at the close of that first grim day at Shiloh, had rushed to report a catastrophe beyond redemption. Or just last week, when a scribbler had raced from Reams Station late in the afternoon to report a handsome victory over the Rebs. Now Win Hancock had to endure the ribbing—all too often jealous and ill-natured—about his "victory" over A. P. Hill.

Well, Hancock would survive it. Wasn't as rough as Shiloh, and expectations were different, sobered up. The news from Atlanta would sweep Hancock's embarrassment aside. And the plain fact was that for all his kicking, Lee had not recovered the Weldon Railroad. Warren sat on the line like a hawk on its nest.

So much more to do after this news. But, for now, it would have to be done elsewhere. Hancock's reverse had convinced him that Meade was right, that the Army needed to rest . . . say, until late September. Then hit Lee again before the election. See if he couldn't take the Boydton Plank Road and cut the South Side Rail Road, force Lee out of Petersburg, and run him down before the vote.

Before Badeau could turn away, Grant said, "If you haven't already had too much of that swill, go over to the telegraph tent and send a message to Humphreys, Parke, and Butler. I want every battery in the Armies of the Potomac and the James to open up on the Rebs at the same instant, with explosive shells. Right at midnight." He smiled to recall his own burst of excitement. "I told Sherman we'd do it within the hour, but I suspect he'll forgive me. A midnight reveille's better suited, I think." He considered the younger man: capable, loyal, and smug. "Understand?"

Badeau smiled.

Twelve twenty a.m., September 5
Headquarters, Army of Northern Virginia,
Violet Bank camp

There would be no attack, of course. The cannonade that had roused Lee from sleep had ended, followed not by the manly shouts of attackers, but by a cacophony of brass bands and delighted hurrahs over in the Federal lines.

He realized that he had not done up the last buttons on his coat. Nor had he brushed his hair. Night revealed men's weaknesses.

"It's true, then," he said at last, addressing his staff confidants, none of whom had dared speak before Lee. "Those people have taken Atlanta. One had hoped the reports . . ."

"It could be something else, sir," Venable said. It was a child's well-intentioned suggestion.

"We must," Lee said, "accept the disappointments the Creator visits upon us. We must bear our trials with grace. Never despair, gentlemen. Never despair." A meager smile cracked his face. "Now I believe we had best return to our beds. There will be work in the morning."

And he turned from them as the nearest Federal band blared out "Rally 'Round the Flag." He'd often thought it a rousing melody, wishing that it belonged to his side, not theirs. A better tune it was, by far, than "Dixie," that minstrel ditty he'd always found unworthy. But the men liked "Dixie," they'd chosen it for their own, and he could not forbid them such a little thing.

Lee undressed slowly, constrained by his arthritis. He prayed a second time, kneeling on the planks, rug cast aside. And after he thanked the Lord for His mercies and goodness, he sought the refuge of sleep but was denied.

Instead, he lay awake, raging. He had beaten Grant, again and again. He'd beaten Meade, Hancock, Warren, all of them. He'd taken their men prisoner by the thousands, he'd slain their legions, humiliated them. Yet their grip tightened like an infernal serpent's. The Weldon line was gone. Wagon trains could bring up the goods from the last safe station, skirting the Union lines, but that would only draw Grant westward again. A season of hunger loomed.

How could he win again and again, only to be pinned in some great cheat? How could the Lord permit it?

There were times, horrid times, when he scrutinized his beliefs, his fateful choices. What if his people had been wrong and slavery *was* a sin? What if the Lord was wreaking His vengeance on Virginia and an ever-bleaker South? What if the Creator had turned away?

Such questions were, at last, beyond Man's ken. And the morning would insist on practical matters. With Atlanta gone, he would need to visit President Davis and face another harangue against the world, with the president unwilling to admit that he himself had erred in any way.

Atlanta . . .

He saw Grant's policy clearly, his brute grip that immobilized the Army of Northern Virginia while his paladins rampaged over the South. He saw it, but he could do nothing about it.

Nothing except hope that, somehow, Atlanta would make no difference, that a war-weary North would elect McClellan and turn Lincoln out, that there would be peace at last. . . .

And if peace did not come . . . they would have to last out another winter and see if the Lord wrought a miracle in the spring.

In the meantime, he had to defend his remaining lifelines, one main road and a railroad.

Beyond the opposing trenches, a band played "Listen to the Mocking Bird."

Seven p.m., September 10
Howard's Grove, Richmond
Surgical hospital for Alabama's wounded

Two aces and three tens," Oates said, slapping down the cards. "Got you beat, don't I?"

Captain Billy Strickland laid down his own cards in disgust. "Not sure you're to be trusted anymore." He shooed a fly with his remaining hand, his wound mirroring Oates' loss. Down the ward, a new arrival groaned. "Back in the regiment, I used to believe you were an honest man. I fear I was deceived."

"Unlucky at cards, lucky in love," Oates consoled him. "Way you charm that old biddy."

"Ain't she a fright? Comes through with the whiskey, though."

Oates eyed his comrade's glass. "You paying up?"

Strickland made a sour face, but his good nature shone through. "Help yourself. To the victor . . ."

Oates grinned. "Don't have the hankering today. I'll content myself with my own ration." He picked up his glass. "Take your IOU, though."

The whiskey was raw and rewarding.

"Well, lookee there," Strickland said, peering through the window. "Off to the races again."

"Fancy ball, more like. That's what I heard. Times I do think I should've followed medicine, rather than reading the law." Oates watched the ambulance, freed of its canvas, pull off toward town with its load of doctors, every one of them in a parade uniform. "Wouldn't mind spoiling a crinoline myself." He pondered for a pair of seconds. "Have to learn to dance with one arm first, get my balance back."

"Hardly seems right, a ball so soon after Atlanta."

"Better Atlanta, Georgia, than Abbeville, Alabama. That's how I'm coming to look at it. Which one of the butcher's boys stayed back, any idea?"

"Mudd, I believe. He was cussing royally earlier."

"Lord help us," Oates said. "Don't sicken until morning, at the earliest."

He reached down to rearrange himself on the bed—and realized, again, that the arm he'd meant to use was no longer there. It was just the queerest thing. There were times when he could still feel a tingling in the fingers, sense a tightening of muscles, even feel cramps. Only the fingers and the rest of that arm were buried on New Market Heights, behind that tree. He'd become part ghost.

Hard to learn how to do things one-armed, harder than he'd imagined. Even playing poker was a challenge. He and Strickland helped each other, but the frustration was always there.

Oates did wonder what a vigorous woman would make of his stump. Ugly as Mammy's behind.

He'd thought himself well along on his recovery, only to swell up and have the surgeons cut him open again to drain the pus. Doc Gaston had done the work himself, and it did seem better now, though the pain came and went.

Out of the blue, Strickland said, "Sure could use a woman. Wouldn't be picky, either."

"Tell you the truth, I've been uneasy with how you've been looking my way."

The captain snickered. "Beards never drew me one bit. Truly, though, I've got half a mind to walk on into town and inspect the merchandise."

"There's always your belle of the whiskey barrel. Just one building over."

"Don't put me off my vittles."

"Well, I reckon we both have a little more healing to do," Oates said. "Shame, though. I share the hankering. Lay here thinking back on this missy and that."

"I do wonder what a fine gal's going to make of a one-armed man. You ever wonder?"

Oates paused a moment before answering, "I do."

"Have to calculate how many men been killed, of course. That smooths the odds. Then you reckon in the men who lost both arms, now there's an impediment to the hallowed deed. Not that it wouldn't be possible."

"Surely." Oates' thoughts dwelt not on highborn women now, but on a colored gal he'd enjoyed the winter before, thanks to Colonel Toney, when he'd been mending up from the wounds to his hip and leg. Contortions had been required, but they'd managed.

"Got to stop talking about it," Strickland said. "Drive myself crazy."

He moved awkwardly, toppling the makeshift table between their beds. Cards flew and glasses fell.

Ever a man of quick reflex, Oates grabbed for his glass. But the arm wasn't there this time, either.

The jerking motion did something, though. Something inside that shoulder. He straightened his back, seeking to regain his balance.

Strickland's eyes went wide.

When Oates looked at his bad shoulder, blood squirted from it like a horse pissing red. Suddenly, he felt weak, faint.

"Doctor!" Strickland screamed. Truly screaming. "Doctor! Get a doctor!"

His friend and comrade struggled to rise and balance himself, clapping his good hand over Oates' stump.

"Lie down, lie down," the captain insisted. Oates sought to comply and Strickland tried to follow along, to keep the pressure on.

He lost his balance and tumbled across Oates.

The other men in the ward who had the strength to call out added their voices, howling like lost and angry souls for a medical redeemer.

Oates was lying on his back. He felt Strickland's hand again. The captain's face and blouse were splashed with blood.

Not like this, Oates thought. *Not after everything. I can't die like this.*

Doc Mudd came running, followed by a male orderly and a matron with nothing else left of her Saturday nights.

Mudd said nothing, but Oates saw his alarm. The doctor slipped his hand in where Strickland's had been, adding more pressure, feeling the wound.

"Ligature slipped. Sloughed off the subclavian artery," he told Oates. As if the information made the least damned bit of difference.

"Joe . . . ," Oates said weakly, "fix me up."

Mudd said nothing for a moment. Then he turned his face to the orderly and said, "Send a rider after Doctor Gaston. Tell them he's needed. Hell, tell them they're all needed, get all the surgeons back here."

Oates wanted to joke that it did sound awfully serious, but found he couldn't speak.

The surgeon sat there by him, maintaining the pressure. All he said to Oates was, "Don't you stir."

Time jumbled itself, veering like a drunk between dreams and waking. Oates careened through long-forgotten memories, vivid, canted, wrenching.

"Can't die like this," he muttered, or thought he did.

Later, during a lucid spell, he heard many voices arguing over his treatment. They all seemed to agree that Doc Gaston should cut into him again and retie the artery.

He heard Gaston's reply clearly, as if spoken from a pulpit on a Sunday, august and irrefutable.

"He'd die. He's too weak, he'd sink under the weight of an operation." The doctor paused. "He's a good young man, fine officer. I want to save him, if possible."

"He's going to die, anyway," an unwelcome voice said. "Might as well try another ligature."

"I'm going to try compression."

"The rupture's too powerful."

"Well, if he's going to die, anyway . . . as you put it . . . I might as well try what I think's for the best."

"Compression will never work."

For the first time in his life, Oates did not care what other men thought of him. He wanted to blurt out, "I can't die like this. I can't." But his lips had no life left.

"Mudd, take over the pressure. Until I get my coat off. Ruined the damned thing already."

"He's gone," somebody said.

Oates had slipped deep into the realm of dreams, a place of brilliant light and of dark, unending corridors, of fractured memories and unearthly beckoning.

He woke up the next afternoon, alive and clotted with gore.

"Don't you move one muscle," Doc Gaston warned him. "Any antics from you and I'll kill you myself."

Three thirty p.m., September 20
Ninth Corps rear, Union lines

Ain't that a pretty sight?" Levi Eckert asked Brown and the others nearby. "Have to wonder what the ladies would make of it."

In a little grove of trees well to the rear, the men of Company C stood about, mostly naked, between rows of packs and rifle stacks. Some of them lazed and some engaged in horseplay, like boys let out from school. Others bent over the troughs set up for them to wash themselves—taking a teasing if they bent over too far. A detail tended the cauldrons boiling their uniforms, hoping to cook the creatures in the seams. Another few men spread their uniforms on the grass to dry. They'd been issued new trousers, nothing else, and sorely needed undergarments and stockings.

Still, Brown felt almost keen again. His splash-up had left him grubby still, but cleaner, almost tolerable. Mild air feathered over his bare skin, soothing the terrible chafing on his thighs.

Sam Losch answered Levi: "If you are washing more and talking not so much, it's better, I think."

"Soap, Levi." Smiling, Brown held out a piece. "Try it, it's a miracle."

"I been and washed."

"I recommend repetition."

"I'm cleaner than any Dutchman ever lived."

All were in good spirits, despite the banter, glad of the filthy water in the troughs. Glad to be relieved of duty for this day. And, at least in Brown's case, glad to be back where a bit of green remained. The leaves in the grove were already browning off and the grass had been trampled, but enough lushness remained to lift his heart. In the three months since they'd arrived in front of Petersburg, the low green hills had been stripped of trees and the earth had been churned to make trenches and traverses, bombproofs and covered ways, until the stretch of land between the lines and for a good mile to the rear was nothing but ruptured dirt and clinging dust. It looked to Brown like Hell in the midst of a drought.

The barrenness wore on men. On him. He dreamed of the wild-grown banks of the Schuylkill Canal.

Didn't help, either, that the stretch of line they'd drawn was one of the mean ones. Here and there, the men on picket duty from both sides agreed to conduct themselves peaceably, trading newspapers, coffee, and tobacco when the officers weren't about and even warning the other side when trouble was headed their way. "Comity," that was the word a colonel had used within Brown's hearing. "We cannot permit such comity with the enemy."

If the word meant what Brown thought it might, he was all for it himself. On their stretch, the Reb sharpshooters were merciless. A man had to keep down, passing his days like a rat.

He stretched his back and considered the oddity of the bodies before him, the flesh grub-white, except where red bites, boils, or carbuncles showed, and hair the more matted for being plied with water. They'd been washing themselves for over an hour, but every man was still foul, just a bit less so, as if they'd taken on dirt that would never come out. And it was strange to see faces, necks, and hands as brown as leather stuck on those pale scarecrows.

"Well," the first sergeant said to him, "maybe soon we go to do more fighting. They do this just for nice, letting us wash. And off we go."

"I haven't heard anything." Brown did wonder, though. It wasn't like Grant to let the quiet last, they'd all learned that much, and it had been over three weeks since things had been lively. Even the Johnnies had only rustled cattle, if a lot of them. A battle had to be on its way, the weather was just too good for men not to fight. "Take what comes, Sam, all a man can do."

"I wash *noch einmal*. Then I go to see about the mail."

"Take your time," Brown told the first sergeant. "You've earned a rest as much as any man. *Ruhe dich doch*," he added in his canal Dutch.

Brown was looking forward to the mail, though. He hadn't heard from Frances in a week. He thought of her in each spare moment, proud and sorry at once that he had insisted on waiting for the war's end to marry. He just didn't want to leave a young widow, there were too many back home wrapped in black already.

He sometimes feared that she might be too fine to be content as the wife of a boatman. Even one who owned his barge free and clear.

Lord, he longed for the clean life he had lived, for muscles strained by honest work, not war. Even the memory of that one bad day, of the boy he'd killed when those fools attacked the first boat on which he'd worked, even that was nothing compared to what he'd seen since 1861. A brother dead, friends slaughtered, all the blood.

Lieutenant George Brown wanted to go home. But he knew he wouldn't, even given the chance. He would not leave these men until the end. So he did his duty as best he could and plodded through the Bible to please Frances.

He'd been surprised at the details in the Gospels, finding Jesus a nice, impractical fellow who just didn't understand the way people were.

Major Schwenk trotted up on a new bay horse. When he spotted Brown, he steered over. The major looked as happy as if he'd just had a real bath in a tin tub. He wore a new frock coat, too, and appeared fully recovered from his wound.

Somewhere along the lines, a band struck up. Then another let loose.

Halting his horse, Schwenk said, "Had trouble making you out. In the guise of Adam."

"Ain't pretty," Brown allowed. The truth was that his nakedness embarrassed him. He'd always been on the shy side about such matters. The old hands on the canal had deviled him terribly during his learning years.

"Hate to interrupt this county fair, but there's news you'll want to hear, it just came down."

Distant hurrahs rippled. Something big was up.

"We marching, Major?"

Schwenk shook his head. His grin revealed the gap where he'd lost a tooth. "Nothing like that. Sheridan beat Jubal Early yesterday. Out in the Valley. Thumped the bejeezus out of him."

"Where?"

"Near Winchester."

"Well, that's good news, sir. That's really good news."

"Not if you're Robert E. Lee." The major's grin just wouldn't go away. "Got to say, Brownie, I like the look of you better in a uniform. You must scare the devil out of the girls." He glanced toward the cauldrons steaming under the trees. "Last time I had my own things boiled, it just gave the lice an appetite."

Six p.m., September 21
Field headquarters, Cavalry Corps,
Army of Northern Virginia

Wade Hampton took the young man's salute, then extended his hand.

"Welcome to the Cavalry Corps, Major Hampton. The adjutant will assign your duties to you."

As he gripped the palm of his eldest son, Hampton felt a heady impulse to clutch him to his breast, to enfold this brawny, bearded likeness of himself in his arms as if young Wade were still an adored child. Instead, he released the hand he would gladly have held for an hour.

Before the adjutant took his son captive, Hampton added, "We acknowledge rank strictly here, Major," a claim that was not quite true. "Your rank will govern your relations with Lieutenant Hampton, of course."

Wade Hampton IV nodded respectfully. *What does* he *feel?* Hampton wondered. Again, he felt the urge to enclose his namesake in his arms, to kiss him in welcome and tell him, "Son, I'm *proud* of you, prouder than I can say."

"That will be all, Major," Hampton told him. And he watched

his scion go, revealing the uproar in his heart to no man. Later, when night fell, he would greet the boy warmly, allowing himself that indulgence. But he would not display the least favoritism, the least affection, before men he might order to their deaths.

Looking around at the other officers who had come out for the welcome, he asked, "Does this headquarters have no work to do?"

The crowd disassembled itself. His other son, Preston, trailed after his brother, bound to be disobedient again. Preston, uncanny reminder of Hampton's adored first wife.

He went into his tent. He, too, had much to do, but he felt the need to sit on his cot for a bit, to discipline his emotions.

When might they all be together again? At Sand Hills? Anywhere? His children and his new wife, his sisters and brothers? There was nothing more important on this earth than a man's family. . . .

He longed to return to Sand Hills, to see Millwood again. He had expected Atlanta to fall, but the news still had come as a shock. Now Early had been beaten, badly, at Winchester. Rimmed by his well-groomed beard, Hampton's lips curled. The praise for his own little triumph had been brief. His "Beefsteak Raid," as the men had already dubbed it, had been a grand caper, showing him the equal of Stuart in the art of raiding. He and his men had slipped behind Grant's lines, riding halfway around the Union army to appropriate twenty-three hundred beeves on the hoof and drive them back inside Confederate lines. The men had been delighted; even Lee had expressed his pleasure. And the Army would eat. But the glory had turned to gloom at the news from the Valley.

His men seemed refreshed and newly determined, though. And Hampton refused to accept that he, Wade Hampton III, would be defeated by anyone. But sitting there on a mild September day, thinking of home and kin, of a future opaque and a past gone like a vapor, he wondered:

How will it end?

September 24, 1864
Boston, Massachussetts

Barlow brayed with laughter. He didn't mean to offend the girl, but he simply could not restrain himself. Sitting nobly at the foot of his sickbed, doing her part for the war by bearing his stink, she had begun her charitable reading with "The Charge of the Light Brigade."

When he mastered himself at last, he rubbed tears of hilarity from his eyes, looked down his long, smothered body at the dutiful amber-haired wisp, and said, "I'm sorry, Miss Shaw . . . forgive me . . ."

Helpless, racked, ribs hurting, he laughed again, though the bout was shorter this time.

The poor child looked bewildered. Left alone in a room with a reeking madman.

"I'm sorry," he said again. "It's . . . simply not like that, war isn't. It's never like that at all."

The girl showed rather more gumption than he expected.

"At least, I made you laugh," she told him. "I wasn't sure it was possible."

Thinking again of the poem's absurdity, he succumbed to a last fit of laughter. He hoped the squirts would not be one result. His condition remained wretched, with the best Boston doctors bewildered. The past weeks had quite surprised him. The military doctors he'd long derided had surpassed the learned sages of medicine: If the butchers in uniform had been of little help, the august physicians ministering to Beacon Hill and Brookline were none at all.

"Well, then," the girl said primly, "not Tennyson. We'll try something else." She chose another volume from the little pile she'd drawn out of her bag.

She was game, he had to give her that. And fond-looking out of mourning. Fresh, unsullied. His mother's behavior was untoward, of course. She'd probably bullied the girl into this nonsense, convincing her that sniffing his waste was her patriotic duty, a tribute to her brother Bob, dead in a ditch with his darkies.

Why was the Shaw girl back in Boston, anyway? Her family had moved to Staten Island so her mother's eyes could be treated. Of course, the girl had relatives aplenty: If the Channings and Barlows were related to half of New England's best families, the Shaws were related to all of them.

In a voice not too afflicted with flint, she tried again:

Five years have passed; five summers, with the length
Of five long winters! and again I hear—

"Oh, God," Barlow interrupted, "please, not Wordsworth. 'Pansies, lilies, kingcups, daisies, / Let them live upon their praises' . . . He can't even get the rhymes right." Almost in rancor, he added, "*All* poems about flowers are insufferable."

The girl's posture never faltered. But her eyes grew moist. Blue eyes, as clear and acute as Bob's had been dull.

His temper had surprised him, and he subdued it. "I'm afraid poetry's wasted on me. I . . . fear I'm not in good form." He attempted a smile. "Never had the bent for verses, really."

But he remembered: Brook Farm, sunlight, childhood. And, later, the way Arabella had recited Wordsworth. And Elizabeth Barrett Browning, whom she adored.

"But you *know* poetry," the girl said.

"I memorized it for a penny a go." With a smirk he could not resist, he added, "I still have my mother's promissory notes, I should call them in."

No quitter, she reached for another book, a small one bound in red.

"Your mother says you were always fond of Shakespeare."

He managed to raise a hand and wave that off. "My mother isn't *au courant*, Miss Shaw. My tastes aren't what they were." He snorted, at once sorry for the rudeness. "Really, I'm not sure I have *any* tastes left."

"Surely—"

"Miss Shaw . . . don't you find this irregular? Not to say compromising? Left alone in the bedchamber of a man you barely know? No, that's not right. A man you don't know at all."

To his surprise, she met his eyes directly, her look as spunk-laden as the stares he'd gotten from very unhappy Southern belles.

"I hardly think, General Barlow, that you're in a state to threaten a lady's virtue."

He blushed, almost laughed, faltered. Then smiled despite himself.

"No, I expect not." Serious again, he said, "It's the appearance of things, though."

"I don't care a whit about appearances."

"You should. This world is unforgiving." He gestured feebly at the bedcover, his shrouded person. "And this can't be pleasant."

"I do not intend to live *my* life amid primroses and celandines."

Surprising and disappointing himself, he answered:

Long as there's a sun that sets,
Primroses will have their glory . . .

It was her turn to laugh, mercilessly.

"Well, General, it appears you earned your pennies. Really, is Wordsworth so awful?"

"Unspeakably so."

She smiled, as if she believed she was gaining ground.

"I think you're just being a bear. To taunt me. You still think I'm that child hunched on the stairs, listening to you berate Bob about calculus. I'll bet you read Wordsworth in secret. *And* Tennyson."

"Assuredly not." At a sudden loss for words, he stumbled on. "Some Shakespeare. Now and then. Not much. Not the sonnets."

Belle had loved the sonnets.

" 'When, in disgrace with fortune and men's eyes,' " she tried.

"Appropriate, I grant you."

"Hardly. You're quite the hero. In men's eyes. And I think you know it. Revel in it, in fact." She smiled with good teeth. "I might advertise my privilege in the papers, to make all the other girls jealous. 'Lately admitted to the Homeric presence of Brigadier General Francis Channing Barlow, who lies in cruel repose after war's fatigues. . . .' I do think I'll take out a notice. I shall be the envy of every well-bred *demoiselle* in the Union." She cocked an eyebrow. "And some of lesser pedigree, I suspect."

Of a sudden, he found her tiresome and presumptuous.

"Best not mistake impertinence for charm, Miss Shaw."

Her lower lip dropped.

Recovering, she said, "You really are a beast. Aren't you? And purposely rude."

"Rude enough to tell you that, whatever nonsense my mother's put in your head, you really mustn't—"

"I don't need anyone's mother to put anything in my head. And I will *not* be bullied by an ill-mannered invalid who can't . . . who . . ."

"Can't what, exactly? Can't even control his bowels? Ah, yes. There we have the essence of heroism, the scent of glory. The disgusting body . . . how much better to read Wordsworth and pretend we all drowse amid flowers." Coldly, he added, "You might go now, Miss Shaw, and spare yourself."

Fighting back tears with all the determination Lee had shown to hold on in the Wilderness, she stood up, her posture that of a sergeant of Regulars, gripped her skirts, and marched toward the door.

"Your books," he called after her.

She turned, slender and ablaze. Better suited to Naples and Vesuvius, to Pompeii, than to Back Bay, she announced:

"They seem to have no value."

Then she was only footsteps descending the stairs.

Why did I do that? Barlow asked himself. For all his mother's harebrained schemes, there was no reason to take his annoyance out on the girl. She really had done her innocent best to be pleasant.

He longed to be well again, hated this confinement, this inability to see to his own necessities. One doctor had thrown up his hands and said his only chance was bed rest, if he hoped to live.

Boston clattered past outside the window, each sound familiar, and yet he was as much a stranger here as any Turk.

He had been cruel these past years. War demanded cruelty, heartlessness. But cruelty without purpose . . . if he'd ever had a soul, he seemed to have lost it. Not Caesar, but Caligula.

He whispered to his pillow, " 'Take physic, pomp; / Expose thyself to feel what wretches feel . . .' "

Well, he felt wretched enough. He longed for the war, his war, loving it for its ultimate simplicity, its beauty, the random clemency. Atlanta had fallen, and Sheridan had won two smashing victories in the Valley. And he was here, befouling his sheets in Boston.

His mouth wrinkled. If Ellen Shaw wanted to experience rudeness, she needed to meet Phil Sheridan. . . .

Astonishing himself, he began to weep. The fit lasted only a moment, but it shook him, loosening something deep, and not in his bowels this time.

He had just brushed the wet from his face when the girl reappeared in the doorway. She looked as though she had been crying fiercely, but that magnificent grenadier's posture, that impeccable haughtiness of carriage, had not relented.

She held a single book.

"If not poetry," she said, "then prose, perhaps? Hawthorne? *The Marble Faun?*"

Gads. Smelly old Hawthorne, ever pawing his mother in the old days.

"I'm fond of Hawthorne, actually," he said.

After the girl had gone, his mother visited him, smug as the cat that finished all the cream. His mother. Even though there was money now, she'd finagled the loan of a fine house on Beacon Hill—if not on the best street—from one of her former *beaux*. The woman couldn't do without adoration. Or the sense that she'd been clever.

"Really, Mother."

"Francis! You stink. Why didn't you pull the bell cord?" She paled. "You didn't . . . while Miss Shaw . . ."

"I'm not certain. Do you think she'd mind?"

"Francis, you're taunting me."

"Ecce homo, Mater dolorosa."

"That's blasphemous. But I don't mind. If you think you can shock me . . ."

Despite the stench, she sat.

"I've been meaning to ask . . . ," he began.

"I've always disliked that construction, it seems weak and indirect. And grammatically awkward."

"Not my academic strength, grammar. Mother, I've had some news. Courtesy of a friend. It seems that my father is somewhere around Philadelphia."

Instantly cold beyond all arctic wastes, his mother said, "We will not discuss that subject. Not now, not ever."

"I only thought—"

"You should concern yourself with your own recovery, nothing else." Ever a master tactician, she turned the subject to one he could not evade. "Francis, whatever did you *do* to Ellen Shaw? You had her in tears like a serving girl turned out."

"Perhaps she found all the perfumes of Arabia insufficient?"

"You're such a little beast."

"That's what she said, coincidentally. The beast part. Not little, though, I don't think."

"She's very fine, Francis. Incomparable, in fact."

Applying a tactic of his own, he said, "I believe the male of the species only applies 'incomparable' to you, Mother."

She sat up with all the grace of Ellen Shaw. "More than one man *has* deemed me incomparable. From an appropriate distance." She smiled as if they shared a splendid joke.

He smiled, too. "Please be serious for a moment. I mean it. You can't go on pressing that girl into fruitless service. Spare her your intentions, whatever they may be. It's . . . unseemly to have her in." He recalled her fineness vividly. "Her reputation, should word get out . . ."

"I don't see that at all," his mother said. "The times have advanced while you've been away, my dear. Even in Boston." She shook her still-lovely head. "A girl of excellent family, who's lost a gallant brother . . . why shouldn't she take pity on—"

"I will *not* be pitied. That's the first thing. I will not have it." He flared still hotter, almost able to rise from his bed and pound the walls. "Second . . . Arabella hasn't been dead two months. It's indecent. . . ."

His mother's face turned as solemn as Hancock's had been when he'd issued the orders for the assault on the Mule Shoe.

"Francis," she said at last, her calm imperious, "I've lived more years than I care to admit. Certainly, I've seen much more of life than you. Be quiet, don't you mock, or I shall slap you. And one thing I have learned is that death is final. Two months, two years, or twenty . . . the dead are dead." Her features tightened in sudden curiosity, perhaps in wonder. "Didn't the war teach you anything?"

Ten thirty p.m., September 25
City Point

Grant sat alone in his cabin, weary. The light of the oil lamp painted the raw wood orange.

He'd issued orders to George Meade by cipher. The next offensive, to start in a matter of days, would follow the same pattern: a blow on the right and a blow on the left, stretching Lee ever thinner. He meant to punch through on the Richmond front, or to cut the Boydton Plank Road behind Petersburg. Or both.

Still dressed, he closed his eyes. One of his headaches threatened. So much to get through, ever more to be done. Sherman needed a better general of cavalry, one who could command infantry, as well. Send him Gregg? Wilson? One of Meade's sons was gravely ill, but

Meade could not be spared even for that. Nor would Meade ask. Stanton wanted a new command for Hooker in the West, but which one? Replace Heintzelman or Rosecrans? Neither had been effective. And Julia still hadn't chosen a Philadelphia house. He'd just written her a letter meant as a nudge.

The good news was that Sheridan's twin victories in the Valley had filled the Northern papers, first the triumph along Opequon Creek, outside of Winchester, then, three days later, the smashup at Fisher's Hill. Shame about Russell, though. His loss would be felt. But atop the news from Atlanta, Little Phil's successes had changed politics across the Union. The election remained in question, bitterly so, but Lincoln had a chance now.

Bill, his manservant, eased in like a cat.

"Where've you been?" Grant said.

"Just doing my doings. Following my orders from Miss Julia."

"That excuse won't play many more hands."

Bill knelt before him, taking up the heel of one of Grant's boots and beginning to tug. Muttering. Pure Bill.

"So . . . what do you think of General Sheridan now? What did you call him? 'Devil man,' was it?"

"He still wicked as Pharaoh. Man a sinner, he just born that way. Any soul looking on knows it, take one look. That man the Devil 'carnate." The first boot came off and Bill went to work on the other. "Feet of yours," he said disdainfully.

"Maybe it takes a devil to beat devils."

"Don't want no truck with no devil, speak for myself."

Grant's other foot came free. Bill wrinkled his nose. "Wash them socks."

"Have a washerwoman in mind? That filly you've been romping after?"

"Just seeing to her protection. All these bad men around."

Grant couldn't help smiling. Bill was a treasure. "Well, what about General Sherman? Seeing *him* in a better light these days?"

"Naw, suh. Naw. That man. He eat the flesh of chillun, nobody looking. Then suck on they bones."

"I've always found Sherman a tenderhearted man," Grant said, lying merrily. "You're a mighty hard fellow to please."

"Folks says the same about other company right here in this room."

"Sherman's freed your brethren from captivity. Thousands of them."

"Ain't my brethren. My people civilized. Good Missouri people. Anyhow, that man don't take to dark folks anytime. Run 'em off, just drive 'em back to the Rebs. Said so yourself."

"He can't let his army be overwhelmed with contrabands."

"None of my business, nohow. You going to get undressed, or you sleeping like that?"

Reluctantly, Grant rose. He tugged off his coat.

"We getting ready to try Bobby Lee again?" Bill asked, slapping the garment.

Grant looked at Bill in surprise.

"You hearing rumors?" If so, it was unacceptable. The plan had to be kept secret, its details withheld until the movements began. He fumbled out of his trousers.

"Naw, suh. We just due for another go at things, way you are. Any fool know."

"If I *were* about to do anything, foreknowledge would be a military secret. And hollering out secrets gets a man hanged."

Bill took the trousers and folded them. "Who I going to tell?"

"All right, then, *General* Bill . . ."

"You set to have your fun with me, calling me 'General Bill' way you do, just deviling. Ought to 'least call me right, call me 'General William Barnes.' You wouldn't call that Sherman 'General Bill.'"

"No, that's true. I would not. Pass me one of those cigars. From the pocket there."

"Miss Julia say you not to smoke in bed, that trash behavior." But he produced a cigar.

Grant took the Habana but didn't bite it. "So tell me, General William Barnes . . . what's your professional judgment regarding our progress? Against General Lee? Think he'll hang on much longer?"

"How you mess these pants so bad, burnt holes in them again? And they new. . . ." Bill shook his head. "Can't say how long Bobby Lee go on frustrating all the great, big Union. No way to tell. But see, it like this here: There's these two dogs. One, he a biting dog, got a fearsome bite, he so proud of his bite, bred high and pretty. Other one, he a gnawing dog, some mix-up hound, just get a holt of a leg and won't let go, keep chewing and chewing, even if the other dog bite his ear off."

"And?"

"Any man ever had him a dog knows the gnawing dog going to win. 'Long as he don't mind the biting too much."

Grant considered that. "So . . . you're calling me a mongrel? I suppose I have fleas, too?"

"Heap of 'em. Anyway, I done heard you called lots worse."

After Grant went to bed, Bill sauntered down to the docks, where the unloading of cargoes continued by torchlight. The colored laborers sang slave songs, the sort that charmed white folks and disgusted him.

When would the day come when he could speak plainly and not resort to minstrel-show banter to live? Even Grant, a good man, expected subservience, took it as his due from the darker-skinned. *Would* the day come when he could stand upright? Emancipation was only the beginning, little more than a word. It might strike off the shackles on ankles and wrists, but the chains in the hearts of men would remain unbroken.

By the banks of the muddy James, bloodied waters of Babylon, he sat down on an idle pier, remembering not a Zion he'd never known, not interested in the past at all, but looking ahead into an unbounded darkness.

How long, Lord? he cried within. *How much longer must it be like this?*

There were times when he wished the war would last until every white man lay dead.

PART
V

THE MILL

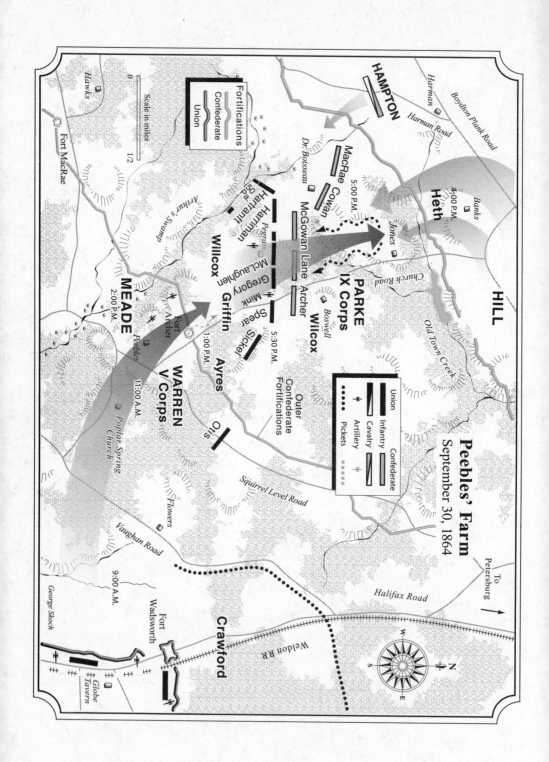

Peebles' Farm
September 30, 1864

Legend:

Fortifications
Union
Confederate

Union | Confederate
Infantry
Cavalry
Artillery
Pickets

Map labels:

HAMPTON

Hawks

Fort MacRae

Scale in miles
0   1/2

Harman
Boydton Plank Road
Harman Road

Dr. Boisseau

MacRae
Cowan
5:00 P.M.

Heth
4:00 P.M.
Banks

Harman
Pegram
6 Ga.
McGowan
Lane
Archer
Jones

Willcox
McLaughlen
Griffin
Gregory
Mink
Spear
Sickles
Wilcox
Boswell

PARKE
IX Corps
Wilcox

HILL

MEADE
2:00 P.M.

Fort Archer
1:00 P.M.

Ayres
Otis

WARREN
V Corps

Outer
Confederate
Fortifications

5:30 P.M.

Church Road

Old Town Creek

11:00 A.M.

Poplar Spring
Church

Flowers

Squirrel Level Road

Vaughan Road

9:00 A.M.

George Skoch

Fort
Wadsworth

CRAWFORD

Globe
Tavern

Weldon RR

Halifax Road

To
Petersburg

N
S
E
W

THIRTEEN

"Well, Major, you're in command, you've got the Third Brigade. Don't expect congratulations," Brigadier General Charles Griffin said.

"No, sir," Ellis Spear responded. "Unfortunate situation."

"One way to put it. Twentieth Maine going to get along without you? I expect so," Griffin added, answering his own question. "Christ, losing Gwyn and Welch. In one piddling attack."

"It was a fine one, though, sir."

"Damn Jim Gwyn. Riding his horse up the rampart, idiotic stunt." Griffin's sandpaper voice grew somber. "At least he'll live. Welch wasn't so lucky."

Letting his mount nose the grass, Griffin nodded toward the Ninth Corps troops passing through his division—while his own men worked to reverse the captured entrenchments. Rather than marching boldly into battle, the Ninth Corps soldiers were barely slinking forward, reluctant as schoolgirls asked to pick up snakes. Their lack of rigor offended Griffin, who would have come down hard, had they been his men.

"Wait a few hours," Griffin told the major. "We'll be fucked for beans again today."

"We did our part, sir. Gave them a good start."

"Isn't the start that counts with Lee, it's the finish."

"Pleasant fighting weather, at least," Spear tried again.

"Going to rain. You wait."

The attack had gone well, Griffin had to admit, although it had taken Jim Gwyn too damned long to get his regiments organized. The 118th Pennsylvania and the 16th Michigan had crossed an open field at the double-quick, with the 20th Maine close behind and not one man faltering, all of them forcing their way through the Reb abatis, going at the obstacle with axes, then hurtling over the walls of the fort with snap. In fifteen minutes of fighting, they'd turned the Johnnies out of their fortifications along Squirrel Level Road. It was all about doing things properly, Griffin believed, and no damned nonsense.

Shame about Norval Welch. The 16th was going to miss him. Hell, they'd all miss him. One more veteran officer gone. But Welch had ended the way a soldier should, topping the enemy's rampart.

"Ellis," Griffin resumed, "the Rebs aren't going to let those Ninth Corps boys just stroll up to the Plank Road and the South Side. You wait. They pass another farm or two, and they're going to get hit, front and flank. Rebs do it every time, you'd think we'd be on to the game." He wiped his thick mustaches. "Not much fight in that corps, by the looks of it."

Yes, he was proud of his own men and saw others as inferiors. But it wasn't pride without justification. As far as Charlie Griffin was concerned, he led the finest division in the Army of the Potomac. Or in the whole damned Union army. And they'd just given the Rebs another taste of it.

Only dismounted cavalry in that fort, though, strung out thin. No more than a fire bell, set out to warn the rest of Bobby Lee's army. Truth was that the ball had barely opened.

"Our plans are just too complicated," Griffin mused to his new brigade commander. " 'Fifth Corps will seize the Squirrel Level Road line and consolidate. Ninth Corps will pass the Fifth Corps line and continue the advance.' Buggering Jesus on Christmas morning, we should have just continued our attack, while the Rebs were reeling. The one thing you can never get back in any battle is time. But no . . . we have to pass the Ninth Corps through and lose a good three hours because Parke's shit-licking recalcitrants are marching like truants headed back to the schoolhouse. Christ, we all know what Lee can do in three hours. . . ."

Ellis Spear almost replied, but Griffin, rarely so talkative, wasn't finished.

"This isn't the Army it was, they have to grasp that. It's no longer capable of intricate maneuvers. If it ever was. Too many of the best officers and veterans are dead, we can't execute the fancy plans they send down. Not even this division. This is a bare-knuckles fight now, not a duel with high-flown rules and rapiers."

"Yes, sir," Spear agreed. His tone signaled impatience. Griffin needed to send the younger man off, to let him get a grip on his new duties.

"Well, just in case I'm right and the high and mighty back in the rear are wrong, you get your boys digging harder. Look at them. Proud as peacocks. After chasing off a handful of underfed jockeys." Cut boneward by long service in the Southwest, his hard face tightened. "I don't just want those entrenchments reversed, I want them improved, and mightily. See to it. And strengthen your skirmish line. Before Powell Hill comes down and plucks our feathers."

"Yes, sir."

"And no damned softness today. Let 'em eat crackers, cooking fires can wait. And straighten the alignment of those rifle stands, this isn't some Mexican cathouse. Those Ninth Corps boys'll come skedaddling and we'll need to patch things up."

Giving the Johnnies three hours, even two, to figure things out was about as helpful as giving a band of Comanches a day's head start.

Spear's posture changed, signaling that he was about to ride off and see to his duties, but first the major asked, "Any more word from the Richmond front? Darkies really do it?"

Griffin cleared his throat and spit. "Seems so. Warren tells me they got farther up the Heights than any white men." He scowled at nothing, at everything. "No doubt their officers will undo it all.

Go on now, Ellis. I've already used up this week's ration of talk. Have your brigade prepared to defend this line or advance at my order. In case we have to go out and save those skulkers." He turned sharply in the saddle. "You there! *You,* soldier!" he called to a Ninth Corps straggler. "Catch up to your regiment, or I'll have you bayoneted."

A squad of his own soldiers working nearby laughed, and one called out, "He means it, laddiebuck. That's General Griffin, it is." The soldiers laughed again. "He's born of the Great Banshee, he'll swallow ye whole."

Griffin rode over to the work party. Hard-faced.

The soldiers slew their good humor and bent to their labors.

Griffin halted his horse. "Did I invite one of you sonsofbitches to volunteer his opinion?"

The soldiers froze. Only two dared look toward him.

"He din't mean nothing bad, sir," the bravest of them said.

Griffin snarled, "Stand up straight when I'm talking to you. . . ."

The men dropped their tools and jerked to parade-ground postures.

"If I'm born of the Banshee, what are you lot, goddamned leprechauns?"

He smiled broadly.

The soldiers eased and laughed. One said, "Oh, sir . . . ye had us afeared, ye truly did."

With a practiced growl, the general told them, "Damned well *better* be afraid of me. And nobody else. You get back to work now, the Johnnies aren't done with us yet."

"Ah, but they'll wish they were," the bravest man told him. "Look to the boys from Cork, sir, and ye'll see doings to savor."

Griffin rode on. Cursing wondrously at the men he loved.

Speaking to his comrades as Griffin passed, another Irishman forged by the Famine declared, "If I live to tell me tale, boys, that buggerin' general's going to steal half the telling, an't he the lovely?" Sighing, he added, "Had we had one such in the '98 . . ."

To the north, skirmishing crackled.

Fucked for beans again, Charlie Griffin swore.

Three p.m.
Boydton Plank Road

It's a gift," Wade Hampton said to Harry Heth. "Fifth Corps just stopped. Hardly bloodied, but they stopped to dig in. Now they're passing the Ninth Corps through to start up again. And no sign of artillery marching with Parke . . . it makes no sense, pushing for the Plank Road without guns. They have to know they're going to face a fight."

Harry Heth had dismounted to relieve himself. Closing his trousers again, he looked up at Hampton. "Like you said, Wade. A gift. God bless 'em, and thanks a-mighty. Trouble enough up there in front of Richmond, with the niggers. Fort Harrison, too. Hard business. Turn a man sick and vicious all at once." He swung back into his saddle. "They're counting on us to keep things right down here. And I reckon we will."

Behind them, along the vital road, the vanguard of Heth's infantry hurried past.

"Whenever you're ready," Hampton said. "I'll give it twenty minutes after you hit them from the front. Then I'll come in on their left, wheel off that swamp. Go deep behind them."

Heth nodded. "Be two hours before my last brigade's up. Just spread so thin. And then I'll need to get it in position. Have to do this right, hit them hard as we can, no room for misjudgments." He glanced skyward. "Beat the rain, if we can. If not, we'll fight 'em wet."

"Wet or dry, no difference," Hampton commented. Hunting that bear with a knife, in the cold rain. Hadn't that been a time? Younger then. Foolish. Were any son of his to attempt such a folly, he would have done more than just berate the boy. The bear would've wept for the lad.

His sons. His heart swelled at every glimpse of one or the other.

Heth's smile was a stingy ornament, but it passed for its purpose. "Myself, I don't mind giving them time to extend themselves, not one bit. Get some distance between them and the Fifth Corps, let them think they've all but done the trick, get their mouths watering. Then scoop them up." The Virginian stretched in the saddle, settled, and yawned. "Almost get tired of thrashing them."

"Never tire of it myself," Hampton said.

Four thirty p.m.
Boisseau farm

Shame.

Brown had never before felt so let down by his own men. The 50th Pennsylvania had never been a quitter regiment, the kind stocked with bounty-jumpers and malingerers. Yet something had happened, something Brown couldn't quite grip. Too many soldiers had just decided that they'd done their part and had enough. The mood was not of mutiny, but of ill-tempered reluctance and thin excuses.

It had gotten so bad that, as they'd marched past the Fifth Corps, some general had chastised a soldier from Company F. And the man had deserved it.

At least, Brown had managed to keep Company C intact, what there was left of it. He'd begun the day's march with thirty-two men, and with Sam Losch, Levi Eckert, and Henry Hill herding them like sheepdogs, he'd brought all thirty-two to this field. He wasn't convinced all thirty-two would fight, though. The newest men weren't worth much.

Sometimes he wondered if the entire army might not dissolve, if Bobby Lee kept refusing to give up, kept drawing blood. Brown had become a Lincoln man himself, but he had to wonder how the election would go, how others would vote. The draftees and bounty men just wanted to go home.

Hard times, no question. Their old brigade had been so reduced that the 50th had been folded into General Hartranft's command. Which was fine, as far as it went. The veterans respected Hartranft, a fellow Pennsylvanian whose rise they'd witnessed up close. But the relationship with their new comrades had yet to smooth out, it was still an untanned hide, with nobody quite sure how much they could trust one another.

The march hadn't even been bad, that was another thing. Brown had understood men dropping away in the August heat. But this was about as pleasant a day as old Virginia offered, even had clouds to keep the sun off a man. But men from the division had shirked by the hundreds.

Pushing through that last stretch of Virginia tangles hadn't helped any, either. Men had slipped away like water through fingers.

But he still had his thirty-two. Because he'd become a hard man, all but brutal, in a matter of weeks. The kind of boss he'd cursed in his learning days. He saw no choice, though. The new men, the draftees and substitutes, were the sort who didn't just steal from the dead but pilfered from each other. He and Sam Losch had applied their fists to break up more than one scuffle.

Now here they were, on an autumn day in Virginia, lined up facing another worth-nothing field on a run-down farm, with yet another stretch of brush beyond, the brigade hemmed in by a swamp on the left and all Rebeldom on the right, every veteran just waiting for the crack of a nearby sharpshooter's rifle, the sprinkling fire of pickets, or a sudden bust-out of howling Johnnies coming their way fast. It wasn't just more of the same, it was too damned much of it.

To the north, on ground held by other men, skirmishers pestered and pricked.

As near as Brown could tell, the 50th stood close to the corps' left flank, which had been refused. Wasn't a good place to be, nor was it a bad one. It was just where they were. And every man with scratches and scars knew the Johnnies wouldn't take it lightly, a Yankee corps pressing into Virginia's flesh again. As the fighting had moved west, it had grown bitter.

There were times when he wondered how he would feel, if he found himself on the other end of things, facing an invading army surrounding Schuylkill Haven or maybe Pottsville, an enemy that reveled in destruction.

But he wasn't in Pennsylvania. He was here, in Virginia, an acting lieutenant with a job to do. And that was that.

War just left men too much time to think.

So Brown waited, along with every other man in the regiment. Wondering if they hadn't received an order to entrench because they were expected to move again, or because some officer failed to pass the word.

Looked like rain, too. And they'd marched light. Be sleeping wet, that was sure.

Two men from the skirmish line dragged in a bearded Johnny. The fellow looked as thin as hunger itself, but cocky, undaunted.

Captain Brumm stepped over. Looking at the passing Reb, he noted, "They're coming. Bet a gold piece."

Wearily, Brown agreed.

He was as tired of all this as any man.

Five p.m.
Banks farm, Boydton Plank Road

Go in," Harry Heth said. "Go in and do God's work. Send those Yankee sonsofbitches to Hell."

Five twenty p.m.
Harman Road

If there was one man Hampton found more unbearably proud than Rooney Lee, it was his cousin Fitz. Born to pride himself, Hampton sought to wear his sense of worth quietly, as a gentleman should. But the rising generation of Lees was rancorous and haughty, without the restrained dignity of the father and uncle they served. Nor did Hampton believe that Rooney, the youngest major general in the Confederacy, would have gained a division command but for his name. Rooney Lee was a very good cavalryman. But he wasn't the best cavalryman. He was, however, a Lee.

Now Fitz Lee lay gravely wounded, a Winchester casualty, and Rooney Lee stood waiting for Hampton's orders. A few hundred yards to the east, the battle had exploded and it sounded as though Harry Heth was doing handsomely.

It was time.

"General Lee, I wish you to go in," Hampton told his subordinate. "Major Hampton will join you. With your permission."

"Glad to have him along. Help with the whipping." Cocky as ever a man could be, Lee eyed him as if Hampton stood on an auction block. "Anything else, sir?"

Hampton shook his head. The plan for a dismounted attack had been discussed and decided, along with the ground to be covered and the goals. No need to waste more time repeating things.

Rooney Lee took off at a merry gallop, followed by his color-bearers and Hampton's eldest son: a major, not a major general.

Hamptons earned their way.

Five forty p.m.
Pegram farm

Brown spun the soldier around and punched him between the shoulder blades.

"Get back in that line, damn you," he told the shaking boy. "You load and fire."

The Rebs had stopped to trade volleys and their line was nearly as ragged as the brigade's. The Johnnies had gained ground so fast that their regiments spilled together, but they still had the numbers and weight. Hooting and calling out threats, the Rebs reloaded with speed but took time to aim. The best Brown could do with the new men who hadn't run off was to get them to fire wildly toward the enemy. Some just kept working their ramrods, as if they couldn't recall what to do next, while others stood frozen, waiting for their mother to wipe their noses. One closed his eyes each time he pulled the trigger.

The regiment had withdrawn twice, once a short distance on order and the second, hurried time after the brigade's Michiganders had come running back through the swamp on their left flank, scampering like kittens thrown in a dog pen.

Now they were trying to hold a shrinking line, with more and more Johnnies gathering to their front.

General Hartranft rode the line, bold as a rich man entering a bank.

"Steady, men," he called. "Steady on now." As he passed Brown's scruff of a company, he said, "That's the way, boys, that's the way you do it."

"Catch himself a bullet, that damned fool," Levi Eckert said.

But the Reb bullets seemed reluctant to strike Hartranft. They laid low many a humbler soldier, though.

Sam Losch collared another runaway, beating and kicking him back into the line. The boy had thrown down his rifle. Losch picked it up and slammed it against the lad's chest. The force of the blow knocked him down.

"Get up and fight, or I'll bayonet you myself," the first sergeant told him.

The brigade was fading away. Soldiers made sudden decisions, turned, and ran. For his part, Brown was just angry and bitter, vicious and cruel, a different man from the one he had been but a month ago.

General Hartranft passed behind them again, calling, "Hold them a bit longer, boys. Let the corps reorganize. Every man who stands here is a hero."

"Like wet shit we are," Levi said. His face seemed to have been sharpened on a whetstone. He aimed, fired, and added, "We're just goddamned idiots, that's all."

A boy's head burst. Brown caught part of the splash. He bent to rub his eye clean.

A Reb hollered, "All your friends done give up aw-ready, Yanks. Whyn't y'all come over here and make us a complete set?"

"Nigger's home diddling your wife, Johnny," Levi called back.

Brown glanced left and right. With the brigade line broken to bits and the remnants withering, the Rebs were working their way around both flanks. The surviving core of the 50th was all but surrounded.

Hartranft still rode the line, though, trailed by his colors and the few staff men who hadn't been shot down.

From nowhere, a rush of blue-coated fugitives appeared and plunged through the line, taking many a man along in their scramble. Brown could not for the life of him figure out how they'd gotten past the Rebs.

But the skedaddlers had done the Rebs' work for them. The 50th Pennsylvania all but collapsed.

Brown sheathed his worthless sword, holstered his empty pistol, and picked up a rifle. He tore a cartridge box off a dead man's body.

"Company C! Stand with me! Hold your ground!"

Worthless ground, worthless Virginia, a useless place to die.

Feeling the weight and solidity of a rifle in his hands renewed Brown's strength. He gave up on rallying runaways, leaving the job to Sam Losch, and banged away, feeling the hard, reassuring kick of the butt against his shoulder, better now than any woman's caress. After one of his careful shots, a Reb officer clutched his belly and dropped to his knees.

Smoke everywhere, writhing around a man's legs and searing his lungs. Gunfire to bust ears. Screaming, cursing. Groans and pleas. Faces spattered with blood and smeared with powder.

The regiment shrank until the colors had crowded next to the dozen men left of Company C. Captain Brumm spoke so close to Brown's ear that Brown felt his breath, his spit.

"Thought you were down, Brownie. Then I saw you playing soldier again."

"Get the colors out of here," Brown told him. "You go. Save the colors."

"We're all going to go."

"No," Brown told him. Adamant. "Save the colors. We'll hold them."

Brumm turned to Henry Hill, who stood beside Brown. As they had stood together in the Wilderness.

"Henry, talk sense to Brownie, would you?"

"Not so minded myself," Hill told him.

Casting aside the niceties of rank, Brown told the captain, "Georgie, get the hell out of here. You're just making it harder."

Brumm wheeled about and ordered the bloodied color guard to the rear. He shielded their withdrawal with scraps of the regiment. Most men just ran.

Company C remained. Brown loaded and fired. With Henry Hill beside him. And Levi next to Hill—Levi, who'd come so far as a man and soldier. And big Sam Losch, a Dutchman so dumb he didn't know when to run high-tail. Five others stood with them. Firing into a gray mass. Buying not minutes, but seconds. Fighting not for the Union or for any high-flown notions, but because they would not leave the men beside them.

At last, an exasperated Reb called over, "Why don't you crazy sumbitches just git?"

"That there's a fine idea," Levi agreed.

The seven men remaining of Company C, 50th Pennsylvania Veteran Volunteer Infantry, withdrew at a walk, their faces to the enemy.

Six fifteen p.m.
Pegram farm

Major Wade Hampton IV found his younger brother. In the depths of the battle.

"Pres, you get out of here now. You're supposed to be in the rear."

"*You're* here."

"I'm under orders. You're gallivanting."

"Just riding to the hounds, Wadey. Like back home."

"We're not hunting foxes, Lieutenant." Bullets *zip-zipped* past. "And you're not at your place of duty." The major wore a look of annoyance and pride. "If Father knew you were disobeying orders, he'd put you over his knee and spank you in front of the entire Cavalry Corps. Rip that rank off your collar, send you home."

"It's not your place to protect me, you know."

"You'll address me as 'sir,' Lieutenant. And I am ordering you to go to the rear. Report to your place of duty. Hear?"

Lips trembling, Preston Hampton pulled his horse about. He gave his brother an exaggerated salute and dug in a spur.

Watching his little brother ride off, the major muttered, "Fool's going to get himself killed."

Six thirty p.m.
Church Road, Pegram farm

Too slow," Charlie Griffin shouted at Ellis Spear. "Double-quick, forward, *now*. Get on that crest and hold it."

On both sides of the farm road, Ninth Corps men fled shamelessly. Griffin followed the rolling snaps of rifle fire as the Rebs pursued the vanquished. Galloping back and cursing the runaways, he directed his next brigade to take a position on Spear's right, as quickly as the worn men could come up. Just to the side of the road, Battery H of the 1st New York Lights awaited orders, limbered up and ready to move. Captain Mink, a one-armed terror, sat on his horse impassively, forcing the fleeing multitude to part to pass around him.

Griffin didn't yet know where he'd need Mink's battery. Everywhere, most likely. He let the captain wait.

Trailed by a skeletal color party, General Warren rode out of the wood line. The corps commander waved to Griffin: *Wait*.

"How is it, Charlie?" Warren asked, breathless.

"Damned mess. But we'll hold. How's the left?"

"Nearly as bad. Hartranft saved them from a complete catastrophe."

"Good man." He looked at Warren, that sallow, high-nerved face. Many a time he'd been out of temper with G. K. Warren, but he always came around. There were worse corps commanders. And if Warren could be slow, he was also methodical. The Johnnies might whip the Ninth Corps out of hand, but they weren't about to shove the Fifth Corps back. Warren already had engineers surveying a new line.

If Warren didn't always move when Meade wanted him to move, he didn't move for Robert E. Lee, either.

"Hold them, Charlie. Parke needs time to reassemble his ruffians. Hold them till dark."

Not a man given to brag, Griffin was in a rough-cut, angry mood.

"Had enough of Harry Heth's shenanigans," he told Warren. "About time for his comeuppance. We'll hold them, all right." Watching the endless rearward flow of quitters, he added, "I'd best get back and see how young Spear's doing. Lot of weight on his shoulders, first day running a brigade. Men might get the jumps."

"Sorry about your losses, Charlie."

Griffin shrugged. "War."

He kicked his horse back to life, riding hard beside the road as his troops double-quicked into battle. As for the Ninth Corps quitters, it was up to them to get out of his way.

As he reached the crest Spear's brigade had to hold, the men had finished deploying. The rise stood barely a hundred yards south of a wood line that still spit blue-coated runaways.

Light fading early. Air growing moist. Rain lurking.

Movement in those trees.

Soldiers emerged from the woods in broken order. Hard to see for the gloom and smoke, but they seemed to be wearing blue uniforms. Rebs had been picking over the dead, of course. Hard to know who was who at times.

Along the line, officers ordered their soldiers to hold their fire. The Rebs didn't hold theirs.

As soon as the Johnnies opened up, Griffin's veterans took action on their own, blasting back at them, quicker than any officer ever born.

Griffin didn't like the brigade's position, but it was vital: Hold the high ground, hold the road. His men were exposed on a naked crest, a perfect target, while the Rebs ghosted through the murk down in the trees, elusive and deadly. But he couldn't fall back and he couldn't risk moving forward, away from the rest of his corps.

The low ridge was trouble for the Fifth Corps artillery, too. The batteries positioned to the rear were overshooting both his men and the Johnnies, accomplishing nothing.

Reb guns had it better, thanks to the lay of the land, and his losses were getting ugly. Griffin rode the line, telling his men, "Pour it into those sonsofbitches . . . this is what soldiering is, boys, this is what it's about . . . show those pissants what a real division can do . . ."

A shell burst above the 20th Maine, knocking down a dozen men and leaving a patch of earth as red as a slaughterhouse.

Waving up his adjutant, Griffin shouted, "Ride back to Captain Mink. Tell him to bring his popguns up here now."

"Sir, you shouldn't be this far forward."

"I'm not forward. Damned Rebs are. Fetch Mink."

Time for some primitive gunnery. Not the prettily calculated sort he'd taught during his single reprieve from the Frontier, when he'd instructed West Point cadets on artillery tactics. This was going to be more like sweeping the causeways at Mexico City—he recalled crazy Jackson commanding a single fieldpiece, clutching his Bible to his breast, and shouting to trim the fuses.

He rode up to Ellis Spear. It was always a matter of balance, of weighing how much of a presence to be with a given subordinate. Spear was doing all right. But even for the finest veteran officer, a midbattle leap from leading a shrunken regiment to commanding a brigade was a hell of a challenge.

Before Griffin could speak, a shell burst gutted a color-bearer's horse and tore off the man's leg.

"Pick up those colors!" Griffin snapped.

The firing had grown so hot that soldiers scoured the dead for cartridges.

"Keep it up, Ellis," Griffin said. "Keep 'em in line. All you have to do is hold this crest."

As if it were that easy. . . .

"Reinforcements would help, sir."

"You don't need them." And there weren't any.

Spear opened his mouth but swallowed the words.

Glimpsed through the smoke, Mink's battery bounced and jingled over a stubble field, unwilling to wait for the last troops to clear the road.

"Just hold," Griffin called as he pulled his horse around. The racket had grown infernal, the casualties worrisome. "I'll see to the guns."

Intercepting Mink, a hellion who rode with his reins in his teeth to free his remaining arm, Griffin pointed to a lowering of the ridge, where the 118th Pennsylvania barely held on.

"Mink, I want one section of your guns ten yards *past* that firing line. The infantry can step aside. Aim at the tree line and give 'em double canister."

A man valiant almost to madness, Mink nonetheless looked shocked.

"I might as well put artillery on the skirmish line. . . ."

"Time to earn our pay, Captain. Get those fucking guns of yours into battery."

Mink recovered, took the reins between his teeth again, and waved his first section forward.

As he rode back along Spear's line, cursing and calling lieutenants and sergeants by name, Griffin kept an eye on the artillery. Mink was sound. In no time, he had the 118th refusing its line while his limbers swung about, the cannoneers jumping down from their seats while the wheels were still cutting dirt and man-handling their fieldpieces to point them toward the wood, the gunners already twisting the elevation screws. Better than any cadets had performed the drill, if not as primly.

In moments, the guns began blasting the grove, making a living hell of the gloom and shadows.

They'd hold, by God. They'd hold and more, they'd drive the Johnnies right out of that wood, make 'em squeal like a survey man caught by Navajos.

Grim and proud, Charlie Griffin paraded behind the firing line, a happier being than he could bear to admit.

As he passed, a smoke-blackened soldier called:

"Din't I tell ye, Genr'l dear, that the boys from Cork do handsome?"

Eight p.m.
Boisseau farm

Hampton stood in the drizzle, contemptuous of the water soaking his shoulders. His temper blazed, but he lacked an object at which to aim his fists. His rigorous carriage barely contained the savage brawler within.

Heth's men had begun to withdraw, frustrated yet again by Yankee stubbornness and the grating, clumsy tenacity of their Fifth Corps, which Hampton had begun to view as the corps that couldn't be pushed from a position, once it was given time to put down roots.

His own men were still fighting out in the brush and the ravaged sorghum fields, in the swamps and groves. They'd taken prisoners aplenty again, but the day was ending, night crowding in, and the Yankee attack had been blunted but not driven back far enough.

So they'd fight again tomorrow. And it would be harder. Warren would have entrenched. And Hampton would have to try to work the flanks more deeply still, while Harry Heth brought up a fresh brigade or two, robbing Peter to pay Paul, thinning the Petersburg lines beyond sensible risk.

His men had whipped the Yankees, beaten them sorely, but they hadn't *won*.

What was it going to take?

He noticed his younger son in a huddle of officers. He'd missed the boy earlier, afraid he'd gone off on another of his unauthorized larks. But no, there he was, oilskin draped on his shoulders, trying to light a pipe in the needling rain, a child playing at adulthood.

As the last, ill-tempered shots of the day pricked the distance, Hampton realized that he was getting drenched.

Ten p.m., October 4
Chaffin farm, Army of Northern Virginia headquarters

The meeting broke up around Lee, leaving behind no merriment and few traces of the genial tone once common. Here, north of the James in front of Richmond, those people had secured their grip on Fort Harrison, repulsing every effort to retake it, while they'd advanced their position on the Heights. West of Petersburg, Grant and Meade had extended their lines another three miles westward, their forward positions barely a mile from the Boydton Plank Road now and little farther from the South Side Rail Road. After three days of fighting and capturing another thousand prisoners, his soldiers had been unable to dislodge Warren.

There were nights when he felt he was a man condemned.

How he longed to strike back, to rout them as he'd done so often before, to maneuver and deliver a powerful blow and then another, appearing where those people didn't expect him and driving them off befuddled, shattered, and shamed. But those days were gone for now, perhaps forever. He lacked the men, he could barely defend these ever-expanding lines. Grant had trapped him. And his army's single unalloyed triumph in months had been Hampton's cattle rustling.

Was that what they had come to? Reduced to cattle thieves? Forced to endure a terrible wasting away, a military version of consumption?

The light rain stopped. Lee left the emptied staff tent. The air was fresh and lovely, yet it oppressed him. His heart fluttered again, leaving ghosts of pain. Camp noises rattled the night.

He missed Beauregard more than he had anticipated. The Louisianan had proved a better deputy—indeed, a fine one—than Lee had expected, based on earlier brushes. And with Beauregard he had been able to speak a bit less guardedly, both of them sharing the terrible weight of rank. But the war in the West was in ruins, and Beauregard had been chosen to put things right.

If things could ever be made right again.

He needed McClellan to win, the Confederacy needed it, Virginia needed it. Scouts and agents reported flagrant electioneering—ever distasteful to Lee—in the Union camps, with soldiers pressed to vote in the election, a privilege long forbidden those in uniform. Now there were reports of entire regiments furloughed to vote in their home states, while other states allowed voting by men in the field. Lee did not trust the outcome, despite the reputed fondness of Union troops for George McClellan.

And President Davis at times seemed all but mad, seized by fantastic schemes. Or else he joined in the spite of the Richmond papers, complaining sharply of Early's defeats, as if the Army had no end of capable generals who might replace him. Lee had sent Kershaw's Division and Rosser's Brigade of cavalry to the Valley, to make good September's losses, but still the odds were against his "bad old man."

Nor did Jubal Early make things easy. Ever cross about something or other, he'd driven John Breckinridge, a decent man, if a proud one, to finagle a new command in southwestern Virginia.

And Sherman sat on Atlanta, a mouser cat digesting a feast and pondering his next meal.

Why did the Lord test the South so?

A raindrop tapped Lee's upturned cheek, and loneliness

overcame him. He sought Walter Taylor's tent, where a lantern burned.

Lee tapped the canvas and lifted the flap. Startled, the aide jerked his back straight in his camp chair.

Taylor began to rise. Lee gestured: *Keep your seat*. Then he extended a hand toward Taylor's cot.

"Please, sir."

The general eased his arthritic bones onto the blanket.

"Writing to Miss Saunders?" he asked, adding, "If the question is not indecorous."

Features taut with guilt, the young man reddened.

"One needn't excuse a letter to one's sweetheart," Lee said. His voice, his bearing, recalled sunlight and laughter, a finer age. "Once duty is answered, of course. Indeed, I should think it another form of duty. If a pleasanter one."

"Do you need something, sir? Have I forgotten—"

Lee waved down the question. "I thought," Lee began his lie, "there might be late news from Georgia."

"No, sir. It's quiet, I believe. Sherman's—"

"Yes, Sherman. But we will not speak of such things. If there is no news."

Lee longed to empty his heart of his many griefs, his mind of his endless concerns. But he dared not speak. Not to this fine young man. Nor to anyone.

Nonplussed by the situation, Taylor asked, "Is Mrs. Lee well, sir? I neglected to inquire."

"As well as might be hoped." What had he to complain of, really? His wife's indispositions? Was he not all but inured to them? His unwed daughters? They might find husbands after the war. His sons were alive, survivors—though not untouched—and that approached a miracle. He and his wife were blessed, indeed, compared to President and Mrs. Davis, who had lost a child unseasonably. Unattended for a fateful moment, the boy had climbed over a balcony, a tragedy made ridiculous by war.

The loss had not smoothed the president's temperament. Or improved his judgment.

At times it was so hard to see God's justice. The heavens, life, all things remained inscrutable and mute. But wasn't the poet right: ". . . presume not God to scan"? Man could not know His wisdom or His glory. To think otherwise was presumption. No, blasphemy.

And yet he longed and prayed for a sign from God.

To break the silence—as heavy as a shell for a naval gun—Taylor said, "I still find it appalling, sir, that the Federals see fit to employ black troops. It cannot suit the conduct of civilized warfare."

Lee looked at his aide and met warm eyes—eyes that surely Miss Bettie Saunders must love. And eyes that, Lee hoped, would remain open and alert for many years.

"In war, Colonel Taylor, 'Right or wrong?' is a fool's debate. I have only learned that with difficulty. If a man aspires to high command, he must ask only, 'Is it wise?' This is a hard truth for all of us, I fear." He looked down at the trampled grass and balding earth of the tent's floor. "Those people would be fools not to find more soldiers where they can. And you see how they press us."

"But it's barbaric. Arming niggers."

Lee nodded. The advent of the Colored Troops troubled him, too, if for different reasons.

"Perhaps so, Colonel. Perhaps that's so. It may even be a sin in the Almighty's book. But let us credit their valor, we must do that much. Their Negroes fought well these past days, with more discipline and result than their paler comrades. They fought . . . sacrificially." Lee arched an eyebrow, seeking clean, clear words. "I do not condone their use, of course. I cannot, it revolts me. But I understand it."

"You'll pardon me, sir," Taylor said, "but it's . . . unworthy of gentlemen. But, then, I suppose the Yankees aren't truly—"

Lee stood up. "I've interrupted you." He forced a smile. "You must write your letter, we must not disappoint our dear ones. Please pass on my good wishes to Miss Saunders."

"I will, sir." Taylor hesitated. "Is everything all right?"

A frightful mood had gripped Lee. Not a foul mood in the common sense, but one imbued with a biblical sense of dread.

"At times," the elder man confided, "I fear that wars might not be won by gentlemen. Not anymore. If ever they were. Good night, Colonel Taylor."

Knees aching, Lee moved to leave the tent, then paused, captive to the grandeur and terror of life, touched for one moment by a force beyond reckoning.

A smile possessed him, a grim smile from the abyss. In a mild voice, a gentleman's fine voice, he spoke again. "When we repelled the Negro troops, when we finally stopped them after those futile charges, that butchery, I saw our error." He recalled the slaves whipped, reluctantly, at Arlington, the boredom with which the sheriff's man wielded the lash, the illusions of his kind, his lifetime, his country. "We consoled ourselves with the shallowness of their faculties . . . and missed the depth of their hatred."

He lifted the canvas to make his way into the darkness.

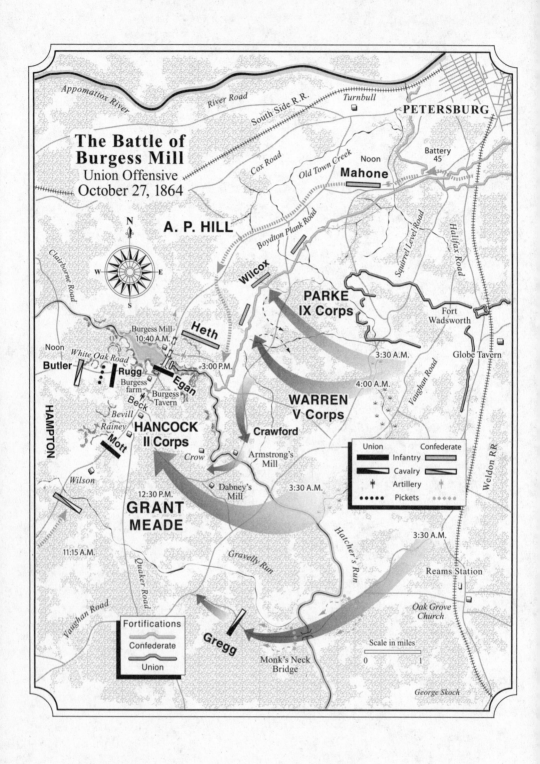

The Battle of Burgess Mill
Union Offensive
October 27, 1864

Appomattox River

River Road

South Side R.R.

Turnbull

PETERSBURG

Cox Road

Old Town Creek

Noon

Mahone

Battery 45

A. P. HILL

Boydton Plank Road

Squirrel Level Road

Halifax Road

N
W   E
S

Clairborne Road

Wilcox

**PARKE
IX Corps**

Fort
Wadsworth

Burgess Mill
10:40 A.M.

Heth

3:30 A.M.

Globe Tavern

Noon
Butler

White Oak Road

Rugg

3:00 P.M.

4:00 A.M.

Vaughan Road

Burgess
farm

Egan

Burgess
Tavern

Beck

**WARREN
V Corps**

Bevill
Rainey

HAMPTON

Mott

**HANCOCK
II Corps**

Crawford

Crow

Armstrong's
Mill

Union		Confederate
	Infantry	
	Cavalry	
✝	Artillery	
••••	Pickets	•••••

Wilson

Dabney's
Mill

3:30 A.M.

12:30 P.M.

**GRANT
MEADE**

Gravelly Run

Hatcher's Run

3:30 A.M.

Reams Station

11:15 A.M.

Quaker Road

Oak Grove
Church

Vaughan Road

Fortifications
Confederate
Union

Gregg

Monk's Neck
Bridge

Scale in miles

0   1

Weldon R R

George Skoch

FOURTEEN

Grant stood alone in the morning light, charged by the smell of bacon. The autumn sun gilded the James below but faltered against the chill. Across the river, trees bared themselves in bright death, and clouds fled across the horizon, as white as flags of surrender. It was a day to make men pause, of wonders insistent.

He bit off the end of a fresh cigar but hesitated to light it and foul the air. For a few fine minutes, all the surrounding contraptions and wealth of war were rendered harmless parts of a greater spectacle. The river churned with side-wheelers and steam tugs. Scavenging gulls swooped between the crowding vessels. On the wharf, hired Negroes passed crates from hand to hand or heaved up barrels, overseen by white men savoring coffee from tin cups.

Better cups of coffee in those hands than whips, Grant reckoned.

He recognized the cough at his back: John Rawlins, his friend.

Stepping close and following Grant's gaze, Rawlins said, "Ask myself sometimes if Lincoln has any inkling what he's done, what's going to happen when millions of them cut loose."

"Less than Southerners fear and more than Northerners want." Grant looked at his chief of staff. "Be all right, most of them. Give them a fair shake. Colored Troops surprised us, no reason the rest of them shouldn't. Just give them a fair shake."

As he'd sweated side by side with Negroes on his Missouri farm, his hands had grown as callused as theirs, his lot fallen almost as low.

Ever the cynic, Rawlins said, "Fair shakes are rare for white men. You know that. Better than I do." He drank from a cup that spread a flowery scent: honey in hot water for his lungs.

"Like breaking a long bone," Grant said, "busting the South and slavery. Take time to heal, I know. Mighty inconvenient and uncomfortable. But many a bone mends stronger."

"You're the unlikeliest optimist I know."

Grant smiled. "I'm the unlikeliest general you know." He turned more fully toward this trustworthy, profane man, whom he feared was dying. "John, something I want to warn you about. I may need you to go back west. In your capacity as chief of staff. Straighten out the St. Louis mess. Settle Rosecrans, see Thomas."

"Just got back, Sam. I'm starting to think my company's un-welcome." He drank, coughed, and drank again.

Grant touched his friend's upper sleeve. "The only person more welcome to me is Julia. And I get more work out of you."

A steamship hooted, a bully among the lighters, coasters, and tugs.

"She settled in, then, the little ones? School business all ar-ranged?"

"Wish it was. That woman . . ."

"Sam, I've never seen a better marriage."

"I suppose."

Rawlin sighed, lungs gurgling. "Washburne's on me about the furloughs again. Sending the troops home to vote."

Grant nodded. "And Stanton's hounding me." He smiled again: Despite all concerns, this seemed a day worth living. "If he thought he could persuade me, he'd probably want me to pack up and march us *all* north. Can't see beyond the election."

"Can you?"

Grant hesitated. "I think it'll be all right. I do, John. Don't want to call down bad luck, but I think it'll be all right. Cedar Creek fight was trumps, Phil pulled it off. Nobody wants to quit when they think they're winning. Atlanta may have been the turning point, but the Valley drove it home."

"Hope you're right. I *think* you're right. People are tired, though. And the Army . . . you saw the desertion figures."

"Saw Sharpe's figures, too. Johnnies are coming across the lines in droves. Hungry, and it isn't even winter. Worried about their home folks. Rather be in my shoes than in Lee's."

"That damned traitor deserves everything he gets."

Again, Grant paused. Then he said, "Being defeated by anyone's the second-worst punishment Robert E. Lee could suffer."

Lowering his cup, Rawlins asked, "What's the worst?"

Grant's eyes sparkled. "Getting whipped by me."

Rawlins cackled. "Sam, there are times when I think you're more of a devil, just more of a wicked scourge, than folks suspect."

"I just know what defeat can do to a man. Knew it long before this war came along."

"You got back up, though."

"Lee won't."

"Sure of that?"

"I lost a potato crop and my commission. Lee's going to lose everything he's lived for."

"*If* Lincoln wins."

"He'll win. Don't say I said so."

Behind the sprawled headquarters, a locomotive got up steam on the military railroad.

"Really wise to have Meade attack again?" Rawlins asked. "With the vote so near? If it doesn't go well . . . Sam, I can hold up that message, that's what I came out to say."

Down on the wharf, two Negroes began fighting. A white foreman watched the set-to long enough for blood to fly before calling on the other coloreds to stop them.

Just need a fair shake, Grant told himself. *Just a fair shake.*

"Meade and Humphreys have a sensible plan, I think it's sound. Three corps this time, swinging well to the west. Test the Rebs along that flank, find the end of their line, and curl around it. And I've made it clear that no one's to assault strong fortifications, no frontal attacks. If we can't get around their flank, Meade's to call it off."

"Things do take on a life on their own."

"Worth the risk. Take Petersburg and reelection's guaranteed."

"And a defeat?"

"Won't come to that. Won't let it. Hancock will be on the far left. Itching to redeem himself after Reams Station. He won't get whipped again."

"He might try too hard."

"Meade's job is to see he doesn't."

A gull swooped near, as if spying.

"George still riled about those newspaper tales?" Rawlins asked.

"Mad as a bear with his hind leg in a trap. Can't say I blame him, either. Lies, start to finish. Do what I can to help him, but . . ."

"He brought it on himself. Refusing to toss the scribblers a bone now and then. High and mighty. It's a different age, Sam. We all have to bow to the power of the press. Pretend to, anyway."

"George Meade can't. He's a gentleman, the old-fashioned kind. Hates journalists worse than he hates the Johnnies, just brought up that way."

"Well, he's paying for it."

But Grant was thinking on Meade the man. "He really can't help himself. No more than Lee can. Can't bear shame. Of any kind." He smiled, not without rue. "Times are I think failure was the best thing happened to me. Taught me a man can outlast just about anything." His small smile sharpened. "I don't recommend it as a practice, though."

Ten forty a.m., October 27
Boydton Plank Road, south of Burgess farm

With his Gettysburg wound oozing through his trousers and paining him to damnation, Hancock watched the Rebel wagons flee. A mile up the road, their canvas tops swayed, just visible through wet mist, heading for the crossing at Hatcher's Run. Had a small detachment of cavalry been on hand, he could have taken them.

At Hancock's side, Brigadier General Tom Egan said, "Well, that's a plum should've been plucked." In temporary command of Gibbon's division, Egan was looking for a fight, Irish to the tips of his mustaches. Hancock was certain he'd find what he was looking for.

"Order Rugg to unfold his brigade and anchor his right on the Plank Road," Hancock said. "His skirmishers will feel toward White Oak Road."

"Shall I have Rugg push out White Oak?"

"Only the skirmishers. Until Mott comes up. I sent Mitchell off to hurry him."

"Yes, sir. Not a bad morning, I daresay." Egan turned to pass on Hancock's orders.

No, it had not been a bad morning, not in the military sense. Just the damned thigh plaguing him again. He hadn't spoken to Meade about it yet, but he feared this would have to be his last attack. Riding was an agony, but walking more than a few steps was unbearable.

How good it would be to go out on a victory. . . .

The men were game, surprisingly so. It was almost as if his veterans had risen from their graves. The corps had advanced rapidly, striking deep and surprising the unprepared Johnnies. Unable to hold even one of the stream crossings, Hampton's cavalrymen had hardly slowed the two divisions Hancock had on the march. And judged by the sound of the scrapping to the southwest, Gregg's mounted division was advancing, too.

He wished he had Miles with him, though, his entire corps, three divisions. But one division had needed to stay in the Petersburg lines, and Miles' soldiers merited the rest.

Miles had turned out to be a solid replacement for Frank Barlow, who was still sick abed in Boston two months on. War was hard on the body, young or old. Even Charlie Morgan, his chief of staff and long of iron health, sat his horse grimly this day, wet through and puke-up sallow, unwilling to stay behind when the corps went forward.

It *had* been a cracking-good morning, though, on-and-off rain be damned. But the hard fighting came in the afternoons and not the forenoons now, so the true test lay ahead. His corps had advanced splendidly, but his progress had opened a gap on his right when Warren's Fifth Corps halted miles behind, stymied by entrenchments. Hancock had been assured that Warren would send up Crawford to cover the flank, but he'd learned to distrust promises. He wanted that division in the flesh.

The flesh was always the weakness, ever the flesh.

Of course, Humphreys' detailed plan had all but collapsed. Plans generally did. On the right of the advance, Parke had met strong works. Then Warren faced the same problem. The Johnnies had extended their entrenchments farther west than scouts and spies had reported. So only Hancock's corps and Davey Gregg's horsemen had found a gap. Now they were striking deep, but unsupported.

If Meade would push Warren to send *two* divisions, not one . . . White Oak Road appeared undefended, the route to the South Side Rail Road naked of troops. Hancock longed to give the order to turn his entire corps in that direction, to move before the Johnnies could react. But first he had to clear out the last Rebs up along Hatcher's Run to secure his flank. And he needed goddamned Warren to do his part, to make an effort.

Quick-marching past the generals, Egan's men showed handsomely, as if the chill in the air evoked better days. And the rain had paused.

To the north, two Secesh guns went into battery but had trouble finding the range.

Returned to Hancock's side, Egan said, "They know we're here now. Some of them, anyway."

"When Willett comes up, deploy his brigade over there, at the foot of that slope. We'll need to clear out those Johnnies on the ridge. And by those buildings. Then push on to the mill bridge, you'll need to take it."

Without waiting for orders, two batteries of the 5th U.S. Light Artillery jangled across a field, swinging their teams around smartly and jumping down to unhitch the guns.

Egan stretched in the saddle. "Rebs are going to find themselves on the dirty end of young Beck. Lad's got the gunner's eye. Ho, there's Smyth."

"As soon as he closes, move against that ridge, Tom. Mott should be up soon, we've got a jump on the Rebs. And if Warren gets his hands out of his damned pockets . . ."

It *had* been a good morning. But Win Hancock needed a splendid afternoon. One last splendid, praiseworthy afternoon.

Lieutenant Beck's guns went into action. In less than three minutes, the Reb fieldpieces pulled off.

A bad leg, but a good day.

Eleven fifteen a.m.
Gravelly Run

The courier's horse threw back more slop than poor-white children got into a pig wallow. Grudgingly, Hampton turned from the rifle pits. His men were holding the crossing against Mott's division. Which meant that his opponent was Hancock again.

Well, this was as good a day as any to finish him.

"Let's see what this is about," he told Matt Butler, one of whose brigades had the duty at hand.

The spattered courier reined up, hailed by a sizzle of bullets. Across the creek, the Federals readied a charge.

"General Hampton . . . Yankees . . . Hancock . . ."

"Breathe easy, son. Where are the Yankees?"

"Behind you. Up on the Plank Road, just south of where White Oak Road branches off."

That wasn't possible. He'd have heard the firing, the commotion.

"Dearing . . ."

Still gasping, the courier told him, "He's not there, sir. General

Heth wouldn't release him, said he needed him. That's what I was coming to tell you. When I near run into the Yankees."

Struggling not to reveal his shock, Hampton turned back to Butler. "Dearing was supposed to cover White Oak. Lord. Matt, pull your boys off, there's no point holding here now. We have to move." As more rain teased, he asked the rider, "Plank Road open anywhere behind Hancock?"

"Couldn't rightly say. Came over the country."

It had been a fool's question, given the courier's path. He had to quell his surprise, to think clearly now.

"Matt, you get along fast. Doesn't matter if the Yankees see your boys going. Just get them mounted and riding, we've got to keep Hancock off the White Oak Road."

Hancock had advanced faster than Hampton thought possible.

"Surely," the brigadier general agreed. "Just have to get there."

"That trail we came down this morning. Take that."

"If it's still open. . . ."

"Chance it. Swing behind Hancock like he swung behind us." Hampton growled low in the throat. "Get them going, Matt. Off the roads, if you have to. Just get them across White Oak Road, as near to your old camp as possible. And *hold* those sonsofbitches."

A cavalryman to the bone, Butler jumped to it and Hampton turned back to the courier. The lad looked downright starved, but he'd done good service. Hampton wished he could recall the boy's name.

"Good work," he said. "Most important message I'll hear all day. Think you could make your way back to General Dearing?"

"Can't rightly say, sir. Try, though."

"Good. Try. Tell him I'm on my way to White Oak Road. He's to join me, as soon as General Heth releases him."

The rain began to sting.

"Reckon he won't," the courier said. "Genr'l Heth has him holding that bridge by the mill, on the Burgess place. Ain't nobody else there to take things up."

Dickinson. That was his name.

"Well, you've done us a worthy service, Dickinson. Just pass on my message to General Dearing. And tell him I wish him luck."

The courier nodded and gave a salute that would not pass on parade, but the boy's eyes glowed.

Butler's men scrambled off the line, dashing through muck and mire toward their horses. Hampton felt they'd already taken too long, though no men could have moved faster. The plan he'd hammered out with Harry Heth to cover the flank was disintegrating.

Gripping his temper, he forced himself to remember that things on a battlefield often looked worse than they were. Even the weather clouded a man's judgment. A leader had to be steady, that above all.

If Mahone came up in time . . . they could still give Hancock a thumping. But Little Billy would have a long march to make from the Petersburg lines, given how far west the Yankee blow had landed. Hampton believed he could hold for a time, for some hours, if he could get his men across White Oak Road. He just wasn't going to hold where he'd thought he would.

And it sounded like Hancock might be exposing his flank.

Already riding at a trot, heading for the path that would lead to another path that might lead this lean brigade to another stand, he waved up his eldest son.

"Major, ride down to Rooney Lee—to *General* Lee—and tell him the plan's changed. Hancock's on the Plank Road, just shy of White Oak. And probably not very shy. General Lee's to come up the Plank Road, straight up from the southwest, and press the Yankee rear. He's not to become inextricably engaged, not yet. He's just to keep them busy. More orders will follow."

"Yes, sir. Anything else, sir?"

Features as firm as a quarry face again, Hampton responded, "When you get back, you keep an eye on Preston. No more of his foolishness."

Noon
Confederate lines, Petersburg

Sergeant Johnny Sale hated marching wet. Wet and cold. Temperature would have been somewhere about pleasant, but for the rain coming back to ambush a man, turning trouser wool to a rawness and everything else clinging. Worked through what remained of his shoes, too.

But marching they were, a ragged, disgruntled bunch, the 12th Virginia, ready to go at the Yankees with their teeth. With any teeth hadn't been lost to them. Time was when they'd been teased as the "Kid Glove Boys," Mahone's entire Virginia Brigade mocked for its tidy dress and general prettiness. Not now, that was sure.

Not three hundred men marching in the 12th, and that many nigh on a miracle, with the lurking sickness and all the dead, those invalided out and the wretches—good men once—who'd slipped off in the night from a picket line. Marching on roads down which they could go blindly, by feel of foot, so many times had they been rushed into battle, quick-marched back and forth until they knew this torn stretch of Virginia as well as any farmer knew his home fields, as well as varmints knew the reach of their burrows.

Today, the roads gripped, pulling on a man's knees and straining his calves. Marching hard they were, bruise-footed, with the officers pained of face and worry-ridden, their gallantry much thinned. Marching on a rain-spanked day that wouldn't behave no better. With the Yankees making an uproar off to the west, still a mean march away, and his job as a sergeant—a sergeant promised a lieutenancy, if this Confederacy could ever make up its mind about one thing—his job was to hurry along these men who couldn't be hurried beyond the grit they already were showing, whose meager flesh couldn't move their enclosed bones to greater speed, who just couldn't go any faster, and he had to tell them constantly to git along, that the blue-bellies were eager to say hello, maybe every man and every louse on that man's scalp remembering better days, times before this death-rich year, this man-breaker, crush-heart time, and Grant grim over there beyond the pickets, Grant whipped and whipped again and just not quitting. How could that be?

Be all that so, and so it was, Johnny Sale wasn't given to over-pondering things he could not bear upon, reluctant to poke much at thoughts beyond the next spoon of beans, for such deep rumi-nations led to doubt, which led Man into temptation. No, a soldier did his duty, best he could, and hoped somebody wiser was think-ing out some sense to the blood and blisters, the friendships torn by death, the cripplings . . . don't think too much on those matters, either, for it did not pay no more than lying with strumpets, which just left a man sour, if not worse.

Sergeant Johnny Sale sought to be a good man, upright in war as in peace, sorry for much he had done, but always and ever set on doing better.

Didn't even think about living or dying anymore, that didn't pay, either. The Lord was his shepherd, that was enough. And he was one mean sheep.

"Hurry up now," he called to the men in his fold. "Yankees be gone before we get a lick in."

"Fine with me," a bent-back soldier told him.

Noon
White Oak Road

Hampton outdistanced Butler's column and crossed a final field, trailed by the few companions and color-bearers who'd matched his pace.

He could see them ahead, the Yankee skirmishers: Their wet blue coats and caps looked black in the murk.

Correcting his path slightly, he spurred his horse again, making straight for the road, judging where Butler's men might defend be-fore the Yankees could close. His horse leapt a ditch smoothly and splashed its hooves in the virgin mud of the lane.

Hampton turned toward the enemy and drew his pistol.

"Mounted skirmish line," he ordered. "Form up, spread out."

His meager band made a line across the road and into the fields, sodden flags held high and pistols cocked. Pure bluff.

Instead of coming on, the Union skirmishers paused to study the new development. Then they took aim and fired. Rounds ripped past, no one buckled. The range was too long.

"They're unsettled," Hampton said. He stayed his horse. "Steady now, everybody."

Several of the Yankees moved forward again, but cautiously. He listened for the hoof-thump of Butler's lead brigade, but heard nothing for the nearer sounds of cannon to the east, the firecracker snap of rifle volleys, and the patter of rain. Hancock was pressing Dearing up on the Burgess farm, pushing for the bridge. Couldn't be clearer.

Looking toward the skirmishers, Captain Aldie said, "We could charge 'em, give 'em a scare."

"I'd as soon not," Hampton told him. It wasn't a day for bravado, but for hard fighting. He did want Butler to bust out of those trees, though. Problem was that his nags were already blown, far from desirable horseflesh for the cavalry.

The South Hampton loved had come down a ways. Wasn't at bottom, though. Hancock would see.

At last, the head of Butler's column emerged from the woodland trail. When Butler reckoned out the situation, he ordered a bugler to announce their arrival, wet lips on wet brass, the call slovenly but effective.

The Yankee skirmish line halted.

Butler waved his men to a gallop, creating a storm of mud. Hampton hoped the guns had fared well on the trail, they were going to be needed.

As Butler's riders approached the road, Matt shouted orders and Hampton added his voice, the two of them working as one, as canny about each other's thoughts as two spiritualists at a table-rapping.

The horsemen fanned out by regiment, stretching their left to a pond to the north and southward across the field. In minutes, Butler's men were throwing up barricades, ingenious at finding materials where civilians would have been stumped.

A few hundred yards to the southeast, a blue column hastened to reinforce the Yankee skirmish line.

It was going to be a long, hard afternoon awaiting Mahone.

Twelve thirty p.m.
Boydton Plank Road

As Hancock issued the order to Mott to move his division up onto White Oak Road, a cavalcade appeared behind his trail brigade.

"Better hold off," Hancock told the division commander. "See what the hell they want. Just get de Trobriand placed. Then come back."

His leg scourged him doubly. He almost felt like pounding his thigh with his fists, to beat out the pus and hammer the pain to death.

Preceded by outriders, Grant and Meade came cantering side by side, trailed by more flags than a Fourth of July celebration in Philadelphia. Behind the banners, enough well-mounted cavalrymen followed to be put to good use, had they not been retained to serve as palace guards. Their uniforms were mud-clotted now, to the delight of troopers less fortunate.

Well, Grant and Meade would find things well in hand, with Egan on his way to the mill bridge and Mott prepared to lunge for the South Side Rail Road *if* that damned prig Warren provided support.

A magnificent horseman, Grant led the way. Meade had a good seat, too, but carefully let Grant keep a half length's lead.

Touching the brim of his hat, Hancock said, "Generals."

"How goes the day, Win?" Grant asked. He was smiling. Grant always seemed to smile after a hard ride, no matter the state of all else.

"Bully, Sam. Caught 'em with their drawers around their

ankles." He turned toward Meade. "That division from Warren? Where the devil is it? Can he send two? Or bring up his whole corps, let Parke hold the line?"

"Just came up from Fifth Corps," Grant answered for Meade. "Crawford's been getting his bunch under way."

"He's to move up Hatcher's Run and secure your flank," Meade added. "Reach out for him with your right."

"That's a jungle down there. He'll be crawling, that's no route to take." Hancock stopped to choose his words carefully, struggling to master his outrage—Crawford should have been on the move hours back and marching up Dabney's Mill Road right behind Mott. He said, "I could use the support right now, George. I just ordered Mott up White Oak Road, all they have holding there's cavalry. But I need solid support, if I'm to advance. All Warren has to do is cover my flanks."

Stern as ever on a field of battle, Meade told him, "That has to wait. For now, you'll hold right here." He nodded toward the sound of Egan's sparring. "Gain the Hatcher's Run crossing, then assume a defensive position, don't let them surprise you. And wait for orders."

Hancock wanted to rip open living creatures with his bare hands. They'd gotten *behind* the Rebs, broken through, done what they'd been trying to do for months. And now he was supposed to stop and hold? Here? Just short of the prize? *Here?* Where he made no damned difference?

Grant eased his big horse closer. "You've had a good day, Win. Don't want to stretch things too far. We'll see what Warren can do, what can be done."

Hancock understood: They'd all failed for so long that success surprised them. And Grant feared a debacle before the election. More than he wanted a victory. They'd all gotten cold feet.

He wanted to curse them down, smack them into the mud. Not least, Warren, with his chronic affliction, the slows. And Parke was worthless. Nobody wanted to fight.

"Choose a good defensive position," Meade repeated. "They'll come at you, no doubt."

No doubt. And he'd just wait for it. It made him want to rip off his shoulder straps and throw them down.

"How's the leg today?" Grant asked.

"No trouble at all," Hancock told him.

One thirty p.m.
White Oak Road

Hampton couldn't fathom it. Hancock had just stopped. His skirmishers kept probing, but there didn't seem to be any force behind them. Even the ongoing fight up toward the crossing sounded dutiful, not impassioned.

Well, he hoped it would stay that way. Until Rooney Lee, who was dawdling, came up and added his weight. He'd sent another messenger to Dearing and one to Heth, asking them to keep the pressure on Hancock up by the bridge, to make it seem the struggle of prime importance. Mahone was on his way, that much was confirmed, but it would be hours until he got into place. Meanwhile, for the plan to work, the rest of them needed to entertain Hancock, to keep him looking north, northwest, and southwest . . . while Mahone worked his way across country, across those damways over Hatcher's Creek, to hit Hancock from the east, striking from the tanglewood well off the prized roads, appearing where a major attack seemed impossible.

And when Mahone struck, whenever that might be, they'd all come down on Hancock from every side. And finish him.

The sky spit another gust of rain, a cloud clearing its throat.

Three p.m.
Boydton Plank Road

Brigadier General Count Régis Denis de Keredern de Trobriand, husband of a New York banking heiress and citizen of the United States by choice since the war's first days, stomped through the mud to spare his weary horse. Horses were splendid animals, but not intelligent, and a good master had to judge the care they needed. He had grown fond of the beasts on his father's estate, after the Revolution of 1830 drove the aging baron from the French army and let him concentrate his substantial energies on his land, his racing stock, his son, a succession of quarrelsome mistresses, and his wife. De Trobriand had learned discretion in boyhood.

Then he had been indiscreet in a *tête-à-tête* with Hancock. Standing on a point of honor, he'd offended his superior, and Hancock was a man who nursed a grudge. Now all de Trobriand could do was to carry out his duties flawlessly, send love poems home to Mary and teasing letters to his eldest daughter, and wait for Hancock to relinquish command.

The *tristesse* of it was that he admired Hancock: The man was a *soldier*. It had been a relief when the Third Corps was dissolved and he had come under Win Hancock's command. Sickles had been a trial, and not just at Gettysburg. The politician had swilled without taste; seduced without grace; and fought with a certain valor but no skill. Inelegant on a horse, Sickles had been no better in a drawing room than in the saddle. And he held his cigars the wrong way. Hancock was better on every count, though prouder than any Frenchman de Trobriand knew.

"No," de Trobriand told the colonel before him. "It must be just *so*. Mud excuses nothing. Rain is the soldier's friend, if he's a good soldier." Preferring explanations to bluff orders, he added, "They will come from there, you see. It is the natural axis. We must refuse the line so. Am I understood?"

"Yes, sir," the well-meaning colonel told him. *"Je comprends."*

"Ah, but when you speak French to me, it makes me sad, *cher Colonel*. The accent . . ."

De Trobriand knew his subordinates found him amusing. And he was glad to amuse them, as long as they fought like demons. And they did.

He led from the front, and they followed. *Simple.*

The American soldier, he was a special case. You could not command, "Do this!" and expect it done. No, the American wished to know why such a step should be taken. And once he knew, he usually performed well. The American was a creature of great curiosity, while the European kept to his own business. Beginning the war with the Garde Lafayette, whose ranks were thick with Frenchmen, it had taken de Trobriand time to grasp the peculiarities of the native-born troops. But once he did, he found them rather marvelous.

The rain stopped, leaving his soldiers soaked and cold—as was de Trobriand. He would not drape a rain cape over his shoulders if his men had none. The day, which had begun handsomely, inched toward disappointment. The corps had stopped. Instead of pressing on with *élan*, Hancock had ordered Egan's division into a minor action, while Mott's division had been carved up like a game pie, with McAllister's brigade sent to bolster Egan, Pierce scattered on the right flank and poking the woodlands, and de Trobriand's own brigade held back to cover the western approaches.

Among his father's endless stock of homilies, one had been, "A man must know when a love affair is over, as a soldier must recognize when an attack is spent." But what of an attack left to decay? A lesson de Trobriand had drawn himself was that the moment an advance paused, it started to fail.

To his father's chagrin, de Trobriand had not chosen *la vie militaire*. But in 1861, in a new land, military life had chosen him, drawing him from a comfortable editorship. Of course, had *cher Papa* been alive still, he would have been more appalled at the happiness of his son's marriage than he had been disappointed by his son's earlier disinterest in uniforms: For his class, a passionate marriage was an embarrassment. Romance was for affairs, lust for kept women or the *maison close*. Wives were to be selected on merits, like horses.

But Régis de Trobriand had married for love—a girl without title, no less, and an American, however wealthy—and here he was on this dreary battlefield, one that would never inspire a martial painting, with his father's ghost at his shoulder, whispering, "But of course! You are my son! War's in our blood!"

Surveying the puddled autumnal fields, the shambling-past men of other commands, and the disorder of wagons and guns massed off the Plank Road, de Trobriand would have done many things differently. But it was not his place—not yet—to make those decisions. All he could do was to shrug, see to his men, and fulfill his disappointing orders.

Nor would he let the errors he witnessed anger him. He had heard much said of the "Gallic temperament," but his kind never indulged in public tantrums—it wasn't done—while American generals blew up at any slight. On the whole, he found Americans far more given to fits than Europeans, even Italians. And as his father, who had served under both Napoleon and the Bourbons, had counseled him at the puttylike age of twelve, a man who could keep a cool head in bed and in battle held the advantage.

Certainly, that admonition had served in his pleasant little duels in Rouen and Paris. A gifted swordsman, he'd never lost and never shamed an opponent more than necessary. When he'd left France for New York on a club-room dare, he'd left behind not only scars, but foes made friends.

De Trobriand paused by a forlorn detail of soldiers, bedraggled men as cynical as French housewives. Choosing a sulking boy, he said, "Ah, but we are fortunate today! Is there any place a soldier would rather be?"

"I can think of a few," a corporal put in.

De Trobriand smiled. "You say that now, *cher Caporal*. With insouciance I must admire. But I tell you, as years pass, you will remember this fondly . . ." He waved a wet hand. "This *fraternité*, this adventure . . ." He stepped between the two men, the broad-shouldered and the narrow, and patted each on the back. "You think, 'This general, he is a fool, he knows nothing of my cares, my misery!' But wait. Your war will be the glory of your lives! You will tell your children's children tales that will swell and soar in majesty. . . ."

"If we live, sir."

"Ah, yes," de Trobriand concurred. "And the best way to live is to slay the enemy first. Don't you agree?"

Three p.m.
Burgess Mill, north bank of Hatcher's Run

Mahone listened.

"They've been forceful," Harry Heth said, indicating the Federals deployed south of the run. "Not fast, but forceful. Methodical. Like they've got all the time in the world."

"Maybe this is all they mean to do." Mahone reached down to stroke his horse. "Might be they spooked themselves, getting this far."

"And well they should be spooked. Leaving that flank open. Billy, you've got to hit them hard. You can rip right through that corps."

"Just waiting for your order."

"I know, I know. And I'm waiting for Hampton to tell me Rooney Lee's up. No more piecemeal efforts. When you hit Hancock, I want him hit from all three other directions."

Mahone looked up at the sky, though there wasn't much sky to see. Just low clouds gray as smoke and a brightness weak in the west.

"You give me the order, it's still going to take me time to get over that dam, it won't pass more than two men abreast. Then I've got to get through that undergrowth, and it's bad—I know that stretch." He curled one side of his mouth. "No wonder the Yankees haven't closed up that gap, it's forbidding to man and beast." He looked at Heth, no nonsense. "I need to hit them before dark, at least an hour before. And dark comes early. Time's burning."

His stomach was burning, too.

"I know that. Just wait, Billy. I'm as anxious as you are."

Across the run, a fresh Union battery rolled up to replace guns with depleted caissons.

"Yankees have been outshooting us today," Heth admitted. "Pains me to say it."

"Too many good men dead. And bad ammunition."

Heth looked across the sodden landscape, over a carpet of clotted leaves, and past half-hidden men in raw entrenchments, bare trees, and busy rifle pits.

"They're going to come at the bridge. Any time now," Heth said. "I'll need Harris here, Dearing's men are tired. But you'll have MacRae's Brigade, along with your own two. Those North Carolina boys will do good service."

"I can do it with three brigades. But I have to move, Harry, I have to move soon. Dark comes early."

A courier arrived: Hampton's eldest son.

Breathless and proud, the major saluted and said, "General Hampton's compliments, gentlemen. I'm to tell you everybody's in position."

Heth turned to Mahone. "Go in, Billy. Go in quick as you can."

Four p.m.
Burgess farm, south bank of Hatcher's Run

Brigadier General Tom Egan had his men ready for the final thrust. He'd swept the Rebs across the farm, artfully and with few casualties, and pushed them from the south bank of the run. But Hancock had been slow to give the final order to take the bridge. As soon as the belated permission arrived, though, Egan had deployed his brigades, as full of fight as he'd ever been in a life spent with his fists up, whether battling rascals throwing rocks at the "Irish brat" or Johnnies hurling bullets at a general.

And then the great flag-flying, star-addled, colonel-ridden, lavishly festooned party had appeared, led by Grant himself.

And Grant said, "Hold up. I want to see how this lies before you go in."

Didn't take a minute for the Reb artillery to celebrate the gift of a matchless target. Explosive rounds burst near enough to wound a pair of riders and kill a man. Reading the north bank through a pair of field glasses, Grant seemed unaware of any danger.

Finally, Grant muttered, "Can't see a thing. Not what I need to see." He looked at Egan. "You stay here." Raising his voice slightly, he added, "Everybody just sit still, I don't need company." He concluded by telling a staff man, "Babcock, come with me."

And Grant, atop a splendid mount, took off along the Plank Road toward the bridge, heading straight toward the Johnnies and riding as smoothly as a tout at a horse show.

Two hundred yards on, Grant stopped. Awkwardly. At a point that made no sense. As Egan watched, the aide wheeled his horse about to close up to Grant.

"The glasses," Egan called to his own aide. He trained his binoculars on the senior officer in the Union.

"Oh, Christ," he said.

Nor was he the only man peering through wet lenses. More than one groan preceded a burst of profanity.

Grant's horse was tangled in telegraph wires that had just been cut.

"We've got to go down there," a voice declared.

"Stay put," Egan ordered. "Damn it, man, if we all ride down there, we're just telling the Rebs the target's important. Any man moves, I'll take my revolver to him."

He raised the lenses again. Grant sat placidly on his horse, as if he'd just had a mind to pause for a stretch, while his dismounted aide worked to disentangle hooves without getting kicked.

To Egan, it seemed as though the world had stopped. One well-aimed Rebel shell . . .

But the artillerymen across the run remained more concerned with the men gathered on the ridge, making it hot for Grant's courtier colonels and hangers-on. Bedazzled by the ball and missing the belle.

"Nobody moves," Egan snapped.

At last, Grant's horse stepped high and free. Still the general waited for his aide to remount before he turned for the rear.

When Grant came up, he looked as though he'd been mildly disappointed by his dinner.

"Saw what I needed to see," he told Egan. "Cancel the attack. Not worth the lives it would cost. Not going that way, anyhow. Just hold the ground you have and wait for orders."

And Grant turned his mount southward, back toward Hancock and the rest of the army.

Four thirty p.m.
Second Corps headquarters, Boydton Plank Road

Goddamn him," Hancock said. "God*damn* him."

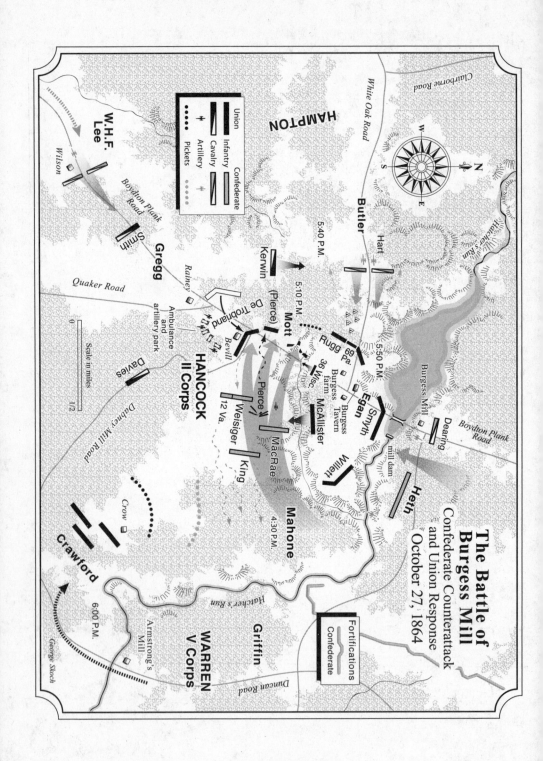

The Battle of
Burgess Mill
Confederate Counterattack
and Union Response
October 27, 1864

FIFTEEN

Four thirty p.m.
Burgess farm, eastern woods

The going was skunk-ugly, them running across a dam lip like bad boys defying their ma. Then came a splash and a nettle-swat through a low stretch not proud enough to be called a swamp, yet more than enough to make wet feet much wetter, cold water clotting worn-through, worn-double stockings. Briars leaping lively at cheek and eye—*Look out, Yanks!*—every man tempered mean as a water snake now, silent past believing. Why? Little Billy said it must be so. There would be no foolery, no brave-me-up chatter, even for the officers: *You all just be quiet.* Lordie-gawd, a man wouldn't put his hounds through this infernal habitat of nothing, not even a drunk man would do it, not in this heathen thicketing upon God's earth, the worst tangles known since the Wilderness, that awful time. October nearing its death couldn't strip this dark green, gray-lit hell of wicked things out to harry and hurt a man.

Forward they went, despite all, just how Little Billy liked things done: that borrowed North Carolina Brigade on the right and Weisiger's Virginians on the left, the 12th Virginia not on the brigade's right—its place of honor—but march-and-countermarch-scrambled on the left now. That felt queer, but a man just did as told and went on forward, one foot, then the other, skin prickly and rashed by foreknowledge, senses all high to skittering. The Yankees were out there, no one knew just where or just how many, but close now close close close—

Stop.

Snaking off through brambles and weed pines, the mighty gray line halted. Silent.

How had Little Billy done it? A thing of wonder. No talk amongst the skirmishers ahead, just hand signals barely seen. And two brigades at the fore stopped cold—wet and cold, for that matter—and surely the Mississippi brigade trailing unseen stopped, too. Why didn't the Yankees cotton to it? The way Old Porte just did the same thing to them every time, two brigades up and one back, slamming into an unwatched, unwatchful flank, the Yankees as inattentive as sluts to their stink.

Mahone rode up to the 12th Virginia, hooves tapping *dumf-dumf.* How that man got his horse through that wicked mire would not be explained in mortal convocations or known to human covenants, another of Little Billy's miracles, though calling it such was irreverent. The general's hat drooped wet.

And Mahone said, softly but within the hearing of Sergeant Johnny Sale, "Colonel, send out your left company as flankers. I'm not in the mood for surprises, unless I cause 'em." Mahone looked down from on high, little-man-big-horse, and added, "Fix bayonets, y'all do it quiet."

And out the flankers went as the lines advanced again, with Sale prowling alongside men he knew and trusted and maybe loved a little, marking off a careful distance from that great gray wave, but ever keeping the 12th's colors in sight, a difficult business here, in this Gehenna.

In mere yards, thickets gave way to an oak grove less tormented by undergrowth. The pace quickened. First shots pocked. Sale imagined the startled faces of skirmishers, Yanks shooting once and running.

This damp day of queer miracles: The flankers had not gone a hundred more feet when a fine-horsed Yankee officer rode right up to them, hailing them, and they let him come on in the spirit of wartime's honest dishonesty, letting him think what he thought, that they were his own men, his advanced pickets, and then all delighting in the look of bewilderment on that ill-starred colonel's face as men in gray greeted him with leveled muskets and invited him to dismount.

Sale relieved the fellow of a pretty sword belt with holster and pistol, but spared the man his fine hat and gold watch. No doubt some rearward fellows would pick the officer clean, but Johnny Sale was a soldier, not a thief, and there were things fair to be taken and things not. Did loop the fellow's haversack over his shoulders, though, that seemed meet and right.

More firing. Cries of alarm. Things happened faster than any men could go.

Keeping to the flank, sharp of eye, blood-quickened if wet and weary, Sale and his comrades popped from the oaks with wet leaves gripping their calves and found themselves before a fence that marked off a broken-stocked cornfield—rotting remains of harvest—just in time to see the Virginia Brigade smash through an addled Yankee picket line, leap that fence, and rush at a raw confusion of Yankee regiments caught facing the wrong way.

Little Billy up on that big horse, waving his hat and hollering. As far as Sale could see in the weakling light, gray thousands advanced irresistibly. A Rebel yell spread from one flank to the other, enormous and thrilling.

Sale had to restrain his men, to remind them of their purpose on the flank. Everybody wanted to go at the Yankees. But duty was duty. So they kept their assigned place, pausing when necessary to see off lingering blue-bellies with a volley or to make a short dash to shoo a bedazzled cluster, leaving more than one Yankee wide-eyed and belly-shot, rump in the mud, astonished, while his too-slow brethren tramped into captivity.

Just to the right, the rest of the 12th dueled briefly with a regiment-size mob of Yankees, then charged into their midst and around their flanks, announcing themselves with bayonets and swinging rifles as clubs. Sale made out First Sergeant Richardson wrestling a Yankee for the Northerner's colors. Richardson won.

But Sale also could see through the wafts of smoke that the brigade was splitting in two, half clinging to the flank of those North

Carolinians as they rushed forward, the other half veering leftward, as if coming over to visit Sale and see what the flankers were up to, and a man could only hope that the split-up was a thing Little Billy intended.

A passel of Yankees blocking his view dispersed. And Sergeant Johnny Sale beheld a sight that lifted his heart.

A few hundred yards ahead and to the left, out by a wishbone of roads, dozens upon dozens of Yankee wagons, ambulances, caissons, spare guns, and even headquarters tents waited to be mustered into Confederate service.

"It's Christmas in October, boys!" a soldier cried.

Five p.m.
Yard of the Bevill house

Those sonsofbitches are *not* going to whip us again," Hancock declared. Turning to General Mott, he said, "Get de Trobriand's brigade across that road, put him behind that fence. He's to hold, no matter the cost, and cover the trains." Exasperated with the world and himself, Hancock added, "*Go,* man, what are you waiting for?"

Turning to Charlie Morgan, who looked malarial, he ordered, "Go find Gregg. I need a brigade of his jockeys across White Oak Road, whoever's closest. I have to pull off most of the infantry and the Rebs will hit us there, too. Not sure why they haven't come on already."

Sick but willing, Morgan lashed his horse.

"And you," Hancock told his last aide, Major Will Mitchell, "get up to Egan. Tell him to reverse his line, as much of it as he can risk, and hit the Rebs in their own flank. I want all of Bob McAllister's Jersey bastards in the attack, but Egan retains control. Understand?"

"Yes, sir."

"And don't get captured before you've delivered the message."

"Will you be here, sir? If I need to find you?"

"I'll be wherever things are in the shit house. My damned job.

Right now, I mean to gently ask fucking Pierce if he'd care to rally at least a few of his runaways."

Hancock pointed his horse at the tip of the Reb advance, where the bastards had almost reached the Plank Road, threatening to cut his corps in two.

Following the departure of Grant's cavalcade, the last order Hancock had received had been to hold his ground overnight and retire in the morning—as if Lee and his paladins would just lean back and let him go unmolested. And goddamned Crawford had never showed up, had not even come close, last located too far south to be useful.

He'd been all but abandoned. Crawford, Warren, Meade, Grant, damn the lot of them.

Well, if he had to fight Lee's entire army with his fists, he'd damned well do it. This would *not* be a repeat of Reams Station.

Five ten p.m.
The Wishbone

Obedient to orders, Régis de Trobriand's brigade still faced to the west. De Trobriand knew those orders would soon change. The fight was to the east, behind their backs, and he was ready. His brigade just didn't *look* ready.

Mott galloped up, followed by a staff already dwindling. A handsome fellow, the general looked as unsettled as a duke who'd discovered his wife in a hussar's arms.

"Good God, man," Mott shouted, "face your brigade about, what are you waiting for?"

"Your orders, sir."

Mott pointed at the melee a quarter mile off. Pierce's men were running. "Hold the junction of Dabney Mill Road and the Plank Road. Take position behind the fence on the far side. You've *got* to hold, Reggie. Hold to the end. Hancock's orders."

"Avec plaisir, mon Général."

With aplomb, de Trobriand turned and snapped out a series of orders in perfect English, taking leave of Mott and trooping his line with inherited posture.

His fellow brigade commanders thought it terribly French and vain that he drilled his brigade in complex evolutions, joking that the "Gaul" loved a parade. Now Mott would see the point of it.

The brigade executed a crisp countermarch by regiment, reversing front with as much precision as speed. De Trobriand extended the line and placed himself in front of his ready soldiers.

Looking back at Mott, he teased his horse to a prance and raised the kepi he favored. After waving the cap a single time, he slapped it back on his head at a dashing cant and drew his sword— the blade so polished it shone on the dankest day. He twirled the splendid weapon to make it shimmer and ordered his brigade forward.

His soldiers cheered.

Five fifteen p.m.
Burgess farm

After making his way through Pierce's debacle, Major William Mitchell found General Egan.

Before hearing out Mitchell's speech, the Irishman interrupted: "Already have them at it, lad. Come along and see for yourself. McAllister's moving upon them, and I'll support him with all the men I can, just keep enough up here to fend off the Johnnies. They'll be coming at us over the run, too. 'Tis clear what they're on to, the shites."

"Yes, sir. Grand, sir."

"We'll see how grand it is, Major. The Rebs will have their say, they will."

And they rode southeast, arriving just in time to see the New Jersey brigade surprise the Johnnies in turn, sweeping over a low ridge and charging across a swale where a branch meandered. A number of gray-clad flankers were taken, and McAllister pushed the Rebs back a hundred yards before they recovered and made a stand.

The Rebs countercharged. They were repulsed in turn. Then McAllister's boys went at them again, dogged and dripping blood. At more than one point, the fight became one of bayonets, rifle butts, emptied revolvers wielded like hammers, and bloody-knuckled fists.

But down behind that struggle, the Confederate attack had stormed across the Plank Road, closing the route that Mitchell had followed only minutes before. Where it wasn't at a stalemate, the fighting still favored the Rebs.

"I've got to see Smyth, one Irishman to another," Egan said. "I'll leave you to pass Win's greetings on to Rugg. Luck of the day to you, Mitchell."

Five twenty p.m.
Plank Road

If Hampton was attacking, Billy Mahone damned well saw no sign of it. He'd driven the Yankees, was driving them still, shattering their attempts to hold the Plank Road. But he needed Hampton to come in from the west and Rooney Lee to do his part from the south, to chop the pig into pieces they could gobble.

His belly burned and acid climbed his throat.

He needed Heth to cross the run as well, to get behind that Yankee brigade that had gotten behind him. And Heth had to move before the drive broke down. It was next to impossible to maintain order in an attack so swift and so successful, almost as hard as controlling men running away.

Davey Weisiger found him.

"General Mahone, I want to push for those wagons, cut those roads. I can do it right now."

"I know, I see it. Don't like to split the force any more than we have to. Hampton needs to do his part, come in and snap them up."

"Well, he ain't. And my boys spotted Federal cavalry riding for White Oak Road. They'll give him a time when he does come, hold him up."

Damn Hampton.

"All right, Davey. Go on. You take those wagons. But keep an eye on your flanks. I'll see to things up here."

Damn Hampton.

He longed for a glass of milk.

Five twenty p.m.
Burgess farm

Charlie Morgan felt puking sick, but he told himself it was no worse than a hangover, a condition of which he believed himself a master.

He found Hancock amid the half-rallied soldiers of Pierce's brigade, cursing, cajoling, and herding strays as if he were a first sergeant. The men were making something of a stand, but the road had been cut. Egan's situation to the north of the Rebs was unclear, but that wasn't the worst of it.

"Sir," he called. But it took a hard moment to get Hancock's attention, to make his way closer. Bullets dropped men all around them, spicing the air with blood and brains and shrapnel chips of bone. A yard ahead, a lieutenant doubled over, pawing his belly and screaming so madly it spooked Morgan's horse to a sidestep.

"Sir," Morgan called, nearing Hancock at last, "I couldn't bring up the Sixty-ninth Pennsylvania. Or anyone else. The Rebs are attacking down White Oak Road. In force. Gregg's men can't hold by themselves."

"Christ. Damn it. I *knew* it."

"Those Philadelphia micks can hold. They just can't be withdrawn."

"Goddamn it, Charlie, I understood you the first time. You there, *you!* Get back on the firing line, you worthless piss-cutter."

"General, you're needed in the rear. You need to be *in* charge, not in a charge."

Hancock wheeled on Mitchell with fury on his face and his shoulders bent forward, an old lion set to maul. "And *you* . . . ," he bellowed. But he stopped himself.

Mitchell waited. He knew when to wait Hancock out.

"Damn you, Mitchell, you know how I hate being wrong."

Five thirty p.m.
The Wishbone

Splendid, boys, splendid! Show them what you're about! Absolutely splendid!"

It wasn't splendid at all, but a bloody mess. De Trobriand reminded himself, as always, that the situation must look as bad or worse on the enemy's side: another lesson inherited from his father, with Eylau tendered as the maxim's proof.

And it wasn't as bad as the Wheatfield. Nothing ever was.

His men behaved themselves properly, never wavering, denying the Johnnies the prize of the junction, with all the spare guns and wagons—and, not least, the corps' sole line of retreat, should it come to that.

He felt pride, of course, but he rationed the emotion. Pride was best indulged in at day's end. And despite the gloom creeping over the fields, he suspected that the day was far from done.

For himself, de Trobriand favored staying alive. He adored his wife and daughters. He had wealth. His health was robust, as sound as a soldier in the field could expect. There were books he intended to write and journeys he meant to take, vintages waiting to be drunk and meals to be had in good company. So he found the bullets aimed his way an affront. Nor was he fearless.

But a man did his duty, or he was no man. That was the entire alphabet of honor. So de Trobriand remained mounted, letting his white gelding prance down the firing line as he encouraged the men he asked to die.

The Rebels charged again.

Five thirty p.m.
The cornfield

Just couldn't move 'em. Damned Yankees. One stubborn brigade behind a rail fence, with fugitive blue-bellies sidling back to join them on the flanks. And that wagon park just at their backs, as tempting as Delilah or Jezebel, as beauteous as the Rose of Sharon, surely. Just waiting to be ravished, food, medicine, all the wealth of Yankeedom. Denied them by one brigade of Philistines, officered by a fellow as wicked as Beelzebub and Lucifer made one, him twirling that shining butcher's knife of his like a circus feller.

Why couldn't nobody hit him? Sale wondered, having failed himself.

They charged again. Feet slop-busting the fading furrows and ankle-kicking away the broken stalks, going at the Yankees with a hoarse cheer, the air wet and clinging, though sparing of rain for now, and bullets singing by, good men falling, and Sale found himself at the forefront, raging, calling on men to come along, it wasn't but a bit farther, just come on, but not enough of them stayed with him and he wasn't given to doing foolish things, so— bitterly, bitterly—he followed the rest of his regiment back into the corpse-specked field, whose middle ground they denied to the Yankees with all the old-mule stubbornness the Yankees were showing to them.

And they just kept on killing each other. Way folks did.

Five forty p.m.
White Oak Road

Hampton had waited, hoping Mahone's attack would draw off some of the Yankees on White Oak Road. As soon as he saw a sign they'd weakened their line, he meant to strike them hard and punch right through, to unite with Mahone's infantry and complete Hancock's destruction. But he couldn't read the field for the trickster light and ghosting smoke, and he remained unsure of the strength of the Federal force awaiting him. All he could tell was that Little Billy had kicked up quite a ruckus, judged by the noise.

Raindrops dabbed his eyes; he could wait no longer. He ordered Butler forward in a saber charge with a dismounted echelon following, the first intended to clear off Federal skirmishers and make the Yankees reveal their strength, the latter to strike their weakest point and shatter them.

In the dregs of the day, Butler led his riders personally for the first stretch of the charge. They advanced with sabers up, the horses slipping here and there as they sped to a gallop, the men hollering like demons. Hampton followed just behind, riding ahead of the dismounted ranks. Positioned on the flank, one of Hart's batteries pummeled Yanks seen and unseen.

Hampton watched his horsemen charge into the murk. Startled Union skirmishers fled in terror. Everything was going right.

A bolt of horror pierced him, followed by fury.

Damned Preston! The boy was unmistakable. Riding amid the foremost horsemen, next to Butler's younger brother Nat.

Hampton resolved to dismiss his son from service. For outrageous and intolerable disobedience.

Turning, he called to his eldest son and pointed.

"Wade! Major Hampton! Go fetch Preston, bring that damned fool back here!"

Young Wade gee-upped his horse and applied his spurs, flinging mud on the staff and Hampton, too.

Hampton quickened his own pace. Forgetting the battle and watching his defiant son.

Preston turned, grinning and waving his hat. His horse's neck bent rearward. He was coming back on his own, he'd had his thrill.

Thank God, Hampton thought. The young fool.

Preston jerked and his hat fell off. He buckled, clutching his groin. Then he slipped from the saddle and dropped like a sack.

Hampton kicked his horse to a gallop.

Young Wade got there first, leaping to the ground and running to Preston. Pivoting to wave for help, Hampton's eldest son toppled over, too.

Zim Davis reined up and slipped to the ground. He bent over young Wade, then slopped on to Preston.

Hampton hurled himself from his horse, landing so hard he almost slipped and fell. The advancing soldiers parted around the scene. Eyeing things warily.

Young Wade was alive and conscious, though in pain. He called for someone to help him sit up, then cried out for Preston, asking if he was all right. Hampton couldn't see a wound on him, didn't see any blood.

He rushed on to Preston, plunging to his knees.

Preston's eyes had rolled back in his head. He breathed in irregular gasps. Bright blood pumped through his shredded uniform, just where his thigh joined the hip.

Hopeless. Hampton knew. And refused to know.

He roared at the rain, the sky. Wordless. Once.

Bending forward, he gathered Preston in his arms, cradling the boy's head with one big hand. He kissed him on the forehead, then on the lips.

"My son, my son . . ."

He held his child against his chest, as if his embrace could transfer the force of life back into the slighter form. The battle his men had joined no longer existed.

The boy's breathing stopped.

"There's a wagon," someone said. Matt Butler, back from his charge. "We've brought up a wagon, sir. And Doctor Taylor."

Holding the boy still tighter, Hampton stopped fighting his tears. Manliness meant nothing anymore.

"Let us take him up," another familiar voice said. Doc Taylor. A hand settled on Hampton's shoulder.

"Save him," Hampton muttered. Unwilling to let go.

Then it was different, all things were different, the world cavernous and bleak. He relinquished Preston's form to men who lifted him—gently—into the bed of a wagon stripped of its canvas.

"Major Hampton?" he asked, remembering. "How is—"

"It's his spine, he's shot low in the back. Rode off himself, though," Butler told him. "Don't know how he did it."

Yes, he would. A Hampton would always ride off himself. If he had breath left.

Hampton wanted to howl and howl. But that was done now, the terrible selfishness. Not the agony. That was only beginning. But the awful sense of being robbed by God had to be subdued, some order imposed on the soul.

Taking the reins from an orderly, he mounted and guided his horse alongside the wagon. Doc Taylor sat in the bed, cradling Preston. The boy's head lolled, unmuscled now, the head of a picka-ninny's doll of rags.

"Too late, Doctor," Hampton said, willing his voice not to break. "But I thank you."

He turned his horse around and went back to his duty.

Five fifty p.m.
White Oak Road

Come on, me darlings," the sergeant called to the approaching Confederates. "Come to Sergeant Danny, ye filthy bastards."

The 69th Pennsylvania stood beside the road, ranked deep, with the men to the rear reloading and passing rifles forward as fast as the front rank could fire.

"An't it a lovely slaughter, though," the sergeant asked those around him. "It's almost as fine a thing as killing Englishmen."

The Rebs came on and they shot them down.

"I do love killing the darlings," the sergeant said.

Five fifty p.m.
Boydton Plank Road

Little time remained before darkness settled, and skirmishing raindrops foretold a proper deluge. As best Major William Mitchell could judge, the fighting remained at a stalemate, with a tilt either way still possible. If Colonel Rugg had only credited Hancock's order and turned to attack southward, it might have turned the tide.

But Rugg had been dismissive, insisting his orders from hours before still stood, and who was Mitchell, anyway? No more than Hancock's pup.

The quarrel had worsened as neither man gave in. Until, at last, Rugg said, "I can spare the Thirty-sixth Wisconsin, nobody else."

Now Mitchell found himself at the head of the shrunken, nearly officerless regiment, leading them down the Plank Road toward the battle, trying to judge where the handful might make a difference.

Wounded men staggered past, not all of them Union. The fighting ahead seemed a chaos, with the opposing lines zigzagging here and gaping open there in swaddling smoke.

The one thing certain was that the Rebs still held a position west of the Plank Road, their deepest penetration.

Well, he decided, charging straight down the road gave him a clear axis, might help keep the men together. And he did think he saw an opening between the Rebs fighting westward and those who had turned north to fend off McAllister.

On the march, he unfolded the little regiment into a line of battle. The veterans moved smoothly, without pausing.

"Fix bayonets!"

The Wisconsin boys did that at the quick-step, too.

Smoke, rain, stray soldiers, a tipped-over wagon with a dead horse atop a living one, the latter neighing madly. Mitchell still couldn't see a Reb line ahead, only a guileless to and fro, with officers struggling to gather their broken commands. Whether because of the dying light or the rain or the smoke or all of it, nobody seemed troubled by his approach.

Not that there was much to notice.

"*Charge!*" Mitchell shouted, waving men on with his saber.

"*Wisconsin! Wisconsin!*" the soldiers yelled.

The Rebs—those who finally noticed them—appeared stunned.

Few reacted before the regiment overran them. And those who did react fled. Or threw down their rifles.

Jesus, if they realize how few we are . . . Mitchell sheathed his sword and drew his revolver.

But the Johnnies surrounding them, outnumbering them, had panicked. It took Mitchell two pistol shots and half a minute to understand why: His charge had excited other Union regiments to join in. On both sides of the road, the attack expanded.

The toughest Rebels fought with rifles wielded as clubs, but more and more withdrew to the east, giving up the Plank Road.

When no more Rebs stood to their front, Mitchell re-formed the regiment, detailed men to march off his haul of prisoners, and turned over the 36th to McAllister—who was spitting happy.

Shaking so badly he could barely holster his pistol, the major rode off to find Hancock. He doubted that he would ever do such a mad thing again in his life.

Less than a half hour later, Mitchell led two more regiments into another attack, with equal success.

Six p.m.
The Wishbone

De Trobriand had all but begged Mott to let him charge the Confederates, but Mott had delayed, still worried about the flank and Hancock's censure.

The order came at last.

De Trobriand leapt his horse over a broken stretch of fence and lofted his sword again, although his arm was tired unto numbness.

"Come on, boys! Those devils started this *soirée,* let us make an end! Oblique order, from the right, by regiment . . . ten-pace interval . . . *forward!*"

The brigade swept over the cornfield, stepping over the dead and skirting the wounded as darkness fell. The Rebs retreated and re-formed inside the oak grove. De Trobriand called for guns to blast them out of it.

Six twenty p.m.
Burgess farm, east grove

Mahone wasn't done fighting. Couldn't be done. Wouldn't let it happen.

He'd done his part, cutting Hancock's corps all but in half, taking whole regiments prisoner, and overrunning their guns. The 12th Virginia had captured three flags.

And what help had he gotten? No sign of Hampton beyond a too-late spatter of firing off to the west. And nothing from Rooney Lee. So little even from Harry Heth that Hancock had been able to turn from Hatcher's Run and counterattack, threatening to encircle brigades intended to encircle him. Mahone had needed to send his bloodied-up horse to the rear and borrow a nag.

Even committing his reserve, his Mississippi Brigade, had done no more than buy time. Time that other men wasted. Now he was in a slashing mood, re-forming his men back in the trees while the Yankees pounded the grove with artillery.

Hampton and all his high-horse, South Carolina pomposity could burn in Hell. Thrown away, another magnificent victory thrown away. What was *wrong* with the damned army?

Weisiger reported. Mahone asked the dark figure, "Ready to have another rush at them, Davey?"

The Virginian hesitated. "Honestly don't know, sir. The men are blown, did what they could. And this rain, the darkness . . . Try, though, if you want."

"I'm thinking on it. Waiting to hear from MacRae, his condition."

"They're on to us," Weisiger noted. "Might be able to do something, of course . . . but there wouldn't be any surprise now. And there does seem to be a heap of them."

Mahone chose not to reply. He had not been so outraged since the day of the mine explosion, when he'd learned the Yankees had sent in their nigger troops. *This* day, they'd had a chance to destroy

the most famous corps in all the Union armies, hardly a week before
the North would vote on the fate of the Ape. And they'd thrown it
away.

A Yankee gun sent a ball through the trees, dropping limbs and
branches. It made a great commotion, but did little damage.

"Must be out of explosive shells," Mahone said. "Empty caissons, almost an invitation . . ."

Weisiger said nothing.

Little Billy Mahone wanted to *fight*.

Within the hour, he ordered a withdrawal across Hatcher's Run.

Eight thirty p.m.
White Oak Road

Hampton sat on his horse in the black rain, calling out elevation
adjustments and fuse lengths. The battle was over, had been. But he
refused to let the artillerymen stop firing into the night, his reso-
lution renewed at each burst of flame from a bronze muzzle, the
man-made lightning.

He *knew* where the Yankees were. His son's killers. He knew exactly where they were. He didn't have to see. The stench of their
vile blood reeked in his nostrils.

"Number two gun, add one-quarter turn," he said in a voice
stripped of mercy. "Explosive shell, fuse cut to—"

"General, we're out of explosive rounds, we're out of near everything."

"Solid shot. Fuse . . ." He stopped. Preston, with his mother's
eyes rolled back in his head. Fool boy.

"Number three gun," he began . . . but couldn't finish.

Matt Butler eased his horse up beside Hampton's mount. Their
riding boots brushed and spurs chinked. Butler reached over and
laid a hand on Hampton's wet sleeve.

"Sir . . . General Hampton . . . it's time for you to come back
now. You're needed."

Hampton almost lashed out at the man, came near to striking him. Instead, he tugged his horse around and nudged it to walk on. Behind him, Butler gave the artillerymen orders to withdraw.

Nine p.m.
The Tangles

Black going, black, black. A man couldn't tell which direction he was headed, once he'd struggled through a thicket or two. Heavy rain punched through treetops, its sting akin to hail. Churchgoing soldiers cursed as they toppled into the mire again or got cat-clawed by briars for the fourth or fifth time. Hadn't taken a hundred yards for the quick-got-up columns to come apart, men losing what little sight there was of each other, some calling out, others afeared to do so, and then came the rifle shots, their crack especially sharp in the rain and the darkness.

Sergeant Johnny Sale did what he could to keep his band together, leading them resolutely, although he was far from sure of his direction, just guiding as best he could by the sounds of other little mobs, trying to keep abreast of Southern voices.

Then there were Yankee voices. Calls for surrender. A volley. Shouts. Deep South voices, Mississippi voices, telling the Yankees they were the sumbitches who needed to surrender. Men killed each other blindly, murdering faceless shadows whose accents were wrong—nervous men judging badly, Sale suspected. And how had Mississippians strayed so far to the right? Or had he led his own soldiers too far left? Where had those Yankees come from?

He tripped over a root and toppled into a waterlogged stretch. Got wet about all over. His few remaining cartridges, too, and his rifle.

Never fond of profanity, he made his men laugh with his exclamations on rising.

Kept hearing Yankees voices. From angles that made no sense.

The black night just grew blacker, the rain heavier.

Sale halted. A man bumped into him.

"Hush," Sale whispered. "Hold up."

Ruckus ahead. But no shooting. And was "ahead" really ahead? He knew how easily men lost their bearings at night, in this kind of undergrowth.

The sounds trailed off.

"Hants," a soldier joked. Not really joking.

It seemed quieter around them now, although there was plenty of shooting in the distance.

"We lost, Sergeant Sale?"

"Reckon we'll find out."

"Yankees probably got themselves lost, too," another man said. "Evens out, most like."

"Just hush up," Sale told them. "Let's go. Little Billy's waiting on us."

"Well, surely I come quickly!" a routine blasphemer said.

But they stayed quiet then. As quiet as their humanity allowed.

When next they heard a fuss, the voices were Upper South, Virginia and North Carolina. Bickering.

Sale led his little party toward the argument. And found that somehow, miraculously, he'd brought his men to the dam they'd crossed on their way into the battle, its berm the route to safety.

The Virginians and Carolinians were squabbling over ownership of a cow.

Ten p.m.
Burgess farm

Message delivered, George Meade's son asked, "Mind if I ride along with you, sir?"

Hancock *did* mind. He was not in a companionable mood. But he said, "Come along, if you want to, Captain. Though a sensible man would get out of this rain. Especially one who's been ill."

Let this captain get a taste for the aftermath of battle, let him smell and hear what he couldn't see, the acrid air resisting the wash of rain and the gut-stink of disemboweled battery teams, the cries for attention from wounded men afraid they would be overlooked by the litter bearers, their voices, North and South, united in misery.

"I haven't been ill, sir," the captain said in a tone of mystification.

"I thought . . . your father said you were gravely ill. Quite recently."

The captain saw the error. "That's my brother, sir. Very ill, indeed." After a pause of a few hoofbeats, he added, "We fear for him."

Hancock didn't know what to say to that. The truth was that he felt little sympathy. He couldn't. There had been so much death in this plague year of war, they'd be finding bones in Virginia's fields for decades. He couldn't feel much for a boy he didn't know. Sorry for George Meade, though.

Christ, what a wretched day. After such a fine start. He smiled grimly, tasting the rain on his lips. He'd wanted to end his field service with a victory and finished it with this purposeless butchery. Well, it was over, he was done. His leg wouldn't let him take the field any longer, he just couldn't do it.

But such a muddled end, the feebleness of it . . .

First, he'd been ordered to hold the ground and withdraw his corps in the morning. Bad enough. Then Meade belatedly offered him the choice of staying to renew his attack on the morrow, promising support from Warren. He'd left the decision to Hancock alone, so any order to retreat would be his.

As furious as he was weary, Hancock had rebelled for all of ten minutes, cursing to make Charlie Morgan wince, swearing he'd stay and fight to show them all. But when he'd queried his division commanders, he'd found the artillery was out of ammunition and the infantry was almost as badly off. Gregg's horsemen, too, had shot up the rounds for their Spencers. Far from being able to attack, he lacked the means to defend if the Rebs struck first.

Struggling in front of his fevered chief of staff, he'd tried to think of a way to hold on, but couldn't. Thanks to Humphreys' plan for a swift attack, they'd advanced with only the cartridges the soldiers carried, and the ammunition trains remained far to the rear. Even had they been closer, it would have been impossible to distribute ammunition in this blackness and rain, with regiments intermingled and officers dead. But the coldest fact of all was that the Dabney Mill Road, his lifeline, could only handle movement in one direction. He either called up the ammunition and hoped the wagons made it through the mud, or he pulled out.

He seethed but resigned himself. He'd given the order to start the corps' withdrawal promptly at ten, leaving behind a few ambulances and a rear guard under de Trobriand, who knew how to put up a bluff. Now, as he rode north with George Meade's son and a weary escort, reluctant to leave his last battlefield, his worn-out soldiers began their southward trudge.

The men were too weary to curse or complain, too drained even to be sullen.

They'd come a long way together, he and the old veterans still in the ranks. He wished he could offer them more than this as he left.

Hancock pulled up his horse by the side of the Plank Road, watching the dark blur of the passing column.

"Take a good look, Captain," he told Meade's son. "I won't claim much, but it's as orderly a retreat as you're apt to witness. They're good men, they deserve better."

The captain said, "But you won, sir. You held the field. After the Johnnies retreated. That means you won."

"Nobody won," Hancock told him.

EPILOGUE

October 31, 1864
Ninth Corps, Army of the Potomac

Acting Second Lieutenant Charles Brown marched Company C to the Ninth Corps headquarters. He'd been warned to have his soldiers looking their best that morning, and the polishing of weapons and leathers, along with futile efforts to smarten their uniforms, had given the soldiers another cause for grumbling. The march to the rear was welcome, though, a respite from Ft. McGilvery: Days on the siege line were dreary, dirty, and dangerous.

Working on buckles and belts the evening before, the men had speculated wildly on what awaited them, from easy guard duty in the rear to a spell in New York City to discourage Irish rioting on Election Day.

Comfortably before the appointed hour, Brown formed his men in two ranks in front of the headquarters, left them standing at ease, and approached the first staff officer he could find to report for duty.

"And who the devil are you?" the colonel snapped.

"Lieutenant Brown, sir. Company C, Fiftieth Pennsylvania."

"Ah, Brown! Sorry. Really, I'm terribly sorry." The officer seemed embarrassed. "So many concerns . . . I'll let them know, of course. . . ." The colonel bolted into the cluster of tents in the farmhouse yard.

Waiting, Brown took things in. More generals and colonels had gathered than Brown had seen in one spot since the Crater fight.

He imagined Levi saying, "Well, *that's* where all those braided shirkers got to."

Guided by the colonel, General Hartranft himself came out to greet Brown.

"I hope you don't mind surprises, Lieutenant. Always liked them myself. The good ones, anyway."

Ten minutes later, Brown stood at attention, facing Generals Parke, Willcox, and Hartranft. An adjutant read the citation for the Medal of Honor, awarded to Brevet Lieutenant Charles E. Brown, 50th Pennsylvania Veteran Volunteer Infantry, for capturing the flag of the 47th Virginia Infantry on the Weldon Railroad.

General Parke pinned the medal on Brown's uniform. Brown was uncertain what he should do next. Salute? Thank the general?

"Just stand there," Hartranft whispered. "We're not finished with you." All three generals smiled.

Better than an execution, Brown figured.

The adjutant next read out an order appointing Brown a *first* lieutenant, with an effective date of rank of November 2.

"Couldn't see holding two ceremonies for one man," the corps commander said. "Brave as that one man may be."

Brown knew what he wanted to say: that he was grateful, mightily so, but Henry Hill was the one who deserved the medal, for what he did that bad day in the Wilderness. Henry . . . and others, too, for what they'd done on so many battlefields. Even Eli. And the promotion was a fine thing, but he knew he'd only gotten it because the better choices were dead, he wanted to tell them that. But he didn't. He just stood there.

The generals didn't ask him to say anything. They went through a flurry of salutes and told him to stand down his company, that there'd be a ration of whiskey for every one of his soldiers in his honor.

True to form, Eli had a comment ready for Brown.

"Bet the whiskey ain't the quality officers drink," he said. "You're not *that* important, Brownie."

"That's 'First Lieutenant Brown,'" the first sergeant told him.

"Not for two more days," Eli said, grinning.

They congratulated Brown with canal-man thumps.

While the whiskey issue was under way, General Hartranft returned and waved him over. The general held out his hand.

Brown took it.

"A good day for old Pennsylvania," Hartranft said. "But don't get too enamored of your new rank. You've already been recommended for a captaincy and General Parke endorsed it."

He clapped Brown on the shoulder, smiled, and left him.

It *was* a good day, that was sure. And winter was coming on, there'd be less fighting. He'd worry about what next year might bring when next year came along.

The promotion meant more money he could save up for his marriage, that was the best of it. He did wish Frances could have seen the ceremony, though. She would have been proud of him. And he *wanted* her to be proud of him.

And had she been there, he could have asked her, quietly, what "enamored" meant.

Ten thirty p.m., November 8
City Point

Grant and his staff sat by a fire on the bluff above the docks, their chairs, acquired here and there, as disparate as their ranks. There'd been drizzle all day, but now it was done, leaving the air fresh and warm for so late in the season. A few hardy flies even scouted the lantern on the general's field table.

The mood was glum. Grant wore a mournful expression as he summarized each telegraph message in turn. The firelight melted the hopes on the officers' faces.

"Massachusetts . . . for McClellan. . . ."

"Connecticut . . . McClellan."

And, later: "New Jersey, heavy for McClellan. Same for Delaware."

Explaining that he would have no disorder, no matter the vote's result, Grant had insisted that every election message the telegraphers received must be carried to him, immediately and exclusively, and not released to any of his subordinates.

"Indiana . . . for McClellan." Grant bit off the end of another cigar.

As midnight neared, the officers drifted away, until only Grant's inner circle of staff men remained. The sentiment around the fire declined from dour to doomed, until no one but Grant bothered speaking, each man studying the fire as if calculating the precise moment when he should hurl himself into the flames.

At ten minutes after twelve, the duty sergeant delivered another message. Grant tossed the stub of his latest cigar in the fire and bent to the lantern.

Shaking his head, Grant said woefully, "Ohio . . . overwhelmingly for McClellan."

That shocked the handful of officers back to wakefulness. Some cursed, others groaned.

But Orville Babcock captured Grant's attention. The lieutenant colonel's eyes had narrowed and he wore a look of temper, almost of outrage.

"By God, General," Babcock cried, rising to his feet, "you've been pulling our legs all night. It's Lincoln, isn't it?"

Grant laughed.

November 27, 1864
Abbeville, Alabama

Sammy Coleman, a Jew fellow, helped Oates down from the coach. Oates remained apt to lose his balance in the course of such doings. Angered him every time. He was grateful for Coleman, an unaccountably good man and former sutler to the 15th Alabama. Coleman had made his way, unasked, to Richmond to accompany Oates on his journey home, an act of kindness Oates vowed he'd never forget.

Good thing Coleman had been with him, too. Hadn't made it

a step farther than Kingsville, South Carolina, when Oates had found himself too weak to go on, his mad heart confined in a beaten-down carcass. A doctor named Oates—no relation, near as either of them could tell—had cared for him over a few days, and most folks had been kind, in Kingsville and beyond. But it had been a hard trip, with the trains infrequent and slow, the nourishment dear and slight, and northwest Georgia ravaged by blue-bellied Ostrogoths.

On his bad days, the South seemed a broken thing; on his good days, just threadbare. And as his journey, by train, wagon, foot, and finally stage, had taken him deeper into his Confederacy, the repulsion he felt at what he saw grew all but unbearable. Every-where, folks lived in fear, and not just of Yankees. Gangs of desert-ers, marauders in gray with a leavening of bluecoats, terrorized farm folk and spooked off the home guards, the "buttermilk rang-ers," motley collections of pimple-faced boys, stay-at-home cow-ards, and dark-of-night score settlers. Thrice, he and Coleman had seen runaway slaves strung up by a crossing, and, once, a young soldier, stripped of his tunic, had dangled from an oak, with a sign hung around his neck that read "Deserter."

Oates had gotten hot, just set ablaze, by the thought of rich-men's hide-at-home sons and verifiable cowards who had never touched war even gingerly hanging that boy as proof of their valor and rectitude.

He had more sympathy by far for those who'd served and fi-nally had enough, now that the war was lost, though no man would say it, more sympathy and understanding for those who fi-nally walked off to see to starving kinfolk than for the yellow-livered men who'd gotten themselves put under orders to stay home and "protect the citizenry" against some frightened coons out in the canebrake.

It had almost brought him to violence in his own state, his Ala-bama, just short of Eufaula, when a detachment of home guards surrounded him and Coleman on the platform at a water stop. The "captain" of the patrollers demanded his papers, all but accusing

Oates of the crime of desertion. Oates seethed. Frail though he was, he was set to reach out from the folds of his cloak with the one big fist left to him and strike the man. He was unwilling even to flick back his cape and reveal himself as one-armed, an obvious invalid. No, he wouldn't do that. Instead, he'd break the sonofabitch's jaw. . . .

Coleman gripped his remaining arm.

The Jew told the leader of the patrol, "This is Colonel Oates, of the Fifteenth Alabama, ordered home on convalescent leave. For his sixth wound of the war, if I count correctly."

"Don't look like no invalid to me. Just scared like. Maybe stole that uniform, killed an officer for it." The captain began to examine Coleman more closely. He was a mean-eyed, long-faced man, the sort who lashed his niggers when he was drunk. Oates knew the type. In his law practice, he'd defended a few of them.

Oates clenched his fist and shifted his feet for balance.

Deftly—maybe with some Jew art—Coleman reached inside Oates' cloak and produced his orders. Oh, he knew where they were, had seen Oates struggle to draw them from that pocket many times.

Oates burned at Coleman, too, now. At the humiliation, the helplessness. Although he knew that his friend was being sensible, that there was no point, after all, in getting themselves shot down or lynched by these vainglorious scoundrels.

The "captain" looked over the much-creased-but-orderly documents, taking his time, while the train waited and impatient passengers watched them from the windows. The patroller could find nothing wrong with the orders.

He handed the documents back to Oates. With hatred in his eyes. Hatred Oates matched and returned with compound interest.

As he and Coleman reboarded the battered carriage drawn by that wheezing, get-out-and-push locomotive, the patroller called after Oates:

"Sad day, when a white man needs a Jew to see to his business. Be niggers next."

Coleman pushed Oates into the carriage before Oates could respond.

That was his Confederacy. A world fallen so low that men were murdered over a deed to five acres.

And now he was home, in Abbeville, dirty, tired, and glad. He'd chosen the town as the right place to make his fortune before the war; it was where he'd embraced the laws that he'd once broken and where he'd bought into a newspaper, the latter endeavor a casualty of the times. The town looked scuffed and bruised, but not yet ravished.

Before he could properly dust himself off, folks he knew came loping over to greet him. Nobody asked for his papers here. On the contrary: They seemed to know more about him than he knew himself. Not all of it true, of course. Maybe not the half of it.

He took a drink with three white-haired men and Coleman, who was known and tolerated. Then, as impatient as he was tired, he said he'd be off to see just how dilapidated his shack had become, if it still had a roof and one window unbroken.

One of the men smiled. As if he knew a thing he wasn't telling.

With only a blanket roll and haversack, Oates walked down the familiar street, touching the brim of his hat now and again as faces passed and muttering greetings, until he reached the corner that would take him around to the little piece of this hurt world to which he held the title.

To his surprise—then concern—smoke rose from the chimney of his one-step-up-from-a-cabin domicile.

If anybody had taken to squatting in his house, he'd . . .

Out of patience with life and drained of all energy but his manly outrage, he strode down the stretch of planks laid above the street mud. Almost losing his balance, he threw open the front door.

Oates smelled stew.

What he was like to say wasn't going to be fit for the town's ears, so he slammed the door shut behind him.

Didn't draw a response, no exclamation or movement, no alarm. He did believe he heard humming, though. Woman-humming.

He marched through a door frame into the kitchen and found old Colonel Toney's Sallie, the dusky gal he'd sported with while recovering from his last wound at Roseland Plantation. More than once, he had recalled her fondly.

"Him jes' come in here like a great, big bull," she declared, speaking to an invisible third person, the way the coloreds did. "Body think he a mad-bit dog, way he act."

Oates said nothing. He was struggling not to cry. He dropped his blanket roll, the haversack, the overcoat.

The woman glanced at him once, took in the armless sleeve, and said nothing about it. Just kept stirring the contents of that pot, languid and easy.

When he did not, could not, speak, she told him, "Heard how you was comin' today, so's I kep' the fire up. Cunnel Toney say you needs to keep warm." She set aside the spoon and turned to face him, one hand on a hip. She was a slender gal, but big where big was useful.

"You hungry?" she asked.

December 25, 1864
Petersburg

Mahone wasn't hungry, but he ate what he could of the Christmas dinner Otelia and her servant girl had scavenged: mutton masquerading as lamb and 'taters in buttermilk. He'd had one Christmas dinner already, what he could eat of it, a frugal meal shared with his officers as they all tried to be merry and failed badly, with good men drinking too much punch too early.

Returned from a round of nursing up in Richmond and working in Petersburg now, Otelia had found a fine house to rent as the population thinned. His wife had thinned out, too, and she looked careworn, not much bothered by the wounds she bandaged but torn apart by the letters home she took down for dying boys. She did remain feisty, though, and Mahone praised the food she put in front of him.

"Billy, you never could tell the difference between good food and bad. That camp cook of yours could put a mud pie in front of you." She shook her head. "All your pretending . . ."

"That isn't true, woman, and you know it. I've always respected my vittles and this here meal is a wonder. Going to turn me into a glutton, that's what you're going to do."

When the slender meal was done, with a portion left for the kitchen girl, he and Otelia moved into the parlor. She'd put up a German tree, a practice she'd introduced into their lives. Every year, she said the same thing about it, that Prince Albert had brought the tradition to Britain for Queen Victoria. And there stood this year's offering, a scrawny thing adorned with a handful of candles of a quality she would not have bought for slaves in the past. A bucket of water and another of sand stood by the pine.

Mahone lit the candles carefully, rationing the lucifer matches gleaned from Union corpses. The little flames did brighten the afternoon, the winter grayness.

"You sit down now," Otelia told him. "You just sit right there."

She went out and returned with a bundle wrapped in plain paper, but banded with ribbons he knew she'd reuse for her hair.

"Merry Christmas, William."

"Well, now, I do wonder . . ."

"Just be quiet and open it. I won't have your fussing."

He untied the ribbons and opened the paper carefully—all things had to be husbanded now.

His wife, beloved beyond mortal expectation, beyond human capacity, sat beside him, eager as a girl.

The gift was a uniform tunic of dove-gray wool, pleated and tapered to his form, the cloth fine under his hand. He saw it would fit without trying it on.

The woman *knew* him.

"Now, how the devil . . . Otelia, this is grand." He held it up by the shoulders. "Robert E. Lee himself doesn't have such finery."

"I won't have you looking bedraggled, General Mahone."

"Now *you* wait here, woman." He went into the foyer, where he'd left his satchel. His gifts were not wrapped as artfully as Otelia's offering had been.

Extending the two small packages, he said, "Do better next year. I promise." And he sat close beside her again.

On the tree, a candle sputtered. The cheap tallow smelled.

She opened the first package—a book, no way to disguise it.

"Why, it's a new one!" she said with pleasure unfeigned. "You know how I enjoy Trollope." She opened the cover and fingered the rough-edged paper. "You've already cut the pages for me, Billy. That was a kindness." Bending toward him, as enthused as a child, she held out her treasure. "Look, there's even a picture by Mr. Millais! How ever did you get it through the blockade?"

"I have my ways." He did not tell her that it came from the saddlebag of a dead Yankee. "Open the other one, might as well."

His other gift was an ivory-colored *mantilla* of Spanish lace. Otelia swept it over her hair and shoulders.

"I shall have to learn gypsy dances," she told him, following up with a kiss. "It's beautiful, Billy. It must've cost a fortune."

It had not cost a fortune. He'd bought it for a pittance in a transaction undertaken by Doc Brewer, his old friend, who shielded the identity of a lady in greater need of food than lace. Nor was pale lace wanted these days, only black was asked.

They sat for a bit as the window light waned.

"I do miss the children," Mahone said.

"No place for them, this isn't."

"I know that."

"They're better off in the country." She looked about to cry.

"I know that. But Christmas . . ."

It wasn't just the living ones who haunted the parlor then, but all those who had died before leaving the cradle. Otelia had suffered a bad run over the years.

"I try not to think about them," Mahone went on. "I can't bear thinking about them. I just shut them out of my mind."

Otelia looked at the candles on the tree. He reached for her hand and she returned his grip with a blacksmith's ferocity. Soon, he would order her to the country, too. Because the Yankees wouldn't wait a day longer than they had to, they might not wait out the winter, and then they'd come on with all their might and things would arrive at a grim and terrible end. Every man who wasn't a damned fool knew it. But they had to fight on, couldn't just give up. Not now, not after everything.

With tears on her cheeks, Otelia smiled. Blushing, embarrassed to be so much a woman.

"I haven't wept since I heard they went for Lincoln," she said.

Billy snorted. "Damn fools, all of us. Thinking it might be different." It was his turn to shake his head, mirroring Otelia's gesture. "After they declared war on us and fought us for nigh on four years . . . it was folly to think they'd just give in when they're whipping us."

A candle on the tree guttered out.

"I'll light the lamp," he said. "Need to snuff those candles soon."

But he didn't rise.

Still gripping his hand, Otelia asked, "What's to become of us, Billy?"

"We'll get on. You're the one always saying it. We'll start over and we'll get on just fine."

Brutally, she twisted free of his hand and got to her feet, stepping toward the window. Refusing to look at him.

"*Don't* you go getting killed," she cried, her voice as sharp as a blade. "Don't you be stupid and get yourself killed, please, Billy." She locked her arms over her chest, gripping his life to her heart on the Belgian carpet. "If you do . . . if you get yourself killed, William Mahone, I swear I'll . . . I'll marry a Yankee!"

Mahone laughed and rose to embrace his wife.

"You'd never find one brave enough," he told her.

February 10, 1865
Columbia, South Carolina

Hampton doubted he'd see his home again. Sand Hills stood just a few miles south, but he could not leave for even a brace of hours, not with Sherman approaching and wielding hellfire. He knew that Sherman would burn Sand Hills and Millwood out of vengeance. Kilpatrick would probably light the fires himself. And that would be that. Hampton only wished he could make a last visit and pass through the rooms one last time, then stand on the porch, look out on the fields, and remember.

It was nearing the end. He knew it, and he refused to know it. He'd assured the governor and mayor he could defend South Carolina's capital. By day, he believed it. At night, he did not.

Preston filled his dreams, calling from his grave. Young Wade had survived, but would never again enjoy time in the saddle or bend without pain. And when Hampton's wife had rushed to Virginia to comfort him in November, marauders—Yankee fugitives or Southern deserters—had ransacked Sand Hills, stolen Mary's jewels, slashed portraits, axed furniture, and scrawled insults on the walls. After that, he had ordered his sisters to leave Millwood for the state's deepest interior.

Hampton had learned hatred. Of a degree he did not know a man could feel.

Only this day had he finally gained full authority over the forces defending Columbia. When he'd sent Hampton to South Carolina in January, Lee had recommended his promotion to lieutenant general but failed to assign him a status, leaving Hampton outranked by "Fighting Joe" Wheeler, whose cavalrymen were brave in a clash but as ruinous as the Yankees between battles. Now, terribly late, Beauregard had confirmed Hampton's authority, but still refused to concentrate all the forces in South Carolina, trying to protect too much and destined to protect nothing.

Beauregard wanted to save Charleston. Hampton wanted to defeat the enemy. Each purpose betrayed the other.

Again, he felt the impulse to ride out and have a final look at Sand Hills. But he didn't do it. He feared that, should he go, he would not be able to leave his home again, that he'd stay there to make a lone stand against Sherman's army.

In Columbia's streets, his soldiers staggered drunkenly, steeling themselves against the end of the world.

February 14, 1865
Rome, Italy

Barlow sat on a stone in the Roman Forum, a volume of Gibbon unopened in his hand. The morning had grown warm, and his frock coat, tailored while he underwent treatment in London, felt as heavy as a soldier's blanket. Beginning to sweat, he gazed at the ruins dutifully.

Arabella would never see them.

He'd removed his mourning armband weeks before. It had begun to seem an affectation. And he tired of the questions, sought no pity. Of course, he should have worn it longer on two counts, for Belle, but also for his father, murdered under opaque circumstances hours after a friend had delivered an offer of help from his son. But Belle had begun to recede—he struggled to mind his memories—while his father's death had startled but not moved him.

An English doctor had brought him back to life, a fellow discovered by luck. Barlow had asked for an open leave to seek treatment in Europe and had been granted an exception to policy, but the spells cast by London's medical wizards had proven as useless as those in New York and Boston. Until a Scotsman furrowed his bushy brows and remarked, "I have a colleague who might take a special interest."

The colleague in question had served for decades in India and believed that Barlow harbored a parasite. The thought was nauseating, the treatment worse. He'd endured hellish cramps and a scorched digestion for weeks, daily swallowing poison. And then, at last, he'd gone a full day without shitting himself. Life resumed, although he had to eat cautiously—plain chops and unadorned noodles here in Rome.

In the Forum's grimy ruins, equally grimy children played roughneck games. Touts roamed, offering counterfeit treasures for sale or presenting themselves as guides. They all went ignored by the English travelers who simply declined to acknowledge them; by the Germans rendered insensate by their guidebooks; and by the Americans perched in Rome for the season, praising Italy's glories and shunning Italians. All of them passed by Barlow, not without curiosity but, somehow, kept at bay by his demeanor. Even those who knew him only nodded.

One fellow surprised him, though, approaching with rolls of canvas or heavy paper under an arm. Italian and a man of middle years, he had graying hair, a damaged smile, and the scent of desperation.

Barlow watched his approach with hooded eyes.

The fellow knelt in the dust and unrolled a watercolor. It showed the Forum, seen precisely from Barlow's vantage point.

"You buy, *signore?*"

"I think not," Barlow said, conditioned to fend off Rome's many classes of beggars.

The fellow appeared crushed by the rebuff. As if he'd risked his soul to approach Barlow. But he didn't fuss or grow noisy, as many did. He merely rolled up the painting and turned away.

Barlow caught himself: He was becoming one more ass on a holiday, closed to the very world he'd come to see. The fellow's picture had been quite good.

He didn't rise, but called, *"Signore! Maestro!"* Thereby nearly exhausting his sum of Italian.

The broken fellow turned, briefly disbelieving that he could be wanted.

Barlow motioned him back, then gestured for him to show the painting again. Eager but protective, the fellow set his two other rolls in a cleft before holding up the painting of the Forum. Barlow hardly considered himself a critic of the arts, but he really did believe the work was good. He laid his unread book aside and bent forward.

The painting could be his peace offering for Ellen Shaw. For Nellie. To whom he'd been a beast, he had to admit. The poor girl had persisted in her visits, never knowing which form of monster she'd meet on a given day. He really was in her debt.

And he'd thought of her. Too often, perhaps. In ways not always seemly. He wished to think only of Belle, to guard her memory, but he strayed.

"How much?"

"Inglese?"

"Yes. English."

"Ah, London!"

"No. I meant I *speak* English." Barlow tapped his chest. "American."

"Ah, *americano!*"

"How much?"

The fellow held the picture high, then pointed to himself. "*I* paint."

"I see. How much?"

The fellow named a figure so extravagant that Barlow laughed. Or brayed. It startled the poor devil.

"For you, *signore,* I make very low," the man said urgently. The price dropped by two-thirds. It was still a bit high, but Barlow didn't mind. He really wanted to have it for Nellie Shaw.

He heard her reading patiently in his room, saw amber twists of hair bowed over a book.

Barlow nodded. "Good. *Bene.*"

"Grazie, signore. Grazie." He reached for another of the rolls. "You look?"

Have I a choice? Barlow thought, amused.

The second watercolor captured the Colosseum rather handsomely. He thought it would be a wry gift for his mother, who had the soul of a gladiator.

"*Sì,*" Barlow said.

The artist reached for the third painting.

Barlow shook his head. "Don't be greedy, old fellow. Two and done."

He paid the man, who tried not to show his delight at putting one over on the wealthy American. Barlow quite liked him.

The artist rolled the two watercolors together and bound them with string. Then, uninvited, he sat down on an adjacent block of stone.

Gesturing at the ruins, the fellow said, "*Bella Roma,* yes?"

But it wasn't beautiful. The ruins were interesting, fascinating. But hardly beautiful. Nellie Shaw, on the other hand . . .

And then there had been the countess, rather a warning about remaining free.

Arriving in Rome after New Year's to recuperate, he'd been welcomed by the American community, whose members feigned restraint and craved sensation. He'd been repelled by his lionization by those who'd gone abroad to avoid the war, feeble young men with wealth and faithless wives. Not least, he'd been put off by the female sculptors, whose oddity surpassed *The Marble Faun*. He suspected at least one, who smoked cheroots, of unnatural habits.

The English, too, had taken him up, fussing over his military record despite their open sympathy for the Confederates. He'd liked them at first, for their sardonic humor and public rigor, but he soon found them petty, vain, and too fond of boys. And the women were awful.

He'd done best with the Italians, for a time. The English and the Americans thought them impossible, but Barlow found them splendidly entertaining. Their balls were smelly and glittering, their *palazzi* in decay and full of life. The women flirted openly, not behind Chinese screens in shabby *ateliers*, and he'd enjoyed the jealous company of two generals, both of them Piedmontese, whose gala uniforms were laden with more medals and orders than any real soldier could gather in a lifetime. Their operatic manners,

Louis-Napoléon beards, and gay accounts of Magenta and Solferino rendered *his* wartime experience indescribable, a horror that occurred in another universe. He listened with his old smirk, letting them brag.

And the countess . . . he'd never seen a woman so wickedly beautiful, as if the word *exotic* had been coined for her. He'd been startled at her interest, suspecting that she found him a mere curiosity, but she favored him at her salons and invited him to her private rooms for tea, where he'd found her alone. She took him to sit for a photograph, which she claimed would be her treasure, and she called him *"caro Francesco"* twice in front of her guests. He'd never found himself carried toward an intrigue before and went about it more cautiously than the countess, which turned out to be wise. On the brink, he learned that the woman was notorious for passing on a loathsome disease to a prince.

It was enough, all of it. More than enough. He didn't fit in with any of them, the war had left him as foreign to their worlds as a Chinaman. They didn't know what men were capable of, didn't understand loss, had no sense of the things that truly mattered, things indescribable in polite society, nameless things. . . .

He despised them more than he despised himself.

Newly arrived, he'd immersed himself in the antiquities, in the ruins, paintings, and architecture. But soon he'd grown avid for the accounts of the war in the London papers, a mere four days late when they reached the English bookseller. Battery Wagner and Wilmington had fallen. Sherman was moving northward from Savannah. And Lee was still penned at Petersburg.

Seen from a distance, things became utterly clear. The crucial point was that the war would be fought to its end in the spring. He *had* to be there, had to be in on the kill.

He didn't belong in Rome or London. Or in Paris, which he had learned to detest in four days. He belonged back in the lines in front of Petersburg.

It was time to return to his war.

The sun passed its meridian. The artist didn't move, but seemed to luxuriate on his slab, as if Barlow had changed his fortunes forever. A band of children erupted from the ruins and scurried past them, shrieking and coming quite close, their bare feet raising dust. The artist clutched the unsold watercolor but smiled in the wake of the boys.

He shrugged and said, *"Ragazzi."*

Barlow realized that his backside ached. But this pain came from sitting too long on stone, not from ill-health. In fact, he felt magnificent, with his strength returned and redoubled. Even his feet had stopped plaguing him.

He stood up and took the watercolors he'd bought.

The Italian rose, too. He pointed at the book Barlow had forgotten. *"Il libro, signore."*

"I'm done with it," Barlow told him.

Author's Note

All novels should challenge their authors—if the authors respect their readers—but this book fought me doggedly. The Battle of the Crater has been written about repeatedly, but not always honestly. Too often, the temptation to leap past the racial viciousness won out, with the result that we think we know how bad it was but really don't. How could I make this account true and bring it to life? What perspectives would best capture this oft told tale with integrity, sparing no party to the carnage and portraying the moral and ethical breakdowns frankly?

The Crater fighting included some of the worst racial butchery in our history, worse than the Ft. Pillow massacre in that some white Union soldiers turned on their black comrades, an act of treachery the passage of time cannot soften. Yet it was the United States Colored Troops (USCT) who first charged into the trenches and traverses, shouting, "No quarter! No prisoners!"

For the Confederates, the commitment of black soldiers in force was a shock that erased inhibitions. Then Brigadier General William Mahone was not an enthusiastic slave-owner. He and his wife shared seven slaves, including three children, and seem to have found them more of a burden than a benefit. After the war, "Little Billy" would ally with black politicians, bringing down the wrath of whites upon him. Yet something in Mahone snapped that morning when he heard that the Colored Troops were committing atrocities. I suspect that his childhood memory of his family's dash to escape Nat Turner's slave uprising—his father's haste and worry, his mother's dread, the crying children, the inevitable rumors of women "shamed" before death—all of that flooded back. And Little Billy gave his own "No quarter!" order.

In that three-sided massacre, we Americans showed ourselves at our worst.

By the summer of 1864, black troops in Union blue were appearing upon battlefields in large numbers—gaining critical mass, in modern parlance—hardening Southern defiance, while exciting a range of reactions from uniformed Northerners, not all approving. As the months passed, the Colored Troops were accepted, grudgingly, as a battlefield presence and contributed notably to the Union victory: The first Federal infantry to enter Richmond's ruins belonged to black regiments (they behaved with more discipline than their paler comrades).

But acceptance lay in the future on that summer day before Petersburg as men struggled to the death in a slaughter pit. This novel attempts to capture the emotions, logic, hopes, and fears of all parties engaged on July 30, 1864, and to do so as fairly as possible. Above all, I sought to avoid that great sin of historical novelists: judging the past by present values, inserting our own sensibilities, and yanking their words from the mouths of the dead to insert our sanitized and approved vocabulary. Our history deserves honesty and our citizens need it. Without understanding who we really were, we'll never quite grasp who we have become, leaving us prey to demagogues and despicable entertainments.

Once this novel fights its way past the Crater, it returns to my standing commitment to highlight forgotten battles and remarkable men who have blurred into history's shadows. Second Deep Bottom, Globe Tavern, Reams Station, Peebles' Farm, Burgess Mill . . . initially indecisive, those contests of arms and souls set the conditions for an ultimate Union victory by eroding Lee's position and depleting Confederate manpower and resources. For most of us, the Petersburg fighting pauses between the Crater and the chase to Appomattox eight months later, but the evolving siege produced a succession of grinding encounters—even more than this book portrays—with the intervals between major bloodlettings filled with cavalry actions, local raids, picket-line forays, and endless, deadly sharpshooting. Once again, I've done my best to help fill in popular history's blanks, adding my bit to the splendid work of historians, National Park Service Rangers, and my friends, the battlefield guides.

The legacy of the Crater haunts us still.

As always, the solitary work of writing has been eased by others. As I struggled to revivify our past, my wife, Katherine McIntire Peters, brought her quarter century of journalistic experience covering government and the military to our battlefield excursions and to her work as my "tactical" editor. Katherine has an unerring eye for the overwrought line or excess word and has done her best to save me from myself (and my passion for Faulkner).

Bob Gleason, my "strategic" editor, has been supportive beyond the call of his formal duties. Bob not only caught the vision for these books, which evolved from a trio to a quintet, but—as one example of his commitment—he personally tracked down the painting I wanted to use on this book's jacket after others had given up hope of acquiring the rights. I had remembered the image from a *LIFE* publication issued during the Civil War's centennial. My father had bought the booklet for me fifty-four years ago and the Crater painting had such an impact on a nine-year-old boy that I never forgot it. I *had* to have Tom Lovell's work on this book. Bob made it happen.

Sona Vogel, an extraordinary copy editor, once again refereed my tug-of-war with the English language. As ever, she has been splendid.

Brigadier General John W. Mountcastle, U.S. Army (Ret.), our Army's former chief of military history and a front-rank Civil War scholar, generously agreed to proofread my draft (and promptly informed me that I had Billy Mahone's date of rank off by two weeks). Over the years, Jack has always been generous with his time, advice, and encouragement, for which I am deeply grateful.

George Skoch created the maps for this novel, as he has for the past two, but this time around the work proved especially onerous for George as I slowly figured out what I really wanted. Of course, he came through: Whatever the reader may think of my words, I trust that he or she will agree that the maps are superb. George's work is essential to these novels.

To Colonel Tom Doherty, Captains Elayne Becker, Emily Mullen, and Whitney Ross, and the rest of the 1st Forge Regiment of Volunteers, thanks for making this book a fine production.

Not least, thanks to the inimitable and irreplaceable Ed Bearss for talking "horse sense" to me.

Following my standard practice, I want to acknowledge some of the key works that I used for reference. This listing is not comprehensive. It's meant as an informal guide to further reading for those who want to explore the men, battles, and issues in greater depth. Some fine books will be overlooked, for which the authors have my apology. Also, given the wealth of works on the subjects engaged, I have excluded any books that I acknowledged in previous novels in this series . . . so Barlow's letters and Lyman's diaries, biographies of Oates, Hancock, and Grant, and many another key work won't be listed in the following paragraphs.

There is no substitute for the words of the men who fought— even when those words weren't strictly honest. Whenever possible, I immerse myself in the *Official Records of the War of the Rebellion* and, especially, in letters and diaries, reading them over and over until I internalize the voices. For this book, *The Papers of Ulysses S. Grant*, volumes 11 and 12, were especially valuable (I'd bought Grant's collected papers when I was an Army captain, a purchase that strained an already tight budget).

First-person accounts of particular interest for this novel included *Our Noble Blood: The Civil War Letters of Major-General Régis de Trobriand*, translated by Nathalie Chartrain and edited by William B. Styple; *Lee's Adjutant: The Wartime Letters of Colonel Walter Herron Taylor, 1862–1865*, edited by R. Lockwood Tower;

Four Years with General Lee, by Walter H. Taylor; *A Pair of Blankets,* by William H. Stewart; *The Veteran Volunteers of Herkimer and Otsego Counties in the War of the Rebellion; Being a History of the 152nd N. Y. V.,* by Henry Roback; and *Seventy-five Years in Old Virginia,* by John Herbert Claiborne.

As for modern biographies, there are two fine studies of Wade Hampton, the man who came closest of any senior Confederate to embodying the ideal of the "Southern cavalier." *Gentleman and Soldier,* by Edward G. Longacre, is a fine, highly readable work that concentrates on Hampton as a soldier. The richly detailed *Wade Hampton: Confederate Warrior and Southern Redeemer,* by Rod Andrew Jr., is a "full" biography of Hampton, with the latter half of the book devoted to his controversial political life after the guns went silent.

Worthy biographies not mentioned in my previous author's notes include the revelatory *"Happiness Is Not My Companion": The Life of General G. K. Warren,* by David M. Jordan; *From Blue to Gray: The Life of Confederate General Cadmus M. Wilcox,* by Gerard A. Patterson; and *A Hero to His Fighting Men,* an excellent life of Nelson A. Miles by Peter R. DeMontravel (although it concentrates more heavily on Miles' Frontier service and later Army duties than on his Civil War experiences).

As for "Little Billy" Mahone, he deserves a modern biography. The Army of Northern Virginia had no shortage of colorful, gifted characters among its generals, but Mahone stands out among the most compelling.

Additional regimental histories consulted for this novel include John Horn's forthcoming *The Petersburg Regiment, 12th Virginia Infantry,* a work of great value. Mr. Horn generously shared his manuscript with me as I completed this novel, and it deeply influenced my account of the fighting around Burgess Mill. Benjamin H. Trask's volume on the 61st Virginia also proved helpful, as did a reprint of *The 48th in the War,* by Oliver Christian Bosbyshell, and *The 48th Pennsylvania in the Battle of the Crater,* by Jim Corrigan. Some of my own early memories of Civil War matters involved tales told of the 48th and the Crater back in Schuylkill County, Pennsylvania, always with a defensive note that "our" miners got their part of the business right. On the other hand, Company C of the 50th Pennsylvania was recruited in my hometown, but that regiment rarely got a mention in kitchen-table discussions—all I knew was that Henry Hill, a relative through an aunt's marriage, had been awarded the Medal of Honor (long after the war—red tape is not a recent innovation).

Fortunately for me—and for all interested readers—there are a number of terrific histories available on the offensives and battles featured in this novel. The masterwork is the two-volume study by Edwin C. Bearss (with Bryce A. Suderow, another gifted historian), *The Petersburg Campaign: The Eastern Front Battles, June–August 1864* and *The Western Front Battles, September 1864–April 1865*. This was breakthrough work, and no individual has done more of the exhausting, exhaustive, get-out-and-get-dirty research and writing than Ed. He's the daddy of us all (although I fear he may view some of us as illegitimate).

Noah Andre Trudeau's single volume on the same period, *The Last Citadel*, is a great introduction to this long, grim struggle. Well organized and always clear, the book underscores why Trudeau remains so popular with Civil War enthusiasts.

In the Trenches at Petersburg: Field Fortifications and Confederate Defeat, by Earl J. Hess, is yet another first-rank study by a Civil War scholar whose works I've often consulted. This is the sort of book that requires a near lifetime of effort to produce. On the Crater specifically, Hess scored again with his *Into the Crater: The Mine Attack at Petersburg*. I found it to be the best single volume on the Crater and used it heavily. A solid runner-up was *The Horrid Pit*, by Alan Axelrod, which made excellent use of the records of the postdebacle court of inquiry.

In the course of writing my Civil War novels, there's always a book that proves especially resonant for a given subject. This time, John Horn's *The Siege of Petersburg: The Battles for the Weldon Railroad, August 1864*, drew me back again and again. It was a true labor of love for Mr. Horn to write about three battles in which the rest of us, wrongly, have shown but little interest: Second Deep Bottom, Globe Tavern, and (Second) Reams Station. His recently revised and expanded edition is, as my old drill sergeant used to say, "mighty fine, *mighty* fine. . . ."

So many combat encounters occurred before Richmond and Petersburg during the months covered in this novel that I could not portray them all. For those who would like to learn more, I recommend Richard J. Sommers' magisterial *Richmond Redeemed,* which examines the battles of Chaffin's Bluff and Poplar Spring Church in such detail that I'm confident his account will never be bettered. A shorter study (though well worthwhile) is *Fort Harrison and the Battle of Chaffin's Farm,* by Douglas Crenshaw. And for a solid work by a promising young historian, seek out *The Battle of New Market Heights,* by James S. Price, a revealing account of the heroism and accomplishment of the U.S. Colored Troops fighting north of the James in the early autumn of 1864. The USCT did their part, but the generals didn't.

Next to last, I have to acknowledge a splendid oddity—the sort of book only a truly dedicated historian would produce—Robert K. Krick's *Civil War Weather in Virginia.* No historian embarks on such a project expecting whopping sales, but if such works of scholarship don't top the bestseller lists, they're a godsend to journeymen historians and writers. Weather is a critical part of this novel (as it is of every war). While eyewitnesses often commented on how hot or wet a day was, it's a fine thing to be able to turn to the meteorologic statistics. "Bob" Krick has many grateful admirers. I'm one of them.

And one final book: *Guide to the Richmond-Petersburg Campaign,* edited by Charles R. Bowery Jr. and Ethan S. Rafuse. A volume in the U.S. Army War College's series of guidebooks to Civil War battlefields, this disciplined, detailed text is a great aid to anyone trying to sort out battlefields brutalized a second time by strip malls and fast-food joints, pierced by superhighways, and ravaged by housing developments (nothing the Yankees did to Petersburg was as destructive as what the city did to itself in the post–World War II decades).

The guide is also helpful for visits to the many battlefields in the greater Petersburg and Richmond areas that have not yet been destroyed. From Deep Bottom to Hatcher's Run and on to Five Forks, efforts by the National Park Service, the Commonwealth of Virginia, private citizens, generous "old guard" families, and a wonderful nonprofit, the Civil War Trust, have preserved an impressive amount of the old lines and battlefields. But we have not done enough. From New Market Heights to Reams Station, more ground can be preserved as great space and green space, honoring the famed, the forgotten, and the fallen.

You can do *your* part. Visit these parks and sites. Feel our history on ground both hallowed and haunted. Let your members of Congress know that you care about our National Battlefield Parks and our nation's heritage. And if you can, please make a donation, however small, to the Civil War Trust.

When we save our past, we save our future.

Ralph Peters
September 11, 2015

Turn the page for a sneak peek
at the grand climax to the Battle Hymn Cycle

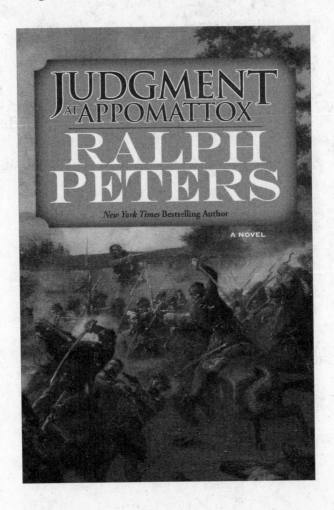

Available August 2017 from Forge Books

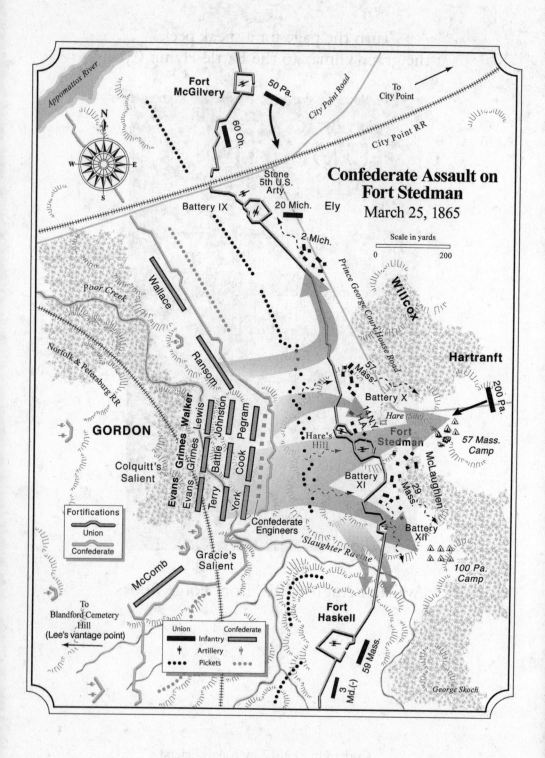

Appomattox River

Fort McGilvery

50 Pa.

60 Oh.

To City Point

City Point Road

City Point RR

N
W   E
S

Stone 5th U.S. Arty.

Battery IX

20 Mich.   Ely

2 Mich.

Confederate Assault on Fort Stedman
March 25, 1865

Scale in yards
0   200

Wallace

Poor Creek

Ransom

Norfolk & Petersburg RR

GORDON

Colquitt's Salient

Evans   Grimes   Walker   Lewis

Evans   Grimes   Battle   Johnston

Terry   York   Cook   Pegram

Prince George Court House Road

Willcox

57 Mass.

Battery X

Hartranft

200 Pa.

14 N.Y. H.A.

Hare's Hill

Hare (Site)

Fort Stedman

57 Mass. Camp

Battery XI

McLaughlen

29 Mass.

Battery XII

100 Pa. Camp

Fortifications
Union
Confederate

Confederate Engineers

'Slaughter Ravine'

Gracie's Salient

McComb

To Blandford Cemetery Hill (Lee's vantage point)

Union   Confederate
Infantry
Artillery
Pickets

Fort Haskell

59 Mass.

3 Md.(-)

George Skoch

ONE

Three fifty a.m., March 25, 1865
Petersburg, Virginia

Gordon stood at the earthen wall, fingers attacked by the cold. Winter still fought rearguard actions before dawn broke. Two days back, a tempest of warm dust had scourged the lines. Now the ill-clad soldiers at his back, fifteen thousand present and more on the way—almost half of Lee's army—shivered as they waited for his signal.

A private knelt beside him, calm in the death-dark. The soldiers who still clung to the Army of Northern Virginia, those who had not deserted to the Yankees or slipped off homeward, breathed the fatalism of Homer's heroes, mythical figures cherished by Gordon and now made real by war. Two hundred yards stretched eastward to the night-draped Yankee fort, ground that might have been the plains of Troy, the waiting multitude *his* bronze-clad Greeks. Fierce, these men would fight. And Major General John Brown Gordon would lead them.

To victory?

Despite the good-tempered confidence he displayed to other men, Gordon was glad of the darkness. Not only would it shield his advancing soldiers, it masked concerns he feared he could not hide. This was *his* plan, his offering, produced at an order from Lee that had been almost plaintive. And the old man had only blessed the scheme for want of better choices: Lee, whose nights were ravaged now, who summoned generals from their beds to talk out the graveyard hours, dreading what might come when he closed his eyes.

The old man expected Gordon to work a miracle, to split the Federal line in two, to roll it up, to slash beyond it, to ravage the Yankee base at City Point, to defy the gods . . .

No longer Agamemnon, but doomed Priam: Poor Lee, grown cantankerous and haunted, complaining of poor lamp oil and bad candles, his fabled self-discipline cracking. By day, he remained a lion to the men, though, all they had left to believe in, the last worth of the Confederacy.

Gordon told himself—insisted—that there *was* a chance this attack would work, bedazzling Grant's hordes sufficiently long for Lee and the army's remnants to slip away, to join Joe Johnston in North Carolina and stretch out the war, combining to beat Sherman and then wheeling to confront Grant. Lee had spoken of Napoleon's strategy of the central position and of Frederick's ultimate victory—despite the fall of his capital—as Gordon listened, nodding but pierced by doubt. At times, Lee seemed unmoored from the army's reality. And all the while Jeff Davis carped and badgered him.

Gordon would not, could not, say no to Lee, that was the gist of it. Not now. Not when the end was near and those who appeared true would retain ascendance over their kind, even in disaster: A victorious people lauded their heroes, but defeated folks *needed* theirs.

The future of the South would fall to those few left untarnished and alive.

A cold gust combed Gordon's beard, which was as carefully groomed as ever. The men behind the rampart rustled, chilled but heeding their orders to keep silent. Aware down deep of how much lay at stake.

Surely word would reach him soon that the last obstacles had been cleared. Then it would all begin at a signal shot.

He had done his best, striving to plan this fight with the guile of Ulysses. He'd studied the Federal lines, selecting the earthen bastion the Yankees called Fort Stedman, along with its flanking batteries, as the attack's first objective. The fort stood where the lines veered close and the road at its back ran straight to the Yankee rear. But the key to ultimate success would be the seizure of a trio of forts half a mile behind the Federal line, masked positions spotted by spies and confirmed, if vaguely, by Union deserters. Take those rear forts and you had that road, and you split Grant's army in two.

They just might pull it off. It wasn't impossible.

Gordon felt he'd done all within human power to craft a victory. And if the attack succeeded, he, John Brown Gordon, stood to be the late hero of the war, an advantage not inconsiderable to a man of high ambition.

Managing defeat would take more skill.

So the plan had been honed in fine detail, key officers taught their tasks. Working in a hush just short of silence, his engineers were clearing lanes through their own side's defenses. When they finished, picked units, relying on bayonets, would rush the Yankee picket line, posing as deserters coming over. With the pickets taken, his best regiments would rush toward Fort Stedman, accompanied by more engineers with axes and grapples to breach the Yankee obstacles. All would be done without firing a shot, for as long as possible. Letting the great blue legions sleep until it was too late.

Following the units tasked to seize the fort and the batteries on its flanks, three columns of one hundred soldiers each, officers and men hand-chosen and led by scouts sent by Lee, would thrust deeper into the Yankee lines to seize those rearward forts and open the road. Gordon's staff had taken pains to learn the names of the Federal officers—Ninth Corps men—along this stretch of line. If challenged, his "Three Hundred" would pass themselves off in the dark as Union soldiers returning from picket duty.

Full divisions, led by his best subordinates, would widen the breach in the meantime, rolling up the Yankee line north to the river and southward as far as possible before dawn.

Once the secondary forts had been taken, more divisions would follow. By first light, a cavalry force would fly down the road to the Union headquarters and depot at City Point.

It *could* work. There really was a chance that it could work.

There had been doubters, of course, not least among Lee's self-appointed guardians, his staff triumvirate of empowered boys. Marshall said bluntly that the plan was too complicated. Taylor reserved judgment, but smirked like a wealthy schoolboy. Worn out by Lee, poor Venable only shrugged.

The thing was, it *had* to work. Or the army was doomed and damned. Along with the Confederacy. It would all end right here, perhaps in weeks, with Grant unleashed by fair weather and the last of them trapped against this played-out city. Not beaten manfully, just beaten down. And *he* might be held responsible.

A voice startled Gordon: a Yankee voice.

"What're you doing over there, Johnny? What's that ruckus?" After a hold-your-breath silence, he added, "You answer real quick, or I'll shoot."

Calm as a front-porch philosopher in August, the soldier beside Gordon rose and drawled, "Ain't no never mind, Yank. Go on back to sleep. Just the boys gathering up the last hard corn, what's left hereabouts. Rations been mighty short."

Cold doubt. Vast night. Waiting thousands.

The Federal called over, "All right, Johnny. Get your corn. Ain't going to shoot a man who's drawing his rations."

Gordon closed his eyes in thanks. But the men clearing off the last obstacles seemed as loud as a stampede.

He flexed raw hands, gloves left behind in his urgency. Why *was* it taking the engineers so long? The attack had been scheduled for four a.m. But he knew without resort to his watch that the hour had passed.

Unbidden, but ever welcome, Fanny swept into his thoughts. Hardly a mile behind him, still in Petersburg, in a lodging just fair and no better, ready to bring their fourth child into the world, a child of war.

Fanny.

Reaching up from the firing stoop, someone tugged his sleeve: his assistant adjutant general, who would lead a brigade this day, at age twenty-six.

Gordon bent down.

"Lanes are clear, General," Major Douglas whispered. "The men are ready."

Gordon straightened. For a moment, he glanced backward, into the complicit darkness, able to make out the nearest troops only because they wore strips of white cloth diagonally over their chests or tied round their upper arms for recognition when the fighting began.

Gordon turned to the soldier waiting beside him.

"Fire your shot."

The signal that would unleash it all.

The soldier delayed. Just long enough to do what he thought fair to a trusting enemy. He called to the Yankee picket, "Halloo there, Yank. Wake up, look out! We're coming."

He shouldered his rifle, aimed high, and pulled the trigger.

Four fifteen a.m.
Hare's Hill

Twas black as an Englishman's soul, this dark, and bleak as bloody Ireland. Danny Riordan rushed out with the rest, the sweet weight of his rifle in his mitts, a rifle left unloaded on bitter orders, but tipped with a bayonet kept sharp as sin. And every wild-elbowed lad, this wave of scrunty Irishmen swept from Louisiana into the war, every man of them hoped he wouldn't be skewered by a messmate, careful to keep the touch of the stinker next to him as feet felt forward in the dark, all the earth black as the cassock on a priest.

Whole lives passed in the seconds it took to stumble and fumble forward in rough silence. Not a man spoke to warn the Yankees, but small sudden noises there were and enough, the brief cries of blue-bellied pickets surprised and not asked to surrender, and the thunk of axes on winter-worn wood, no shots yet but a terrible tapping of hundreds—nay, thousands—of shoes worn thin as muslin, thin as famine dead.

One shot, two. The grump of a bucko tripped up. Riordan

himself legged wild at a trick of the ground, recovering to leap the berm of a rifle pit, sensing his way uncannily in the dark: a very acrobat he should have been, gone off with the circus, larks! A landing foot found a belly, its man-meat tension recognized from battles and prisons and brawls.

Dead, that one was.

Shouts of struggle tore at the surprise.

"Jaysus," cried the man next to him, a comment on this world and the hereafter.

More shots.

"Help the colonel," cawed a Leinster crow.

Riordan turned from curiosity—a vice more trouble than drink—and lent a mitt to Colonel Waggaman, who commanded what the war had left of them: not much, that was, not many. A hurry of hands pulled the colonel out of the clabber, and hard he snarled, mud-covered in the cold. The high marsh grabbed at Riordan's shredded shoes.

Waggaman cursed, a priest run out of the whiskey.

But why were they running downhill? Their purpose was to attack a fort or the like, but even a fool would not put such on a downslope. Had they mistaken their way in this devil's dark?

In answer, an officer's voice—so different they sounded, you always knew the high lads—called out, "Half-left, *half-left*!" and then came lightning, the bright spew of cannon, a greeting.

By the flash he saw murderous faces. Like his own.

By another gun's flare they spotted the rampart ahead. Sworn to silence still, they raced for the earthen wall, fearful of waking cannon to their front. But there were none, or none tended.

Up and over. A few men howled from habit, but soon were hushed.

Forms dark against darkness. The white bands his kind sported helped, but unreliably. Instinct led his rifle as he blocked a blundering man. One who wore no ribbon.

Too close for the bayonet. Riordan slammed the butt of his rifle into the man's belly, bending him to a gasp. The wood of an ill-managed weapon grazed Riordan's head and clattered down. He gave the doubled-up fellow a knee in the face, then brought the butt down onto the fellow's shoulders or parts similar, beating him to the ground.

When the Yankee had been laid out properly, Riordan smashed down the butt where the bugger's head should be. And he heard the lovely crack of splintering bone, not even a last cry from the fallen Federal.

"That's for Point Lookout, ye bastard," Riordan grunted.

Men packed around him, dangerous, querying each other in hushed brogues.

By the light of a last Yankee musket flash, he saw Daniel Keegan before him, bereft of his tin whistle now but with stripes sewn to his sleeve, promoted while Riordan rotted in Yankee prison pens, one and then another, taken not once in the war, but twice, to his mortification, and worth a fight it was when a man claimed that he'd been swept up *three* times, for third time there had been none, just sickness in a hospital hungry for corpses.

"Cripes, I almost killed ye," Riordan told him.

"Take a bolder one than you, it will."

The donnybrook was done for the moment, though. Officers hissed at them to re-form, still lacking the light to know the east from west.

Whispers ran down the regathered line that the colonel had welcomed a bayonet in his meat. As like from one of their own as one of the Yankees, and damn the confusion. Captain Bresnan took over, unbothered.

"Come on," he called, though still not battle shouting.

They filed out of the fort's rump, most of them in some order, though others went over the walls just for the pleasure. What were they now, this handful of men that remained of the proud Louisiana Brigade, melted into the Consolidated Brigade, with Company E, the old Mercer Guards, as Irish as want and pride, reduced to a mere handful of ragged wraiths?

Forward they went. Or someone believed it was forward.

A rumpus of shooting rose to the left: a tougher time for Grimes' lads in their glory, and let them keep it.

"We should've held back till the Yankees cooked up breakfast," a soldier griped, voice unfamiliar. "I've got the hunger on me, I do."

Riordan snorted. Hardly a man knew hunger as he did. The prison rations at Point Lookout, spare enough, had been a feast compared to the black years in Ireland. Many a man in the army claimed he was starving, but you never heard that word from Irish lips. Hunger, yes. Starvation, no. Starvation was a girl got thin and dried out as a woman of fourscore; starvation was a village abandoned to corpses—those not dead of chewing winter grass gone black with the cholera or flecked blue with typhus, starvation's eager companions.

Yankees. Surprised. Surrendering.

Some fought, though. A ragged volley crackled ahead.

"Load, load!" Bresnan's voice. But the boys were after more than that, for they'd gotten into a white maze of tents, pitched foolishly close to the line. And tents meant treasures.

"Time for that later," the captain pleaded.

When Riordan had been exchanged in January—a surprise to all concerned—he'd grown so thin the Yankees had counted him done. And more than a friend or two had suggested he come along into the byways as winter bit, for they'd had enough, those buckos, and were either going home or going over. It made sense, Riordan allowed. Why fight for an army that wouldn't trouble to feed you? But he'd come back stubborn from the camps, with a mind to kill at least a few Yankees before the fiddler stopped and the jig broke off.

Away they'd gone, all those who'd had enough, but Riordan stayed. A fool, they called him, an idiot. But the army pleased him better than digging ditches, addled with Louisiana's heat and Irishmen valued so low they put them to work next to chained-up niggers. Used to the heat, like animals, the darkies had mocked the misery of white men. Nor were the sons of Africa the worst of it:

Shoveling along the levees, a man learned fast that Pádraic had driven the snakes out of Ireland only to pack them off to Louisiana. Seamus McGintey had reared up sudden with a monstrous gurgle, gripping a great serpent, its fangs so deep in his neck that it couldn't free itself, and Seamus danced out his minutes, swinging the snake back and forth, until he yanked it off and fell over and died.

A rifle was a finer tool than any pick or shovel.

They got themselves into a maze of trenches, tripping and tumbling. Officers whipped men with the flat of their sabers to drive them on.

Back up on a spit of flatland, the line re-formed, ragged but pressing on. Was there a newborn paleness on that ridge?

Horse hooves clobbered the earth, telling men of the nearness of a road. Yankee prisoners cried, "Don't shoot! Don't shoot me, Johnny!" as they clumsied past, headed rearward into their turn at captivity.

The last sons of Erin and Louisiana exchanged volleys with an enemy who could only be glimpsed by muzzle flash. They'd gotten themselves down another slope. Or perhaps the same one a second time. The earth was dry here, though. Riordan wondered whether a single officer had one sound idea where in the world they were, for he had none himself.

To the left—the north?—artillery grew busy, boding ill.

Their officers stopped the Louisianans, confused and waiting for orders.

Four forty-five a.m.
Union lines

Brigadier General of United States Volunteers Napoleon Bonaparte McLaughlen approached Fort Stedman on horseback, wishing for daylight so he could get things settled. Of course, the Johnnies would probably withdraw long before that, unwilling to be caught in the open on one of their picket raids.

As an enlisted man in the 2nd Dragoons before the war, McLaughlen had learned when to trust a horse. He was glad of that knowledge now, since he couldn't see one damned thing beyond an occasional rifle flash. The dark was so thick you could bite it. The horse knew the roadway well, though, and kept to it even when spurred.

Horse stink, man stink.

McLaughlen had suffered several bad minutes, fearing that the Rebs had struck in force. He'd even sent off his staff to rouse reinforcements. But he'd found Fort Haskell secure in trusted hands, its frontage quiet and no one alarmed, so now he just needed to stiffen up Fort Stedman. Make sure all those sluggards were under arms in obedience to his orders.

His horse shied around shadows.

He thought the sky looked paler. Then it seemed black again.

Somebody had gotten the jumps to the north, up between Batteries IX and X, by the feel of things. The Johnnies might have staged more than one simultaneous picket raid, out of either boldness or desperation.

Grinding his parts against a saddle before the sun came up always reminded him of his frontier days. Damned well hadn't suspected back then that he'd one day become a general. Even sergeant had looked a long way off.

A frontier soldier got his coffee, though. Before he put a horse between his legs.

This Reb disturbance annoyed McLaughlen, not least because he'd been working on his own plan to strike the Johnnies from Fort Stedman. He'd been trying, thus far without success, to interest his superiors. And this didn't help, suggesting that the Rebs remained alert.

He spurred the horse again, spending a bit of the anger he felt at the Johnnies. They were defeated and done with, but too proud to admit it. Anyone could see that Lee was finished. Everything from here on out was a needless waste of blood.

McLaughlen was determined to take charge, to get his lines

under control and end the nonsense before the morning muster. And find some cook fire where the coffee was boiling.

Again the horse swerved to avoid shadows in motion. Shirkers, the general reckoned. Some of Hartranft's green bunch, most like, straying in the dark. Their officers needed to get them under control.

Too near, a cannon discharged and startled his horse. It made no sense. Had his mount grown confused? The direction of that flash seemed all askew.

More noise than there should have been. Yet, not the bang and rumpus of a real fight.

The slope stopped climbing and leveled out. It *felt* like the rear of Stedman. Smelled like it, too, that latrine stench. Matters seemed calmer here. The riflery, which had snapped down the line minutes earlier, had fallen off to isolated shots.

Queer business, though.

The horse took him right into Stedman, where the soldiers sounded disorderly and rambunctious. And seemed excessively plentiful. As if they had been reinforced too heavily, packed together uselessly. Perhaps they really were Hartranft's new volunteers and dregs of the draft. That would explain the indiscipline.

A cluster of man-shapes approached. McLaughlen reined up.

"You there," McLaughlen called, "you're going the wrong way, soldier! Get back to your posts, every one of you."

Laughter.

A voice that was utterly wrong replied, "Well, now, it does seem to *this* body that we're heading just where we'uns want to go. That right, boys?"

"Are you . . . a Rebel?" the general asked, bewildered.

"I do prefer 'Confederate.' But 'Reb' does nice enough. Now you git down off that long-legged cow and surrender."

Outraged—not least by his folly—McLaughlen demanded, "Are you an officer?"

"Don't matter one lick. You dismount right now, or I'll blow your head off."

McLaughlen sensed a pistol rising toward him. A merry, unforgiving crowd had gathered.

The general got down. "I'm General McLaughlen and I demand to be treated with proper respect."

"Your pistol. Give it here."

McLaughlen handed it over, but insisted, "I can only surrender my sword to a fellow officer."

The men crowding close whooped at that.

"Well, I'm Lieutenant Guinn, Thirty-first Georgia. But you hang on to your letter opener. You can give it to General Gordon, he'll be tickled." A big, unpleasant shape, the lieutenant turned. "Bradwell, take this high-flown gent on back to General Gordon, with my compliments." He chuckled again. "Rest of you, let's go. Sportin's over." But he turned once more to warn, "I don't want him picked *too* clean, Bradwell. Hear me?"

The private nudged McLaughlen through a reeking mass of Confederates. The two of them joined a stream of Union prisoners flushed rearward between advancing Rebel columns. McLaughlen let fly with his feelings for the world to hear.

The soldier given charge of him finally said, "Genr'l, I never did hear a man cuss so powerful. Where'd you learn them words?"

McLaughlen grunted. "I was a goddamned private just like you. And lucky if they don't make me one again."

Five ten a.m.
Union Battery IX

First Lieutenant Valentine Stone, 5th U.S. Artillery, leapt from his horse, blouse flapping, and shouted, "Load spherical case!"

Mack MacConnell had already had the men wheel a section of guns to point due south.

In the first gray tease of light, Stone saw them coming: a long, uneven line of Rebs sweeping northward, half inside the Union works, the rest driving up the ground between the lines. Scampering ahead of them, small bands of his kind raced for safety.

Those boys had put up a fight, though. He'd heard it from the innards of Fort McGilvery. Remnants of the 2nd Michigan they'd be.

Within the battery walls and along the traverses, the men of the 20th Michigan, charged to protect the battery, cheered on their fellow Wolverines, urging them to run faster.

There did seem to be a plentitude of Rebs. He wished those Michiganders would go to ground so his guns could fire.

"Under four hundred yards, sir," MacConnell called.

"I see that. Damn me. Open on the Rebs outside the lines."

MacConnell shouted the orders. The gun crews were all but ahead of him. Muzzles shot flame, carriages recoiled, and smoke rose in the half-light.

One round hit perfectly, tearing a gap in the line. The Michigan infantry cheered.

Farther south, toward Stedman, it looked and sounded as though the Rebs had blown a significant hole in the line, with episodic encounters flaring and fading. More guns joined the fray, firing in multiple directions

The boys from the 2nd Michigan figured things out. They either scooted off to the east or dove deep into trenches. So Stone's artillerymen could do their work.

"Left thirty degrees. Load spherical case. Ready canister. Fire at will."

There were just more Johnnies than Val Stone needed to see of an early morning. Yipping their high cry now. Flags whipped back and forth in the morning twilight, urging on the graybacks.

To Stone's immediate left, Al Day got his Michiganders ready. Waiting for the Rebs to close within two hundred yards. Not that Stone put much faith in musketry, even in good light. Artillery, that was the thing.

First volley. Johnnies fell. Not enough.

They screeched that ghastly wail. And on they came.

The gun crews slammed in the canister rounds, while infantrymen reloaded with the speed of veterans who meant to live.

A high Reb voice cut the tumult: "Best give up, Yanks. No use now, you're beat. Throw down them rammers."

"Fire!" MacConnell told his gun sections. Before Stone could give the command.

The Michiganders, too, fired another volley.

Through the smoke, Stone saw the Johnnies wavering, some stepping forward still, others hesitating.

First real light coming on. The field looked like hell on a Saturday, as far as Stone could see into the smoke.

Reb officers rallied their men. One grabbed a flag. Urging his Johnnies to resume the attack.

Stone's gun crews fired without need of commands now. Pouring in the canister.

A fuss of grunts, pounding feet, and jangling metal rose behind the battery. Colonel Ely had brought up reinforcements from Fort McGilvery. Stone recognized Captain Brown of the 50th Pennsylvania in the lead. No sword, just a revolver in his paw. Good man, Brown. His raggle-taggle veterans were barely half-dressed, but every man had his rifle, bayonet, and cartridge box.

The Rebs stopped advancing, but appeared determined to hold their ground. Firing in support, artillery opened from the Confederate lines, able to identify targets now. And they knew the ranges, both sides had known them for months.

It looked set to be an ugly morning in godforsaken Virginia. But Valentine Stone barely gave a damn about what might happen elsewhere on the field. This was *his* ground. And he meant to hold it.